Chris Throsby

ADMONITION

Limited Special Edition. No. 6 of 25 Paperbacks

Chris Throsby was born in Chatham, Kent, and lived in the Medway Towns until 1990 when the relocation of his Civil Service job led him into moving to Winsford, Cheshire, where he still lives today. Redundancy in 1998 provided Chris with the opportunity to return to education and in 2004, he was awarded a 1st-Class Honours Degree in English Literature and American Studies.

In 1990, only months prior to moving to Cheshire, Chris was diagnosed with Multiple Sclerosis, which, despite its progressive nature, hasn't prevented him completing his first full-length novel, *Admonition*.

I dedicate this book to Lesley, my wife, who has supported me through every stage as *Admonition* took shape and has been there for me in life no matter what. Also to my son, Sam, who pressed me to write in the first place and didn't stop until I sought publication. I love you both.

Chris Throsby

ADMONITION

AUSTIN MACAULEY PUBLISHERS™

LONDON • CAMBRIDGE • NEW YORK • SHARJAH

A CIP catalogue record for this title is available from the British Library.

ISBN 9781528933346 (Paperback)
ISBN 9781528967433 (ePub e-book)

www.austinmacauley.com

First Published (2019)
Austin Macauley Publishers Ltd
25 Canada Square
Canary Wharf
London
E14 5LQ

I would like to thank my sister, Judy Halliday, for her support, encouragement and critique of early drafts and for being strong enough to say "I don't like that bit", a rare and valued quality.

My long-suffering friends Christine Brookes and Sheila Wigley, both unstinting in their support, interest and encouragement, who still asked how the book was going at a time that was well beyond the call of duty.

Michelle Roberts, whose first question when she walked in the house seemed always "How's the book going?" and proofed all my biblical references.

Debbie Bootz, who kindly provided me with 'Lolly Hamlet' in name and stature, though definitely not in character!

And finally, Amanda, Amy, Dad and Carole, and anyone else I've forgotten.

I hope you all enjoy *Admonition* and think it's worth the wait!

Thank you.

Now all these things happened unto them for ensamples: and they are written for our admonition, upon whom the ends of the world are come.

1 Corinthians 10:11

Part One

William
The Admonition

Payday always went one of two ways.

On the good days, Dad came straight home from work, gave Mum his money, told her about his day and usually collected his conjugal reward when they thought we were asleep. But with all of us sleeping in one room, we were used to hearing Mum's quiet murmurs of encouragement and the muffled sounds as they tried to smother their conclusion.

But on the bad days, diverted by the call of the Boar's Head, Dad left Mum hoping the little money she'd managed to siphon away would feed us until next payday. The Boar was the nearest pub, and according to Mum it was only there because it lay between the salt pans and our village. She said it sold bad ale, drunk only by men made thirsty by salt and heat.

The truth is the ale isn't too bad, but the Boar's reputation is not for its ale, but as a place to trade salt without questions or tax. The Excise knows what goes on there but they've never caught anyone – Dad told me their local man is well paid by the Boar's landlord, Jabez Payne, not to watch too closely.

Anyway, on the bad days we'd go to bed early to keep out of the firing line when Dad got home. It was always the same. Mum wouldn't have minded if he just had a couple, because she knows salt panning is hot, thirsty work, but he'd come home roaring drunk and broke. Bed was different as well; Dad's slow repetitive movement as he lay on top of Mum seemed endless. He'd hold her hard and when, with a low grunt he finally finished, he'd roll off her, fall asleep in moments and then begin the snoring that would disturb our sleep until morning.

On those nights, the only sound louder was Mum's silence. She couldn't refuse him her body. She knew what would happen if she tried to do that, but she could deny him her presence. Unmoving and making no sound, she'd lie there waiting for him to finish, desperately hoping he'd remember his promise; sometimes he did, sometimes he didn't. Only once had she tried to pull away, but he'd grabbed her even more fiercely and all of us heard as she couldn't stop herself from crying out.

It was because of a night like this my little sister was born; certainly that's what Mum spat at Dad when she found herself pregnant for the seventh time. Mum had lost one before I came along, but when the one after Sally was stillborn, she told Dad she didn't want any more. Dad agreed. The truth was he'd never been that interested in us – at least not until we were old enough to work. But on that night, drunk, he'd forgotten what they had agreed.

It was always Mum who named us, and she guaranteed no interference by giving me, their first–born, my father's name, William, and as a second name that of my grandfather, John. When my brother came along, she sealed matters by calling him John William. Any faint interest Dad had in us ended there; his heir would make sure his name would go on and just in case something happened to me, a suitable replacement waited in the wings. From then on, he didn't ask, just waited for an announcement from Mum.

Sometimes it took weeks for Mum to decide on a name. She said she needed time to get to know us and to find a name that suited. But I believe she first wanted to see if we survived. Experience had taught her it was just a little harder to say goodbye to a person with a name than to a nameless baby. It was never easy for her I know, but anything that eased the pain, even a little…

As I said, Dad never asked. He just waited for a decision. He didn't usually comment either – a grunt meaning he'd heard was all she got. So when my baby sister was born, it was a surprise that Mum named her almost immediately. It surprised my father even more when she announced,

"Your baby's name shall be Admonition."

She sounded like Reverend Grace who terrified us on a Sunday with tales of Hell and Damnation. She watched for his reaction and when she was sure there would be no argument, nothing more than a sharp turn of his head, she spoke to us. She knew none of us had ever heard of the name, so before any of us could ask, she explained.

"Your sister's name has a meaning. Admonition means 'a right telling off', so every time your father sees her or hears her name, that's what he'll be getting – a right telling off."

We were all too young to understand 'rebuke'; that would have confused us even more, but we'd all had a right telling off at some time or other and because we'd all heard Mum's cry and so believed we knew the reason, none of us asked why Dad was getting his admonition. As she spoke to us, Mum remained looking fixedly into Dad's eyes until, finally, he looked away. Soon after, unable to endure the silence that followed Mum's announcement, he left for the Boar's Head. That night he came home late but I believe sober, because he went to bed quietly and shortly after all we could hear was the rhythmic breathing that meant he was asleep.

While I can't say he never again came home drunk, I can say that Mum bore no more children – Admonition made sure he never again forgot their agreement.

Why I woke early that morning, I don't know. It may have been Dad's snoring – he'd come home drunk again – or perhaps just the bite of the cold morning air. Whatever the reason, I'd got up whilst the others slept, and still comfortable in the only world I knew, walked down the gennel to the privy.

The houses in the gennel were all single rooms made cheaply from clinker left by the salt pan fires. Dark grey and separated by less than a brick's width, they stood in two parallel rows, rows so close together, there was barely room for a horse to draw a cart between them, but because they ran from east to west, they saw little sun and always seemed to be in gloom. However our house wasn't in the gennel, nor was it made from clinker, instead, made from oak but still just a single room, it stood beyond the gennel and sideways to it, facing south across the fields towards the sun and the salt pans.

On any bright and dry morning, Mum cooked our breakfast outside, so as I returned from the privy, I hoped to catch the tell–tale smell that would tell me our porridge was almost ready. But that morning, as I walked back up the gennel, a loud and unfamiliar noise sent me hurrying to the end. There, I was just in time to witness my home disappearing into the ground, taking with it my family, my home and my life as I knew it. Looking back, it seems the last fragments of my childhood slipped away that morning along with everything else.

For a moment I was transfixed, then, knee–jerked forward, I was drawn towards the chasm that had swallowed my home. Blinded by dust, I stumbled over the rubble that had escaped the chasm's draw. Fortunately, though I may not have thought so then, I was halted by a familiar voice.

"Wait!" A hand grabbed me. "They're all gone Will, and the ground's still slipping. If you go any closer, you'll go the same way."

It was Tom Rider who worked alongside me and Dad who had pierced my shock. I have to admit that just at that moment slipping away with the rest of my family seemed like the best thing I could do. But it was then from behind me I heard,

"Will?"

It was such a small voice.

"Adie," I cried, reaching for her, "You're safe."

Standing there in her dirty and torn nightgown, my little sister appeared unhurt. Amazed that she was still alive, I asked her,

"But how did you escape?"

"Don't know," she mumbled, "… was asleep… then I was here."

"I saw what happened," Tom said. "I called for your dad; state he was in last night, I thought he might need a little persuading. He'd just appeared, looking as bad as I knew he should, when there was a fearful tearing sound. We both looked around and saw that a great split had appeared down the front of your home. I couldn't believe my eyes, still can't really, 'cos then the whole house began to move and juddered slowly forward, it also started to sink."

Stunned by what he'd witnessed, Tom clearly needed to tell his tale.

"Your dad swore and reached for the door. It wouldn't move. It was already too far out of square, but the window had popped, so squeezing through the hole it left he vanished in the dust. All this time the house was moving and sinking, still making that awful tearing sound whilst the hole left by the window was twisting and getting smaller. Then part of the roof collapsed, some of it falling towards me, but most falling into the house which was slowly becoming shrouded in thick dust and I thought your dad was lost along with the rest of your family.

But suddenly the shroud parted and like a popped cork your sister flew out from what remained of the window. Your dad had pushed her through and as I pulled her quickly away from the house, he poked his head out and seeing she was safe, disappeared again. That was the last time I saw him, because moments later a chasm appeared in front of your house and swallowed it whole. It happened so quickly no one else stood a chance."

Without thinking I said,

"So Dad died saving Adie?"

As soon as I spoke, Adie's face changed and for the second time that morning, I wished the ground would swallow me as well. A dark cloud crossed her already leaking eyes and I knew that, thanks to me, the burden of guilt she already shouldered was now almost more than she could bear.

"Why?" she said. "Why did he save me?"

Wishing I could take back what I said, I tried to find words to console her.

"I suppose because he must have found you first."

I couldn't hide the desperation in my voice.

"That can't be true." She looked lost. "You know Sally and Ann share the bed nearest to the window."

I knew she was right; I didn't know what else to say.

But then Tom spoke again.

"Your dad died trying to save the rest of your family, not you; remember after he'd saved you, he went back."

He managed a sympathetic smile. Well almost.

Adie looked at him and seemed to accept what he said. She didn't stop crying or look any less bewildered, but I was sure the cloud I'd caused had lifted just a little, and though I could tell there was something more he hadn't said, I was grateful to Tom for that.

Jabez
A Hard Road Travelled

I've never touched hard liquor. Hard to believe I know, me being a pub landlord. So let me explain.

All who met her said Mum was a beauty, but the bruises, cuts and burns – a hot poker his weapon of choice – left her broken, and barely five years with him left her unrecognisable from the bride he'd married.

They had been married for seven years when my mother died and she hadn't been well since giving birth to my sister. But I think the death of Ruth, barely three months after she was born, was too much for Mum to bear. As for me, I'd long since learnt that crying only provoked my father and although I always tried to hide my tears, when Mum told me Ruth had died, I couldn't help myself. I'd loved my little sister since Mum first sat me down and showed me how to hold her. Then, when she was about six weeks old, Mum trusted me enough to leave Ruth with me whilst she did other things and I would sit happily for as long as Mum let me, mesmerised by the way, rarely blinking, Ruth stared into my eyes. Mum said she already knew me, but wouldn't believe me and said she was too young, when I told her Ruth had smiled at me; but *I* knew she had, and so when her death came suddenly, I was overwhelmed.

One day, Mum told me Ruth had a fever and I wasn't to hold her until she was better – but she didn't tell me I couldn't look at her lying in her crib. So the first time I looked, I was shocked; whimpering and tearing at her clothes, Ruth's face was very red and just standing by her, I could feel the heat coming from her little body. It was three days later I noticed she had gone quiet. Mum had just stepped outside, so I went to her crib and was happy to see she was sleeping peacefully and her fever seemed to have gone completely. Excited, I ran outside and called Mum. She was talking to a neighbour, but when I told her Ruth was asleep and I thought she was getting better, she didn't smile or say anything, just rushed into the house. She picked Ruth up and looked at her, but she didn't smile or make the clucking noises she normally made. Instead, she began to wail in a way I'd never heard before, have never heard since and hope I never will again. It wasn't like when Dad set about her or even how she was after he'd finished with her. Confused, I asked her what was wrong and when she didn't reply, I tugged at her skirt and asked again. She pulled herself away from me and screamed,

"She's dead!"

I didn't understand. How could it be true? I'd seen Ruth moments before and she'd been sleeping; how could she have died so quickly? But when I asked Mum, she set her teeth and spat,

"You stupid child, she wasn't sleeping. She was already dead."

Pulling at her arm, I made her show me, but when I touched Ruth's face, it was cold and she didn't move at my touch. Then I noticed her little chest, which I was used to seeing move rapidly in and out as she breathed, now was motionless and I realised Mum was telling the truth. The shock forced me to my knees and as I buried my head in Mum's skirts, the tears began to flow.

For what seemed forever, Mum left me there sobbing, but finally, after putting Ruth back in her crib, she bent down and pulled me gently to my feet. She pleaded with me,

"Your father will be home soon. You don't want him to catch you crying, do you? You know what he's like, so dry your eyes now and be a brave boy."

I knew she was right about my father, but I'd lost my little sister and I was very far from being ready to be a 'brave boy'. So instead, I ran out the front door and kept running until I was safely in the woods that surrounded our village. There I threw myself on the ground and cried myself out.

When I returned home a couple of hours later, Dad was already there, but neither he nor Mum wanted to know where I'd been. Mum only asked me quietly whether I wanted something to eat. I said yes, but then ate only a couple of mouthfuls. Normally I'd be forced to eat the rest and when I finished, my reward would be a beating from Dad, but this time Mum just took my plate away and Dad said and did nothing.

I never saw Ruth again and when I noticed her body was no longer in her crib, Mum explained that she'd already taken her to get her ready for burial. And as they didn't take me to the funeral, I never had the chance to say goodbye.

When Mum died, Dad took to drinking whatever he could, wherever he could get it and it was only a few months later that he abandoned me. I learnt later that two more years of that life had found him dead in a gutter.

I was barely seven years old and my father hadn't taught me much. But two things I had learnt from him that I would never forget: how cruel men could be to women and the way drink could destroy their lives and the lives of those around them. In time, I came to realise that life had put my father at the bottom of the pile and fate had conspired to keep him there. Mum had been the one bright shell that had washed up on life's otherwise cold beach. Beguiled by her looks, he believed she would lead him to a better place. She gave him no reason to think that way and couldn't be blamed for her looks – she certainly never flaunted them – but when he realised that nothing would change, her looks became a taunt to him and the passion to destroy them became as strong, stronger even, than the one that had dazzled him in the first place.

Dad drank too much to keep any job and I became used to being woken in the dead of night and moved from one dank hovel to another even worse. Finally, when there was nowhere Dad didn't owe rent or where his reputation as a bad payer didn't precede him, we spent an uncomfortable night sleeping under a hedge.

Early the next morning, I awoke cold and hungry and we found some uncollected windfall apples, left presumably because they were beginning to rot. Making sure the maggots, already started on their own meal, didn't become part of ours, we breakfasted on those morsels we found that were still edible.

Meagre as it was, that meal turned out to be the only food we had to eat all day and after spending the day wandering aimlessly and not finding anything better, that night we returned to the same hedge. Huddled close to Dad, though cold and aching with hunger, I was so exhausted I slipped into fitful sleep. But then, in the middle of the night, Dad woke me.

"Come on son, wake up. I know what we're going to do."

As I struggled to my feet, lying in the cold and damp had made me very stiff, Dad said,

"We're about three miles from town and there are some people there who'll take you in and look after you. You'll have to be really quiet when we get there though, 'cos we don't want to rouse them 'til they're ready to take in a newcomer."

Without another word, he started walking away and bleary-eyed, there was nothing I could do but follow.

18

It was still dark when he stopped outside a high gate. He spoke in a whisper.

"This is the place then Jabez; in a couple of hours, they'll open the gate to let a few people out."

Pointing at the flint–fronted building that lay in darkness beyond the gates and so quietly I could barely hear, he breathed,

"When they see you, they'll ask why you're here and all you have to do is tell them the truth. You just explain that your Mum's dead and I've gone to find work. Tell them that and they'll take you in, feed you and give you a bed until I've got things sorted out and can come back for you."

I was frightened to be left alone and the building, which in the night looked windowless and unwelcoming, filled me with foreboding. But I didn't want to spend another night under that hedge and I was so hungry that the thought of food, any food, overcame my fear.

When I think back, my father actually looked relieved as he said,

"Right then son, I better get going. Remember, I'll be back as soon as I can."

I sat down by the gate and waited for someone to appear. I think, even then, I knew I'd never see my father again.

'What the devil are you doing there boy?'

A voice had interrupted my dreams, and opening my eyes I saw a man stood at the gate jangling a large set of keys in his hand. Struggling to my feet, I said what Dad had told me to say, fully expecting the man to open the gate and welcome me in. But the gate stayed firmly shut as he sneered,

"So your father's left you here, has he? Expects us to feed and clothe you, does he? Put a roof over your head 'till he feels like picking you up? Now you get on your way and catch up with your father and when you do, you tell him – and make sure that you do – you tell him we're not here to look after any of his waifs and strays."

I was confused. I didn't understand. Dad had said they would just take me in. So not knowing what else I could say to change his mind, I said,

"Please sir, I haven't eaten for days, or slept in a proper bed."

Looking down at me, he remained unsympathetic.

"That's not our problem, is it lad? It's your father's job to look after you, not ours. Now the sooner you get after him, the sooner you'll catch him up and when you do, you tell him what I said; tell him I don't want to see either of you back here. Do you understand me?"

I just stood there not knowing what to do. His unforgiving face told me I'd never change his mind and as if to confirm my thoughts, he added,

"I said get on your way otherwise I'll call a constable."

I started to walk away; I didn't know where I was going but there seemed to be little else I could do. I was so hungry; my stomach hurt. So tired, I was light–headed and worst of all, I felt so very alone.

As I walked, my head began to swim and reaching for a wall, I missed and fell. I must have fainted because in what seemed moments but must have been longer, I found myself being picked up by a man I didn't know. I was too weak to struggle and, to be honest, I couldn't see the point; whatever fate this man had in store for me, it couldn't be worse than the one I was already facing.

I slipped in and out of consciousness, so I remember only slivers of what happened next. I've never met that man again, so I've never been able to thank him and tell him that that morning he probably saved my life; he certainly changed it for the better.

Ignoring the porter's protests, he called,

"Nurse Cole."

Repeatedly he called for her. He wouldn't give up and eventually she appeared. Just out of bed, her hair dishevelled, she'd clearly dressed in a hurry. Looking very displeased, she demanded,

"And who is it making enough noise to wake the dead? Who thinks they have to drag me out of bed at this ungodly hour?"

Then she must have seen me and, ignoring the porter's scowls, told him to unlock and reopen the gate.

"Bring the boy here," she told my rescuer.

He carried me in and, at Nurse Cole's instruction, put me down. I tried to stand but my head started swimming for a second time. I staggered and would have fallen if he hadn't caught me up again. With a note of resignation, Nurse Cole said,

"Very well, bring him inside and take him to the infirmary."

Carrying me in, the man laid me on a bed and after wishing me well, disappeared. Despite my hunger, I fell asleep instantly and whilst sleeping was overtaken by a fever.

Most of the next week was nothing to me but fevered dreams, broken occasionally by Nurse Cole trying to make me drink a little water. Again and again I had the same nightmare; I was in a darkened room where Mum gave me a basket full of apples and every time I took a bite from one of them, it turned rotten. When I turned to ask Mum why, she was the same, her face rotting and covered with maggots.

The fever broke after four days and later Nurse Cole told me she'd seen many, both young and old, who'd had a lower fever than me but hadn't survived. Nevertheless, once the fever broke, I started to recover quickly and thankfully as my temperature fell, so the dreams became less frequent until after a week they stopped completely.

After ten days, I was given a bath (I hadn't bathed since Mum died) and some fresh clothes. The clothes were rough, but at least they were better than the rags I'd arrived in. In all the time I spent in the workhouse, that was the only time I bathed in clean water because usually, one by one, we all used the same water and if you were far enough down the line, it could be thicker than the gruel they fed us every morning. Nevertheless, they always fed me, clothed me and put a roof over my head. The bathwater might have been dirty most of the time, but it was always at least lukewarm and usually took off more dirt than it put on. After bathing, although still weak, I was moved into the main dormitory and joined the same routine as all the other young paupers.

So for the next six years, the workhouse was my home and although I was often reminded how fortunate I was that the parish had taken me under its wing, in all that time I was never again asked any questions about my father, or the circumstances that led to him abandoning me outside the workhouse. I suppose, like me, they knew he was never coming back.

'Bend with 'em and you'll be alright.'

That's what Joseph whispered to me the first night I was in the boys' dormitory – I've often wondered why he later forgot to follow his own advice, but I'll come to that.

Beds in the dormitory were arranged in two lines down opposite walls and I was given the last one on the left with Joseph next to me. The ceiling was high, as were the two small windows that provided the room's only light. The walls were unbroken distemper, unbroken but for a small fire in one corner which, even when lit, threw heat no further than the two nearest beds.

But for me it was everything I could wish it to be. I had a dry bed, a pillow, a sheet and a blanket. The pillow may have been hard and the blanket thin, but they were more than I had enjoyed for a long time and by simply pulling the covers over my head and curling up in a ball, I found I could create enough warmth to make me comfortable on even the coldest nights. So on that first night and most that followed, I slept soundly.

The next day, as he showed me how to pick oakum, Joseph introduced himself. He told me, in that straightforward way we all have as children but lose before we become adults, that his name was Joseph Levy, he was eleven years old and that he had come to the workhouse with his mother after his father had died.

"But you can call me Joe," he said. Then, lowering his voice, he added, "Now, remember what I told you last night. I'll make sure none of the other boys give you any trouble and the men and women here probably won't have anything to do with you. They keep us separate from them nearly all the time and most of 'em have enough troubles of their own not to be bothered with the likes of us."

For reasons I only understood later, it was clear Joe had decided to take me under his wing.

"No, it's some of 'em who run this place you've got to watch out for. Nurse Cole's alright. She growls a lot, but she don't bite. Mr Deeming, our tutor, is much the same, as long as you learn your letters and get his sums right, he'll give you no trouble. The ones you've got to watch out for are the Master and Matron. You're best doing anything you're told by a member of staff, but with those two, you'll do better if they don't notice you at all. They hate everyone who's in the workhouse and as far as they're concerned, we can never do right.

Matron is usually with the women and girls, but Mum says she's much the same as the Master. They call us slackers and sluggards and never miss a chance to punish us, even if we haven't done anything wrong and it don't seem to matter to them that without us they wouldn't have a job. I haven't been allowed to see Mum for three weeks because every week when he does his dorm inspection, the Master says my bed's not made right. He pulls on the sheet really hard so it's bound to come off; I've never seen him do it to anyone else."

I didn't say anything, just wondered why Joe was treated differently from all the others. Surely the Master could have done the same thing with anyone's bed?

"The others are alright most of the time, but o' course you've already made your own enemy."

Confused, I asked him,

"How can I have made an enemy? I haven't spoken to anyone in here apart from you and Nurse Cole?"

After looking round to check he couldn't be overheard, he said,

"But you were let in after the porter refused you entrance, weren't you? Nurse Cole overruled him in front of some of the paupers and according to him, 'undermined his authority'."

I was still bewildered.

"How can he blame me? I walked away when he told me to. It's not my fault that I passed out and someone carried me back."

"But that's just it," Joe said. "He's convinced himself you were acting. 'Like summat outta Shakespeare', he said, ''e shouldn't be in 'ere. 'E should be on the stage'."

"But I wasn't acting," I said angrily. "I was starving."

"I know, but you won't convince him. Don't worry though, as long as you stay away from the gate, you shouldn't need to have anything to do with him. His name's Platt by the way.

Anyway," he continued, "we'd better get some more of this oakum picked before the dinner bell rings – they won't let us eat if they don't think we've picked enough."

Like everywhere else in the workhouse, the walls in the classroom were painted white, but unlike everywhere else, two good-sized windows in the back wall meant the room was well–lit on all but the gloomiest days. A fire, which Mr Deeming ensured burnt whenever it was cold, made sure the room was always tolerably warm. I sat at the back next to Joe.

When Mr Deeming breezed in, the class, which was already quiet, fell silent, and after glancing round, his gaze settled on me.

"You, the new boy, we don't want you sat at the back, do we? At least not until we know you're not sitting there just to avoid working."

I think he smiled, though it looked more like a grimace.

"What's your name then lad?"

After I told him, he said,

"Right then Payne, come and change places with Camden here in the front. On your way to the back Camden, hand out the slates, will you?"

The slates were in two neat piles on Mr Deeming's desk, and without a word, Ben Camden collected the first pile and handed them out to those nearest. Picking up the second pile, he distributed them as he made his way to his new place next to Joe.

When I'd settled at my new desk, Mr Deeming handed me a piece of chalk, but seeing the clumsy way I held it, he said, "You've not learnt to write yet, have you boy?"

I knew my face was turning red; all the others were looking at me and I wasn't used to being the centre of so much attention, so I could think of little else to say other than,

"No sir."

"And can you read at all?"

The truth was Dad couldn't read or write, so there was no possibility that I was going to learn.

"No sir."

Expecting that reply, almost as soon as I spoke, he said,

"Right, give me your slate and we'll start you at the beginning."

As he wrote on the slate, he told me,

"I've written the first five letters of the alphabet, A B C D and E." He pointed to each one as he named it.

"Now I want you to hold the chalk like me and copy them. They're to look exactly the same as mine, the same height, all the lines joined but none running over another and all the letters in a straight line. If you make a mistake, rub it out and start again. When you've finished, put your hand up and I'll come and look at what you've done. I don't want to see them 'til they're perfect, mind."

With an emphasising rap on my desk, he handed me back the slate; I was already holding the chalk as he had. Starting the first downward stroke was the hardest, but once I sat back and saw it mirrored Mr Deeming's, I grew more confident and the other lines followed easily. Though he made no comment, I think Mr Deeming was surprised at how quickly and accurately I completed the letters. Finding no fault, he took my slate, wiped it clean and gave me the next five to copy. I found copying letters quite easy and it wasn't long before I was copying simple sentences. I don't know exactly when it was I started reading what I was writing, but I do know that within a year I was trying to read anything I could lay my hands on. In time I also gained a working knowledge of numbers, but it's a love of reading that has stayed with me all my life.

The first bell of the day was at six. On a Monday morning, it was followed at half past by dormitory inspection and it was the Monday after we'd first talked that I witnessed the Master's treatment of Joe. I not only discovered the reason he treated him differently from everyone else but also why Joe had befriended me.

Before the bell stopped clanging, Joe leapt out of bed and ran for the broom which stood behind the door. Running back and whilst urging me to get up, he swept all around and under his bed. By the time I was dressed, the rest of the dormitory were up as well and as Joe handed me the broom, others started calling for it.

Joe, who by now was tugging furiously at his sheet, trying to make sure it was tucked in as tightly as possible, looked up at me and in a loud whisper hissed,

"Hurry up."

There was an edge of panic in his voice.

"They want the broom and you've still got to make your bed."

His fear was infectious and I swept frantically around and under my bed. After handing over the broom, I'd only just finished making my bed when the door burst open and the Master strode in. To my alarm, he was followed closely by Platt.

We all stood nervously by our beds and whilst the Master began pacing slowly between each pair, Platt remained standing silently in the doorway.

The floor and apparently every bed passed inspection until he reached Joe's. Standing with his hands gripped behind him, after first glancing at Platt to make sure he had his full attention, he turned to Joe's bed and said,

"So, let's see if the dirty Jew has done any better this week."

With that, he kicked Joe's mattress which of course raised a great cloud of dirt. In anger, he released his hands from behind his back and with one pull, removed Joe's sheet. Disdainfully, he said,

"Once a dirty Jew, always a dirty Jew, can't make a bed, can't clean a floor. Simple things any boy bought up civilised learns from when they can walk. What say you, Mr Platt?"

"You're right as always, Master."

"So why do you think this boy ain't been bought up civilised then, Mr Platt?"

"'Cos he's the son of a Jew Master, that's why."

"Exactly, Mr Platt, exactly. But not any Jew, oh no, he's the son of a workhouse Jew. All of 'em are either robbin' you blind with their money lendin', or in the workhouse takin' advantage of the Parish's generosity.

Though you can't really blame the boy, you just have to teach him. Ain't that right, Mr Platt?"

"No one else is going to teach him, Master. 'Specially not that mother of 'is."

"Why's that then, Mr Platt?"

They were obviously working together, walking down a well–worn path. Joe's face had reddened, but he'd said nothing, just stared at the wall opposite. But then Platt must have strayed from the path and entered forbidden territory because when with venom he said,

"Because she's a dirty whore, Master, as well as an uncivilised and ungrateful Jewess."

Joe went past the Master so fast that there was no chance he'd be stopped. He flew into Platt, fists flaying and shouted angrily,

"You shut your filthy mouth. My mother's a good woman and it's not her fault we're in here. You're only working here because the Parish pays you to look after us; otherwise you'd be livin' in here just like the rest of us."

With the first volley, Platt had stepped back in surprise and although Joe stopped hitting him quite quickly, he carried on shouting and for a fleeting moment, I wondered whatever happened to 'bending with 'em'. But I suppose things had been building up inside him for a while.

By this time, the Master, who had got over his initial surprise, snapped at the porter,

"Get hold of him, Mr Platt, and take him to the refractory cell. We'll see if a couple of weeks in there won't teach him to show some respect for his elders and betters."

The Porter was a big man, well–fed and used to carrying heavy loads. Joe, on the other hand, was a wisp and like most of us, short for his age. So once Platt had recovered from the initial onslaught, Joe was no match for him. In fact, after that first outburst, the fire seemed to go out in Joe and even though roughly handled by Platt, he put up no resistance as he was marched away.

Joe had gone, but the rest of us still stood transfixed, wondering what would happen next. Once again, the Master paced slowly up and down the dormitory. As he went, he looked directly at each boy. I think he wanted to ensure we were equally affected. He needn't have worried; we were all terrified.

Finally, as his gaze landed on me, I noticed Platt, still puffing from his exertions, had returned and was again standing in the doorway. Later I discovered from Joe that Platt had raced him to the lock–up, thrown him in and without another word locked the door. Joe said he'd heard him moving rapidly away and guessed that he must have known he was still needed – an opportunity he clearly had no intention of missing. In fact, I think the Master and Platt knew exactly what they were going to do next and they also knew it would involve me.

The Master walked slowly to the end of my bed and to a small boy he looked fearsome as he thundered,

"So, here's the boy who says he's been abandoned by his father. What do we think about that, eh, Mr Platt?"

With one movement, the Master pulled the sheet off my bed and let it fall to the floor.

"We think he's a liar, Master. Said he was ill. Put on a great show to play on your generosity."

"Well boy, what do you think of what Mr Platt has to say? Are you a liar playing on my generosity?"

What I thought was, *'why does he keep talking about the Master's generosity? Him and his wife get paid to run the workhouse. We're not costing them anything.'*

But all I said was, "No sir." My heart was racing.

"Then are you calling Mr Platt a liar?"

He glanced at the Porter; I thought I saw a smirk flicker across his face.

I remembered Joe's advice.

"No sir. I just think he's mistaken."

"Did you hear that, Mr Platt? He thinks you're mistaken. We'll just have to see about that, won't we? I've got my eye on you lad, so you'd better watch your step.

Now you get the floor swept and make that bed up properly. If I've got time, I'll be back to check and if you haven't done it properly, you'll be joining that Jew in the cells."

27

With that, he marched back up the room and left, followed closely by Platt and leaving us unsure if he would return.

One of the others swept under the bed for me and Ben helped me make it again. Of course the Master never returned. He knew he'd had the effect he wanted and I'd learnt Joe's words of advice had been good ones, even if he hadn't followed them himself.

The Master had picked on me because I was the new boy, but because I'd taken Joe's advice and provided no reaction, offered no resistance, the Master paid me no further attention.

It was a pity the same could not be said for Joe.

Joe returned to us after two weeks, a little thinner perhaps but otherwise unchanged. He thought the Master might leave him alone now, but he couldn't have been more wrong; the Master was about to persuade Joe to sign his own death warrant.

He said that the worst thing about the refractory cell was boredom. The cell contained just a stool, a thin mattress and a bucket, the tedium broken only once a day by an early morning delivery of bread and water. For the first couple of days, Joe tried to talk to the pauper who brought him his food, but the old man just kept his eyes cast down, said nothing and only once on the first Wednesday, looked up and shook his head; it was clearly part of Joe's punishment that he was forbidden to talk to anyone.

The only variation from the daily monotony happened on the first Sunday of Joe's incarceration. The Chapel Bell had just announced Morning Service when Joe heard the cell door unlock. It burst open and in strode the Master. He seemed to enjoy the drama of bursting into rooms, and Joe told me he entered the cell with a smirk on his face and a Bible in his hand. He placed the Bible carefully on Joe's mattress with the front cover open and then, saying nothing, left.

When Joe looked more closely at the open cover, the Master had written, "1 Thessalonians 4 11–12." Joe's mother had taught him a lot from the Old Testament, but he had never even looked inside the New Testament, but as he said, he had all the time in the world to look. I told him that I knew a little about the New Testament but I had never heard of Thessalonians. Fortunately, Joe had found and memorised the passage, so with a deep breath he pronounced,

"And to aspire to live quietly, and to mind your own affairs, and to work with your hands, as we instructed you, so you may walk properly before outsiders and be dependent on no one."

Neither of us really understood the passage, nor why the Master had especially chosen it for Joe. But shortly afterwards, it became clear that it was nothing more than a cruel hint of what was about to befall Joe and I'm sure he used a passage from the New Testament just to rub salt in Joe's Jewish wounds.

Over the next fortnight, Joe came to believe his punishment had truly been served; and he had good reason. At consecutive inspections, both he and his bed had passed without comment and of much greater importance to Joe, that meant he'd been able to spend time with his mother. Family meetings, if they were allowed to happen at all, were on Sundays straight after Chapel and although neither Joe nor his mother attended Chapel, they still had to wait until the Service was finished before they could meet.

Joe didn't talk too much about those meetings, although he displayed a new calm that told me they had gone well. One thing Joe did say with great enthusiasm was that his mother was very keen to meet me. So on the third Sunday following his release, I joined Joe, who'd been waiting impatiently for me outside Chapel and met his mother in the yard.

Like most paupers, the strains and worries of life had clearly taken their toll on Mrs Levy. Thin, even by workhouse standards, her hair was grey and her face bore a crisscross of worry lines drawn by that enthusiastic artist, poverty. Her face nevertheless lit up when she saw Joe and her smile temporarily erased some of those lines. Joe ran to her and I must confess feeling a twinge of envy when they hugged. Mrs Levy, who stood facing my direction, looked past Joe and saw me standing there. Though she may not have recognised my envy, she must have seen my awkwardness, because she peeled herself away from her son and said,

"Joe, we're forgetting your friend. Now, aren't you going to introduce me?"

Joe blushed; in the excitement of seeing his mother again, he'd forgotten I was there. So in a desperate attempt to regain what he felt was his adult status, he put a finger and thumb to his mouth, whistled loudly and hailed me over. This would have been fine, had I not been less than twenty feet away from him and looking straight in their direction. Mrs Levy smiled at me knowingly and cuffed Joe lightly round the back of his head. Joe looked disgruntled as I sidled over, but I think he would have felt better had he realised that by his actions he'd already broken the ice between me and his mother.

Joe had explained to his mum that my mother was dead and that my father had left me at the workhouse gate. In fact when Mrs Levy finished telling all she knew about me, there was little more that I could add. Lowering her voice, she said,

"Now Joe, there's something I need to tell you. You too Jabez; come close both of you. I don't want us to be overheard."

We moved close, her sudden change of tone making us curious,

"What is it Mum?" Joe said.

"Now look, I don't want to raise your hopes," all humour had left her face, "because nothing may come of it."

Joe was used to disappointment, but I could see something in his mother's tone had raised his expectations and her warning went unheard.

"What Mum? What's happened? Are we getting out of here?"

Mrs Levy looked concerned at Joe's reaction. Taking hold of his shoulders, she spoke firmly.

"No, nothing has happened – not yet anyway. It's just that I've written to my cousin Abram who I haven't seen for over twenty years. I was still a child when he moved to London with his parents. His father fell out with your grandfather, over what I never knew. I don't know how Abram heard of your father's death, but when he did, he sent us a note of condolence and the note contained an address. Now, although I don't know how matters lay with Abram, it may just be that he's a little better off than us. I'm hoping so and that the note containing an address means he wants to let matters from the past rest in the past. Anyway, I've written to him explaining our plight in the hope that he'll be able to help us. I can't say anything will come of it, Abram may not be in a position to help us and even if he is, he may not want to."

She gripped Joe's shoulders even tighter and said,

"So it's important you don't get your hopes up; do you understand me?"

She held his eye until he nodded and muttered,

"Alright Mum."

She let go of his shoulders and, turning to me, said,

"And Jabez, if you like, should Abram write back, I can tell him I want to adopt you. Then perhaps he'll take you as well. No promises, mind."

She gave me an encouraging smile, but I was dumbstruck. I didn't know what I thought. But before I could say anything, Joe spoke.

"Mum, does that mean he'd be my brother?"

Mrs Levy looked a little taken aback.

"I'm not sure Joe, but I suppose it would. Anyway, we don't know whether Jabez would want you as his brother. You'd have to ask him."

Joe turned to me and for the second time that morning, his face reddened. Mind you, my face felt hot, so I suppose we were both blushing.

"Well, what do you think?" he muttered.

Too embarrassed to meet his stare and with my eyes fixed firmly on my feet, I just said,

"I s'pose it'd be alright."

And with that understated reply, it seems that at least briefly, we became family.

The rest of the time we had that morning, Joe and I spent excitedly planning our future lives together, probably in London. Neither of us had anything but the vaguest idea of what London was like, but that didn't stop us from taking the smallest fragment we had and building a world around it.

The Tower of London was our main topic of discussion. Neither of us new very much about it, but we did know that it held England's darkest criminals. We knew of it from class, where Mr Deeming had an illustration on the classroom wall. He used to point at it, especially the nightmarish Little Ease cell, and tell us how in there, even for small boys like us there wasn't enough room to lie down or stand upright and if we misbehaved, it was where we would end up.

In the way young boys unite, Joe made us both laugh whilst remaining just a little afraid. Imitating Mr Deeming, he pointed at an imaginary picture on the yard wall and with a voice full of menace, said,

"Remember boys, anyone who's sent in there never comes out alive."

Mrs Levy left us to dream and play and I'm sure it gave her great pleasure to see us taken out of our workhouse lives, even if it was only for a short while. But all too soon, the dinner bell rang and we had to part. I waved goodbye to Mrs Levy and told Joe I'd see him inside. Deliberately I didn't look back. I knew Joe would be embarrassed if he thought I'd seen their inevitable farewell hug. But, unbeknown to both Joe and his mum, that meeting was to be their last.

Next day's class was interrupted by the Master who, in his usual manner, burst into the classroom and announced,

"Mr Deeming, the boy Levy needs to come with me."

Though clearly annoyed by the manner of the interruption, Mr Deeming just said,

"Alright then, Levy. You heard the Master. If you're not back by the end of lessons, I'm sure Payne will clear your desk and bring back to the dormitory anything that's yours."

Looking straight at Joe and in a menacing tone, the Master said,

"Oh, he won't be back. You can be certain of that Mr Deeming. In fact, he won't ever be coming back."

Joe, who had already stood up, looked excited.

"Has my mum heard from her cousin? Are we going to London?"

The Master was a little taken aback. This quite obviously was not a response he had expected, but recovering he said,

"I don't know about any cousin but you're certainly not going to London. I've got somethin' special for you m'lad. You're off to be a pauper apprentice in the lead works at Gladlys; keep you nice and warm that will."

He laughed to himself. We all failed to see why but I noticed Mr Deeming wasn't sharing the joke.

"If I'm leaving, I'll have to tell my mother. I don't know where Gladys is and Mum will need to know where I am."

"You don't need to worry about that. I'll make sure she knows; and it's Gladlys, not Gladys. You don't want to start by giving a bad impression, do you?"

31

Without waiting for a reply, he said,

"Right, come along then boy. There's a cart waiting for you at the gate."

Taking a firm grasp of Joe's arm, the Master led him from the classroom. Joe only had time to glance back pleadingly in my direction before he disappeared. But I understood. I knew that whatever the Master had said, Joe wanted me to seek out his mother and tell her what had happened.

He needn't have worried though because, as Mrs Levy later told me, the Master was as good as his word and as soon as he knew Joe was well away from the workhouse, he took it upon himself to break the news to her. Taking great delight from telling her that Joe had, that very day, signed up for a seven-year apprenticeship in the welsh lead mines, he went on to tell her she could visit him just as soon as she left the workhouse. Joe of course would not be able to leave Gladlys until he had served his time. The Master's cruel pleasure was extended as he went on to explain how Joe would spend his days dragging ore from the mine to the surface, breaking and washing it and then helping with the smelting.

When Sunday finally came around and I was able to see Mrs Levy, it was clear she was deeply upset. Looking more careworn than she had when last I saw her, the lines on her face seemed etched more deeply than ever. But she put on a brave front and told me she still hoped to hear from her cousin who she was sure, when he heard of Joe's fate, would buy out his indenture. I had no idea what an indenture might be, but even at seven, I could hear the desperation in her voice. She asked me if I might come and see her every Sunday; just in case, she said, one of us had some news of Joe. I believe she thought I held memories of Joe that I could share and would enhance her own recollections.

Enclosed by high grey walls on all sides and dubiously decorated with streaks of green slime, the yard was a stark place. The long and narrow walkway that led through to the yard from the workhouse, tunnelled even the balmiest breeze into a bone chilling wind. Despite the cold, the yard was filled each week with couples and families huddled against the conditions, prepared to endure any discomfort in order to spend time together.

Each week, we found a spot to meet and in time learnt to manoeuvre ourselves to a position where others protected us from the worst of the wind. But our greatest problem wasn't the cold. It was that after only a few weeks, I had nothing further to add to the picture of Joe Mrs Levy had so preciously retained. Though we had learnt a great deal about each other, I'd spent barely three weeks with Joe, so there were few recollections or golden moments I could tell her that she didn't already know. In fact, if just once Mrs Levy had suggested that we met only if we had fresh news of Joe, I would have gladly agreed. But that suggestion never came, so each week we met, we told each other we had no news and I shivered whilst Mrs Levy, to whom the cold seemed unimportant, continued to look worse than she had the previous week.

Save for the warming weather, months passed without news or change and although my weekly meetings with Mrs Levy meant I never forgot Joe, workhouse routine ensured that my mind was mostly occupied with other things.

Each morning was filled by breakfast, then work and finally lunch, whilst every weekday afternoon was spent in the classroom. Like everything else, our food followed a routine. Some grumbled and it's true there was never enough, but it was always hot and usually edible. I especially liked Friday because on Friday they gave us what they called Irish stew. We never knew exactly what was in it, though some of the boys talked darkly of missing cats, but there were always bits of meat and enough potato to take the edge off your hunger.

But what I remember most about Friday is that it was on a Friday Nurse Cole told me that Joe had been killed. That morning, she had found me in the garden where I'd been sent to help raise some potatoes. Calling me to one side, she said,

"I'm afraid I have some bad news for you Payne. The workhouse has just received notice from the headman at Gladlys that Joseph Levy was killed in an accident last Thursday. That's all the note said, but the boy who delivered it told me Joe had been killed when gunpowder had ignited prematurely, causing a rock fall."

Quietly she added, as though it would bring me some consolation,

"He said Joseph was killed instantly when a large rock crushed him and that he wouldn't have felt a thing."

But she had brought me no consolation because my friend, my brother, was dead. I was excused work for the rest of the day and allowed to return to the dormitory and it was there something remarkable happened.

The dormitory was empty of course and the others would not return until evening, so I threw myself on my bed and wept. Of course I cried over Joe, but I also cried over losing my mum and even over being abandoned by Dad but, strangely, most of all, I cried again for Ruth, the little sister I never really knew.

After a while I must have cried myself to sleep because the next thing I knew, someone was gently shaking my shoulder. I woke with a start. The dormitory was already in darkness, but in the gloom I could see clearly Mr Deeming standing over me. Struggling to get up, still in sleep–induced bewilderment, I thought I should be in the schoolroom. As I tried to rise, I began to apologise.

"Sorry sir, I'll be there right away… I don't know…"

He pushed me gently back on the bed.

"Stay where you are Jabez, you're not in any trouble. Nurse Cole told me what happened to Joe and I know you boys had become friends, so I thought I'd come and talk to you."

I had only been in the workhouse a few months, but one thing I had learnt was never to expect kindness from any member of staff, so Mr Deeming had done nothing to clear my confusion. As again, I tried to rise and began to speak. He pushed me back putting a finger to his mouth to silence me. Then he said, quietly,

"Now Jabez," his voice was a little sterner, "I want you to lie still and listen to me. Will you do that?"

I nodded; I was fully awake, now. He said,

"I've only just heard about Joe and I knew you would be upset. As you have no family in this place, I wanted to give you some advice.

When you have time to think about the manner of Joe's death, you're going to want to blame someone and I'm here to tell you that would be a mistake. Finding someone to blame for his death will be of no value to you because you'll be powerless to do anything about it. I think Joe would have agreed with me when I tell you that in your life it is important you look after yourself, because no one else will. You must also use any skill you possess that might give you some advantage over your circumstances.

Now, although you have only been here a short while, I've noticed how well you've taken to reading. In fact, I may tell you that of all the young paupers who've been in my classroom, you have shown the most promise. So I want to lend you a book; you won't be able to read it yet, but in time you will. *Robinson Crusoe* is about a man who's the only survivor of a shipwreck and lives for many years on a desert island. The story is full of adventure and I think when you have learnt enough to be able to read it, you'll enjoy it. But I hope you'll also see that along with all his adventures, the most important lesson

Crusoe learns is that he can rely upon only himself to survive so, as I said, that's the lesson I want you to learn."

He handed me a green–covered book, the corners of many of its pages bent; clearly, it had been read many times.

"The book is mine and it's the only copy I own, so look after it. I'll want it back before you leave this place."

With that, he turned and left. I opened the book, but it was already too dark to read, so I hid it under my pillow; I knew the other boys would be coming to the dormitory shortly and I didn't want them to see the book until I could give them a reason why it was in my possession that didn't cause any bad feeling.

The following day, as soon as we were released from the classroom, I made for the dormitory and retrieved the book from under my pillow. Sitting on the edge of the bed, I opened it eagerly, but whilst I recognised a few words, most were just a jumble of letters. Disappointed, I put the book back under my pillow and waited for the others to join me.

The next afternoon at the end of lessons, Mr Deeming told me to wait and when the others had all left, he asked,

"So, tell me, Jabez. Have you tried reading Robinson Crusoe yet?"

"Yes sir, but it's too difficult for me."

He smiled and said,

"Remember I told you, Robinson Crusoe had to learn to do things for himself. He did that in three ways; first, he took things he'd already learnt in life and applied them to his new situation. Second, he learnt by using guesswork and sometimes using a little of both made a third. Now, each day in class you're going to learn more new words and new sentences and each day I want you to take what you've learnt and try to read the book. Be patient and, in time, you'll recognise enough of the words to have a good guess at those you don't know and that way be able to read the whole book."

He was right of course and after about a year, I had learnt enough to make a fair guess of all the words I didn't know.

I had come to an arrangement with the other boys in the dormitory. When I shyly showed them the book, it was passed from one to another and their reactions ranged from curiosity to jealousy, but they all had one thing in common: none of them could read it, so I promised that as soon as I could, I would read it to them.

Eventually, after three or four months, I felt confident enough to offer to read the first chapter to them. My offer was met enthusiastically. They had after all waited patiently for what must have seemed a long time for this moment. The boys had left me alone when, each evening, they had seen me settle down to read and though this surprised me at first, I came to recognise that they'd seen the book and knew how hard the task I'd taken on was.

I had moved to one end of the dormitory and, feeling apprehensive and with trembling legs, climbed onto the only chair that we had. But as I looked around at all the eager and attentive faces, nervousness left me. The trembling in my legs drained away and was replaced by a comfortable solidity; I opened the book and began to read,

"I was born in the year of 1632, in the city of York, of a good family, though not of that Country, my father being a foreigner of Bremen, who settled first at Hull."

My voice sounded strange to me. It was clear and strong and when I glanced up, I saw only expressions of awe looking back at me. Although I had read the first chapter to myself more often than any other, I still stumbled over many words. But I pressed on, sometimes making complete guesses and at length, read,

"Til at last I quite laid aside the thoughts of it, and looked out for a voyage."

I had finished the chapter; my legs ached and by the end, my voice was reduced to a hoarse whisper. I closed the book and looked up. All the faces looking back at me were transfixed. At first there was silence but then, one by one, they began to clap quietly.

Flushed with success, I told them, or tried to tell them, I would read the second chapter the next evening. Fortunately, though my voice was reduced to a whisper, the boys nearest, who could still hear me, passed what I'd said on to those who hadn't heard.

And that's what happened. The next day, with my voice recovered, I read chapter two and on the following evenings a chapter or on occasion, when a full chapter was too long, only half of one. In reality, my reading ability was still limited, but whilst I continued to make mistakes, stumbled over words and guessed or made up many others, encouraged by the other boys, I persisted. And after a few weeks I had completed a, no doubt, unique but generally true to the substance of the tale, reading of *Robinson Crusoe*.

I had no sooner read,

"All these things, with some very surprising incidents in some new adventures of my own, for ten years or more, I shall give further account for in the Second Part of my Story," and explained I didn't have the second part of his story, before they clamoured for me to start reading from the beginning again. However, as it was already getting dark and reading the last few pages had been quite a strain on my eyes, I was glad to say I would start again the next evening.

I read to those boys every day and over the time I was in the workhouse, I probably read that book to them, from cover to cover, a dozen times and each time with less and less guesswork.

Reading was important to me then and, before I left the workhouse, was already shaping my life.

The Sunday after Joe was killed, I went looking for Mrs Levy. As usual, the yard was crowded with couples and families keen to be with each other for the first time in a week or more, but Mrs Levy was nowhere to be seen. I waited for about a quarter of an hour hoping she'd arrive, but when she still failed to appear, I began to make my way back indoors. I had just entered the walkway that led back to the workhouse when she appeared at the other end. Straight away I could see something was wrong. The sight of her careworn face and her thin body, thin even for the workhouse, had become a familiar sight. But now her walk was slow and laborious and she appeared to be talking to herself. I'm certain had I not spoken to her, she would have walked passed me without a word.

"Hello, Mrs Levy."

"Mmm. Oh, hello Jabez. Have you heard about Joe?"

"Yes Mrs Levy, Nurse Cole told me on Friday. This is the first time since then that I've been allowed to see you."

She started to walk ponderously towards the yard again, but I grabbed her arm and said,

"I'm so sorry, Mrs Levy."

I didn't know what else to say. She gave me a strange smile.

"He was blown up, you know; didn't feel a thing."

She continued towards the yard. I didn't follow; it seemed though she said my name, she didn't really know me, so instead, I just returned to the workhouse.

The next week I went back to the yard, determined I would talk to her and discover why she had acted so strangely. But even though I waited for the whole hour we were allotted, she never appeared.

As I stood in the yard keeping the whole length of the walkway in clear view at all times, the following week appeared to be heading the same way. I was concerned that she might decide to come to the yard and then lose courage, so I was ready to run and stop her, determined that we should speak if she appeared. It was then I noticed a man and women arguing, and both of them were looking repeatedly in my direction. Clearly, in some way I was the cause of their disagreement. Eventually, the woman started walking towards me and though the man tried to stop her, she shrugged him off.

As she came towards me, she started talking.

"You're looking for Rebecca, aren't you?"

Disappointed, I told her I wasn't and that I didn't know any Rebecca.

"I mean Rebecca Levy." Then as she reached me, her voice dropped and she added, "Joe's mum."

Now realising who she meant, I nodded and asked,

"Do you know her? Do you know why she hasn't come to the yard?"

"Yes son, I know her and I know why she's not here. It's 'cos she's not in the workhouse no more."

Before continuing, she looked around to make sure she wasn't overheard. She needn't have worried. All the people there were from families who'd been torn apart by the workhouse system and for whom this hour on a Sunday morning was the nearest they had to normality. In fact, this woman, who was kind enough to tell me about Mrs Levy, had given up her own precious time with her husband to speak to me; the reason, no doubt, he continued to look highly agitated. Certain that we were being ignored by everybody else and after pulling a defiant face at her husband, she continued,

"Rebecca was affected terribly by Joe's death. The shock broke her and by the end of last week, she was refusing to leave our dormitory. Instead, she just stood in the corner rocking to and fro and banging her head against the wall.

The Master reported to the workhouse governors that Rebecca had gone mad and needed to go to the madhouse. The governors would have done it as well, 'cos they always do what the Master says. But luckily for Rebecca, before the governors had their next meeting, who do you think turned up at the gates, large as life and took her away with him?"

"Her cousin?"

Nonplussed, the woman said,

"How did you know that? No one else is supposed to know about him. I just happened to be in the dormitory when he came to collect her. That's why I was arguing with my husband. The Matron told me not to tell anyone and he told me I should keep my mouth shut."

She gave a cursory nod in the direction of her husband.

"But I told him I'd seen you with Rebecca every week and you had a right to know what had happened to her."

I thanked her for telling me and explained that,

"Mrs Levy told me and Joe about her cousin weeks ago. She said she'd written to him and asked if he could help her and Joe get out of here."

I didn't tell her that I was supposed to go with them. What this woman told me just seemed to confirm Mr Deeming's words of advice when he found me in the dormitory.

And so it was that, punctuated by bells, for the next six years my life followed an unchanging routine. From the bell that woke us to the bell that told us to go to bed, every day, except Sunday, was an endless repeat of the day before.

But reading took me away from the dull routine. Every night for about three months, I read aloud a chapter or so from Robinson Crusoe, and even though they were becoming very familiar with the story, the boys' keenness to hear me read never waned. Like me, I'm sure in their imagination they loved to escape to the hot, dry isolation of that island and to be where, unlike in the workhouse, they had the luxury of seclusion.

Mr Deeming had said nothing to me about the book since encouraging me to persevere, but one day, just as he had on that occasion over a year before, he asked me to wait behind at the end of the day's lessons.

"So Jabez, how have you been getting on with Robinson Crusoe?"

With the confidence the other boys had given me, I said,

"Very well, I think, sir."

"Well then, I think you should bring the book to class tomorrow and read it to the others. What do you think?"

Finding it hard not to smile, I agreed.

It was always hard to tell what Mr Deeming was thinking, but as I left the classroom, I thought I saw that he too had the trace of a smile on his face. Now, when I think back, I believe he knew exactly what was going to happen.

When I reached the dormitory, I told the others Mr Deeming's instruction and because they were all as familiar with the story as me, they had little concern. They knew, or thought they did, that when I stopped reading, whatever questions they might be asked about the book, they would know the answer.

So the next day, straight after our midday meal, I rushed to the dormitory and collected the book. By the time I got to the classroom, all the boys were sat quietly at their desks and Mr Deeming was at the head of the class.

"Ah, Payne, glad you could join us."

"Sorry sir," I panted, "I had to fetch the book from the dormitory."

He continued.

"Well then, when you're ready, perhaps you can begin to read to us. Start at the beginning."

I had barely finished the first paragraph on the second page when he told me to stop; I wondered where I'd gone wrong.

"That's fine Payne. You can stop reading now. Now, who's next?"

He surveyed the class, his eyes finally coming to rest on Ben.

"Camden; let's hear from you."

Ben said nothing but strode confidently to the front and took the book from me; it was still open at page two. He started, to 'read'.

"Being the third son of the family and not bred to any trade..."

As I suspected, Ben had heard me read the adventure so often that he now knew large parts of it off by heart. But he soon discovered learning that way is not the same as reading.

Again, Mr Deeming intervened.

"No, not from there, Camden. Turn to page eight and start reading from, 'Though my mother refused to move it to my father…'"

Ben, whose face had carried a look of assurance now, as he found page eight, bore a look of panic. Desperately, he scanned the page; I could see he was trying to remember how the story went from there.

Impatiently, Mr Deeming said, "Come on now Camden, let's begin."

A combination of a little of what he'd learnt in class, loud echoes of the story he'd heard me read many times and cold fear, led him to believe he'd found the right place. So, falteringly he began, or so he thought, to read.

"Though my mother refused to move it to my father… she told me it would be to no use…. to tell my father anything. That he knew."

"Stop," Mr Deeming bellowed.

The mood of the whole class had changed. Everyone knew Ben had gone wrong, but they all knew, if asked, they would have the same difficulties.

Mr Deeming continued, though in a slightly lower tone.

"What do you think you're doing, Camden?"

"I'm trying to read the book from where you said, sir."

"No you're not. That's nothing like the piece I asked you to read. It sounds more like you're trying to re–write the story. Is that what you're trying to do, Camden? Do you think you can write a better story than Mr Defoe?"

"No sir."

Ben looked defeated. Clearly, he feared what punishment awaited him. But Mr Deeming just told him to sit down and then, turning to the class, asked,

"So, is there anyone apart from Payne, who thinks they could do better than Camden?"

The class was silent; things were definitely not going as they expected.

"As I thought, no one. I'm not surprised. You see, on occasion, since I lent Payne that book, it's proved necessary for me to pass your dormitory in the evening."

I could see no reason why he should need to pass our dormitory. The corridor led nowhere other than back to the main rooms of the workhouse.

"And each time, without fail, I've heard Payne reading this book to you."

He held the book out in front of him.

"And I've not heard one of you even *trying* to read it."

To ensure he still had our full attention, he slammed the book down on his desk. The class froze, uncertain as to what would happen next.

"You've all been happy just to leave it to Jabez."

He'd never before called me Jabez in front of anybody else; I hoped none of the other boys had noticed.

"Now, I'm going to give the book back to Payne."

He placed the book back on my desk; I was just grateful he hadn't called me Jabez again.

"This time I want you each evening to read a piece yourselves and in a month's time we're going to repeat this exercise and see how you've all got on."

With that, he changed the subject and we spent the rest of the afternoon reciting our tables and I was left wondering what the night would bring.

I wasn't taunted too much. Mr Deeming had used my first name only that once and anyway they were all relying on me, or at least they thought they were, to help them read *Robinson Crusoe*. Of course, they had all been learning to read in class and they had become very familiar with the book, so reading *Robinson Crusoe* themselves was largely a matter of confidence. Nevertheless, when a month later, they were each able to read a few pages of the book to Mr Deeming's satisfaction, my approval in the workhouse amongst my peers was assured.

However, my greatest security came from the familiar daily routine. For another five years, life continued with little variation or incidents, but then the day arrived which would take me from the workhouse and shape the rest of my life.

Whilst in class one afternoon, the Master entered in his usual brusque fashion and without invitation said,

"Mr Deeming, can I see you for one moment?"

With that, he stepped back out of the classroom, expecting to be followed. Mr Deeming looked around the class, all of whom had frozen when the Master entered.

"Right boys, carry on working. I'll be back shortly."

He followed the Master from the classroom and when he returned after only five minutes, he said nothing. The afternoon's lesson continued as before, but when the class was dismissed, he told me to wait because he needed to speak to me. When the others had all left, he told me to sit down again and explained the reason for the Master's earlier interruption.

"The Master has been approached by the landlord of the Boar's Head, Mr Dodds. The Boar's Head is an inn about fifteen miles north of here and Mr Dodds is looking for an apprentice. The Master asked for my advice because Mr Dodds can't read or write and so requires a boy not only to help run the Inn, but also to check his accounts and ensure his suppliers aren't swindling him. The Master asked me whom I thought was best suited to the job and I told him you."

I suppose I knew I would leave the workhouse one day. After all it was usual that those who didn't leave the workhouse with their parents or were taken by other members of their family, all became pauper apprentices by the time they were fifteen.

Mr Deeming continued.

"Mr Dodds is spending the night in town and is going to meet you at the workhouse gates at eight o'clock tomorrow morning."

So that was it. One more night in the workhouse and I'd be starting a new life wholly unknown to me. Although I suppose I knew I could be made to leave at any time, I harboured a vague hope that somehow, I had formed no idea how, I would be able to stay indefinitely. I knew there must be many questions I should ask, but all I said was,

"I'll go and get *Robinson Crusoe* for you, sir."

For the first time in the six years I had been in the workhouse, I saw Mr Deeming definitely smile and he said,

"That won't be necessary Jabez. Take it with you. Who knows, perhaps you'll have time to read it to Mr Dodds."

So, the next morning, having gathered my few belongings and eaten my last workhouse breakfast, accompanied by the Master I went to the gate to meet Mr Dodds.

To a thirteen-year-old, the man waiting at the gate was ancient, although Jack Dodds was in fact only in his mid–forties. In appearance, it seemed he'd concentrated all his effort into growing tall and neglected to save any for developing his girth. Consequently, he was at least nine inches taller than anyone I knew, either pauper or workhouse staff member, but looked like a stiff breeze would snap him in two.

Before I left, the master gave me my indenture papers and a quill and, forgetting that I could read, showed me where to sign. So, whilst I had very little time to read before I was pressed to sign, I did have time to see that, like Joe, I was signing for seven years. Over the years since he'd been killed, my memories of Joe had faded, but I still remembered enough to hope I would enjoy a better fate than him.

The porter opened the gate and as I stepped out, I heard him mutter that I would come to no good and something about how Mr Dodds would live to regret taking me. For me, it was the first time since I'd been carried exhausted and starving into the workhouse that I was on the outside and even though I had feelings of anxiety, those of nervous excitement were stronger. I scowled at Platt but said nothing, even at this late stage I was afraid Mr Dodds might change his mind and I would be sent back into the workhouse. Fortunately, the Master was as keen for me to leave as, by then, I had become to go, and he concentrated all his attention on Mr Dodds. So handing him the signed paper he said,

"There he is then, Mr Dodds, Jabez Payne, our tutor says he's the best reader and writer we've got. Now, he's got no family as far as I know, told us he was abandoned by his father at this very gate and out of kindness our porter took him in; that's the case, ain't it, Mr Platt?"

Platt looked startled. I don't suppose he expected to be involved in this conversation, but he rallied,

"As you say, Master, starvin' and fevered he was when I found him; so weak he had to be carried in. Still, fully recovered now though, ain't you lad?" He forced a smile.

Although, barely eight years old at the time, I'll never forget the feeling of desolation and loneliness I felt when Platt refused me entrance, nor that it was only the kindness and persistence of a man I never knew that had won me access. Stunned, I remained silent; freedom was so close. I think it was to avoid further awkwardness that Mr Dodds intervened.

"Well Master, if there's nothing else, we'll be on our way. Come on lad, the cart's just around the corner but we've got a long journey."

With that, he began to walk away from the entrance. I suppose he thought he was walking at an ordinary pace, but for me, his long loping stride meant I had to break into a trot just to keep up. We turned the corner and were just walking by the high wall which marked the boundary of the workhouse, when a small black door in the wall opened. Over the five years, I think I had explored every corner of the workhouse, so I realised it had to be the rear entrance to the kitchen. What was a complete surprise to me was seeing Mr Deeming standing in the doorway. Startled, I stopped in my tracks.

Clearly anxious not to be seen by anyone in the workhouse, he kept glancing over his shoulder. He spoke urgently.

"I wanted to see you before you left, Jabez. I'm glad you're going with Jack Dodds. He's a good man."

Glancing in the innkeeper's direction, he said,

"Work hard for him and I know he'll treat you well.

Now, if you have any time to yourself, then I want you to read this."

With that, he handed me a book. It seemed brand new. I looked at the cover and read: 'Travels into Several Remote Nations of the World'. It said it was written by someone called Lemuel Gulliver. For the second time in only a few minutes, I was lost for words.

Having checked again there was no one behind him, he said,

"I know you must have read Robinson Crusoe so many times by now that you know it by heart, so I thought you might like that one. But be careful. It isn't all it seems."

I was intrigued, but he hadn't finished.

41

"Gulliver sees things differently to Crusoe and it's important that we learn to understand different points of view. Anyway Jabez," he grasped my free hand and shook it vigorously, "work hard for Mr Dodds, help him in any way you can and I'm sure he'll teach you his trade so that, in time, you will be able to support yourself."

With that, he let go of my hand, gave a final nod to Mr Dodds and slipped back through the door, shutting it behind him. I found myself mouthing 'thank you' to a black, blank door. I don't know how long I would have stood staring at it and wondering what had just happened (me, a workhouse pauper and he had just shook my hand!) when Mr Dodds spoke.

"Very well then lad. Keep hold of that book and let's press on. The cart's just up ahead."

Pulled back to reality, I once again broke into a trot.

The journey to the Boar's Head fascinated me.

The horse that pulled the cart had been dozing when we reached him, but ambled off without complaint when roused. There was still a chill in the morning air, so Mr Dodds spread a blanket across our laps; little else passed between us for most of the journey.

Leaving the workhouse, we headed towards the town and as we didn't talk much, I had time to absorb the unfamiliar world I barely remembered. When we reached the edge of town, we passed a number of houses so decrepit and rundown that it seemed only desperation kept them standing. Some of their occupants, mainly women holding babies with barefooted scraps hanging round their skirts, stood looking at us hopelessly as we drove by. We turned into the High Street and entered a world of bustle and commotion and I was thankful to leave the desolation behind us. We now met carts, their drivers shouting warnings to careless pedestrians, keen to make their way into town. As we drew towards the town centre and the array of shops it contained, the number of people and carts increased in number and urgency, and it was fortunate that our horse knew only one slow, unruffled speed. Fortunate, because as the road became more crowded, so it became more deeply pitted, with that and many more people darting across our path, our slow progress ensured Mr Dodds had sufficient time to steer the horse on a safe course.

I had never really seen a town before. Even when Dad brought me through this one, it had been in the dark dead of night and I had seen nothing. Now, the urgency with which people appeared and disappeared through shop doorways, mingling with numerous goods and smells that spilled out onto the path had me mesmerised. I was fascinated by the throngs of people who stood talking to one another, some who met in greeting, others who stood and argued, whilst the greatest number just stood together in comfortable familiarity.

For me, one pair of eyes was never going to be enough to take in all there was to see, but a glance at Mr Dodds told me he was wholly unaffected by the spectacle. With concentrated disinterest he looked only forward, his eyes on the horse and the road ahead and the only time he or the horse reacted quickly was when two brawling drunks fell from a pub into the road directly in front of us. Startled, the horse had reared, raising the cart behind him and only an instinctive grasp of the cart's side saved me from being thrown into the road. But Mr Dodds held on tight to the reigns and, by talking firmly but evenly to him, brought the horse back to his usual rhythm. Memories of my father's drunken violence made me grateful that Mr Dodds ignored the drunkards' swearing and kept us moving through the town.

Soon after we passed the pub, the town began to peter out and before long we were in the solitude of the country. A long bend in the road brought us to a junction where, turning left, our path began to climb. As we progressed, trees which had been scarce became increasingly more numerous, until woodland enclosed us on both sides. After we'd travelled for what must have been a further half hour, I noticed that the road had levelled and that whilst the woodland to our right now rose high above us, to our left we looked down on the tops of even the tallest trees; clearly, our path was taking us round a hill. As we moved away from the town, the road surface improved, so now only rivulets, bound to their downward journey, occasionally eroded the road's surface as they crossed our path.

We met only one other cart as we rounded the hill and when we did, to me it seemed the path wasn't wide enough for us to pass one another. But Mr Dodds and the driver of the other cart knew better, so whilst the other driver drew his cart as close to the inner bank as he was able, Mr Dodds moved us towards the outer edge. This left me overseeing nothing but tree tops and pointlessly gripping the cart again, praying that the wheels unseen beneath me would remain on the road. But I needn't have worried, because two experienced horses, driven by two skilled men, inched passed each other without incidence and with only the faintest acknowledgement of each other by their drivers.

I forgot I was still holding the side of the cart until some minutes later when Mr Dodds glanced in my direction and said,

"The road's wider now. It'll stay that way 'til we reach the Boar."

Not wishing to show my embarrassment, I bent down to check my bootlaces then, sitting up again, rested my hands in my lap. Mr Dodds said nothing, though I'm sure I saw a hint of a smile.

After we rounded the hill the path descended, the woodland thinned and a further hour brought us to another junction where, turning right, we once again entered a world of activity. Moving with us was a steady stream of empty carts, whilst moving in the opposite direction were others all fully loaded with salt.

Mr Dodds seemed to have read my thoughts.

"They're from the salt pans."

He seemed to expect me to understand, but I'd never heard of them.

"The salt pans?"

"That's right. Our living depends on them. Most of the men who drink in the Boar work in the pans and those who don't make their money from those who do."

This was the most Mr Dodds had said to me since we met; it was clear the salt pans were very important to him and though I wasn't to know it then, in years to come they were going to be even more important to me. Five minutes later, we left the traffic and turned into a tree–lined lane and I could see that at the end of the lane stood a solitary building. As we drew closer, I could see above the building's entrance a drawing of what had to be a Boar's Head.

Mr Dodds led the way inside and headed straight upstairs. Unsure if I should follow, I hesitated, but not hearing my footsteps behind him, Mr Dodds returned to the top of the stairs and called down.

"Come on lad, this way."

When I reached the top and turned the corner, in front of me there was a dark corridor containing two doors. Mr Dodds had passed the first and was waiting for me by the second. Opening it, he invited me in saying,

"This is your bedroom Jabez, mine's next door. When you're ready, join me downstairs and I'll show you where we work."

With that, he stepped back from the doorway, shut the door and I heard his steps retreat down the corridor and fade away as he descended the stairs. Transfixed, I stood in the middle of the room. For as long as I could remember, I had only slept in a dormitory, but this room was to be mine and mine alone.

Turning slowly, I took in the room. Apart from a bed beneath the window, the room contained only a chest against the far wall and a chair by the bed. I put the book Mr Deeming had given me and my few other possessions on the chair and knelt on the bed to look out the window. For so long I had seen only the confining walls of the workhouse, but now from the bedroom window I could see out across the Inn's orchard to the fields beyond. The horse that had brought us to the pub was grazing on the grass that grew long around what, looking down, I could see was a deep well. The last time I'd seen an orchard, the trees had been largely bare and the only evidence that they'd once borne fruit were a few maggoty apples lying in the grass. But here, as it was May, there were no signs of fruit, but every tree was full of white blossom; to me, it looked like a sudden snowstorm had struck the field and by some miracle, all the snow had caught in the trees.

As I marvelled at the view, Mr Dodds called for me from the bottom of the stairs and broke my reverie. Panicking, I leapt from the bed, wrenched the door open, ran down the corridor and headed down the stairs, descending three at a time. Only because Mr Dodds stepped back smartly into the bar was a collision avoided, instead I skidded to a halt just short of the front door. I had barely stopped and was still turning to face Mr Dodds, when I began apologising.

"Sorry sir, I was distracted by the trees outside my window, I've never seen…"

But I was astonished into silence; Mr Dodds was laughing.

"There's no need to apologise lad, and no need to call me sir. Mr Dodds will do just fine. Remember, you're not in the workhouse anymore. I called you because I just wanted you to know there's a few victuals down here if you're hungry."

Relieved that I wasn't in any trouble, I realised suddenly how hungry I was. The only food I'd eaten that day was the bowl of thin gruel they'd given me for breakfast at the workhouse and now, sat on the bar, were a hunk of bread and the largest piece of cheese I'd ever seen. Mr Dodds poured a mug of ale and passing it to me, said,

"I need to tend to the horse; he needs food just like the rest of us. You stay here and eat some of that bread and cheese; eat as much as you want. It looks to me like you need fattening if you're going to give me a decent day's work. When I return, I'll show you what I want you to do."

Though it was simple fare, to me that bread and cheese was the finest food I'd ever eaten and by the time Mr Dodds returned, I had devoured most of the bread and half the cheese and I was just draining the last of the ale.

"You finished then, lad?"

Still swallowing, I could only nod.

"Right then, let me show you what I want you to do."

He told me that in the morning he wanted me to clean and tidy the bar room and wash out the jugs and mugs, in the afternoon I was to help him with any odd jobs and in the evening I was to work behind the bar. Then he surprised me by saying I need not start until the next morning.

"Seven o'clock sharp, mind. I'll give you a call at a quarter to. Until then your time's your own, so if you want to go out into the orchard, maybe introduce yourself properly to the horse, or make a start on that book Mr Deeming gave you. It's up to you."

Bemused, I'd never had so much freedom; I remained where I was.

Mr Dodds smiled and said,

"Why don't you go out to the stable? Just inside the door you'll find a box of windfalls. Take one and give it to the horse. He loves 'em and it will be a good way for you two to get acquainted. Only give him one mind, too many makes his belly swell. Have one yourself if you want, but make sure you give him his first. He won't like it if he thinks you've stolen his apple."

So that's what I did. Going back outside, I went across the grass and into the stable. The horse, which by this time had wandered to the far end of the orchard, at first took no notice of me, instead, he stood dozing and enjoying the day's sun. But when I came out of the stable, an apple in both hands, he behaved very differently. First, having recognised what I held, he came quickly towards me. He was only trotting, but it was the fastest I had ever seen him, or any other horse, move. Not knowing what else to do, I closed my eyes tightly and with my arm outstretched, held one of the apples in the palm of my hand. The next thing I knew, he'd snatched the apple from me leaving my hand completely untouched. I opened my eyes and there he stood in front of me, apple juice dripping down either side of his mouth; Mr Dodds was right, he definitely loved apples.

The horse showed no interest as I began to eat the other apple, seeming only to want to enjoy the taste of apple that remained in his mouth. I reached out and cautiously rubbed his nose and he responded by putting his head down to make my reach easier; encouraged, I rubbed more firmly. For a while, whilst I rubbed, he pushed hard against my hand, but then tossed his head and moved away. I didn't know why, but later I learnt from Mr Dodds that he loved to have his ears fondled and that's what he was expecting me to do. Despite my failings, in time we nevertheless become firm friends and Mr Dodds was not only to give me full responsibility for his care, but also taught me to ride him.

After the horse moved away, I drifted to the top of the orchard and there, overhung by long grass and reeds, found a sizeable stream. Slow–flowing but clear, I wondered why I hadn't spotted it when I'd looked out earlier from my bedroom window. It was only the next morning, when looking out the window again and knowing the stream was there, I spotted an occasional glint from the water as the morning breeze fleetingly parted the grass. Otherwise, the stream was completely obscured and once I had located it from my bedroom, became of little interest to me, remaining so for many years and only much later in my life taking on a greater significance. I spent the rest of the afternoon wandering aimlessly around the field, exploring the stable and finally dozing under a tree.

It was dusk when the sound of Mr Dodds calling dragged me awake.

"Are you coming in lad? I've just heated some soup if you want it."

Running in, I followed Mr Dodds straight into the bar, where I stopped abruptly. I had forgotten the Boar was an inn as well as my new home and there, sat by the unlit fire, were two men sharing a jug of ale. I must have looked startled because one of them spoke to reassure me.

"It's alright lad. We don't bite; you must be the new apprentice Jack was tellin' us about."

I smiled nervously.

"So what's your name then son?"

After I told him, he said,

"Well Jabez, pleased to meet you. I'm John Bostock and this here is Gilderoy Smith. If you stay here, you're probably going to see quite a bit of us. Ain't that right, Gil?"

They both laughed at something which, at the time, I didn't really understand. But then John stopped laughing and said,

"I hope you turn out to be what Jack's been looking for, but just now, you'd better turn around because I think you're wanted."

I swung round just as Mr Dodds finished pouring a bowl of steaming soup. Putting the pan down, he said,

"Here you are then Jabez." He put the bowl on the table in front of me. "If you go out the back, you'll find the rest of that bread you had earlier."

The soup was thick with potato and full of pieces of meat and with the bread was more, even though I tried, than I could eat. I put down my spoon, fearing what would happen; I still remembered how things had been with my father. But Mr Dodds just said,

"You had enough then Jabez? I've only ever had to feed myself. I've never had to feed a boy before. Still, I suppose there's quite a lot we're going to have to learn about each other."

A little later, he poured me another mug of ale and I think the ale, along with the rest of the day's events, made me very weary. Mr Dodds must have seen how tired I was because as soon as I finished, he said,

"Right lad. Let me light you a candle and then you get yourself off to bed. Work starts in the morning, remember."

To calls of 'night Jabez' from the others, I left the bar, and with candle in one hand, stair rail in the other, began to climb. As I reached the top and turned the corner, exhaustion rolled over me. Supported by the wall, my legs leaden, I made it to my bedroom where, pausing only to place the candle on the chest and without even removing my shoes, I lay on the bed and fell into a deep sleep.

My day had started full of anxiety, containing an array of bewildering new experiences. But when I was woken the next day by the early morning sun shining through the window, something told me my life was about to take a new and better path.

Just like in the workhouse, life as an apprentice was mostly routine. Six years in that place had got me very used to six o'clock starts, so when on that first morning, there was a rap on my bedroom door, I was already dressed and kneeling on my bed looking out the window. The curious thing was I couldn't remember undressing the night before, but that morning I'd found my clothes all folded neatly on the chair.

Telling myself I'd probably been too tired to remember getting undressed, I answered the knock by wrenching the door open and saying,

"I'm up and dressed Mr Dodds, and ready to start work."

Mr Dodds was standing there holding in one hand a jug of hot water and in the other, a folded towel that I was to discover hid a piece of soap. He stepped back and said,

"Steady there Jabez, we've got a few minutes before we have to start. Lift the lid on that chest, will you? I'll pour some water into the basin for you."

I looked at the chest and as far as I could see, it had a solid top, four identical drawers and a fifth slightly bigger one at the bottom. I looked back at Mr Dodds.

"Go on lad, before this water gets cold."

Still unsure, I reached for the top; it opened easily and Mr Dodds poured water into the basin which replaced the top two drawers. Leaving the soap next to the bowl, he put the towel on a rung which ran along the side of the chest and stepping back, emptied the jug into the bowel. Before leaving he added,

"Right. When you're finished, just throw the water out of the window, then come down and we'll have some breakfast."

So that was that. Every morning, there was a knock at my bedroom door and Mr Dodds would bring me in a jug of hot water. And every day, after washing and dressing, I would join him in the bar where he would have already poured me a bowl of gruel; but his gruel was *always* made with milk.

On that first morning and most that followed, after breakfast I started work, but I was to find that compared to the workhouse, my duties at the Boar's Head were light and most days I was finished by midday. For the whole of that summer, after I checked with Mr Dodds that he didn't need me for anything else, I found my new book and if the weather was fine, I spent the afternoon lying under a tree in the orchard reading. If it rained, as it did on a few occasions, I'd kneel on my bed and read whilst still, every so often, gazing out of the window.

In the main, Mr Dodds left me alone at these times, just occasionally needing my assistance maybe to position a new barrel at the back of the bar or help stack some hay bales that had just been delivered. It was only after I'd been at the Boar about six months that a real change occurred. It was now autumn and though the weather was dry, it was too cold for me to sit outside, and so I spent most afternoons in my bedroom. However, in mid–October, the weather changed and for about a week summer returned. Glad for the opportunity to sit outside again, I found my favourite old apple tree, which now carried a few apples but also still had a fair covering of leaves, and even though the sun sometimes shone surprisingly strongly, lying beneath them I received only a dappled warm glow.

Originally, as Gulliver had been the sole survivor of a shipwreck, I thought that despite what Mr Deeming had told me, the story would be like *Robinson Crusoe*. But I soon became fascinated by the tales of his adventures in the land of the Lilliputians and I had only just begun to read of his time with the giants of Brobdingnag, when a shadow fell across my book. I looked up and saw Mr Dodds, looking down at me and nervously rolling and unrolling a piece of paper he held. I shut my book and stood up, annoyed I hadn't seen him approaching, but before I could say anything, he asked me,

"Can I see that book you're reading?"

He held out his hand and I gave him the book. I knew he couldn't read, so I supposed he was taking it to punish me for something I'd done wrongly or forgotten to do at all; life in the workhouse had left its mark. But as I stood wondering what it was that I'd done wrong and what was going to happen next, he slowly flicked through the pages before handing it back with a sigh and saying,

"So you can read that book then, can you?" I nodded. "And you've got to be a good reader to read it?"

I found my voice. I had relaxed the moment he'd given me back my book.

"I'm alright I think. It gets easier with practice, but I'm definitely not as good as Mr Deeming."

I looked at the paper he still held, that since he'd given me back my book he'd gone back to rolling and unrolling. Then it dawned on me.

"Mr Dodds, would you like me to read that for you?"

In an instant, he had offered me the paper.

"If you can?" he said. "I can't read you see; never learnt."

I told him I already knew and that was why I had been chosen to be his apprentice. I unrolled the paper, but one glance told me I would have great difficulty reading it. It wasn't like a book – printed, regular and each letter always the same. No, this had been handwritten using a quill and by the look of the scrawled, irregular letters, each carrying an incomplete mirror of itself, the nib of the quill must have been split. Not wanting to worry him, I tried to sound confident when I asked Mr Dodds if I could have the invoice (I had worked out that much) for the evening and let him have it back in the morning. Just happy he may have found the solution to a worry that gave him sleepless nights, he said,

"Of course lad. There's no hurry. It's just the bill from Esther Barton. She's been supplying me with most of the drink I sell here for years. I'm sure it's alright, just seems a bit steep, that's all."

That night, I burnt a new candle until it guttered, working out exactly what the bill said. However, the next morning after we'd had breakfast, I was able to explain it all to Mr Dodds. He listened quietly as I told him the bill covered six months and made no comment when I told him the quantity of beer Esther Barton said she'd supplied. He looked surprised when I told him how much she'd charged him for gin, but when I told him how much five bottles of whisky and the same amount of brandy had cost him, he looked at me sharply and said,

"Are you sure that's what it says, five whisky and five brandy?"

I admitted that those entries had been particularly hard to read, but I was certain I'd read them right.

"And that bill's for six months, you say?"

I nodded.

"I knew that vixen was trying to cheat me," he said. "I'm lucky if I sell a bottle of either of them in a year; too expensive for my customers, you see. Comes to that, how much did she charge me?"

I told him, eighteen shillings for the whisky and a pound for the brandy.

"One pound eighteen shillings. That must be a quarter of the whole bill. Right. That settles it. I'll go and ready the horse. Then you and me can go and see dear Esther and find out what she's got to say for herself."

I must have looked alarmed because he added,

"It's alright lad. You can wait with the horse. I won't need you inside unless she argues. I'm not expecting her to do that because if she does, I'll tell her we haven't checked all the old bills she's sent me yet and we won't do as long as she corrects this one. I haven't kept any of the old bills; didn't seem any point as I couldn't read them."

Then he grinned and added,

"But she isn't to know that, is she?"

With that, he went to fetch the horse and cart and we drove into town.

Mr Dodds was right, of course. Though she made several dark glances in my direction, when he returned to the cart, Mr Dodds was delighted to be able to show me a corrected bill and I was happy to be able to confirm that everything now appeared to be in order.

It became my job to read every piece of paper Mr Dodds received. I did ask him once whether he would like me to teach him to read, but he said he was too old. What he did enjoy, though, was for me to read to him. Of course I read *Robinson Crusoe* and *Gulliver's Travels* (as most people called it), but one day, almost shyly, he handed me the biggest book I'd ever seen and asked,

"Do you think you could read that to me, lad? It belonged to my mother."

Fortunately, as we were in the bar, I was able to rest the book on the nearest table and turning it round read the beautiful gold letters:

The Bible
King James Authorised Version

Of course, I told him, I would be very happy to read it for him.

So that's what I did. Every afternoon, about an hour before we opened for the evening, we'd sit in the bar, rest the Bible on a table and I read to him. Starting at Genesis and heading for Revelation, every day for several months without omission, I read each and every page. There were many exciting stories and of course other passages that were less interesting, but whether I was reading about David and Goliath, or struggling through all the 'begetting' in *Chronicles*, Mr Dodds never said anything other than 'thank you Jabez', when I stopped. That is until I reached *The Psalms* and in particular *Psalm 27*. I had just read, *be of good courage, and He shall strengthen thine heart: wait, I say, on the Lord* when he said,

"That was my mother's favourite; she knew it off by heart."

Surprised that he'd spoken at all, I looked up and was even more surprised to see there were tears in his eyes. Not knowing what else to say, I asked him if he wanted me to stop, but he just shook his head and said,

"No, no. But, I wonder, would you read that Psalm again for me?"

He smiled and of course I said I would. Wiping his eyes, he said quietly,

"My grandfather gave that Bible to my mother on her wedding day; he'd already taught her to read. But father said it was a complete waste of money and if mother wanted to keep it, she'd better make sure it stayed hidden. When I came along, she was forbidden by my father from teaching me to read and although she never disobeyed him, she did teach me to recite all the pieces of the Bible that she knew; I don't remember most of 'em now but, as I say, Psalm 27 was her favourite.

I believe my grandfather was quite a rich man, made his money from shipping. But he didn't approve of my father, told mother she'd married beneath herself and when he died, her brother inherited almost everything. My mother only inherited a few pieces of my grandmother's jewellery, keepsakes my mother said, not worth anything other than sentimental memories."

Shortly after he told me all this, there was an impatient rap at the front door; the first of the day's thirsty customers were keen to get to their first drink. Mr Dodds went to open the door and I hurriedly put the Bible in the back kitchen, where it would be safe enough until we went to bed, when Mr Dodds could take it back to his bedroom.

51

Things changed again that day because from then on, Mr Dodds talked to me a lot more. He asked me many questions about my life in the workhouse and told me much more about his life, and it soon became clear to me that he thought of me more as a son than as an apprentice. He seemed to take great pride in telling his customers, and more importantly his suppliers, how well I read and he was delighted to find that, over the next year, whilst others complained about rising prices, many of his bills actually went down.

Content as I was, I did regret that I had nothing else to read. I'd read two books for many years and although I'd been reading the Bible for less time, it contained only so many exciting stories and many of those I'd heard before in the workhouse chapel. So it came as a pleasant surprise when I discovered that the bottom drawer of my dresser, a draw I'd never used, was lined with newspaper. It wasn't much, but at least it was something new to read.

Yellowing and fragile, the outside pages broke into pieces when I took them out of the drawer. But when they broke away, they revealed a second folded set of four pages that were in much better condition. Leaving the broken pieces in the bottom of the drawer, I took the whole ones and laid them carefully on my bed. Kneeling, I began to read.

The first thing I noticed was the date of the paper – 15 January 1763, which made it almost four years old. It was full of how cold the weather had been and at the time of writing, that there were several Cheshire villages still cut off by snow; worst affected, it said, were those on the edge of the Peak District. Although I read every inch of those pages, there was little else of interest. So, disappointed, I folded the paper and took it back to the drawer.

Bending to place the paper carefully back in the drawer, one of the broken pieces, larger than the others, caught my eye. Still only a fragment, though I lifted it gently, little flakes came away from the edges. Nevertheless, the main piece containing the article that I'd noticed stayed intact. Once again, I carried the paper carefully to my bed and knelt down to read it. The article told how a family of six had been found, frozen solid, in the basement of a house in Chester. It went on to say that these deaths raised the total number of people in Cheshire who had been killed by the cold since Christmas, to twenty–four. It ended by demanding that county authorities ensured tragedies like this never happened again.

Having read the article, I gently lifted the fragment and placed it back in the drawer. The way I held it meant I returned the fragment to the drawer with the article face down, so it was only as I was shutting the draw that I saw the name which stopped me in my tracks. Reopening the draw, I pulled out the paper and once more took it back to my bed. Stunned, I stared at a small entry at the bottom of the fragment: 'Vagrant found frozen in Nantwich High Street.' But the headline wasn't what caught my eye; it was the next line. 'The man was believed to be one Oswald Payne.' I sat on my bed and read how the vagrant was well known in the area, often being seen helplessly drunk in the streets of Nantwich. The article went on to say that his death 'was regrettable, but no surprise to those for whom he had become a familiar and shameful sight.'

Sitting on the bed, the article next to me, I thought, 'So that's how he died.' When, after a year Dad hadn't returned for me, any faint hope I might have harboured of ever seeing him again had disappeared. So reading of his death was no surprise. What did surprise me was how I reacted. My father was dead; the paper said he'd been a "familiar and shameful sight", who'd been too drunk to save himself from being frozen to death. But it all meant nothing to me. For me he had died many years before and his place, I realised, was more than filled by Mr Dodds and that's what surprised but also pleased me. After a long moment, I stood up, took the article and crumbled it into small pieces before throwing all of them out the window, where a light breeze blew them away. Shutting both the window and the draw, I went downstairs, meeting Mr Dodds who was just coming in; he'd been shopping in town.

"Everythin' alright then, Jabez?"

Laden, he strode past me and headed for the back kitchen. I don't think he expected much of a reply.

"Everythin's fine, Mr Dodds. Everythin's just fine."

He must have heard something in my voice because, stopping, he turned and faced me.

"That's good then lad – that's very good."

For just a moment, we both stood and smiled at one another. Then turning back, Mr Dodds continued into the kitchen, while I went through and lit the fire to warm the bar in time for our first customers.

Part Two

Elizabeth
Between a Rock and a Soft Place

It stands to reason, there's always been a few of 'em, but now rock pit holes are appearin' everywhere and one of em's made a grave for Bill and most of his family. Do the owners care? 'Course not. They say it's nothing to do with them 'cause no holes have appeared near the shafts, but the pillars aren't anywhere near the shafts and that's where the trouble comes.

This is how it works. First, they dig the mines three hundred feet deep, leaving the roofs held up by nothing but pillars of rock salt. Then the mines slowly fill with water. The water dissolves the salt in the pillars which weakens them until finally they collapse. Without support from the pillars, the roofs soon follow, bringing down with them anything, or anyone, unlucky enough to be sat above 'em. So what I want to ask is, if they know all this, and they must do if I do, for the love of God why do they keep diggin'?

Tom says that's an easy question to answer – money. He says the mine owners are making a fortune and the Government's taking its share, so no one's going to stop them, at least not 'till things get a lot worse. And do you know what I think? I think he's probably right.

I don't worry about the boy. He'll look after himself, but I'm not so sure about Adie. At first I thought it was just the shock of the accident that meant she didn't cry all week, but even today when she has cried, it still seems to be for all the wrong reasons. Well, not wrong exactly, it's just that she doesn't seem to be that upset about losing most of her family and I know it might be a terrible thing to say, but when she did cry, I think it was only because I showed her a little kindness. To be honest, I don't think she's seen much affection in her short life; you only have to look at the way she pulled in so close when I put my arm around her.

Just an irritating noise, that's how she's been treated – especially by her mother. I know Hannah was angry with Bill because he accused her of seeing another man. He refused to tell her who she was supposed to be seeing mind, and then to make matters worse, he made her pregnant again. Including herself and Bill, she already had six mouths to feed and the amount Bill spent down the Boar, Tom told me how much he drank, only made things worse. It wasn't the child's fault. Hannah knew that. But she still gave her that name – the poor child was a constant reminder of what Bill had said and done and though she was blameless, Hannah punished Adie on every possible occasion.

And what about that name? Admonition. It was supposed to be a punishment for Bill. Hannah made no secret of that. But even though they're both gone, for Adie nothing has changed; for her, it's still a lifetime's punishment. All her life people who know what 'admonition' means are going to ask why it's her name and if they don't know, they'll be curious and when they find out, then *they'll* ask why it's her name. I'll tell you something though, she'll never hear me call her Admonition and I'll make sure Tom doesn't either. She'll be Adie here and nothing else.

The salt pans are dangerous places. Tom's worked there most of his life and seen more than his fair share of deaths and injuries, so usually he's unaffected, but this time is different. This time I can see he's been hit hard by the accident; you only have to look at what he's done since. He brought those children straight back here, let me feed 'em and didn't argue when I suggested they should stay the night. In fact it was Tom who said we should give up our bed for them, even though it meant we had to make do with chairs.

The next day, he left it to me to find out from Will if he knew of any relatives who might be able to take care of him and Adie. I was worried Will might think I was saying they weren't welcome, but he was fine about it. He told me he didn't know anything about their dad's family, but thought some of their mums might still live over Macclesfield way. He couldn't tell me anything more, 'cos as far as he knew, his mum hadn't been there since his aunt died of scarlet fever, which happened when he was very young and long before Adie was born.

Anyway, I told Tom all this and the following Sunday, the first day he wasn't working, he walked all the way to Macclesfield and back; well over twenty miles it was, and when he returned, we went outside and he told me all he'd learnt. We agreed what we should do. He said it would be best if I told them what he'd discovered and then explain our idea. Tom's not very good with children. He's not had much experience and that's why I was amazed he bought 'em back here in the first place. So, thinking he was probably right, I took a deep breath and followed by Tom, went back indoors. Both Will and Adie were sitting silently on the bed, waiting to hear what Tom had discovered, so I squeezed in between them and began to repeat what he'd told me.

"You know that Tom went to Macclesfield today to see if he could find any of your family and see if they could take you in."

They both nodded, so I continued.

"Now when he got to Macclesfield, he didn't know who to speak to, so he decided he'd start by speaking to the Church Minister. Luckily, Reverend Lingard remembered your mum from when he first came to the Church and she sometimes came to the Sunday Morning Service with your Aunt Eleanor, but he didn't think he'd seen her since Eleanor's funeral.

Reverend Lingard was deeply saddened to hear what had happened to the rest of your family. He asked Tom to tell you he'd remember you in his prayers and would ask his congregation to do the same.

He understood your Aunt had been married, but that her husband had left her before he'd come to the Parish, so he suggested they spoke to the verger because he'd been involved with the Church since before the spire was taken down back in 1740. Reverend Lingard explained to the verger why Tom was asking about Eleanor's husband and after thinking for a few moments, the verger, who Tom says was very old, said…"

"As old as Methuselah."

Tom's interruption caught me by surprise, but I think he was just letting me know he was listening 'cos straightaway he lapsed back into silence. Speaking suddenly like that he'd thrown me, but I gathered my thoughts again and carried on.

"Yes, as old as Methuselah, but as Tom told me, his memory was still really sharp. He said that Eleanor's husband's name was Nathaniel Watson and that he'd left her about a year after they married. Unfortunately no one had seen or heard from him since, although because he'd been a sailor when he met your aunt, most people thought he'd probably gone back to sea. I'm afraid it seems your mum was probably the only other close family Eleanor had."

I put my arm tightly round Adie and grasped Will's hand because I wanted them to know that what I had to say next came from my heart.

"Now, we've talked about what we should do, and we've come to a decision. We think that, even though we haven't got much, Tom and me would like you both to stay with us. Isn't that right, Tom?"

Tom still didn't turn round. He seemed lost in his own thoughts, but he murmured his agreement.

I felt Adie begin to tremble and I sensed she was about to cry. She hadn't cried at all since she'd come to us, so I thought that my poor offer had at last made her realise how much she'd lost. Desperate to make things right, I turned her gently so we were looking at one another and said as softly as I could,

"Adie please don't cry. I know I'm not your mum but I'll try and do my best for you. We both will, won't we Tom?"

Before Tom could speak, Adie said something that surprised me. Starting to cry, she buried her head beneath my arm and between sobs, hiccuped,

"That's not why I'm crying… I miss my family… but… but you've been more like a mum to me than mine ever was."

She dissolved completely and I held her even closer, trying to comfort her. Eventually her sobs subsided and apart from an occasional rasp, her breathing became more settled. After what felt like an age, the nature of her breathing told me she was asleep. Tom must have noticed the change as well, because finally turning from the fire, he beckoned Will to join him and they both stepped outside. I could hear a murmured conversation and later that evening, Tom told me how they'd talked about Will's return to work.

We hadn't had any children, Tom and me, and after ten years of marriage, it was unlikely that we ever would. To tell the truth, Tom had never really been very interested in me that way and after a couple of years, had lost interest altogether. I told myself I was lucky. I'd seen so many babies die before they could even walk. Hannah had lost two before Adie was born and I'd seen mothers go as well – sometimes with their baby, other times leaving orphans. But for all that, I knew deep down I yearned for a child of my own. So, as I sat with Adie, her head pressed against my breast, asleep and trusting, I realised she might be my one chance. I had no reason to feel guilty I told myself, after all, I had nothing to do with the accident. Even Tom's best efforts to find any relatives who might take in her and her brother had failed. Anyway, it was plain to see this child needed a mother and I didn't think anyone else was going to offer to fill that role.

My dreams were broken by Tom and Will's return, so I laid Adie gently down on the bed, put a blanket over her and got on with making dinner. I said nothing to Tom or Will because I wasn't sure either of them would be happy with me becoming Adie's mum. Uncertain of Tom because I knew he was quite happy with us being childless. I was equally unsure of Will, as Adie's last words would still be ringing in his ears and I didn't want him thinking I agreed with her about Hannah. No, much better to say nothing and let things take their own course.

William

Lies

Going back to the pans was easier than I thought. Dad and Tom had rented a single pan between them producing fine salt – although the hardest to produce, fine salt paid the highest rate. I'd worked with them for almost a year and John had joined us a few weeks before the accident. I know Dad was pleased to have both his sons working with him and proud to see us following him, just as he had followed our grandfather. Once John had learnt all the tasks involved in producing the salt, Dad had told me it was his intention to rent a second pan.

Most of the work in the salt pans takes place inside a long, low shed, with only storage (the finished salt is kept in a separate, dry storeroom.) and the loading of barges, taking place elsewhere. The work is hard and dangerous and whilst the shed keeps out the weather, the fires that heat the brine in the pans mean it is always hot and steamy. Every hour of every day from Monday to midday Saturday, those fires keep the brine bubbling away and as the water evaporates, the salt that remains is dragged to the side to be scooped into moulds. When most of the water has evaporated and the salt removed, the pans are again filled with brine and the whole process starts all over again.

Although we worked stripped down to no more than decency required (some said beyond even that), as the brine bubbled, so did we. Although the sides of the shed were slatted, providing us with some relief, sweat poured from us freely even before we started work and the heat and the salty steam left us permanently thirsty.

For those who passed the Boar's Head on their way to work – and most did, life was made more tolerable by Jabez Payne, the inn's landlord, who allowed them to draw water from his well. The well had been there longer than anyone could remember and its water had always been clean. Jabez allowed us to take the water for free on the understanding that, at least occasionally, every worker would stop on their way home and buy some of the Inn's more traditional refreshments. Most did, driven not only by thirst but by the need to wash the taste of salt from their lips. Apparently, this arrangement was introduced by Jabez' predecessor, Jack Dodds. Jack, who in the first few months he was landlord, had already become popular with his locals, sealed his popularity when he allowed free use of the well. After his death, fond memories meant Jack's reputation grew, so that now he is generally held to have been the Boar's greatest landlord in its two-hundred-year history. Whether or not his reputation was deserved, we were all grateful for the free water.

Of course, the fires under the pans had to be watched and fed all the time and although I said nothing to Tom, I couldn't see how just two of us could manage all the work. I also worried how people would treat me when they saw I was back; I hoped they would carry on as if nothing had happened.

I needn't have worried on either score. Although everyone knew what had happened, when they arrived in the shed, though some mumbled a few words of condolence, most just got on with their work. How they really felt started to become clear after we'd been working for about half an hour.

Like everyone else, our first job on Monday was to remove the common salt which had formed in the cooling pans since they were last used on Saturday morning. We had just drained the remaining brine from the pan and were about to start work on removing the salt, when a young lad appeared at Tom's side. Like all the children working on the pans, he was pale and skinny.

"Ma dad said I should come and give you a hand. I'm not so good with the sledge', but I can use a shovel if you can let me have one."

"What's your name, son?" Tom asked as he handed the boy a shovel.

"Charlie, same as ma dad."

He puffed his chest out when he answered, it was clearly something he was proud of and I saw the trace of a smile on Tom's lips when he said, "Well Charlie, thank you and when you go back, thank your dad for me, will you?"

Tom might not have recognised him, but I knew Charlie from the village. He'd been living there with his parents ever since, like so many others, they'd lost their farm. I liked his father; in a way the older Charlie was a bit like Mum. Watch him and often you'd catch him staring who knows where – certainly somewhere distant. I'd seen Mum doing the same thing and when I'd asked her why, she'd laughed and said she was just remembering her childhood on her parent's farm and not to mind her.

Anyway, Tom told Charlie what he wanted him to do.

"If you can go and get us a box barrow, me and Will can start breaking up the salt with the sledgehammers. When you get back, I want you to start shovelling salt into the barrow."

With Charlie gone to find a box barrow, me and Tom started breaking up the salt which lay thick in the bottom of the pan, and by the time Charlie got back, we'd broken up enough for him to start filling the barrow. But even though he worked like a demon, he couldn't keep up. The trouble was the barrow stood much taller than he did, so he had to throw each shovel-full high above his head. Although he managed to do this quite quickly, I could see he was slowing down as his arms became more and more tired. I was about to suggest that I should switch jobs and give Charlie a hand, when Tom called a halt so we could all have a swig out of the water jug he'd filled at the Boar. Charlie pulled so hard on the jug that I wondered if there'd be any left for me and Tom and I was about to make my suggestion, when a voice hailed us from across the way.

"Hey Tom, looks like you could use an extra pair of hands. If it'd help, I don't need my lad 'till the tide turns and that Liverpool barge comes in, so can you make use of him?"

"Thanks, George. This lad looks fit to drop." Tom put his hand on Charlie's shoulder. "If your boy can help us for a while, we might get the job finished."

When George's son loped across, he looked more my age than Charlie's and he didn't look too pleased to be joining us. But he'd brought his own spade with him, and without a word he started shovelling the salt into the barrow.

Tom sent an exhausted Charlie back to his dad and the three of us were soon joined by one of the women who worked on the pans. Like Charlie and his parents, Sarah and her children lived close to us in the village. At about five foot eight, she was a tall, imposing woman, but it was her strength that was the most remarkable thing about her, though given the size of her arms which compared well with any man on the pans, not surprising.

Two years before the accident that killed most of my family, Sarah's husband had slipped on one of the hurdles that bordered the pans and fallen into the boiling brine; he was dead before they could pull him out. They had raised a big family and two of the boys were already working with their father when he was killed. Sarah loved her husband

and mourned his death deeply, but she had worked on the pans before the children started coming, so barely a week after she buried him, she took her husband's place, leaving her eldest girl in charge of those still too small to work. Since then, two more of her boys had grown enough to join her. Sarah wasn't happy that her children were working with her, especially when some were still so young, but she had little choice if she wanted to keep her family out of the workhouse.

I know when her husband was killed, Dad had helped Sarah, quite a few though not everyone did; there were still some who had a disliking for Jews. Yet even though Tom had been one of those who hadn't helped her, it was clear Sarah wanted to return Dad's favour by helping me.

First she helped us finish clearing the pan. Tom had our chipping paddle and Sarah had brought her own, so with them clearing the rims of the pan and me and George's lad shovelling out, the last of the salt was soon cleared.

Before she came over to us, Sarah had helped her boys with their first draft, leaving strict instructions that the youngest ones should stay well back from the boiling brine. But now their first make was about ready and she headed back to help them with what was one of the toughest jobs in the pans, dragging the salt from the bottom of the pan to the sides. From there, using their skimmer, the still hot salt would be scooped out and put on the far side of the shed to dry.

But before returning to her family, she took me to one side and said,

"Your dad was a good man Will. I know he was proud of you boys. What happened to him and the rest of your family was awful, a terrible tragedy that should never have happened.

Still, it's good to see you back. It's what your dad would have wanted."

Lowering her voice, she said.

"Tom's not to be trusted. He'll keep you and your sister whilst he thinks he should and for as long as you're of use to him. You must know he isn't very popular here and though there's only rumour and suspicion about him without any proof, that's enough for some. We all talked about it last week after the accident and agreed that we would help if you came back. People are coming to help the pair of you because you're Bill's son. But I have to tell you Will, there were already a few who didn't want to help Tom. So you'll probably get help for the next month or so. After that, me and my boys will help you as and when we can, but apart from that, you'll be on your own."

She glanced at Tom, who was already beginning to look at us suspiciously and added,

"My advice to you Will, is as soon as you get a chance to get out, you take it. You hear me?"

Tom wasn't the most popular person on the pans, I knew that, but by now he was looking straight at us and I knew I couldn't ask her for any more, so bowing my head so he couldn't see what I said, I muttered,

"I hear you."

When she left, Tom came straight to me.

"What was she talking about then?"

I hadn't had time to think, so I just said,

"Oh, you know, she was just saying how sorry she was about Dad and everything."

He looked at me suspiciously.

"Is that all? She was talking for a long time."

"She was saying how grateful she was to Dad for all the help he'd given her when her husband was killed and that she would help us whenever she could."

This seemed to satisfy him because he said,

"Alright then Will let's get on. You take that barrow out to the yard and I'll get another draft started."

Life in the salt works carried on just as Sarah said it would. When I started, people had told me I'd get used to the heat, which wasn't true. I don't think anyone got used to it. They simply learnt how to cope. So every day despite the heat, we raked, shovelled, lifted and loaded tons of salt, and every day support would be offered or, especially with the young ones, just appear. They'd stay for at least a couple of hours, sometimes all day. There were never more than two, but rarely were we left to work on our own.

I noticed that none of the men ever helped us. There were boys of all ages, a few girls – always with a brother or a mother – and some of the women who came alone, but no men. It didn't worry me though, I was sure if you'd asked them, the men would have said it was because, apart from working the pans, they also organised the rest of their family and made sure the youngsters kept out of danger. Whether that was true or not, I'm certain it's what they would have said, and at the time I wouldn't have doubted them.

Anyway, we soon settled into a routine and even when the extra help first dwindled then stopped completely, we still managed to produce enough salt to make sure Tom and Elizabeth had enough money to feed all four of us. We worked hard, but we would never have coped when help declined, had Tom not made a crucial decision.

When help diminished, Tom gave up producing fine-grained salt and switched us to a common pan. The common pan produced only coarse salt but the fire beneath it needed much less attention than the one we'd been using. To produce fine salt, the brine had to be kept boiling at all times, but for common salt it didn't need to be quite so hot. All that was needed were banked fires attended to by a shared fireman. Once made, the salt was transferred in barrows straight to storage ready for delivery, by land or water, to whichever firm had bought it. This way, although the work was still hot and hard and the salt we produced was worth less, we managed to get by with just the two of us.

Sarah stayed away and what she'd told me slipped completely from my mind. For the next three years, not knowing the truth, life for me in the salt works continued uneventfully and it was much the same at the Rider's. We worked hard together, me and Tom, and never argued. In fact Tom treated me as a workmate. For him, I think, I became a replacement for Dad. At the same time Elizabeth and Adie got on well and as she got older, Adie was able to help Elizabeth in more and more of her chores. Yet, in the end, it was their relationship that was to cause a rift between me and Adie, a rift that has never healed completely.

"Oh Will, I've really upset Mrs Rider. I know I have."

That's how Adie greeted me when I walked through the door. After fourteen hours of shovelling salt and pushing a box barrow, my response wasn't too kind and I'm sure I sounded more than just a little irritated when I said,

"So what did you do to upset her?" Looking round I added, "and where is she, now?"

My tone made her worse and now in a fearful voice, she replied,

"I don't know. I never meant to upset her Will. She's always been good to me. Whatever I've done, I'll do anything to put it right. Anything.
You've got to tell me what to do; I must be a terrible person.
Perhaps we should leave, run away before Mr Rider comes home."

She was on the edge of panic and I could think of only one way to stop her, so in the sternest tone I could muster, I said,

"Admonition, stop it. Whatever you've done, I'm sure it's not that bad. Now think, what have you been doing today?"

This appeared to work; she had been close to tears, but now she began to think back over her day.

"Well, we were doing our usual jobs. When we'd got back from the woods where we'd been gathering mushrooms, we took down the washing. All the time we talked just like we always do. I love it when we talk. It doesn't matter about what. It just makes me feel special. I s'pose she won't ever want to talk to me again."

I could see she had again taken herself close to tears, so I said quickly,

"Now come on, crying won't help. What else did you say to her? Think."

Holding back the tears, she said,

"The only other thing I remember is after we came indoors, I needed to go down to the privy, but before I went, I asked her if it would be alright for me to call her Mum. She smiled at me, but didn't say anything; she didn't look angry though. Anyway, I really needed the privy and I just couldn't wait any longer. I thought she'd give me her answer when I got back. I wasn't gone long, but when I got back, she'd disappeared. I thought she must have just popped out because she'd left the washing in a pile and she'd never do that if she was going to be out for long. When she didn't come back, I went looking for her, but I couldn't find her anywhere…"

With that, I saw the light dawn in her eyes, but with it came the dark clouds that never seemed far away.

"Will, that's it, isn't it? That smile hid her real feelings. She isn't my mum and she doesn't want to be, does she? She's been good to me and now I've spoilt everything."

I know I was weary and Adie's first words when I came home had felt more like an assault than a greeting, but I don't think they were the reasons I reacted as I did. The fact was I'd lost my parents too, yet I was expected to put that behind me, stride back into the world and return to work as if nothing had happened. All the while Adie could remain a child, behave like one and be treated as one; she could even think about replacing Mum. So I aimed both barrels at her and fired.

"What the devil made you do that? Mum's dead, so is Dad. Tom and Elizabeth haven't got any children and I don't expect they want anybody else's calling them mum and dad."

I could see I'd hit home, but my anger hadn't diminished; I knew I had to get out of the house before I said too much, so I just said,

"Right. Now I'm going out to try and find her, see if we can't sort this out before Tom comes home."

I turned to go, but as I did, there was a light tap at the door. I opened it a little too forcefully and a startled Betsy Grimes took a step back. Old and wizened and bent nearly double, making her stand hardly taller than Adie, Betsy Grimes had delivered all the children in the village for as far back as anyone could remember. She'd had no children of her own and had never married, although she did like to say that all the children in the village were hers, which I suppose, in a way, was true, she'd certainly met them all before even their mothers had. Now past eighty, it was still to her, anxious dads would run and mums cry out, when their baby was ready to be born. Though Elizabeth had never had any children, she and Betsy were great friends. Mum said it was *because* neither of them had any children that they were close; they could talk about things other than children.

In my anger I'd forgotten that Betsy's was the most likely place for Elizabeth to have gone, so having apologised, I explained I was just going out but asked how I might help her.

"Actually, it's Adie I was looking for," she said. "I have a message for her from Lizzie Rider. She thought Adie might be worried after the way she left this morning without a word and hasn't come back. So is Adie here?"

Because she was so small and I was still standing in the doorway, she couldn't see Adie, who anyway had retreated to the bed.

I said,

"Yes, she's here."

Now that I'd remembered Betsy and Elizabeth's friendship, I imagined I knew what this was about, so I added,

"And as soon as she sees Mrs Rider, she's going to apologise to her."

Taken aback, Betsy said,

"Young man, she has nothing to apologise for."

She called out, "Adie, can I have a word?"

Adie came and stood close behind me. Smiling, Betsy reached past me, grasped her arm and said,

"I have a message for you dear, from Mrs Rider."

Adie tried to pull away. She still believed she'd upset Elizabeth and as old age had robbed Betsy of most of her teeth, her gummy smile did little to reassure her. But Betsy's grip was surprisingly strong, so holding firm she went on.

"She said I should tell you that what you asked her this morning was the nicest thing anyone has ever said to her and if you still feel the same, she'd really love you to call her 'mum'."

Adie looked confused. Betsy, who had already begun her slow walk back down the gennel, called back,

"Well, so what shall I tell her then dear? Do you still feel the same?"

Adie's face was transformed, the clouds already replaced by the brightest smile.

"Please tell her yes," she said. "I'd very much like to call her mum. And can you tell her I'm sorry if I upset her."

Betsy made a strange sound. I think it was a chuckle but it sounded more like the honk of a goose flying home.

"I'll let her know your reply dear. Anything else you want to say to each other can wait 'til she's back home."

As Betsy slowly walked away, Adie turned to me and started to speak,

"Will, she wants to be my…"

But interrupting her, the anger I felt turning to rage, I slammed the door and fired again.

"So that's it then, is it? Mum and Dad are dead, and Dad got killed rescuing you, remember, your sisters are dead and so is your brother, but you'll be alright, *you've* got a brand new mum and no doubt you'll want Tom to be your new dad."

I knew that I'd hurt her, but I hadn't finished; I couldn't help myself. As I stood there clenching and unclenching my fists, I shouted,

"No new brothers or sisters, though. And I'll tell you Adie, if you go through with this, you'll lose the only brother you have, 'cos I won't want anything to do with you."

I didn't expect her to change her mind, but I did expect her to cry, plead with me or perhaps ask me to try to understand, but she didn't do any of these things. She was only eight years old, but the girl who looked at me wasn't my frightened little sister anymore. She was somehow older and darker. Calmly looking straight at me, she said,

"But they weren't like a mum and dad to me, were they? Not really."

I was about to object, but she wouldn't let me.

"Oh come on Will, you know it's true. Dad was so wrapped up in why Mum had given me my name, she made sure everybody around here knew as well. He hardly ever spoke to me. Mum did though, oh yes, she spoke to me all the time; but she was never kind, was she? She was always blaming me for something or other. But, do you know what I really think?"

I said nothing. This was an Adie I'd never met before and she hadn't finished. Dry-eyed she said,

"I think she really blamed me for being born and that's why she gave me my name. And even though I've never really understood what it means, I've been ashamed of being called Admonition for as long as I can remember."

Although she didn't say it, I was sure she blamed me, John and even her sisters for going along with Mum, and to confirm my thoughts, she finished by saying,

"And if you don't want to be my brother, that's alright, I don't mind. I'm used to being alone."

All she said might have been true, but I was still angry; they had, after all, been *my mum* and dad, *my* brother and sisters. I didn't argue with her. In fact I didn't say anything, just turned and left as I'd meant to do a few minutes earlier. But now I didn't go looking for Elizabeth. Instead, I turned the other way and headed towards the pans. I hoped to meet Tom and walk back with him. He was doing a few extra hours helping to load a barge and I knew he should be finishing soon.

I met Tom about halfway to the pans. He looked a little surprised to see me but said nothing and we walked home together. He told me they'd managed to fill the barge before the tide turned forcing it to leave. He added that another was due the next day, so everyone was going to be busy again, making salt in time to be sure this one left full as well. It was important to make sure any barge didn't leave under-loaded, because then we'd lose money and we couldn't afford to do that.

By the time we got home, I hadn't forgotten my argument with Adie, but listening to Tom talking about work, I had been distracted. When we walked in the house, Adie and Elizabeth were in each other's arms. Clearly, there was no longer any misunderstanding between them. Then, as Elizabeth explained to a disinterested Tom what had happened, Adie stared at me unblinking; daring me it seemed, to voice my objection. But I said nothing; I'd decided that as long as neither of them wanted me to call Elizabeth 'mum' and as I was sure Tom would never want me to call him 'dad', I supposed I'd have to put up with their new arrangement. But, as I've said, it placed a rift between me and Adie that's never quite gone away.

Today, for the second time, my life is in turmoil.

Three days ago it came as a surprise when, as I pushed another full barrow into the warehouse, out of the darkness and from behind a line of empty barrows, I heard a sharp whisper.

"Will!"

Turning instinctively in the direction of the voice, I could see no one. All around me people were pushing full barrows in or taking empty ones out of the storehouse. It seemed no one else had heard the call. They were ignoring it if they had.

"Will, leave the barrow, Josh'll take it up the line for you. Come over here, I need to speak to you."

With that, Joshua, Sarah's eldest, came out of the darkness and without a word started pushing my barrow. Still no one else reacted, though they must have heard Sarah the second time she called me. Bewildered, I entered the darkness; Sarah was between two wagons. She looked anxious when she spoke.

"Josh will take as long as he can to empty your barrow, but when he returns, you'll have to take it straight back inside. It means we haven't got long, so I want you to say nothing, just listen to what I've got to tell you."

She looked to see if she had my full attention; she needn't have worried. I was intrigued, particularly as no one else had reacted to her call and memories of what she'd said to me two years before were already returning. But she still wasn't ready to tell me what she knew.

"I'm going to tell you something about Tom and I think it'll shock you. I know it did me. But I want you to promise me that when I'm done, you'll go back to work and carry on as if nothing has happened, no matter how you feel."

I didn't know what she was going to say, but as I've already said, Sarah was a strong and imposing woman used to being listened to, as I'm sure all her children would agree, so I nodded my agreement.

"No matter how you feel?"

"No matter how I feel."

Satisfied, she started to tell her tale.

"Now, you know that for some time before the accident, your mum and dad hadn't been getting on too well?"

I said that of course I knew and that it was something to do with Adie, but I couldn't see how it could have had anything to do with Tom. Sarah smiled, but I had a feeling I wouldn't find what she was about to tell me funny.

"Well that's not exactly true; your poor sister was only the result of things that had already gone wrong. I know you think he's a good man, but when I've finished, you'll see how Tom is right in the middle of what happened.

I'm sure you know that before having Adie, your mum had lost two babies shortly after they were born. It was before the second of those babies was born that Tom told your dad your mum was seeing another man. Your dad would never tell your mum who she was supposed to be seeing, or who had told him. No one even knows if Tom had given him a name, but it doesn't matter because it was all just a pack of lies.

69

I discovered the truth when I visited my sister over in Macclesfield. While I was there, her husband, Jack, told me a tale about a man who walked into his local, the Black Lion. He'd been drinking alone when the stranger walked in and stood next to him at the bar and ordered a jug of ale and then offered Jack a refill.

In no time they were chatting and the stranger said he'd had some business in Nantwich that morning and it was clear to Jack that whatever it was it must have been successful, because he seemed to be in the mood to celebrate. After they finished that jug, Jack ordered another and it was only after Tom called for a third that his tongue started to loosen and Jack began to wish he'd had nothing to do with him.

With a sparkle in his eye, he told Jack he'd just spent the morning with his favourite moll, a girl of thirteen who granted him favours his wife could never imagine. It seemed that he wanted Jack to share the pleasure of this recent memory, but sensing he wasn't changed tack; Jack thought he wanted to justify his morning's experience. He said he should never have married Elizabeth, that the truth was he'd had his eye on a girl called Hannah from when she was very young, long before she married her husband, Bill. He had never told Hannah how he felt and was sure if he had, she would have married him instead.

I had thought Jack was just telling a tale, but now that I knew who he was talking about I paid special attention. It wasn't long before Tom reminded Jack of the accident that killed most of your family and explained how he and his wife, Elizabeth, had taken you and Adie under their wing. He told Jack that he'd wanted to put a breach between your mum and dad, hopefully one wide enough to let him in. So he told your dad that your mum was seeing another man, and he said it would have worked in time, but that no one expected the accident. I think he was wrong. I don't think his plan would ever have worked, yet it did bring unhappiness to what had been a happy marriage. But the fact is Tom was telling a pack of lies and in the end, I think your dad knew that – the trouble was he couldn't find a way to tell your mum.

Jack said he'd been glad when Tom left. He'd taken a dislike to him and I'm telling you Will, when he told me, it fair made my blood boil. So I've spread the word around this place, and now there are plenty here who want to punish him. People have had their doubts about Tom for a long time, but now they're all very angry. Apart from anything else, they know that what Tom told him started your dad drinking heavily and some have been saying, though no one can really know, that if your dad had come home sober the night before the accident, he might have saved more of your family than just Adie. I don't hold with that. I can't see how it would have made any difference, but that's how some are thinking. Now they know Tom lied and that he did it just to make trouble between your mum and dad and because many of 'em have young daughters, they don't intend to let matters lie. That's why you've got to get out and why it's got to be soon – if they know you're leaving those who want to punish Tom for what he's done will wait 'til you're gone. But they *are* going to punish him and they know he'll tell Elizabeth it was an accident, 'cos he won't want her learning the truth.

Now in three days' time, the Liverpool boat that's just finishing loading will be back for another load, and when it leaves again, you need to be on it.

I've spoken to the captain and he'll drop you at Marshall's mine. I hear they're taking people on and they especially want people who've worked in the salt, so you shouldn't have any trouble finding work."

I realised Sarah was right. I could no longer live with this man. But then it struck me. How could I leave Adie with the Rider's knowing what that man had done?

Sarah must have read my mind because she took my arm and said gently,

"I know what you're thinking, but don't worry. Adie will be alright. You must know Elizabeth adores her and will look after her. She'll be in more danger if you stay, especially if Tom thinks you knew about his punishment and didn't warn him.
No, you must tell them you're leaving. How old are you now Will?"

"Seventeen, nearly eighteen," I told her.

"Well that's old enough. Now, you tell all three of them you're leaving because you want to start making a life for yourself. They won't like it, but they'll understand.
Anyway, here's Josh back with your barrow. He knows what's happening and he'll offer to take your place until those who intend to punish Tom feel the time is right. Promise me you'll act as if nothing has happened and just make sure you're on that boat. But remember, whatever else you do, for Adie's sake, don't tackle Tom yourself."

Stunned, I had no time to take in what Sarah had told me before returning to work. When I returned to the pans, Tom had just finished racking out the next load.

"Busy was it Will? Always the same when the boat's in. I think we'll hold this draft and start the next one. It should be easier to move the barrow once that boat's gone."

Relieved that he'd answered his own question, I forced a smiled and helped him to finish loading the barrow.

I knew what Sarah had said was right; there was no alternative for me but to leave without confronting Tom. If I challenged him over what she'd told me, I would still need to leave and I'd have no choice but to take Adie with me. Whether I liked it or not, whilst we had grown apart, Adie and Elizabeth had grown close, really close. So I knew if I took her away with me, Adie would be losing her mum for a second time and I couldn't do that to her.

Once before, my life had seemed certain, yet had crumbled and collapsed before my very eyes and now it was happening all over again. But this time Tom, who had taken me and Adie under his wing helping us to rebuild our lives, now was responsible for their destruction.

71

Somehow I kept my own counsel and finishing the shift as if nothing had changed, that evening when we'd eaten but were still all together at the table, I told them I was leaving in three days' time. I told Tom and Elizabeth I should always be grateful to them for taking Adie and me into their home after the rest of our family were killed. I even said I was pleased Elizabeth and Adie had become like mother and daughter. I looked at Adie as I spoke. I wanted her to believe I accepted their relationship and although her face was ashen, she did manage a faint smile. Finally, I told them I believed that I was old enough now to begin making my own way in the world.

It was Elizabeth who first broke their stunned silence.

"Come on then Will, tell us, where are you going and what are you going to do?"

I'd had no time to plan beyond Sarah's instructions, so I just explained that I was heading for Marshall's. Clearly taken aback, Elizabeth said,

"Marshall's! You're leaving us to join the miners, joining the ones who were responsible for killing your family in the first place."

"Don't know why you're surprised, Lizzie," Tom said, "plain selfish, that's what I call it. Says he's leaving in three days, eh, wonder if he's given any thought as to how I'm going to earn a living on my own?

Oh, and he expects us to keep his sister after he's gone. He talks all that drivel 'bout you and her being like mother and daughter, but I reckon it's just to make you feel guilty in case we make him take her with him; which we should, as it happens."

"Now Tom, don't be unfair. You know it's not Adie's fault, 'spect she's as upset as we are about her brother going; ain't you Adie?"

I think at the thought she might lose Adie, Elizabeth became anxious. In reply, Adie stared fixedly at the table and shook her head.

Surprised, Elizabeth said,

"You're not upset?" But again Adie shook her head.

"You're not going to miss your brother?" Now there was desperation in Elizabeth's voice.

Finally provoked, Adie said,

"Of course I'm going to miss him. How could you think I wouldn't? But I've known for a long time he would leave one day, because he's often told me he needs to make his own way in the world. But he's also told me," at this point she lifted her eyes and looked at me, "that one day, when he's made something of himself, he'll return and take me away to live with him."

Her eyes asked the question, so I smiled, hoping she would be reassured. Shifting her gaze, she answered Tom directly.

"I don't know what would have become of us if you and Mum hadn't taken Will and me in and I'll always be grateful to you both for that. But if you're saying that if Will leaves I'm no longer welcome here, then I'm sure Will will take me with him. Won't you, Will?"

She looked at me expectedly, I didn't know what to say, but clearly taking Adie with me was never in my plans. I needn't have worried though because, before I could answer, my thoughts were interrupted by Elizabeth.

72

"Adie, I'm sure Tom didn't mean anything like that. You're welcome to stay as long as you want. That's right, isn't it Tom?"

I think Elizabeth was a little afraid of Tom, but the fear of losing Adie was stronger. Tom ignored her question. Instead, he turned to me.

"You still haven't explained how you think I'm going to earn enough to feed the three of us once you're gone."

I knew it would be unwise to mention Joshua. Tom might be many things but he was no fool and if I told him Josh would be coming to replace me, he was bound to realise there had been some planning and any planning had to involve Sarah.

So I said what I thought would be safe.

"Remember Tom, I'm not leaving for three days and I'm sure once people know I'm going, you'll get offers of help; you remember how much help we received after my dad was killed."

Tom's face showed he was unconvinced, so I added,

"But if in that time I can't find you help to replace me, I won't go until I can. I'm the one who's leaving and it's only right that I find you a replacement."

I wish I hadn't made the last remark. It may have sounded a little more confident than I wanted; certainly I could see that Tom was about to say something more. Fortunately, before he knew what he wanted to say, Elizabeth spoke.

"There you are dear. Will says he won't leave until he's found you his replacement. You can't say fairer than that, can you?" I could see Tom wasn't convinced, but though he muttered under his breath, he said nothing out loud.

Whether I was at work or at home, the next three days were anxious ones for me. It's true that after a morning of asking for help from people I knew would refuse, when I told Tom that Joshua had agreed to help him after I'd left, he accepted it without suspicion and life at work became a little easier. But at home, Adie seemed to become more and more distant from me so that eventually, on the last evening before I was due to leave, I asked her if she would come for a walk with me. Though it was raining quite hard, Elizabeth obviously thought this a good idea because she immediately offered Adie her cape, and though much too large for her, the cape was oiled and would keep her dry. She said nothing, but rose from where she'd been sitting on her bed and took the cape.

Stepping outside, we turned our backs on the rain and started walking up the gennel in the direction of the pans. At first we walked in silence, a silence I thought I was going to have to be the first to break, but with her face hidden by Elizabeth's cape, it was Adie who spoke first; it was the first time she'd spoken to me since I'd announced I was leaving.

"You will come back for me like you promised, won't you Will?"

Before I could try to reassure her, she added,

"Because even though I don't mind living with Mum and Mr Rider, I've always hoped that one day you and me would live together somewhere on our own."

I stopped walking and took hold of her arm; she turned and faced me. Despite the rain, which was falling even harder, I pulled back the hood of her cape so that I could see her face. Though she often seemed much older than her years, Adie was still very young and hadn't begun to conceive that one day, either one or both of us might marry and others then become our priority. But now was not the time to explain this to her. Instead, I held her face gently in my hands and looking straight into her eyes, said,

"Adie, you're my sister and I love you. I know I've said some hard things when I've been angry, but I want you to know I'm pleased you and Elizabeth have grown close and I'm glad she lets you call her mum. But I promise that as soon as I have a roof of my own and I'm earning enough to keep two, then I shall come and fetch you."

This must have satisfied her, because for the first time in three days I saw Adie smile. Raising her cape again, as we were both very wet, I suggested we might make our way home. Shivering, she made no objection, so we started the short walk back and although the rain was falling even harder now and drove into our faces, I was happy because Adie held my hand all the way back. I knew now she would let me go with an easy heart, and that was all I wanted.

Elizabeth
Forgotten

Adie's fine and that's the main thing. It's been a month since Will left and you'd think he'd have sent a note or something just to let her know he's all right, but we've heard nothing from him. Never mind, as I say, his leaving doesn't appear to have had much of an effect on her. It's true that for two or three days after he left, she seemed to be a little quieter than usual, but since then she's been back to her normal self, in fact, since he left, I think we've become even closer.

I can't say the same for Tom. He's always been a quiet one, but now he sometimes goes for days without really speaking. Really you'd think he'd be fine because, just as Will promised, that young lad Josh has been helping him. The lad's a couple of years younger than Will, but from the little I've managed to get out of Tom, I know the boy's a good worker. But I don't think it matters how good he is, it won't make any difference 'cos I think Tom just misses Will. If you asked him, he won't admit it, mind. He says Will's let him down, that he only ever thinks of himself. Whatever he says doesn't matter because I know I'm right. For one thing, and it's as plain as the nose on your face, he misses talking to Will, especially about what goes on in the pans. Of course it's natural he talked to him about their work more than he does with me. I just wish, now that Will's gone, sometimes he'd talk to me about his day; I'm sure he'd feel better for it if he did.

He's strange with Adie as well. Though he rarely talks to her, I've often seen him just staring at her. Once, when I asked him, he denied doing it and said he was just looking out the door. Although it's true that I had just opened the door when I asked him, it wasn't the first time I'd seen him staring at her that way and it certainly wasn't the last. I'm not too worried though, 'cos I think I know why he does it.

Tom has never made friends easily and I think Will had become like his father before him, Tom's only real friend in the pans and the straightforward fact is he misses him. He resents Adie because every day she reminds him of her brother, but unlike Will who worked, he thinks she just sits here costing him money. Of course that's not fair and in his heart he knows it; she's still young and I won't let her work in the pans. But it's not true to say she does nothing because every day, never complaining, she helps me with all my jobs.

I think in time things will be alright. Tom will forget Will and then his anger toward Adie will fade. Until then I'll keep an eye on him, make sure he doesn't confront her like he did when Will told us he was leaving. I'm sure everything will be fine.

Jabez
A Meeting of Minds

It began like any other Monday.

Although experience had taught me it was a decision I would regret, I ignored the bar with all its usual mess; empty and mostly empty tankards, ale–soaked tables and ash where some had missed the fire or not even tried. Instead, before setting off on the four mile walk into town, I went out to the barn and fed the donkeys and then released them into the orchard. When I reached town, I settled some debts I could no longer avoid, ordered more ale and then bought myself enough victuals to last me the week. Finally, after paying what was left of my week's takings, which wasn't much, into the bank, I began my journey back to the Inn, unaware that a morning begun like any other was to end by changing my life for ever.

The Boar's Head lays about half a mile beyond the village I needed to walk through in order to get home. It was just as I was passing the village church, walking slowly because I knew the mess I'd left behind would be patiently awaiting my return, when from a narrow gennel a young girl flew out. She ran into me full–square, knocking the breath out of me and leaving me hanging on the church gate. I didn't know who she was, but even as I tried to catch my breath, I could see she was really agitated. Recovering enough to speak, I used a few choice words and that started her crying, but then I realised what I'd taken for agitation was, in reality, fear and a few moments later I saw why she was afraid and knew she had good reason.

I knew Tom Rider from the Boar, although if all my customers were like him, I'd be broke in a month. Years past, before the accident, he used to come in with Bill Bostock and though he never drank like Bill, he still used to share a pitcher with him. I reckon Bill filled his tankard three times as often as Tom, but Tom didn't seem to mind. I think he was grateful to Bill because all my other regulars steered clear of him. There was something about him that made them wary. I had asked a couple of them once what it was they didn't like about him. They told me they didn't really know, but they believed his reserved manner hid something he didn't want other people to know.

On seeing him, the girl stiffened noticeably, then remembering her original course, tried to break away from me. Instinctively, I caught her arm, but before either of us could speak, Tom called out,

"That's right Jabez. Just hold her there for me will you, she's been carrying on something shameful, cussing and swearing. Old Bostock used some choice words and I reckon she must have picked them up from him, but me and Lizzie don't hold with that kind of talk and the girl needs to be punished."

It was in that moment I understood two things; first, I realised who the girl was and second, it was clear to me Tom was lying. You see I'd heard men talk, especially when they were drunk, about women and girls and what they'd like to do to them. But with them, talk was all it was and by the time they sobered up, they'd forgotten everything they'd said. But sometimes there were those who never spoke of their feelings, whether drunk or sober and keeping their thoughts inside, dreamed, planned and listened closely to the others. They were the dangerous ones, and Tom was one of them and I was certain that was the reason Admonition was running from him, not because she'd done anything wrong.

I whispered to her,

"If you can just trust me Adie, I think things will be alright."

The truth is I really had no idea what I was going to say or do, but distracted, I think because I knew her name, she relaxed slightly, allowing me time to say the first thing that came into my head.

"So this is Bill and Hannah's girl, is it Tom?"

Tom, who'd stopped running when he saw I held Adie, had now reached us. Still out of breath from his exertions, he panted,

"That's right. Me and Lizzie took her and her brother in when the rest of 'em were killed."

After stopping to catch his breath, he added,

"Will was alright, takes after Bill I suppose. He worked with me and tried to pay his way. Mind, he's long gone, went to work down Marshall's mine; told us he wanted to find his own way in the world. That's all very well, but he left us with that one."

Now fully recovered, he stabbed an accusing finger at Adie.

"And she's nothing but trouble; sits in the house doing nothing and if, like this morning, Lizzie asks for her help, she just gives her a mouthful of abuse."

I felt Adie stiffen again and I knew she was about to speak and I didn't think she was likely to help her situation, so I said quickly,

"Perhaps you should put her to work Tom. Get her out from under Lizzie's feet and bring a little extra money into the house."

"I would if I could find her any," Tom said, "but Lizzie doesn't want her to work in the pans. Says it's too dangerous and there's no other work for her around here."

I thought about all the mess waiting for me back at the Boar and realised here was an opportunity that might benefit me as well as Admonition.

"I'll give her some work Tom. I could do with help looking after the Boar. I won't be able to pay her much mind, but I'll treat her fairly and at least whilst she's with me, she'll not be troubling Elizabeth."

Surprised, Tom faltered, so before he could reply, I added,

"Of course, I don't know what Admonition thinks about the idea."

I looked at Adie, hoping she understood I was trying to help her, but Tom had found his voice.

"She'll do as she's told Jabez, but I'll need to talk to Lizzie first. I'll come and see you when I've spoken to her."

Looking coldly at Adie, he said,

"Right. Come on Admonition, let's get you home."

Adie showed no sign of moving, so I said,

"Why don't I come with you both and then we can all hear what Elizabeth has to say?"

Not waiting for a response from either of them, but still with a firm hold of Adie's arm, I started back towards the gennel. Adie came without resistance; she later told me she would have accepted any situation that saved her from being alone with Tom. For his part, Tom had little choice but to follow.

Elizabeth looked surprised to see the three of us, but once I'd explained my suggestion and a glance at Tom told her he had nothing to add, she voiced no objection. I filled the awkward silence that followed by telling Adie that because the Boar was usually open until late, I wasn't in the habit of rising early, so I wouldn't expect to see her until about nine o'clock. Finally I added,

"So if we're all agreed, I'll see you in the morning."

I hoped I sounded matter–of–fact and that Adie would see my smile as reassuring, but whether she did or not didn't seem to matter because Tom intervened.

"You don't need to worry. Like I told you, she'll do as she's told and she'll definitely be there by nine."

A barely noticeable nod from Adie told me she agreed. So as there was nothing more to say, I made my goodbyes and got on my way.

I didn't know it at the time, but my relationship with Admonition, one as unusual as her name, was born that day.

William
Chance Meetings

More than three hundred feet:
That's how far underground the tub took us, with nothing but a tallow candle to scratch the darkness. Barely a yard wide, the tub provided the only way in or out of the mine for both miners and salt. What's more, if the steam engine that operated its winding mechanism broke down, then anyone in the mine was stuck there until it was fixed. Of course, if miners underground were trapped, it also meant that any miners still above ground couldn't work and didn't earn a living. So when the engine broke down, which it seemed to do about once a week, the miners preferred to be underground stockpiling for when it was working again; they told me the winch was able to lift twelve hundred pounds at a time, so a backlog could soon be cleared and they lost little, if any, earnings.

I'll never forget the first time, after descending by the light of that one dim candle, I entered the mine's main chamber. Having descended well over two hundred and fifty feet in a chimney barely wider than the tub, I hadn't imagined the mine to be anything like the sight that now presented itself. I'd expected it to be small, really nothing more than a tunnel, and I only hoped that I might be able to stand upright. But when without warning the tub left the chimney, I found I was still about thirty feet above the floor of a cavernous chamber, and as, gently swaying, the tub completed its descent, I looked around and was fascinated by halos of light dotted all over the mine. Also, between the pillars of rock salt which provided doubtful support for the roof, I saw ghost–like figures loading tubs led by ponies, or prising away boulders of salt for others to break.

As I headed slowly towards the chamber floor, I realised that wherever a candle was placed close to a wall, and many were, salt crystals in the rock cheerfully reflected the candle's light. These reflections created the 'halos' that had taken my eye when I'd first descended into the chamber. But then, just as I do now, I thought they appeared out of step with what otherwise appeared to be a sombre place.

It didn't take long for me to get used to the sudden jolt as the tub reached the ground and I quickly learnt that simply grasping its side prevented me from being thrown across the tub. What took me much longer to get used to were the miners themselves. Many, just as they did in the pans, worked as a family. But unlike in the pans, where everyone went home at the end of their shift, many of the mining families stayed underground all week, only going home on Sundays.

In the pans I'd been used to the sound of brine boiling, salt slapping into moulds, carts filling, pans being scraped and workers shouting across to each other. They were relaxed with each other, always laughing and joking and I think because the heat forced them to wear very little, it would be impossible to do the job wearing more, it also gave them a freedom which allowed them to be much more familiar with each other. They worked hard, very hard, but what united them was that they depended on each other for their safety.

The miners were different because, whilst the mine echoed loudly to the sound of them working, the miners themselves said very little. Salt mining may have been hard, grim work, but it was also constant and methodical with little danger, whereas the pans were hot, frantic and dangerous places. These things all reflected in the miners' different nature and although they spent so much time together, I found little sense of people working with and for each other; rather, the cavernous nature of the mine with the hushed tones of the miners reminded me mostly of a church with a complacent congregation.

I can't deny I missed my old work or that life in the mine made me lonely, but even though I was friendless, for me there was no choice and there could be no going back. So for a little more than a year, I broke up rock salt, filled trams, led ponies, or transferred the salt from the trams into tubs to be hauled to the surface.

Before leaving the salt pans, Sarah had told me that drift-masters were responsible for hiring everyone who worked in the mine. So when I arrived at Marshall's, I was surprised that I was taken not to a drift-master but to the mine owner's mother. Mrs Marshall told me her son, as he often was, was away in London completing some legal work and when he was away, he left her in charge of the mines. She told me it was her way (and I gathered not her son's) to decide for herself who to hire. Her brother had worked the salt pans all his life until he recently retired and for as long as she could remember, he had told her that pan workers were the best workers in the world. She smiled when she told me and admitted she wasn't sure if that was true, but said she'd never taken on anybody from the pans who hadn't turned out to be a good worker. Once I explained I had worked in the pans for three years, I was hired without further ado. So whatever the reason, Sarah's words proved true: Marshall's were keen to employ salt pan workers.

Before taking me to a drift-master, Mrs Marshall saved me from the need to find somewhere to live because, at the same time as telling me I could start on the day shift the next morning, she gave me details of a place in Northwich (one of many owned by Marshall's), where I could find lodgings. I had a long walk into Northwich on that first day, but once I had taken a share in a room with another miner who only worked nights, I found there were coaches which ran to serve shift changes both night and day.

I worked a fourteen-hour shift and unless the rock face was to be blasted and we needed to find cover, stopped only once all day and that was to eat my baggin'. Usually, before returning exhausted to my lodgings, I would call at the Cock o' Budworth, a nearby coach house, staying only long enough to eat some pie and wash away the taste of the day's salt with a mug of ale. Hopefully, when I returned to my room, my fellow lodger would have already left for work, leaving the bed free until I rose again at five the next morning. George was much older than me, but other than that, and you might think it strange as we shared the use of a bed, I knew little about him. In fact our paths rarely crossed and when on occasion they did, lack of sleep and plain exhaustion made us both too tired to exchange more than a few words.

It was only when loneliness finally overcame pride and I had resolved to return to the Rider's, whatever might have befallen Tom, a chance arose for me to escape the mine. Just as in the pans, much of the salt from the mine was carried by boat to the Mersey Docks for export, and it was from there that, one morning I heard *The Mulberry* was in the Docks waiting, once its cargo of salt was loaded, to leave for America. Normally this would have caused me little interest, but on this occasion I was spurred into action by the word that went round that the ship was short of crew.

I didn't hesitate; I told the drift-master I was leaving, returned to my lodgings to collect my few belongings, then went to the Cock O' Budworth and caught the afternoon coach bound for Liverpool.

The journey to Liverpool seemed to last forever, though it really took little more than two hours. The coach's last stop was at the Exchange and I had been told the ship I was looking for was berthed in the Old Dock. Not knowing which way to go, I hailed a chair and asked its driver how much he would charge to take me there. He said he ought to charge me a bob, but as the distance to the dock was just over a thousand yards, it would only cost me a tanner. I told him I was in a great hurry and that if he made double speed, he'd get his shilling.

Inviting me to 'hop up', I'd barely gained my seat before he took off. Clearly not wishing to miss his shilling, he careered through backstreets, shouting at those who crossed his path to clear the way. Without losing any speed and almost toppling the chair, he rounded the last sharp bend and came to a halt outside the dock gates. Breathing hard and holding on to the arms of his chair for support, he gasped,

"There we are then sir, the Old Dock, as fast as I could make it."

Stepping unsteadily from the chair, I thanked him for travelling so speedily and paid him his shilling.

The gate to the dock was unattended, so I walked straight in. Although I ran back and forth trying to find *The Mulberry* amongst the forest of masts that filled the basin, the ship was nowhere to be seen. Anxious that I might have gone to the wrong dock, I enquired at the nearby Custom House, only to discover that the information I'd been given was wrong; or at least the ship had been there in Old Dock, but fully loaded and fully crewed, she'd left on the morning tide. Downhearted and not knowing what else to do, I began walking back into the town.

As I walked, I considered my situation: I had little money, perhaps enough for a couple of days, but only if I could find cheap lodgings and victuals and I didn't know who might hire me, as the nearest I'd ever been to the sea was walking by the stream that ran behind the Boar's Head. It seemed there was no other option for me but to return to Marshall's and see if they would re-hire me, or head back to the Rider's.

I'd walked quite some way without really taking note of my route and found myself completely lost. Stopping, I decided to look for a chair or hackney cab to take me back to the docks. I knew there wouldn't be any more coaches until morning, so I hoped to find a bed for the night in one of the many inns I'd seen as I flew through the streets on my way to Old Dock. But as I was about to hire a cab whose driver was clearly looking for trade, across the road I spotted offices belonging to one Thomas Marshall Esq. Although I couldn't be certain that this was the same Thomas Marshall who owned Marshall's Mines, I knew it had to be a possibility.

Negotiating the traffic and disappointing the cabbie, I crossed the road and entered the office, hoping this might finally be the stroke of good fortune I was seeking. As well as being surprisingly deep, the office was quite narrow and sparsely furnished. Standing at the back were two men leaning over a table, both completely absorbed in the paperwork laid out before them. At the front, looking down from a high stool raised on a plinth and set behind a desk, sat a thin, pinch-faced clerk. Clearly lording it over the office, he appeared less than pleased that I'd entered his kingdom.

On seeing him, my first thought was to make my apologies and leave, but if there was any chance of finding a place on another ship, I was determined not to miss it. So avoiding his bad-tempered look, I asked the clerk if the Thomas Marshall named on the office's door was the same as the one who owned the salt mines. In a voice that made it clear, he considered the fact to be common knowledge for anyone who might be worthy of asking, he confirmed that it was. Ignoring his tone, I explained I had, until that morning, worked as a miner for Mr Marshall and before that had spent three years working on the pans. But before I could say any more and louder than he needed, I imagined to impress the two men at the back of the office, he told me that he knew of no positions in Liverpool that might suit a miner and that he certainly didn't have any himself. After starting with such hope of new opportunity, my day had been full of nothing but disappointment and so, defeated, I thanked him for his time and left; his attention had already returned to his work. As I turned to leave, I saw one of the two men at the back of the office glance up and appear to notice me, but as he may simply have been distracted by the clerk, I thought nothing more of it.

Night was falling and as I knew there would be no chance of finding employment before morning, my thoughts returned to my search for a cheap bed for the night. I'd noticed several places close to Old Dock selling liquor and offering lodgings, and by the look of them I'd guessed they would be cheap. So having no alternative, I decided to make my way back there.

Most shops were closing for the night, and as they shut, so the many ale houses and gin shops that had stood unnoticed in the darkness, were springing into life. I'd started my journey back to the Old Dock thinking I might again find a cab or chair to take me. But as I pressed on through the increasing crowds, hoping I was heading in the right direction, it became clear I would be fortunate to find one free. If I saw a cab discharging passengers seeking Liverpool's dubious night time pleasures, before I could hail it others, who presumably wished to avoid the same delights, would claim it ahead of me. So having no other choice but to walk, I knew that at least the shilling I'd save in fare would allow me a better supper.

As I pressed on, the aroma of gin, ale and of food cooking filled the air, but I suppose because it was still new to me, the smell of the Mersey persisted and signalled the way to the docks. I was unused to the size of the crowds that buffeted me as I tried to make my way, so I stepped off the path and walked in the gutter. Even though it was full of filth and most others avoided it, by stepping carefully over the worst, I at least managed to move a little quicker in the direction I thought I needed to head.

Because I was still unsure I was going the right way and was still looking for somewhere I recognised, the first time it happened I imagined the girl was only being friendly and helpful, if a little forward.

"Evenin' chuck. Looking for somewhere to spend the night?"

It took me a moment to understand she was talking to me, but when I realised what she'd asked, I was keen to know if she could help me.

"Just you come with me darlin'," she said. "If you've got a guinea to spend on a girl, I'll keep you warm all night."

Looking at her properly for the first time, I saw how gaudy she was, wearing clothes and colour to attract her clients, I realised the girl's trade. Feeling a fool, I made my excuses and walked hastily away, the girl's laughter ringing in my ears. No longer surprised, I ignored the women, some in groups, others on their own and all seemingly drunk, who tried to stop me with similar questions.

Happily, as the smell of the river grew stronger, I knew I must be approaching my destination. Emerging from the town onto Duke's Place, I could see the river and turning towards Salt House Dock knew the Old Dock was just around the corner. So excusing myself from the unwanted attentions of yet another woman offering her services, I was passing between the dock and a salt works when suddenly, coming from the works, a man stepped straight across my path. Although I managed to stop before either of us came to any harm, he'd emerged too close to me for us not to collide.

Muttering minor apologies to each other, we both set off again, me towards Old Dock and because he crossed over, I knew he could only be heading for Salt House Dock. I'd gone only a few yards further when I heard someone call. Though I had no reason to think it was me being hailed, instinctively I glanced back over my shoulder and was surprised to find that the man I'd just collided with was looking straight at me. As I turned round fully, he called out.

"Hold on their lad, can I have a word?"

His face was familiar but for a moment I couldn't recall where I'd seen him. From his dress I could see he was well-to-do, so, curious to know why he would want to speak to the likes of me, I waited as he crossed back over.

Joining me, he said,

"You won't remember me."

It was at that moment I remembered where I'd seen this short, rather rotund man before.

"No, no, I remember you," I said. "You were in Marshall's this afternoon. I hope I didn't disturb you."

"No, not at all." He gave a wry smile. "Can't say the same for that sour-faced clerk."

Pulling me from the edge of the path and saving me from being struck by a carriage trundling up the narrow road behind me, he said,

"Look, I overheard what you said to that clerk and I think we may be able to help each other. That's if I'm right to assume you're still seeking employment?"

When I told him I was, he said,

"Good... Forgive me, I haven't introduced myself. My name is Wade Stubbs," pointing out the salt works he added, "and amongst my business interests, I share ownership of this place with Tom Marshall."

I told him my name and hoped he might be about to offer me employment in the salt work, but what he said next took me completely by surprise.

"I also have an interest in a West Indies' plantation that's owned mostly and run completely by my brother Thomas. Tom has plans to start a salt producing venture on the plantation, but he needs someone who understands salt panning to help him run it. The ship carrying supplies back to the plantation leaves tomorrow and up until now I've been unable to find anyone suitable who's also willing to take their chances in the Caribbean. Seeing you again down here in the docks, I guessed you might still be looking for a ship and remembering you told that clerk you had worked in the pans, I put the two things together and wondered if we might be able to help each other."

He looked at me questioningly, but I was still trying to take in everything he'd told me. Sensing my confusion, he said,

"Anyway, let's not stand here. If you think you might be interested, we can go over to the ship and then I can tell you more about it. If, when you've heard all I've got to say, you're not interested, then just walk away."

I knew little about the West Indies and nothing of what this 'salt production venture' might be, but I couldn't see that I had anything to lose.

The *Bridget* was a hive of activity and was clearly being made ready to leave on the early tide. Picking my way carefully between piled boxes of provisions yet to be stored and stepping gingerly over ropes not yet properly coiled, I followed Mr Stubbs below deck. Here, every spare space seemed already to have been used for storage and I wondered how room was ever going to be found for all the supplies still waiting on deck.

As we worked our way through the ship, we passed several sailors packing still more supplies into every nook and cranny, squeezing themselves into the smallest of spaces to allow us to pass. Finally, when I thought we must have reached the stern, Mr Stubbs stopped and knocked sharply on a door almost hidden by two improvised pillars of boxes.

In answer to a commanding call to enter, I followed Mr Stubbs into the Captain's quarters. Immediately in front of us, the Captain sat behind a desk, charts spread out in front of him. His bunk ran the length of one wall and above it a chaos of logs and more charts filled two shelves of similar length to the bunk. On the opposite wall, fixed next to the cabin's only porthole, a lamp provided light to the whole cabin. I squeezed into the only remaining space with Mr Stubbs. He was the first to speak.

"Evening Captain; I don't want to hold you up, just wanted to check everything was on schedule."

"Evening Mr Stubbs. Aye, we'll be ready in plenty of time to catch the morning tide."

Mr Stubbs clasped his hands together as if he was about to offer prayer and said,

"That's excellent Captain, excellent."

Looking my way, he said,

"This young man is Will Bostock and I'm hoping he's going to help my brother run the plantation. If he agrees to my proposal, you do have a berth for him, don't you Captain?"

"You told me you hoped to be sending a passenger Mr Stubbs, so I've kept a cabin free down on the orlop."

I sensed the Captain was a little irritated, but satisfied, Mr Stubbs turned to me and said,

"Come on then lad, let's go and find this cabin, then I'll tell you all about the plantation and Tom's plan for producing salt."

Telling the Captain he'd be back in the morning to see him off, Mr Stubbs shepherded me from his cabin and back through the ship.

We weigh anchor within the hour and though I'm not sure how I'll find the journey, Mr Stubbs told me to expect some nausea until I get my 'sea legs'; at least I can look forward to a better life when we reach the Turks and Caicos Islands. I'd never heard of them before, but Mr Stubbs showed me a map of all the West Indies and though these islands look quite small compared to some of the others, he told me that the Cheshire House Plantation is the largest in all of the Turks and Caicos.

Last night, he also told me all about the plantation and then went on to explain his brother's plan. He said that for some time Tom had seen how the slaves on the plantation trapped pools of sea water and after the water evaporated, scraped up the salt residue that remained and used it to flavour their food. He believes it will be possible to create much larger pools and produce salt on a commercial scale. He thinks he'll be able to export what he produces to the southern United States and I've agreed to help him set up and run the venture.

This morning, Mr Stubbs returned to the ship for the last time and before he left, he asked me if there was anyone he might tell where I was going. In all that's happened since yesterday, I hadn't given a thought to Adie or the Riders. Adie can't read and I'm not sure about Tom, but I know Elizabeth can, so I've written her a note explaining where I'm going and Mr Stubbs says he'll make sure she gets it.

Things can change so quickly and often at times and in ways you least expect. Take me for example. Yesterday, as I made my way back to the docks, I'd been thinking I might have no choice but to return to Marshall's or even the Rider's – I didn't look forward to either prospect, and for different reasons I wasn't at all sure how each might receive me. Now, not even a day later, I'm about to travel thousands of miles to a strange place I didn't know existed until yesterday, where I'll work for a man I've never met. It seems no time at all had passed since I was strolling back up the gennel, expecting my family to be up and that I'd be leaving shortly with Dad and John for work. Instead, they and most of my family are dead and here I am saying farewell to England not knowing when, or indeed if, I'll ever return.

Part Three

Elizabeth
All in a Name

How she's changed; it's wonderful to see. When Adie came to me, she was pale and gaunt and feared speaking in case it brought her trouble. Always quiet, she seemed to live in a world of her own. But now, with long black hair, dark skin and soft chestnut eyes, she's growing into a beautiful, young woman, full of life and always ready to speak her mind. I thought Will's leaving would set her back, but although she appeared a little quiet for a day or two, she grew even closer to me after he'd gone.

I suppose it must be four year's since Will left and all we've ever had from him was a scribbled note saying he was joining a ship bound for the West Indies. He said that when he got there, he was going to be in charge of salt panning on a plantation. Tom says he's never heard of such a thing, that he's sure there's no salt panning in the West Indies and I must have read Will's note wrongly. But Tom can't read and he's always hated that I can – he says it's a waste of time – anyway, whatever he thinks, I know I read that note right. Mind you, in a way I wish I hadn't because Will said nothing about when he might be back or, if he was staying in the West Indies, when he expected to send for his sister to join him. Although Adie never said, I know she hoped to hear more because when I read her the note she only asked,

"Is that all he said?"

When I replied that it was, she looked crestfallen but said nothing. But as I said, she seemed to quickly put it behind her. I suppose she'd made up her mind that either he'd write again when he was ready for her to join him, or just turn up at our door.

She's a fiery soul and now she always says what she thinks, no matter the consequences; I suppose she'll have to learn a little caution as she gets older, but I hope she never lets that fire go out. She isn't selfish mind. She may have her own opinions but that's not to say she isn't a great little helper. She seems always to want to do for me the best job she can – it makes my heart ache to see her; even if I ask her to do something for me that's completely new to her, she always does her best to get it right.

Yes, and she's not so little now, either. I believe if she grows as fast in the next six months as in the last six, she'll be taller than me by Easter. Mind you, her dad was a tall man and Hannah wasn't small, so I suppose I shouldn't be surprised.

As well as being a great help, she's good company too. When we work, jobs go more easily and time passes quickly because we chat and laugh and tell each other our dreams. Of course, I've never told her my greatest dream, but I have every hope that one day it may come true; I know she thinks of me like her mum and sometimes I dare to believe she might even think of me *as* her mum.

The other day I felt the time was right to talk to her about her name. In the years since the accident, despite all we've talked about, that subject has never been raised and I've kept my vow and we've always called her Adie.

It was a beautiful autumnal day and we were walking slowly back from town. In the morning there had been quite a sharp chill, but in the early afternoon there was a balmy sun shining, its light glowing in warm colours that matched the russets and reds of the autumn leaves; we walked slowly because we knew Tom wouldn't be home for hours. It was then it struck me how comfortable we were with each other and how confident in each other's love we'd become, so it was then that I said it; there was little forethought and certainly no malice.

"We haven't ever discussed your name, have we Adie? You know, your full name I mean. We've never talked about why it was given to you and you've never asked, but I think you know yours is not an ordinary name, so I wonder would you like me to tell you what I know about it?"

First hesitating, she then carried on walking and I kept silent because I could see she was thinking. Finally, she spoke,

"We get along, don't we? You and me I mean."

Surprised, I said,

"Of course we do. You know we do. Why would you ask such a thing?"

She stopped, turned, looked straight at me and declared,

"Because I think my name's a curse and only brings trouble. It brought trouble to Mum and Dad. It left you and Mr Rider stuck with me, and all the other children in the village taunt me about it; they still don't want anything to do with me. And worst of all, I think it's why my family was killed, so I don't talk about it 'cos I don't want anything bad to happen to you."

I'd wondered if she thought something like that; the truth is most people in her life *had* treated her like she *was* cursed, so I knew whatever I said next was important.

"Adie, your name is not a curse and it is definitely not the reason your family was killed. They were killed because a salt mine, which should not have been dug where it was, collapsed under your home.

But your name is a burden, or at least it will be if you let it. Your mum gave you your name as a warning to your father that he must never again treat her in the cruel ways he had. And that's what your name means; it's a warning. But it isn't a warning to you. It was meant only as a constant reminder to your father and perhaps one other. It is not a curse and nothing like what happened to your family is going to happen to me and Tom.

Your name *is* unusual. That's why people notice it and they always will. But you need to see that it will be up to you what they make of it."

She seemed interested and now as curiosity overcame worry she said,

"I suppose so. I remember Dad once told me something like that when I was very young, at least he told me people would always talk about my name. But I never knew he'd been cruel to Mum though. Do you know what he did to her?"

I'd promised her the truth, so even though I knew it would be hard for her, I told her the tale Tom had told me. I took hold of her hand and as we started walking again, I said,

"Adie, what I'm going to tell you now is something Tom told me. I promised him I'd keep it secret and I've never mentioned it to anybody, but I think you have a right to hear it."

I took a deep breath and told her what I knew.

"Now, before you were born, there was a night when Tom and your dad came home from the Boar's Head roaring drunk and singing. You probably know that your dad came home like that quite often, but I'd never seen Tom in that state. Anyway, your dad left

Tom at the door and when he came in, he was still singing. He slumped in his chair by the fire and as his singing petered out, he started talking. You know Tom isn't one for talking much, but the drink had loosened his tongue."

I glanced at Adie to make sure she was alright. I didn't want her believing I thought badly of her father, but she just gave me a nervous little smile. It was clear she wanted me to go on.

"At first I thought it was just the drink talking. He talked about how I was a good wife and how he knew he could trust me, all that old nonsense men come out with when they're drunk. I didn't pay much attention to what he was saying. I worried more about how I was going to get him into bed; I thought I might have to leave him where he was.

But then he appeared to make a huge effort to pull himself together and looking at me closely, in a whisper, he asked me if I could keep a secret. He put a finger to his lips to emphasise the point. I didn't see why we were whispering, because other than us the house was empty, but I didn't want to discourage him. After all, it was nice to have Tom confiding in me like he was, even if it turned out to be just the ramblings of a drunkard. So I whispered back that of course I could keep a secret and that's when he told me why your dad was so angry with your mum.

'Bill told me summin' tonight that's goin' to surprise you, but you must promise never to breathe it to another soul. Do you unnerstan'?

I was beginning to lose my patience. I told him that, of course, anything he told me I would keep in the strictest confidence; he was my husband after all.
That seemed to convince him 'cos he carried on.

'Sally isn't Bill's child an' he thinks Annie might not be as well. He wouldn't tell me who she's been seein', but he says it's someone she knew from before they were married. Apparently, it's been going on for years. '"

Adie went pale, so I said hurriedly,

"Oh, I told him that couldn't be true. I'd known your mum from the day she and your dad were married and I swear she never looked at another man.

So I asked him what made your dad think that way. Apparently he wouldn't say, but Tom thought someone must have said something to him. I tell you Adie, if I found out who that person was, I'd give 'em a piece of my mind, 'cos they sowed a seed of doubt into a good marriage and that's unforgivable. It's also the reason your mum gave you your name; it was the only way she could let your dad know how she felt about his accusation."

I looked at Adie to see if I'd upset her, but whether I had or not, her reply was defiant,

"So you're saying the only reason I've got my name is because Mum wanted to settle an argument?"

I started to reply.

"Well, that's partially true…"

But she interrupted me.

"So, even though it wasn't my fault, I was the one she really punished. She's dead; it don't matter to her anymore. But me, I'm going to have to live with it, with the teasing by the other children, the strange looks people give me – all my life I'm going to hear them, whispering and giggling whenever I'm near.

'Admonition, that's a strange name.

Oh, don't you know, her mother gave her that name to punish her father.

Punish him, punish him for what? …'

Like I said, she's dead and it doesn't matter to her anymore. But I'm stuck with it. I hate her and I'm glad she's dead."

I suppose I shouldn't have been shocked, but I was, so I said,

91

"Adie, you don't mean that, you're just upset."

She hadn't finished and by what else she had to say, it was clear she certainly was upset.

"I do mean it. I do. She always called me Admonition. Always. And she made all the others do the same whenever she was around. Mine isn't a name. It's just a punishment. You've never called me Admonition. You always call me Adie, 'cos I think you think the same as me.

And do you know the first time I remember someone hugging me? It was the day of the accident when Mr Rider first brought me and Will back to you and you hugged me. She never held me, she only ever hit me, told me I'd done wrong. She was never a mum to me. Never."

She finally burst into tears.

What could I say? I knew the child deserved honesty and I believed what she'd said was right. But somehow, for her sake, I needed to soften the truth.

Gripping her hand more firmly, I said quietly.

"I shan't argue with you, Adie, but things were made hard for your mum in a way she couldn't have seen coming. She loved your dad but he had unfairly accused her of doing wrong, of being unfaithful. He never gave her the man's name, so she couldn't defend herself.

Can you imagine what that was like for her? Just think, to be completely innocent, yet treated as guilty and punished accordingly by the person you loved the most in the whole world. It made her very angry and she struck your father in the only way she could. When we're as angry as your mum was, we sometimes make mistakes. She was thinking only of your father when she gave you that name. If you could talk to her now, I'm sure she would admit it was wrong.

Life will bring you many experiences; good and bad, short and long. They won't shape your life, but how you react to them will. You're growing into a beautiful young woman, but if you let it, that name will twist your looks along with your nature."

She stopped again and looked at me.

"You really think I'm beautiful?"

I laughed, mostly with relief.

"Of course you're beautiful, didn't you know?"

I'd never before seen her blush, but she did then and with her eyes cast down, said quietly,

"No one's ever told me that before. How was I to know?"

I knew that was probably true.

"Trust me, it's true. But Adie, don't forget the other things I've told you. They're just as important, more even."

This time she squeezed my hand and, for the first time since our conversation began, gave me a proper smile and said,

"I won't."

We were almost back at the gennel, so slipping my hand she skipped ahead and I chuckled to myself; despite all that had happened to her in her short life, Adie was still a child.

Jabez

The Salt Road

I stayed an apprentice for seven years and through all that time I continued to read for Mr Dodds who, for his part, made sure I learnt all he could teach me about running a pub. And it was from standing behind the bar with him, watching and listening to how he handled his customers, that I learnt the important things about being a publican. Through him and my own lifetime behind the bar, I learnt to read my customer's every action and reaction. I especially knew my regulars, knew their work, their fears, I knew their whole lives really. But the real skill I learnt from Mr Dodds was that whatever they wanted to talk about, no matter the subject, they all thought I agreed with them. The truth is of course, I never agreed or disagreed with any of them. Like Mr Dodds I just listened and gave them a sympathetic ear, because usually that's all they want.

Mr Dodds never mentioned that I was an apprentice in all the time I was with him; at least not until the day my apprenticeship came to an end. That morning, just like every other, he woke me with a smart knock on my bedroom door. But this morning when he entered, he wasn't carrying a jug or towel, instead, accompanied by a beaming smile, he carried a piece of paper I hadn't seen for seven years; my papers of indenture. Handing them to me he said,

"There you are Jabez. Today your indenture is complete and you're no longer an apprentice. You're free to leave any time you like, though I must admit I'm rather hoping you'll stay."

The paper he handed me seemed so insignificant, nothing notable apart from the signature I barely recognised of a young boy I hardly remembered. But by giving it to me, Mr Dodds had finally separated me from the workhouse for ever. So returning his smile I said,

"Thank you Mr Dodds, I've loved my time here and I hope never to leave."

Stepping out of the room, he came back with the jug of water and towel he'd left outside my door and said,

"That's good to hear. Now, when you're washed and ready to come down, there's something else I want you to read."

I thought he had a bill, notice or some such that he needed me to read, so I washed and finished dressing without any particular urgency. Most mornings Mr Dodds left my breakfast at one of the tables in the bar and was usually to be found seeing to the horse, feeding and grooming him and sometimes mucking out his stable, although this last duty usually fell to me. But this morning was different because when I walked into the bar, Mr Dodds was sat at a table and in front of him was, I assumed, the document he wanted me to read.

Taken aback I said,

"I'm sorry Mr Dodds, I didn't realise it was urgent otherwise I would have been quicker."

As I sat down opposite him, he slid the document in front of me.

"It's not urgent lad, or at least I hope not, but it is important that you read it."

It took only a glance for me to realise that this was his Will, so I asked him whether he really wanted me to read its contents. In reply, he just turned slowly to the first page and passed it to me. Looking down, I could see there were very few words and of those, even fewer were of significance. The phrase that carried everything was,

'To Jabez Payne I leave all my worldly goods. '

I must have looked as shocked as I felt because, even though I hadn't yet had time to form them, he then seemed to answer all my questions in one,

"As far as I know I have no family living, so you're the nearest thing I've got. I've taught you all I know about running a pub so I know, when my time comes, I'll be leaving the Boar in good hands."

Standing, he said,

"That copy is yours to keep. Make sure you put it somewhere safe because my copy is with the solicitor who wrote it and I haven't known young Carlyle long enough to be sure that he can be trusted."

I told him I didn't really know what to say, but that I was very, very grateful.

He smiled and said,

"Right then lad. You go and find somewhere safe to keep your copy and I'll go and get us some breakfast."

Not really knowing what else to do, I took the will to my bedroom, took my clothes out of one of the chest draws, lifted the lining paper and placed the will underneath. It stayed there until long after Mr Dodds died. In fact it might have stayed there forever because Carlyle turned out to be as honest as the day's long and had the will ready to be read at the earliest opportunity after the funeral.

Although he never said, I believe Mr Dodds already knew he was ill when he had the will drawn up, because it was only about a year later he was laid to rest in the village church cemetery and at the age of twenty-two, I became landlord of the Boar's Head.

It's hard to believe how the years slip away. I had been the Boar's landlord for twenty-five years and in all that time, the inn had just about paid its way, but now it was in trouble. Since the mines started opening up, work at the pans had steadily reduced. As a result, many of the men had gone to work in the salt mines, even taking their families with them and all of them eating and sleeping underground and only coming home again on Sunday. I'm not saying what they did was wrong, but now they hardly ever came to the Inn. For those who stayed at the pans, there was a lot less work and less work meant less money and of course that meant they had less to spend on ale. Not for the first time I was mulling this over, as usual without reaching any solution, when my first customer of the evening walked in.

Joseph Bayley was a rare visitor to the Boar and though I thought I knew the look of trouble if it decided to walk through the door, just this once it was so well disguised that even I didn't recognise it, so instead I welcomed Joseph in.

"Evening Joseph."

"Evening Jabez"

"Small beer, isn't it?"

I was curious, there had to be a reason for his visit. But there was no point in rushing him, I just had to leave the door open. If he'd got something to say, he'd walk right through; but only in his own time.

"No. Give me a gin, will you Jabez? I need somethin' a bit stronger."

I poured him his gin, took his money from the counter and then served a couple of my locals who'd come in just after Joseph. I'd only just finished serving them when Joseph called for a refill. Without comment, I served him again.

It was only when, five minutes later, he again called for a refill that I invited him to step through and tell me what was on his mind.

"You're not usually a gin drinker, are you Joseph?"

I knew he wasn't, but my question had the desired effect.

"Thirty years I've been a baker. Worked with my father from the age of seven and took over the shop when he died and like him, I've always produced good bread. No rubbish in my bread, just good flour and now it looks like I'm going to have to close down.

People have moved away or just stayed away, and the rest are buying less bread because they can't afford it. If they'd just cut the salt tax, it might give me an edge, but I hear that if they're going to do anything, they'll put it up even higher."

I gave him his third gin.

"Take it slowly, eh Joseph. Something may turn up."

It was as if I hadn't spoken.

"See, my bread's better not only 'cos I use good flour but because it's tastier. And do you know why it's tastier?"

His eyes were beginning to lose focus.

"It's 'cos I use a little more salt. Mix it wrong, you kill the yeast and the bread won't rise, add too much salt an' it tastes 'orrible."

The gin was having its effect.

"Tha's a trade secret, thad is. I'm telling you cos I know you'll keep it to yourself. Now gimme another gin, will you Jabez?"

What he'd said was true; his secret was safe with me. Far more likely, especially as the bar became busier, was that others would overhear his slurring, but liberated, tongue and I knew there were some who had access to cheap salt and they weren't all fair men. Deal with the wrong ones and I knew Joseph might end up in real trouble, so although I knew he'd had enough, I also knew, as he wasn't used to it, another drink would knock him out cold. So I served him.

As he slumped onto the bar, I arranged to get him home. If they lived locally, I dealt with all my regulars when they'd had too much to be able to walk, in the same way. Although he wasn't a regular, Joseph was local, so I got a couple of the stronger lads to sling him across one of the donkeys and take him home. I'd already taken money out of Joseph's change to stand them both a drink on their return, a practice which was generally agreed to be fair.

I liked Joseph and I felt sorry for him, so I thought I'd have a word with a couple of pan workers I knew I could trust and see if we couldn't help solve his problem. Men from the pans often smuggled small amounts of salt past the watchmen and sold it to residents and shopkeepers from the town. But I always made sure I neither saw nor heard anything and I didn't ask any questions when a small parcel of money was dropped at my door, nor did the revenue's local officer when I passed half of it on to him. But now, for the first time, I became involved in supplying contraband salt and that held the danger I hadn't foreseen.

A couple of nights after he'd been in the Boar, Joseph had a visit from two men he didn't know. With few words, they dropped a bag containing a bushel of salt in front of his counter.

"That'll be eight shillings," one of them said.

A bemused Joseph paid him and the stranger said,

"If you want any more, just tell Jabez."

With that, according to Joseph, the two of them slipped away into the night. An insignificant encounter for them, but those final words were to mark the start of my life in the world of salt smuggling. What started simply enough with me operating as the link between Joseph and his salt suppliers, in not much more than a month, had me embroiled in a serious smuggling operation.

And so it was that about a month after Joseph had last been in the Inn he walked in again. I wasn't surprised to see him but pretended I was.

"Good evening, Joseph. Twice in a month, keep this up and I'll be calling you one of my regulars. What can I get you, a drop of gin?"

I thought I knew why Joseph had called and it definitely wasn't for gin. From what I'd heard, he'd not only been hung–over for two days, but his headache had been made a lot worse by his wife who didn't let up for a full week. Her mood hadn't been improved when a few days later she was woken in the dead of night by two complete strangers delivering contraband salt.

So I wasn't surprised by Joseph's reply.

"No! No gin, just give me a small beer, will you Jabez?"

He looked around furtively, why I don't know because, apart from the two of us, the bar was completely empty.

To encourage him, I said,

"So is there something else then, another reason why you're here again?"

In an urgent whisper, he replied,

"Do you remember how you helped me out last month?"

96

"With the salt you mean?"

Nearly spilling his beer and with panic in his voice, he breathed,

"Shsh! Someone might hear us."

Even though I knew we were on our own, I found myself looking all around; his nervousness was contagious.

"Joseph, believe me, we're completely alone and we'll hear if anyone approaches. Now, what is it you wanted to say?"

Still in a whisper, he said,

"Well, that salt you arranged for me has made all the difference, see. I've been able to drop my prices and still make good quality bread and most of my customers have come back to me. They're not buying as much as they used to, because they're earning less and everything else is more expensive, but at least they're buying enough to keep me in business."

"That's good to hear. Another beer?" I also had a living to earn.

"Well, just another small one."

"A small one it is then Joseph and while I pour it, you can tell me why you're really here."

I gave him what I hoped was an encouraging smile and he took courage and launched in.

"It's just that I've almost run out of salt and if I don't get some more, I'll have to pay regular prices for it, then I'll have to put my prices up as well. If I do that, I'll lose my customers again and no matter what I do, I'll never get them back a third time."

He seemed close to panic, so to ease his fears I said,

"Joseph, if you want some more salt, just say. I'm sure it can be arranged. Didn't the men tell you that when they delivered the last lot?"

Sheepishly, he admitted that they had and said he should ask me.

"Well, there you are then. Just leave it with me." I passed him his beer and told him,

"Expect a knock in the next few days."

But Joseph wasn't the only one who was about to receive a late-night visitor.

Saturday night was a busy one. It was just a few days after my conversation with Joseph and the bar was full. Just like old times, most of my locals were in and my takings were good. But in addition, sitting at or crowded around one of my tables, were eight men I'd never seen before. I kept a close eye on them when they first came in, but they were no trouble. They kept themselves to themselves, got a little rowdy as the night grew old, but any disquiet they may have caused me was more than compensated for by the quantity of ale they swallowed. Paying as they ordered, it was clear money was not a problem for them.

As my regulars began to realise these strangers were only here for ale and each other's company, they started to relax and the strangers' high-spirited mood became contagious. I'm sure some of my locals had aching heads when, the next morning, they tried to explain to disgruntled wives where all their money had gone.

Anyway, when I finally called time at about one o'clock, I was concerned that this might be the point our newcomers would cause trouble, so I positioned myself within easy reach of my billyclub and watched them very closely. But I needn't have worried, because after all my regulars left in good humour; loud but happy enough, the strangers drank up together, got up together and quietly left all together, a manner I found somehow disquieting. Only one delayed his departure, a tall, thin man, he wore a black greatcoat and looked not only to be the eldest, but something in his manner, told me he was also their leader.

Speaking in a husky-edged whisper, he said.

"You won't need your billyclub Jabez. You won't be getting any trouble from us. But you *can* expect another visit from me."

Giving me a grim smile, he gave the bar a concluding rat-tat and, without another word, left to join the others. He left me greatly unnerved; certainly I had questions for him, such as how had he seen the billyclub? And how did he know my name? But what unnerved me the most was the way, at the end of the night and without a word, the whole group had moved in unison. I'd only once seen men move with such accord and that was a group of acrobats I'd seen at the Knutsford fair; but whatever these men were, they weren't acrobats. No, something else drew them together and it was wondering what that might be which left me uncertain.

But then I shrugged and said to myself,

"Jabez, you're becoming a fanciful old fool. Of course he knew your name. Your locals call you by it all the time and, after all, you've been here over twenty years; there's no mystery there."

I finished clearing the bar and as I went, thought some more about this man and what he'd said. I realised that the Billyclub was probably just a lucky guess. He must have seen me glancing under the bar and put two and two together. I told myself,

"You need to remember that the billyclub is the favoured weapon of all publicans in these parts. No, stop your worrying, go to bed and just be grateful that you've had the best night's takings since Christmas."

Reassuring myself it was nothing more than a sensible precaution, I grabbed the billyclub, bolted and locked the door, took most of the night's takings from the till and placed them in a money bag. Having extinguished all but one of the candles, which I took to light my way, I headed for bed. But before getting in, I lifted a small mat that lay in front of my bed, removed a loose floorboard specially cut for the purpose and put the money bag under the floor, pushing it completely out of sight. After replacing the floorboard and the mat, I blew out the candle and, billyclub in hand, finally got into bed. Sleep wasn't a long time coming after my long and busy night, but as I drifted off, my last thought was of those men who had moved together like well drilled soldiers, yet something told me they had nothing at all to do with the army.

Pulled from sleep by a familiar rat-tat at the back door, I was halfway down the stairs before I was awake enough to realise I'd forgotten my candle. I could have gone back for it, but my eyes had adjusted sufficiently to what was a familiar path for it to prove unnecessary. So having negotiated my way along the corridor that led to the back exit, billyclub at the ready, I unlocked and cautiously opened the door.

Peering into the dark, I could see nothing. Softly cursing, I was about to shut the door when the darkness spoke.

"Hello Jabez."

Grasping the billyclub more firmly and speaking with all the authority I could muster, I said,

"Whoever you are, show yourself."

Movement by the well indicated where the voice came from.

"I said you didn't need your club Jabez."

As he spoke again, I recognised the voice of the stranger who had spoken to me earlier that evening. He stepped forward out of the shadows and, though I still kept it in a firm grip, I lowered my club.

"Let's step inside. I think it's best for both of us if we're not seen."

He spoke with the assurance of one who was used to being obeyed. He appeared to be alone and to pose no threat, so I moved back from the doorway to let him in.

Shutting the door behind him, he said,

"Can't be too careful. Usually those Excise men are too idle to be around at this time, but things are a little different at the moment."

It may have been almost as dark in the hall as it was outside, but for me a light was beginning to dawn.

"Let's go through to the bar," he said. "I'll introduce myself and explain why I'm here."

"Let me go first," I thought it best I showed the path. "I'll light a candle when we reach the bar."

When I thought about it, I was sure he was very used to finding his way in the dark. Nevertheless, a gesture with his hand told me I had his permission to proceed.

When we reached the bar, I lit a candle, made sure no light could escape the window blind and then we sat at a table furthest from the window; I noticed he made sure he sat in the shadows.

My offer of a drink was declined.

"Thank you, but I never drink when I'm working."

There seemed little value in mentioning the copious amount consumed by him and his friends earlier in the evening. He then introduced himself, although I already had a good idea of who he was.

"My name's Sam Baker. By day you'll find me working the pans at Nantwich. But nights I have a different trade."

I looked straight at him and said,

"You smuggle salt, you and the rest of your gang."

The notoriety of the Nantwich Gang and their leader, Sam Baker, was spread throughout Cheshire and beyond. But although their identity was well known by the authorities, nothing had ever been proven against them and any possible witnesses to their work were too afraid to come forward, even if they wanted to. It had always been my intention to avoid any involvement with the Gang if at all possible.

It was as though Sam could read my mind, although I imagine he was just a good reader of men.

"Look, I know you're going to tell me you don't want anything to do with us and our work, that our reputation goes before us and you don't want any trouble. But, you see, I have a problem and I think you may hold the solution.

The Excise has brought in a new Supervisor and they've doubled the wage for the job. I've talked to him and he's made it clear he knows what we're doing and he intends to make his reputation by catching me. He's learnt he can't trust the night watchmen. They're all in my pay and can be relied on to be somewhere else when I need them to be. Besides, they all live around here and they've all got families who they wouldn't want to come to any harm, if you understand me."

I understood him alright and wondered vaguely what he'd have in store for me if I didn't do whatever it was he wanted. After all, as far as I knew I had no family still living. Torch the Boar, perhaps? Whatever it was, I knew it wouldn't end well for me.

He continued.

"He's hired two men from outside the County to work for him. Pays them out of his own salary I hear, promised them a bounty if they catch any of us with salt and a larger one if the 'someone' they catch is me.

Now we don't have any problem getting the salt out of the sheds and safely storing it locally. Our problem is moving it on to our customers. This man and his sidekicks work nights and although they can't cover every route at any one time, our luck must run out at some point.

So that's where we need your help. You want to help us, don't you Jabez? I hear you've started providing your own supplies, undercutting our prices."

There was no menace in his voice, just that hoarse whisper, but he still scared me; maybe it was because I wasn't at all sure whether he'd asked me a question or issued a command.

I wanted to explain that Joseph was an exception and I'd only helped him because he was desperate. I certainly didn't want anything to do with undercutting Sam's prices, but he didn't wait for a reply.

"I need people unconnected with us or the pans to work relays out to my customers. Covering short distances reduces the risk you see.

I want you to work the first of a run to my biggest customer in Liverpool. I have a cousin who runs a small farm by Foulk Stapleford, that's about three miles from Chester, and I need you to take the salt to him."

I was bewildered. How did he expect me to transport large quantities of salt without being seen?

His answer was simple.

"Jabez, you've got two working donkeys. If one of them spends the night delivering a load of salt, then no one's going to notice if the next day there's only one out in your field because the other one's resting in your stable."

Of course, he made no mention of when *I'd* get some rest.

"Two of my men, two of those you saw tonight, will come here for a drink. They won't stay long and they won't talk too much, but you can take it as a signal to expect a delivery that night at about this time. You'll need to store the salt until the next night when you'll take it to my cousin; he'll be expecting you. When they come for a drink, the men will leave a map showing my cousin's farm; remember, you must memorise and then destroy it.

So are we clear? We wouldn't want there to be any misunderstanding, would we?"

No, everything was clear I told him. I didn't tell him what was clearest of all – that he was giving me no choice.

"Right, I'll be away," he said. "You can expect my men in the next week."

With that, he got up and made for the corridor. I hurried after him with the candle. When he reached the door and before opening it, he turned to me and said again,

"We're not going to have any problems here, are we Jabez?"

That was the third time he'd asked me a question that sounded more like a command. I shook my head and muttered that of course there wouldn't be any problems.

With one hand on the latch, he paused and added coldly,

"Because we wouldn't want anything to happen to the Boar, would we?"

Despite the danger, I was getting annoyed because that was the fourth question he'd asked me that sounded like so much more. So I said,

"If you don't think you can trust me, why ask me?"

"Oh, I know I can trust you, I just wanted to make sure you remembered why."

With that, he gave me another grim smile, unlatched the door, stepped out and in moments, had once again disappeared into the darkness.

Returning to the bar, I sat at the nearest table. I sat for so long my candle guttered and I made no attempt to re-light it. It was hard to take in all that had happened in just one night, but sitting in the dark I knew one thing for certain. For good or for bad, I was about to become a salt smuggler.

The following Thursday at nine o'clock, two of Sam's men walked in. Just as he'd told me to expect, they spoke very little to each other and apart from ordering their drinks, said nothing to me or anyone else. After only a couple of pints, they left, but before leaving one of them slipped me a folded piece of paper which I slid into my trouser pocket. I had no need to examine it. I knew what it was and knew I'd have time to study it closely after the pub shut.

I also knew that whatever the temptation to do otherwise, it was important I behaved normally because I didn't know who might be lurking in the darkness watching the inn. If I was to deliver the salt to Foulk Stapleford and return before dawn, the following night would be sleepless. So when I'd cleared the bar, locked and bolted the door and extinguished the candles, I retired, determined to get a good night's sleep.

Determined or not, I didn't sleep at all. All night my ears strained for any sound that might indicate Sam's men were abroad. But apart from the call of a lone owl seeking a mate, there was only silence.

Nevertheless, when morning finally dawned, I rose, dressed and headed straight out to the stable. There, in the middle of the floor, were four five-bushel sacks of salt. I stepped inside and quickly shut the door. It was unlikely that anyone would be passing this early but I wasn't taking any chances – it was a good job I didn't.

Both donkeys were restless, anxious to be out. But before I released them, I moved the salt into a corner of the stable and surrounded it with straw bales. Only then did I let the donkeys out and with one last look back, followed them. Hearing a branch to the side of me snap, I turned and saw Tom Rider standing by the well; he was looking straight at me.

"Mornin' Jabez. I was just passin' when I heard a noise in your stable. I thought it must be you attendin' to your donkeys, but it went on for so long I thought you might have burglars. I was just about to take a look."

I laughed – I hoped it didn't sound strained.

"Morning to you Tom. No, I was just moving some straw I had delivered yesterday. But thank you. It's good to know you were looking out for me. Come in tonight and I'll stand you a beer."

I hoped my offer would assure Tom that nothing unusual had occurred. Thankfully, he seemed to accept what I said and, after saying he might see me later, went on his way. Anxiety meant I never asked him why he was outside the Boar so early.

The rest of my day was uneventful, as was the evening. My worries that I wouldn't be able to clear the bar or that one of the donkeys would be needed to get someone home proved unfounded. Tom Rider never appeared which didn't surprise me because after Bill Bostock's death, I'd rarely seen him.

I'd stabled the donkeys at dusk and resolved to wait until one o'clock before setting off. When it was time to leave, I loaded the salt onto one donkey and riding the other, headed out for Foulk Stapleford. I should have liked to wait another hour, so I could be sure of not meeting anybody on my way out, but I knew the return journey would take me at least six hours by the shortest route. In October, leaving the Boar around one should see me return at just about daybreak. I wasn't sure what I would do in the summer, but between September and April, I was confident I could complete the whole journey in darkness.

Whilst sleepless the night before, I had noticed the moon was full, providing me with another reason to worry. But fortunately, the following day it rained continuously and although by nightfall the rain had stopped, the sky remained overcast, clouds completely masking the moon and meaning I was able to travel under the cover of darkness. Avoiding the roads was obvious, but I decided even the lanes presented too much of a risk that I might be discovered. So I was lucky that whilst studying the map Sam's men left me, I realised it would be possible to travel across country, staying close to streams and rivers. I knew Foulk Stapleford was close to the River Gowy and by studying the map, I found a route, starting from the stream that lay behind the Boar, which would take me to the Gowy, just three miles outside Foulk Stapleford.

I'd also decided to use both donkeys. That way I hoped they would have plenty of time to rest before they were again called upon to work. Also, I would need to do all my usual chores and still be ready to open the Inn as normal. I didn't relish the thought of working after six hours walking as well as a second sleepless night.

Knowing there was no escape from the night's work, at about quarter to one I loaded one of the donkeys. Covering her with a blanket, I still knew that if we were stopped by the Excise men, there was no possible way of disguising the load; I could only hope that my chosen route wasn't one of theirs. Joining the donkeys with an old linking rein I'd found in the stable and disregarding my pounding heart, I mounted the unladen beast and we set off.

In the dark, as we headed for the stream that I hoped would mark the beginning of an incident-free journey, the only sound to be heard was that forlorn owl still searching for a mate.

Reaching the stream, we followed the path which ran alongside. With the water reflecting a shade of darkness on one side of us and a hawthorn hedge, wet with the day's rain, a lighter shade on the other, I felt confident enough of our way to push the donkeys into a trot. Our progress was interrupted only by occasional stray branches which, as if conspiring with the donkeys, dragged their thorns painfully across me, trying unsuccessfully to slow our progress. Otherwise our path was uninterrupted and we encountered no one else on our journey; no one that is until we joined the Gowy.

We had made good time following a number of deserted streams and I hoped to return to the Boar early enough to get a couple of hours rest before beginning my day. Apart from a couple of sleeping narrow boats, which we slipped quietly past, even though by now a river rather than just a stream, the Gowy also appeared to be deserted. Sam had told me his cousin would leave a lantern burning outside his farmhouse to indicate our destination and I believed from memories of studying the map Sam's men had left, that when we rounded the bend that lay just ahead, the lantern would be visible. I was becoming more hopeful that we would reach our goal without incident

But it was then I heard a noise up ahead. I froze and as the disinterested Gowy continued to flow past, the sound continued getting nearer and I recognised the murmur of two men whispering. Although what they said was unclear, it was evident from their tone that they were arguing. It was also clear that in moments they would round the bend and I would be directly in front of them. Unarmed, with the river to my right and an unbroken hedge to my left, there was nothing I could do but stand and face whoever was approaching. So stopping the donkeys I dismounted, just as the men rounded the corner.

Still arguing, they were both taken completely by surprise when they found their way forward blocked by a stranger leading two donkeys. Only one of them appeared to be armed and although clearly flustered, he hurriedly took the musket from his shoulder and pointed it at me. It occurred to me the weapon was unlikely to be loaded but, particularly at such close range, that was a possibility I was not inclined to test; besides, there were two of them so they could probably overpower me with or without a loaded gun.

Looking past the man with the gun, I saw that the other had on his shoulder a very full sack. It was obvious these men were poachers and the full sack indicated they'd had a successful night's work. Regardless of how the night had gone for them, I was sure they had no desire to risk drawing attention to themselves. So, making sure I was as far away from the water's edge as possible, I pulled the donkeys against the hedge and offered the men a clear path. Cautiously, never taking their eyes from me and with the musket still pointed in my direction, they moved past me. They clearly understood that I also had no desire to draw attention to myself, and whilst they might be curious to know what my wide-girthed jenny might be carrying, they could be sure, travelling at this hour, I wouldn't wish to explain.

Remounting, I once again headed towards the bend in the river, but before I reached it, I paused and looked back. I was concerned that the temptation to relieve me of my donkey and her load might overcome the poachers' caution. I needn't have worried because when I looked, I could just make out two shapes hurriedly disappearing in the direction from which I had just come.

Relieved, I pressed on and as I hoped, when I turned the bend I saw set back from the path by about a hundred yards, a light shining out of the darkness; I knew this had to be my destination. Another twenty yards along the path and I came upon a break in the hedgerow where a small track led towards the light and as I could now just make out its outline, the farmhouse.

Emerging from the track I recognised, standing in the lantern's light outside the farmhouse, one of the men who had accompanied Sam Baker that first time he'd appeared at the Boar. Thickset and leather-skinned from a lifetime spent outside, Sam's cousin put a finger to his lips to indicate I should be silent. Taking down the lantern, he led the way to a barn at the rear of the farmhouse. I stayed mounted and, still leading the other donkey, followed him. When we reached the barn, he opened the door and taking the donkey's rein from me, led her inside. I started to dismount so I could follow, but as I reached the ground, the barn door shut and I heard a bolt being drawn. It was clear I was not invited to join them, so I had little choice if I wanted my animal back, but to wait for them to reappear.

It began to rain again, so I drew my mount into the shadow and shelter of the barn and waited. After five minutes, the door of the barn re-opened and the rein of a much slimmer donkey was handed back to me. Indicating I should remount, he lit the way back to the track that would return me to the Gowy. Slapping the haunch of my mount to send us on our way, he turned and headed back towards the farmhouse.

The light from the lantern meant my eyes were no longer fully accustomed to the dark, so at first I made sure we went slowly. As we made our way, it struck me that not only had Sam's cousin not said one word all the time I had been at his farm but, as Sam hadn't told me, I didn't even know his name. Of course, when I thought about it, it was obvious – clearly the less I knew, including the name of Sam's cousin, the safer we all were. The man had insisted on silence presumably not only because he couldn't be sure there wasn't someone lurking in the darkness waiting for one of us to incriminate ourselves, but also because it kept him anonymous.

By the time we reached the Gowy, my eyes had adjusted fully, so I tried to spur my donkey on. Unused to travelling more than a couple of miles and clearly weary, he was very reluctant to speed up. The jenny, on the other hand, seemed keen to get home and was following very close behind us. So stopping, I switched the saddle and mounted the jenny, and with my new mount glad to be leading and unaffected by my extra weight, she set off towards home, whilst the jack, relieved of his burden, was content to follow.

The return journey was wholly uneventful and we made good time, and as the rain had stopped by the time we reached the Gowy, all three of us were dry long before we got home. Quickly and quietly I stabled and fed the donkeys and then made my way back inside the Boar. As I walked back in, I could see that the sky was just beginning to lighten, and I knew dawn was still about half an hour away. That meant I had about two hours before I would be expected to be seen up and about; in other words, two hours rest and I wouldn't see my bed again for another sixteen. Still the main thing was that I'd delivered the salt and returned without incident and hopefully Sam Baker wouldn't pay me another visit for a while.

As I shut the door, I was sure I heard a noise, so I paused and straining my ears waited for another sound. But hearing nothing more and telling myself it was probably just a badger or some other nocturnal animal on its way home, I turned and headed for bed.

Looking back, I have to admit that first delivery went without a hitch. It's just that for a full week from the moment two of Sam's men had entered the bar, I expected Excise men to come and arrest me.

I was sweeping when she walked through the door. She didn't say anything, just took the broom from me and finished the work I'd started. I stood and watched as she methodically swept every inch of the bar floor. When she'd finished, she turned to me and asked,

"Is that all right? I will get better with practice, and quicker."

I heard the nervousness in her voice, but glancing around, I saw that every corner was clean and she'd demolished the lifelong homes of several spiders. I laughed and said,

"Admonition, I've lived here since I was fourteen years old and I swear I've never seen this floor so clean. If you do the rest of the bar as well as you've done that floor, my locals will think they've come to the wrong pub."

She giggled and said,

"So does that mean you still want me to come back tomorrow?"

I looked straight at her. I wanted her to be certain I was serious and why.

"Adie, I've already offered you work and I did it so you wouldn't be so beholden to Tom. So yes, I definitely want you to come back tomorrow. You'll be safe here."

She smiled.

"When she asked me why I wanted to work for you, that's what I told Mrs Rider; I knew I'd be safe with you. I think that's why she agreed."

"So you don't feel safe at the Rider's?" I asked.

Her face flushed and turning away, she said,

"I never said that. The Rider's took me and Will in when we were left alone and homeless, and Mrs Rider's always been like a mum to me."

"Until now?"

I spoke without thinking. The truth was I didn't really know anything about Adie's relationship with the Rider's, but what I did know was that there had to be a reason she ran from Tom and an explanation for the coldness towards her from Elizabeth that didn't fit Adie's description of her.

She turned back to me and with eyes lowered, said quietly,

"Until now."

But then she straightened, looked me in the eye and declared,

"Right. No point me standing here talking, why don't you show me where you keep all the things you use for cleaning and then show me anything else you want me to do."

She barely knew me, so it was no surprise she didn't want to talk about her relationships with Tom and Elizabeth, but I was pleased she felt she'd be safer with me.

So that's how we left things. I showed Adie what I wanted her to do: clean the bar, wash up any mugs, jugs and tankers still dirty from the night before and clear up any mess left outside. It was barely two hour's work but over the next six months, despite our age difference, we talked a fair bit and she usually stayed the whole morning and that's the way things might have remained if it wasn't for Sam Baker.

Although he still only required me to take salt loads to his cousin in Foulk Stapleford, now it was three times a week with double the load. I still followed the same streams and river because, despite the risk not changing my route brought, it still seemed the safest and quietest. But I couldn't ask either of the donkeys to carry the whole load, so I split it between them and walked alongside. Now, not only was I losing most of a night's sleep three times a week, but also having to complete the outward journey on foot. In addition, the nights were getting shorter and even though familiarity with the route meant I could travel faster, I knew it wouldn't be long before part of my journey would be in daylight. Of course, that would be on my way home, by which time I wouldn't be carrying anything I shouldn't, and I could handle any awkward questions, but I just didn't want the Excise getting suspicious.

But the worst problem I had was exhaustion and it was becoming increasingly difficult for me to appear normal when Adie made her appearance each morning. So I suppose I shouldn't have been surprised when one morning the inevitable happened. Struggling in from Foulk Stapleford at about six, I was too tired to care that it was already broad daylight, and so after stabling the donkeys, I'd stumbled into the inn and made straight for my bed. With my boots still on, I'd fallen asleep immediately.

The next thing I knew, my shoulder was being gently shaken. Opening my eyes, I was surprised to see Adie.

"I'm sorry Jabez, the front door was wide open when I arrived so I came in. I called for you, but when you didn't answer, I was worried, 'cos I thought you might have had a break-in. I called for you all through the pub and I don't understand why I didn't wake you; it's almost ten o'clock you know."

I tried to get up, but sat back on the bed; the sudden movement had made me light-headed. She told me,

"You look really ill. Lie down again and I'll go and find you some breakfast."

I was too tired to argue and just laid back down. I think I was asleep again before Adie left the room and I only resurfaced when I heard her talking urgently to me.

"It's one o'clock now Jabez, I've got to go. Mum will be wondering what's happened to me."

The shock of hearing the time brought me to full consciousness. Sitting up, I said,

"Of course, you must go. I'll be fine now. But thank you for staying so long."

I struggled to my feet and even though I still felt drowsy, I did feel much better.

Adie looked at me critically,

"Alright, but you've been looking very tired for a few weeks now, and I've been thinking, perhaps tomorrow we should talk about how I might be able to help you a bit more."

I had time before having to give a reason why that couldn't be, so I just agreed we should talk in the morning.

Satisfied, she said,

"Alright then, as long as you're feeling better, I'll be on my way."

With that she left, but as she descended the stairs, I heard her call out,

"I've left you some food on the bar and drawn you some water from the well. I hope that's alright."

I'm sure the sound of my grateful reply, still dampened by sleep, went unheard, but moments later I heard the door slam. Aware that if I laid down, I might fall asleep again and knowing there was much to do before I opened for business, I got up and headed downstairs.

Of course there wasn't much to do at all. Adie hadn't been idle whilst I was asleep and all that was left for me to do was to change the barrel, which had run out late the night before, and replenish the gin which was running low. So before heading for the cellar, I took the jug of water that Adie had left into the back kitchen, filled a bowl and washed my face. Refreshed, I took the jug back into the bar and poured the remaining water into a pint pot, then settled down at the bar and started on the food she'd left.

Whilst I ate, I thought about her offer. Clearly, Sam Baker wasn't going to stop expecting me to deliver his salt for him, and I had to admit the additional income had made all the difference. But I also knew I couldn't go on in the same way, driving me and the donkeys so hard.

So might Adie provide the solution, after all? I certainly felt a whole lot better after a few extra hours sleep and it was also clear that she would have to know why I was so tired in the morning, even if I didn't take up her offer. I believed I could trust her and that telling her about my night time excursions wouldn't be a problem. But I also knew it wouldn't be right to let her get involved.

Anyway, I didn't have time to dwell on the subject. I had a barrel to get ready for opening time. One thing I couldn't get off my mind though, I was sure Adie had said she'd found the door to the pub wide open and I was sure I'd shut it when I came in; I can't have been that tired, could I?

Next morning, I was sat in the bar when she walked in.

"Morning Jabez, you're looking a lot better today. The extra sleep must have done you good."

Smiling, she found the broom and started to sweep the bar. Admiring her industry, I recalled Tom's lies and in a moment made a decision.

"Adie, put that broom down and come and sit here with me, will you?" I pulled a chair out for her. "I need to talk to you."

She stopped sweeping and turned and looked at me.

"Is it about yesterday?"

She looked anxious, so I tried to look encouraging as I said,

"Yes, in part."

I'd clearly failed because she said,

"I knew it was. I should have just shut the door and left, shouldn't I? I'm sorry Jabez. Honestly, I didn't tell anyone anything about what happened. Mr Rider was at work when I got back home and I just told Mum you asked me to do a bit extra."

She surprised me. I'd worked out what I wanted to say to her but now I couldn't do that without first reassuring her about the previous day's events.

"Adie, you couldn't be more wrong. If you had just shut the door and gone away then who knows when I would have woken and in what state the bar would have been come opening time. No, come and sit down. I just want to explain why I've been so tired recently and after I've told you then you can decide whether you're still willing to work a little bit more for me. In fact, after I tell you, I'll understand if you say you don't want to work for me at all."

She looked at me curiously, but then without another word put down the broom and came and sat in the chair I'd offered. Before I could begin, she said,

"You don't have to tell me anything, you know. Your business is your own."

I couldn't tell what she was thinking, so I pressed on.

"It's only fair that I explain to you exactly what I do. If you're to help me any more than you already do, you're bound to see things and then I'm going to have to ask you to keep secrets."

She smiled and said,

"Jabez, I think you're a good man and you've shown me nothing but kindness, so if there's any way I can help you, then I want to. Mind you, I'm sure that whatever you're doing can't be that bad."

I still needed her to understand what she'd be getting involved with.

"Well, I think you should wait to hear what I've got to say before making up your mind. You see, what I do isn't strictly legal, in fact, to be truthful, it isn't legal at all."

I looked to see her reaction. She was tense but her face betrayed nothing.

"There's no other way to say it. I smuggle salt."

She relaxed and her face broke into a smile again.

"Is that all? I think everybody who works on the pans takes a bit of salt. Tom's always bringing some home for Mum."

"Yes, I know, but I'm not talking about a bit of salt to use at home. I think even the Excise man's not too worried about that. No, what I'm talking about is as much salt as two donkeys can carry, and that three times a week. If I'm caught, it will mean prison, or worse.

And that's not all. Have you ever heard of the Nantwich Gang?"

When I think back that was the one and only time I ever saw her shocked. Her smile vanished and the colour drained from her face.

"What you're doing isn't anything to do with them, is it, Jabez? When I was young, Will used to frighten me with stories about them. He said he'd heard that they sometimes kill people."

As an afterthought, but mainly I think because she'd scared herself, she added,

"But I don't think that last part's true. I think it was just Will trying to frighten me."

I didn't see any point hiding the truth from her.

"Don't doubt it; it's true. I know of two men who 'disappeared' after falling foul of the Nantwich Gang and they say there are others and yes, that's who I'm involved with. But I've got no choice. Their leader, Sam Baker, came to see me and told me that he needed my help. Believe me, if you don't want to 'disappear', when Sam Baker asks for your help, you'd do well not to refuse him.

But Adie, you do have a choice and I definitely don't want to involve you in smuggling. If you're to help me, then it must only be to run the pub."

I went on to tell her how I'd managed in the beginning because, although I was always afraid of being caught, it had been only one, sometimes two deliveries a week, but that now it was usually at least three. I explained how, at first, I only needed to load one donkey and ride the other but, as the months passed, not only had the number of deliveries increased but so had the loads. So now, I told her, I was forced to split the load between the donkeys and walk beside them until after I'd made the delivery.

She looked at me thoughtfully then said,

"And I suppose with nights getting shorter, you're not getting home 'til after dawn."

Which, of course, was right.

"And that means you're more likely to get caught." Admitting this was now my main concern, I could see she was thinking things over. But what she said next took me completely by surprise.

"So would it help you if I came and lived at the Boar?"

My surprise must have shown because she added,

"It seems to me it would make sense. I wouldn't need to be involved in the smuggling, but there's all sorts of other ways I could help make things easier for you."

Her enthusiasm made me wonder if something more had happened with Tom, providing her with her own reasons for wanting to move in with me. But I said nothing and let her continue.

"If I stayed here, before you had to make a delivery, I could slip out to the stable and prepare the donkeys. Then, when you've closed the inn and are ready to go, you could get on your way while I cleared up the bar. That way you'd be back long before dawn. I could finish cleaning the bar in the morning like now, and you'd be able to get a lot more rest."

I could see the advantages, but there were obvious questions.

"Adie, it's one thing working mornings for me, but if you live here, people will ask questions and anyway, what do you think Tom and Elizabeth would say?"

She looked at me and appeared to make a decision.

"Would you like another cup of tea? I'll make us both one and then I'll explain about Mum and Mr Rider."

110

Getting up, she took my empty cup and disappeared into the back kitchen; I had a feeling I was about to have my suspicions confirmed. She returned with the tea and, putting the cups on the table, sat down again. Pushing her cup forward and resting her arms on the table, she said,

"You've been honest with me Jabez, but I haven't told you everything. I've wanted to, but it never seemed the right time. But now, when you've trusted me over the salt and everything and you still need convincing that me moving in here is a good idea, it seems to be the right time."

Taking a sip from her cup, she began.

"You asked me once if my relationship with Mum had changed. Well, I almost told you then, but I wasn't sure I could trust you; I didn't trust anybody. I'd thought I could trust the Rider's but I found out that wasn't true either.

Anyway, do you remember how we met?"

Laughing, I said,

"How can I forget? You ran straight into me."

She smiled. "Yes, but do you know the reason I was running."

"You were running from Tom."

"That's right, but I never told you why, did I?"

I shook my head.

"Mum's never talked about it and I've never told her, but I know she's seen from the corner of her eye how Mr Rider stares at me when he thinks she's not looking. I know she has, because whenever she sees him doing it, she asks him to help her with something or other or sends me on a pointless errand.

For all the time I was growing up, everything was fine. I spent every day with Mum and there was never a cross word between us, but once he'd started with those looks, she changed towards me. I don't think she really blames me. I just think she's panicking. Now everything I do is wrong – in her eyes anyway. She never says anything nice to me anymore, calls me names, crewdlin', stupid, especially when he looks at me that way. There's never a kindness.

I was thirteen when he started with those looks; I knew what they meant and I knew he wasn't going to wait any longer than he had to. He might be a quiet man, patient even, but with Will gone, I reckoned he was just biding his time, waiting for his chance. Then I knew he'd be a lot different."

I wasn't sure she wouldn't one day regret confiding in me, so I interrupted her.

"Adie, you don't have to tell me everything, because even if you think you should now, don't you think one day you might regret it?"

She shook her head and said,

"I know I don't have to tell you, but I want to, and I don't believe you'll ever make me regret it. I think you've guessed some of what has happened, but you've never asked, just gave me a place where I feel safe. Now, if I'm to move into the Boar, I think it's only right that you should know everything."

Having swallowed a little more tea, she continued.

"When I bumped into you, things had just come to a head. In fact I don't know what would have happened to me if you hadn't been there."

"Bumped into me! You almost knocked me off my feet; you definitely winded me."

She giggled. "I know. I remember thinking how you sounded a bit like the bellows on the church organ."

Serious again, she said,

"But I was very scared. You see I was helping Mum with the cooking and we needed more firewood, so she asked me to go out and find some. The gennel seemed deserted as

I headed towards the wood, but suddenly Mr Rider stepped out of a doorway's shadow and grabbed me. Even though he's quite small, working in the salt has made him wiry-strong, so once he'd got hold of me, although I struggled, there was no way I could escape.

Then he really frightened me. He put his face close to my ear and I could feel his hot breath on my neck as he whispered,

'I've seen the way you look at me and I know what you want. It's alright. Lizzie doesn't need to know and I won't tell her. It'll be our little secret.'

I didn't say anything. The truth was I was so scared I *couldn't* say anything.

He carried on, he was still whispering but his voice had softened,

'It'll be alright. I'll take care of her. Make sure she's out. Then we'll be alone together. You'd like that, wouldn't you Adie?'

I think he believed what he was saying because relaxing his grip, he added,

'Everythin'll be just fine and you'll be my special girl, won't you Adie?'

He started to stroke my hair; Jabez, it was horrible, but it broke fear's hold on me. I tore myself away from him, ran out of the gennel onto the main street and without looking ran full bat, straight into you."

Smiling through the tears that had begun to fall, she said,

"I swear I never gave him any encouragement. I've never thought of him that way. If you hadn't been there, I don't know what would have become of me."

Not knowing what else to say, I said,

"As I remember, all I did was to make you cry."

"Honestly, Jabez, I would have cried whoever spoke to me. But you were different. You didn't even know me, but as soon as Mr Rider appeared, you seemed to take my side; you're still doing it and I don't even know why."

She looked at me questioningly and I knew I'd have to tell her how I'd felt about Tom. So I took a deep breath and plunged in.

"It's not easy for me to explain, but I'll try. You see I've had my doubts about Tom for some time and when you've been a landlord for as long as I have, you learn how to read men. As far as Tom is concerned, he had the same look I'd seen in other men's eyes. I've heard men talk, especially when they're drunk, about women and girls and what they'd like to do to them. Now with them, talk is all it is. It's not very nice but by the time they sober up, they forget everything they've said. But sometimes, a very few times, there are others who have a darker look in their eyes and never speak of their thoughts. They keep it inside, dream, plan and listen closely to the other men – they are the dangerous ones."

I picked up my cup, but before raising it to my lips, added,

"I knew Tom was one of those men."

Even though her voice trembled, she looked straight back at me and said,

"But you've never said anything. I've been coming here every day for six months and you've never said a word."

I knew I'd upset her and I wanted to explain.

"How could I?" I said, "You hadn't said anything and I had no other proof. But I did hope that if you came here regularly, Tom would think twice before he tried anything."

She seemed to accept this.

"Well, that's true. He didn't do anything for a while after I began working here, and things seemed to have gone back to how they'd been. He was quiet an' everythin', like he used to be, but over the last month he's started again."

She'd already told me all I needed to know, so I tried to stop her.

"It's alright, Adie. I think you've told me enough now. You've already persuaded me that you moving in here would be the best for both of us. I really don't need to hear any more."

It was as if I hadn't spoken.

"I just wanted things to be like they were.

You might think it unfair, Dad having saved my life and everythin', but I'd felt happier with the Rider's than I ever did with Mum and Dad. They haven't any children of their own and I think Mrs Rider saw us as a chance she never expected to come her way. I don't know how else to put it. It's just that for me, she felt like a real mum. So when everything seemed to go back to normal, I told myself it had all been a misunderstanding between me and Mr Rider.

But then one morning when the two of us were alone in the house, he started again. Mum was round with old Betsy Grimes. She's the kind old lady who once told a frightened little girl that Mrs Rider didn't mind if I called her mum. But Betsy was sick, not long for this world Mum said, and so she was spending several hours each day caring for her.

Whilst she was spending so much time with Betsy, Mum asked me if I could do some of the jobs that we usually did together. I loved that she trusted me and every day I did all the jobs she asked and every day I glowed with pride when she told Mr Rider that I had done this or that job better than she could do it herself. I'm sure that wasn't true, but at least I never actually saw her go back over something I had already done.

One day Mum asked me if I thought I could manage to do the washing on my own. This was a job we usually did together every week and me and Mum agreed it was the hardest job we had. The copper had to be very hot and the dolly stick was really hard to move with the weight of the wet washing.

Mr Rider was dozing in a chair and I paid him no mind. But when I stopped turning the dolly for a moment so I could catch my breath and rest my tired arms, I glanced across at him. He wasn't asleep anymore. He was looking straight at me and he had a look on his face I'd never seen before, sort of smiling, but not at anything funny; I didn't like it.

He looked me straight in the eye, making sure he had my attention, and then his eyes tracked slowly downwards until suddenly, I realised where he was looking. I put my arms across my chest and turned away; I'm sure my face reddened. You see the steam from the copper had made my shift stick to me and I'm sure he was able to see all the contours underneath.

Then he laughed out loud and said,

'You're a growing girl, ain't you Adie? I can see I'm going to have to keep a close eye on you – a very close eye.'

Then he laughed again. His eyes never left my shift.

Not knowing what else to do and even though my arms were still tired, I quickly took the washing out of the copper, put it in the basket and went out to hang it on the line. I was still hanging it out when Mum returned. Her eyes were red from where she'd been crying. She told me that Betsy had passed away and though it's a terrible thing for me to say, I was glad she had because it filled Mum's thoughts and she didn't notice how upset I was. I've got no other choice, I know I'm going to have to leave that house before he gets another chance."

It was clear she was right. She'd have to leave the Rider's home, but I was still worried that moving in with me would only cause her more problems.

"But what are you going to tell them? After all, a young girl going to live alone in a pub with a man in his forties, they're sure to object."

Standing, she said,

"It doesn't matter what they say. I'm going to have to leave. If I don't go now, then I'm always going to be on my guard and if I keep finding ways to refuse Mr Rider, I know he'll turn Mum against me and they'll throw me out anyway. If I leave, Mum might be a bit upset at first, but I won't be far away and even if she doesn't want to admit it to herself, she'll know the real reason I'm leaving."

With that, she turned and went back to sweeping and I found I had learnt two things; first, it was clear, as far as she was concerned that the matter was closed, and second, that despite her youth, Adie was a great deal more single-minded than I had imagined. Nevertheless I still worried about the reaction she'd get at the Rider's.

"I'll go with you," I said. "Make sure there's no misunderstanding."

She shook her head.

"No, it'll be alright. I'll tell Mum as soon as I get home. I'll make her see it makes sense and then we can tell Mr Rider together when he gets back from the pans."

I wasn't sure she was as confident as she sounded. I knew I wasn't. But I could tell she was determined and there was no point in arguing any further, so I finished my tea and went out to the stable where I knew the donkeys would be expecting to be fed. Adie finished her work and headed home and I was left hoping she hadn't been too optimistic about her reception.

In the early part of the evening there were only a few in, and after Adie left, the rest of my day had been unmemorable. Now just a handful of my regulars sat quietly together around the unlit fire. So the surprise when the door burst open and, propelled by Tom Rider, Adie flew across the bar, becoming entangled with the first table and chairs that crossed her path, was greatly amplified. Obviously unhurt, (clearly, the loud crack had been wood, not bone) she regained her feet but her temper remained off balance. She turned to face Tom and I could see there was no fear in her face and when she spoke I heard only blind fury.

"You're an evil man, Tom Rider, and one day everyone's going to know the truth about you; starting, God help her, with Mum."

Tom sounded equally angry.

"Mum, Mum. My wife is no mother of yours; you've made sure of that."

He turned to the men sat round the fire who were all transfixed by the sudden and unexpected developments, circumstance having made them an uncomfortably captive audience.

"We gave her a home, me and Lizzie. Lizzie even let her call her 'mum' just because she felt sorry for her. Now the ungrateful little slut says she's leaving us to come and live here with Jabez.

What do you think of that, eh? She's fifteen and she's going to live in a pub alone with a middle-aged man. I tell you, she's broken my Lizzie's heart."

His audience either looked at each other, drank their ale, or just stared at the floor, anything to avoid his eye. Luckily, Adie, who was far from finished, relieved their awkwardness. Her face pale with anger, she said,

"Don't you dare say anything about Jabez. He's a kind man and he knows all about you."

The others were still all looking anywhere but at Tom, so I think I was the only one other than Adie who saw Tom react, but she made sure they were all fully informed.

"Yes, that's right, well might you flinch. I've told him everything about you and I know I can trust him – unlike you."

Tom turned to me and with a look of disdain said,

"Oh, so that's it. You've fallen for her lies, have you Jabez? I thought you'd know better."

I didn't expect to have to use it, but my hand gripped my billyclub below the bar. I spoke calmly, or as calmly as I could.

"We don't want any trouble, do we Tom? You're right I am middle-aged and even though I don't like to admit it, as I get older I find running this place on my own gets harder and harder. Adie's offered to help me and as there's plenty of room, she can do that a lot better if she lives here. That's all there is to it."

I looked steadily at Tom, hoping he understood I was giving him the chance to back down. Unfortunately he wasn't yet ready to take up my offer, because turning again to his audience, he said.

"And that's what we're supposed to believe, is it? She's just going to help poor old Jabez run his pub."

The anger inside me was rising but I knew, for Adie's sake, I needed to keep it dampened. So ignoring his taunts, I tried again.

"I don't suppose Adie's got much that she can call her own, has she Tom? But I expect she's got a few bits we can arrange to collect?"

Tom spat back.

"She's got nothing of her own. She's lucky we've let her keep the clothes on her back."

I raised the billyclub and rested it deliberately on the bar; I thought this ends now or the club ends it for me. I said,

"Are you sure about that, Tom? Perhaps you should go home and discuss it with Elizabeth and if you find anything, clothes, nightwear, that sort of thing, then you could bring them back here tonight. Of course, if you want, I could go and see Elizabeth tomorrow when you're at work and apart from picking up Adie's belongings, we might talk about everything she's told me about you. After all, I think it would be a shame to miss the chance to hear what Elizabeth has to say about Adie's 'lies' as you call them, don't you?"

I held the billyclub more firmly; I expected him to back down, but if Tom was going to react, it would be now.

Unfortunately he definitely wasn't ready to retreat. Instead, he stepped towards Adie, who instinctively moved back. Ignoring her, he took hold of the chair she'd broken in her fall and wrenched from it an already mostly detached leg.

Turning, he let forth an almighty cry and simultaneously swept the chair leg along the full length of the bar, completely clearing it of all bottles, mugs and glasses. He then raised the chair leg high above his head and with a second emphasising cry, brought it down on the now cleared surface.

I moved back smartly when Tom swept the bar, but kept hold of the billyclub. When with surprising agility, he leapt on top of the bar, I swung the club and made contact with his legs just below his knees. They gave way, and with a cry of pain he landed at my feet. Without a second thought, I swung the club again and caught him a blow on the side of his head. He lay senseless.

For some minutes, I had seen nothing other than Tom but now, when he no longer posed any kind of threat, I surveyed the bar. With her back against the wall, Adie was holding the broom she used daily and presumably had intended to use to defend herself. To a man, my customers sat looking at me with various expressions of astonishment and I realised, as it was many years since I'd last used the club, it was a sight most of them had never seen.

But now I had a senseless man at my feet I needed to move, something I couldn't do on my own. So first I spoke quietly to Adie.

"Adie put the broom down will you? And go out the back and bring me a jug of water. We need to bring Tom round."

Hesitating for only a moment to gather her senses, she put down the broom and hurried into the back room. Whilst she was gone, I asked a couple of the men sat at the table to go and saddle one of the donkeys and bring it around the front.

Looking down I could see Tom was stirring, but looking up again I was too late to stop Adie leaning over the bar and pouring a full jug of water directly over Tom's face. Cursing and spluttering, he struggled to get up, so I put my foot on his chest and said,

"Now we don't want any more trouble, do we Tom? Let's just take things slowly, shall we?"

He looked at me defiantly, but his body hadn't yet regained the strength to match his eyes, so he gave up the struggle.

Turning to Adie, I said,

"Now he's awake, can you go and get a cloth so he can dry himself?"

She lingered for a moment, smiling down at Tom and I felt him move beneath my foot. I looked sharply at her but she was already making her slow way to the kitchen.

John, who'd gone with his father to fetch the donkey, came back into the bar to tell me his dad was out the front with the tethered animal. John was a big lad, so with his help I had no problem raising a still groggy Tom and guiding him out to the donkey where, with the additional help of John's father, we assisted him onto its back. Finally, before they left, I instructed them to make sure Tom got inside safely and not to just leave him at the door.

With that, they set off and it was only as they were about to turn onto the main road, I remembered to call after them that they should ask Elizabeth for anything she could let Adie have; I hoped she'd hold a different opinion from Tom.

When I went back into the bar, Adie had cleared up most of the mess and wiped up the water that hadn't remained on Tom. Now smiling as though nothing had happened, she was serving my remaining customers with a round of drinks. They, for their part, were all talking to her at the same time and whilst it was difficult to identify what any individual was saying, it was clear they were all welcoming her to the pub.

I joined her behind the bar and helped her finish the round. Not quite sure of how they felt about my use of the billyclub, I told them,

"By the way lads, this round's on the house; make up for the inconvenience of this evening's little, er, incident."

I think in the end there had been more entertainment than inconvenience, but I was pleased they had been so welcoming to Adie. Although there were only six of them, I knew their opinion of Adie was important because the next day everyone in the pans would know all about my new barmaid. In the meantime, as Adie was obviously fine holding the bar, I wandered back outside and waited the return of John and his father. As it turned out only John returned leading the donkey, so it was with some anxiety I asked him,

"Your dad's not come back with you then John? Tom didn't give you any problems, did he?"

"No, everything went fine. Dad's gone home 'cos he's got to be up early."

John's father, Harry, was the local blacksmith, had been for years but, since enclosure had swept through the county, the now much larger farms employed their own smiths and work for Harry had dropped significantly. So recently, he'd found some extra early morning work for him and John in town, clearing horse muck and other rubbish from shop fronts before they opened. There wasn't enough work for two, so they took it in turns and the next day must have been Harry's.

John told me what had happened when they got Tom home.

"I think Tom's head still hurt because he went like a lamb and after we saw him inside, he threw himself on their bed and went straight to sleep."

"How was Elizabeth?" I asked.

"Well, she wasn't pleased when she heard what you'd done to Tom, but I don't think she was surprised. She said that the last thing she told Tom was not to hurt the girl or get into a fight with you, so at least she was thankful when Dad told her both of you weren't hurt. Anyway, she said I should give Adie this."

He raised a small bag he was carrying. Pleased that Elizabeth clearly didn't feel quite the same about Adie's decision as Tom, I said,

"Let me take the jenny and while I put her in the stable, you go inside and give that bag to Adie. Tell her I said to give you a pitcher; you deserve it."

117

He handed me the rein and then, bag in hand, headed into the pub. I stabled the jenny and joined him and the others. The rest of the evening went by uneventfully and after I shut the pub, Adie discovered that in the bag, along with her nightdress and a few items of clothing, Elizabeth had sent a hurriedly written note wishing her well and hoping they might see each other soon.

Adie was accepted quickly despite her age, and she took to her new role as if she'd been doing it for years. She soon came to know every customer and not only did she know their names, she also learnt what each one drank and what hours they worked, so their drink was always ready and waiting for them when they appeared. My customers who were the first to meet Adie, pump–primed the rest and as I had hoped, curiosity brought men in to see the new barmaid. But I hadn't anticipated that because of Adie and her personal touch, my regulars became more regular, occasional customers became regulars and all of them started bringing in their wives now and again, just to prove the girl they'd been talking about was all they said she was but nothing more. Whilst the women could see Adie was young and attractive, they also saw she treated all of my customers, including the women, with equal friendliness and attention. As far as me and Adie were concerned, I think you could say that our shared secrets meant that any slight awkwardness between us soon disappeared.

As I've already mentioned, Tom Rider was an infrequent visitor to the pub, so his absence was unsurprising. More surprisingly, I heard from others from the pans that he hadn't been seen for a couple of days after the incident. Because I was out of practice, I worried I may have hit him a little harder than needed, so I was pleased when I heard he had returned to work. But when he returned, they said he'd been quieter than ever and there had been no mention of that night and no explanation of the lump, which they told me was clearly visible, on his temple.

Adie's only regret was that whilst she didn't care whether or not she ever saw Tom Rider again, she had never seen Elizabeth since being dragged to the Boar by him. But she never showed her sadness to my customers, instead reserving it for when we were closed. I decided that I owed it to both of them to find a way of bringing them together.

Meanwhile, behind the bar, Adie sparkled. But while she shone, I still had a darker role to play and it was no surprise to me when Sam Baker visited me soon after Adie moved in, concerned that his operation should remain watertight. I was in the stable when he first arrived, so Adie was alone in the pub, and when I returned, Sam was standing talking quietly to her. She told me afterwards that although she hadn't known who he was when he came in, there was something about Sam that made her pay him special attention.

All my other customers had either moved to the ends of the bar or were seated at a table. I thought I was standing outside his vision, but I had barely taken a step inside the bar when he spoke to me.

"Good evening, Jabez. I've just been getting acquainted with your new barmaid. Admonition isn't it?"

He looked at Adie,

"People usually call me Adie."

Disregarding her, Sam said,

"Well, Admonition tells me she's living here now."

When she moved in, I knew this day would come. I also knew it was important I handled the situation well if I wanted to avoid any serious consequences. Turning to Adie and trying to sound as relaxed as I could, I said,

"This is Sam Baker, Adie. I've told you all about him."

Later, she told me that I'd only confirmed what she'd begun to suspect, but what I was really trying to do was show Sam that I trusted her and that he could as well. For the moment, he appeared to be satisfied.

"Alright then Jabez. We'll talk about this later." Then turning to Adie, he said, "Right then Admonition. How about another mug of ale?"

He pushed his empty mug towards her.

"As I said, most people call me Adie."

"Alright then. Another pint of ale please, Adie. Most people do still call it ale, don't they?"

She parried his sharp-edged smile with one of her own and it was becoming clear to me this girl feared little. Like me, Sam, who I'm sure was used to people being afraid of him, must have been surprised by her reaction to him because he took his ale and went and sat at a table on his own. For the rest of the evening, every time I looked in his direction he was looking at Adie, but I couldn't fathom out what he was thinking.

Probably because of Sam's presence, the pub cleared quite early, until he was the only one who remained. When the place was otherwise empty, Sam said,

"You can lock up now Jabez. Then we can discuss what's to be done about young Admonition here."

Going out the front, I locked and bolted the door. I'd been thinking about this inevitable conversation all evening, but only as I walked back into the bar did I decide what I should say. All evening I'd been watching Sam looking at Adie and I remembered how she had met his smile, so before he could say anything more, I answered him.

"There's nothing to be done about Adie. I told her about the work I do for you before she moved in. She had to leave where she was living and she's here because I make all the trips you require and still run a pub on my own."

He then asked me,

"Why did she have to leave her old place? She was living with the Rider's, wasn't she?"

Clearly, he knew a little more than he'd let on, so I told him,

"That's right. The Rider's took her and her brother in when their house collapsed, killing the rest of their family. The reason she had to leave she told me in confidence and until she tells me otherwise, it will stay that way. Mind you, as I hold her secret, I think you'll understand that she won't break my confidence; I'll keep her secret. She keeps mine."

"And I'll keep Jabez' confidence because he's always been kind to me. I don't know why, but he's never asked me for anything in return and I mean anything." Her tone made sure Sam knew exactly what she meant, "So I'll help him in any way I can."

Sam's face broke into a smile and for the first time it was genuine. Then with another first for me, he actually chuckled and said,

"Alright Adie, I believe you. In fact I think I believe you more than him." He glanced in my direction. "You see I've been watching you all evening and seen how you get on with all of Jabez' customers. I've been asking myself why, even though you're young, all of 'em, and let me tell you there are some awkward cusses amongst 'em, why all of 'em seem to like you. I think I've worked it out; you've got an open and honest face. You treat them all the same and you always say what you believe to be the truth, unlike Jabez here who always tells them what they want to hear."

Though I made to defend myself, Sam wouldn't let me.

"Don't deny it Jabez. You know it's true. Anyway, apart from working in the bar, what else does he have you doing?"

Adie didn't hesitate.

"Well, he won't let me have anything to do with smuggling, if that's what you want to know, but there are lots of other things I can do. You've seen me work in the bar, but when he comes back exhausted after he's spent the night working for you," she paused to make sure Sam understood the emphasis before adding, "I let him sleep while I take care of the donkeys and after I've seen to them I see to the bar."

Sam turned to me and said,

"You didn't tell me about this new arrangement and I'm not happy about that. I don't expect any changes in any of my arrangements unless I agree them first."

Apparently unafraid, Adie answered him for me.

"Yes, but if he had told you what he was going to do you never would've agreed, would you?"

Sam looked at her. He was clearly annoyed, but meeting his eye, she carried on.

"You need to understand that Jabez was just about done for, so no matter what you did to him, he would have had to stop making all these trips and then none of your salt would have been delivered, would it?"

I was astonished at her defiance, but she still hadn't finished.

"And another thing, he was getting too tired to look after the donkeys properly, so they were suffering and soon would have broken down as well. But now I make sure they're cared for, Jabez gets enough rest and because of that your salt gets delivered, so everyone should be happy."

I held my breath. I was sure no one had ever spoken to Sam like that, but she just smiled defiantly. Sam turned to me. His smile was gone and in an unnaturally quiet voice, he said,

"I was going to say that I don't expect any changes in any of my arrangements unless I agree to them first, but as this seems to be secure and to have some advantages, I'll say no more about it. But let's be sure, shall we Jabez? No one talks to me like that girl's just done. She's young and she doesn't know me very well, so I'll let it pass this time. I admit she is engaging, but if she speaks to me like that again, she'll be very sorry; you both will. Is that clear?"

He looked at both of us. Adie still looked defiant, but to my great relief, she just nodded and I said,

"Yes Sam. She'll be fine. Everything will be fine; another load tomorrow, is it?"

I didn't like how I sounded, but this was a new experience for me; I had another to protect. Sam, who was heading for the back door and appeared to have lost interest already, just said,

"I'm not sure, but you'll find out in the normal way."

As he left, I was very glad to be able to shut the door behind him. I breathed a sigh of relief, but before I could speak Adie, who had followed me, said,

"Look, I know you think I said too much, but I don't think he knew how far he'd pushed you. That's the trouble with men like him. People are so afraid of 'em that they never get to hear the truth, so they make mistakes."

She still echoed with defiance, which worried me, so I had to be sure she understood that he meant what he said.

"Yes, but Adie I'm not sure you understand exactly how dangerous that man is. Promise me you'll never cross him again."

Smiling, she said,

"Oh, I understand very well and you needn't worry. I won't cause you any trouble with Sam Baker."

I could see that she meant what she said, so I relaxed.

"Alright then," I said, "but look, it's getting very late, so let's call it a night. We can clear up the bar in the morning."

There was no argument from Adie and after she'd helped me snuff those candles which were still burning, we made our weary way to bed. I had little trouble falling asleep, but before I did, still thinking about how Adie had spoken to Sam, I smiled and said to myself,

"Well Jabez, I think you underestimated that girl and whatever comes of it, she definitely gave Sam plenty of food for thought."

As I expected, another delivery arrived the next night, but now Adie insisted she should assist me. For some time I had ensured I kept a good supply of straw, and with her help I was able to hide the salt in a way that only a thorough search would expose. So in the evening, while I attended bar, she said she was retiring early and went to load the donkeys.

Although I objected, reminding her she shouldn't get involved, I must admit I was glad not to feel so alone, convincing myself that her involvement could never be proved. That night, and those that followed over the next few months, went as smoothly as that first one. Also, because the donkeys were already loaded, I was able to leave promptly and return earlier. It was not the smuggling, at least not at first, that disrupted our arrangements.

Congratulating myself on another straightforward trip, completed in good time despite earlier rain making parts of the route slippery underfoot, it was only when I returned that I realised something wasn't right. Clearly distressed, Adie was standing in the doorway to the Boar talking to someone inside the pub. Although, I knew they were tired, I kicked the donkeys into a fast trot, the nearest thing they had to a gallop, and called out to Adie. But as I got closer, I realised she was shouting at the person in the pub and either didn't hear me or was too occupied.

I reached the door and dismounted as Adie stepped back from the doorway and Tom Rider appeared. Wielding what I correctly assumed was my billyclub and clearly blind drunk, he swung at Adie. She dodged out of the way quite easily and his momentum almost made him fall, but regaining his balance and focus with equal difficulty, his vision fell on me.

"So Jabez, where have you been on this fine morning?"

I was concentrating too closely on the billyclub he was swinging to point out the sky was overcast and it had just started raining again. Instead I said,

"I've been exercising these beasts, Tom. It's the only time I can do it."

He was struggling to hold focus and clearly wasn't listening to what I was saying and moving in my direction, he started swinging the billyclub with more purpose. Seeing how drunk he was, I stood my ground knowing I could easily evade the bat when he attacked me, which he surely would. As he approached, he started cursing me; his language was slurred, but I could get the gist and it seemed Elizabeth had triggered his visit. He took a swig from a bottle he held and said,

"Liz says it's my fault. She says if it wasn't for me, Adie would still be with us an' I can't make her see it's 'cos of you. I don't know what it is but tha' girl's..." He waved the club in a wide arc, but I assumed it was supposed to have pointed at Adie.

"She's left a perfectly good home to come and live in sin with you. Why won't Lizzie unnerstand that?"

All this time, like a rabid dog, Tom had been meandering slowly towards me. But now he broke into a run to cover the short distance between us. Instinctively, I stepped backward, caught my heel on a tree root and fell into the mud. Looking up, I saw Tom above me. His eyes had cleared and for a moment he was sober. As there was nothing else I could do, I shut my eyes, raised my arm to protect my face and waited for the impact of the billyclub already poised to strike.

But the blow never came. Instead, a familiar voice said,

"I don't think you want to do that, do you Tom?"

Opening my eyes, I was in time to see Sam Baker wrench the billyclub from Tom's grasp. But Tom held on just too long and losing his balance, in a moment went from standing over me to sprawling in the mud beside me. Bemused, I struggled to my feet and looked to Adie, who was still standing by the door.

"He hasn't hurt you, has he Adie?" I called.

"No, I'm fine," she said, although she couldn't prevent her voice from betraying a slight quiver, "but I can't say the same for the bar."

That Adie was unhurt was important and anything broken in the pub was replaceable. Relieved, I think my mind cleared for the first time since I'd returned, so turning to Sam who still stood over Tom, I said,

"I think you can let him up now. It doesn't look like he's going to cause any more trouble."

Sam looked down. It was almost as if he'd forgotten Tom was there, and slowly stepped back. I was surprised because Tom failed to move, but moments later, all became clear when he began snoring loudly. Sam laughed and said,

"You know Jabez, I think you might be right."

Tom was no longer my main concern. I wanted to know why Sam was outside my pub so early in the morning.

"I'm grateful you were here Sam, but what I don't understand is why you were here so early."

"Oh, that's easy. I had reports that this one," he toe-poked Tom, raising a snort which only interrupted the rhythm of his snores momentarily, "had been seen hanging around a few times, so I decided to take a look for myself. When I got here, I could hear a lot of noise coming from inside the pub, but I wasn't sure what was going on; it might have been the Excise Supervisor and his men. It was only when Admonition appeared and I could hear a drunk voice that I knew something else was happening.

Now, I think we should throw him onto one of your donkeys and then, if she's in agreement, me and Admonition should take him home. She can tell his wife what's been going on and I can tell her what will happen to him if he causes any more trouble."

With that, he got hold of Tom's ankles and started dragging him towards the donkeys. I hurried after him, took hold of Tom's shoulders and between us we carried him to the Jenny and lay him across her. Sam called Adie,

"Let's go then girl. I want to get this man home before he wakes up."

Adie didn't move. She was clearly reluctant to go, so I said,

"Come on, Adie." I urged, "You've been hoping to see Elizabeth since you moved here. Now's your chance."

She looked at me and said,

"That's true, I do, but not like this."

Leaving Sam securing Tom to the donkey, I walked across to Adie. I'd never held her before but now I held her tight and said,

"You know you're going to have to tell her the truth at some time, don't you?"

She said nothing, so I added,

"And you know there's never going to be a good time, don't you?"

Pulling away from me, she said,

"But she may never talk to me again."

She buried her head in my chest and although I knew she was crying, I pulled her gently away from me again and, putting my arm round her shoulder, walked her to Sam's side. Before letting her go, I said,

"Remember, Adie, if you don't explain how things have been with Tom, *he'll* make sure you never speak to Elizabeth again."

Leaving her with Sam, I asked him to make sure she stayed safe. He gave me a slight nod, enough to let me know he would, and began to lead the donkey towards the road which would take them to the village. With Adie following reluctantly, I stood and watched them go and then, after leading the remaining donkey to the orchard, thinking I'd stable and feed them both when Adie returned, I entered the pub to survey the damage.

Things were not as bad as I feared; in fact it was plain to see that damage followed a trail caused by a chase with the billyclub, rather than from a concerted effort to cause destruction. So there were chairs flung aside from a path across the bar leading from the door, odd tables overturned that had smashed some of the pots and jugs left on them over night, and of course the dregs they contained were now soaking into the floor. But tables and chairs outside Tom's path were unscathed and the bar and all its contents were completely untouched; Adie had obviously had the good sense not to get trapped behind there.

But as I went, following the trail of things damaged or smashed by the swinging billyclub, my mind turned to how it must have been for Adie; clearly she had kept her wits about her, but she must have been terrified. The further I went, clearing the mess Tom had created, the more a picture of what had happened formed in my imagination. The clearer, more detailed the picture and more vivid the image of Tom chasing an increasingly desperate Adie became, the greater the anger in me grew. Finally, to nobody in particular, I shouted out loud,

"What makes him think he owns her?"

I decided there was only one way to resolve the situation and, suddenly certain, I waited impatiently for Adie's return.

125

But impatience didn't hasten her return and over two hours later, having cleared up the mess, restocked the bar and stabled the other donkey, I was reduced to pacing the ground outside the front door when Adie finally returned. She was leading the jenny and it cross my mind briefly to ask her why she wasn't riding, but only briefly, because from still some distance, I could see she was very upset. Running quickly to her and after taking the donkey's tether, for the second time that day, I pulled her close. It clearly wasn't the time to talk. The details of her visit could wait. For now, I just took her gently towards the pub, quickly tethered the donkey and led her inside.

Seating her at the nearest table, I brought her a small gin from the bar. She looked at it, then picked it up and after hesitating for a moment, emptied the tankard in one go. The time she took to swallow it, seemed more than the time it took to return, and was now accompanied by a coughing fit. The gin, having made a rapid reappearance from the back of her throat, completed its escape not by heading back to the tankard it came from but by making straight for my face. Adie looked at me and despite the distress her visit had caused her and the obvious gin-created discomfort she was suffering, when there was room, her coughing was interrupted by laughter. Although her laughter was at my expense, I was glad to hear it and after the initial shock of the juniper scented shower had passed, I found myself laughing with her.

When she recovered, she said,

"I'm sorry Jabez, I didn't mean to spit in your face, but I've never tasted gin before – and it's horrible. But you do look funny."

With that, she started laughing again, but this time I resisted joining in and instead went out the back to find a cloth to dry myself. I washed most of the gin from my face and having used the cloth to dry, returned to the bar and sat down again. I thought the time might finally be right, so I asked her,

"Do you think you're ready to tell me what happened this morning?"

She was ready she said, but surprised me when she began because it was Sam not Elizabeth or Tom she talked about first.

"He's not all bad, you know. Sam I mean. I didn't really want to go with him and it's only 'cos of what you said that I did. I was already about twenty yards behind him when I set off and because I was walking really slowly, it must have been about fifty when he turned the corner. I didn't go any faster 'cos I thought he'd lose patience, speed up and go on without me and I thought then I'd be able to come back to the pub. But when I turned the corner, he was waiting for me. At first, he just looked at me thoughtfully. He seemed to be considering what he should do next. But then he made his mind up and with it apparently mine for me as well because when he spoke, his voice was firm and I remember he said,

'I don't know what's been going on between you and Tom and to be honest, I don't really care, but I do know that whatever it is, I don't want it interfering with my business; his wife's name's Elizabeth, isn't it?'

I said that it was and he told me,

'Well, Tom needs to know that he's not welcome at the Boar anymore, and the best way for that to happen is for you to talk to her; explain what it is between you and him.'

I suppose I must have looked unsure 'cos he smiled at me and said,

'Don't worry. I'll make sure she gives him the message.'

And then his smile disappeared as he added,

'If he doesn't believe her, I'll make sure she knows what will happen to him. It'll be up to her to convince him.'

He looked me straight in the eye. I'll never forget it because when he looks at you like that, his gaze pierces right through you, and then he said,

'You have my word. You'll come to no harm while I'm around. In future, I'll make sure someone's watching the Boar every time Jabez is on a run.'

With that, he began leading the donkey towards the village. I was still unsure I was doing the right thing, but I followed him because there was something reassuring, something certain, about the way he talked."

I wanted her to tell me what happened when they saw Elizabeth. It was clear from the way she was on her return; things had not gone as she hoped. But I could also see that she wanted to tell it her way and that pushing her wouldn't help. What I had to say to her could wait a little longer, so I was patient and just let her continue at her own speed.

"I couldn't believe my ears because as we walked, he started to tell me about his life."

That was a surprise to me as well. As far as I knew, Sam was a closed book, so this would be interesting. I let go of her hand and waited for her to carry on. But then she got up and said,

"Give me a minute, I must get some water. That gin and all this talking have given me a dry throat."

I sat back and waited for her. Returning from the kitchen, sipping her water as she came, she sat down again and said,

"Now, where was I?"

I reminded her she was about to tell me what Sam had told her of his life.

"Oh yes, that's right.

Well anyway, he said that like me, he'd lost most of his family when he was very young. In fact he'd been little more than a babe. He was born in Macclesfield and his family had been wiped out by typhus. I don't know if I ever told you, but I had an aunt from Macclesfield who died before I was born, and Will told me she'd died of typhus as well."

She hadn't, so I shook my head.

"Anyway, I didn't tell him about that, I didn't want to interrupt him."

She looked at me curiously because I couldn't help smiling.

"He told me he'd had one surviving sister who was married and lived nearby in Walker Barn. She was visiting the day his mother spotted the first signs of typhus in one of his brothers. She knew the family would be quarantined when the authorities found out, and she also knew that would probably be a death sentence on them all. So she bundled Sam up and gave him to his sister, telling her to keep him hidden and not to return until it was safe to do so. Of course, by the time Macclesfield was clear, there was no one left for his sister to take him back to. But he said things hadn't been so bad for him because his sister had brought him up as her own child. He made me laugh 'cos he said, 'You might say that when she took me from my mother, I had my introduction to smuggling.'

"I tell you Jabez, until just now, that was the only time today that I've laughed. But then, without thinking, I asked him how he got involved with salt smuggling in the first place.

"He began to answer me, but then he stopped and I nearly ran into the back of him. I thought I'd gone too far, but when he turned to me, his face wasn't telling me anything. He wasn't smiling but there again, he didn't look angry either and when he spoke, his voice was even. He said, 'Donkeys don't tell what they overhear, but their riders might.'

"He looked meaningfully at the body slumped on the donkey. Looking the same way, I noticed that Tom's eyelids were fluttering. Listening to Sam's story, I'd completely forgotten Tom was there and now I didn't know whether he was awake or just dreaming. Everyone knows what Sam and his gang do, but if the Excise had a witness who'd actually heard him discussing it, I dread to think what might happen. Anyway, Sam turned and started leading the donkey again as if nothing had happened, but now, instead of the leisurely pace that we had been walking, he went so quickly that the donkey, who'd been enjoying the stroll, brayed her protest as she was now asked to go at a steady trot.

"I didn't care about her complaints, but what did worry me were the moans now coming from her passenger. The noise from the donkey and the rougher ride had woken Tom fully and he was struggling unsuccessfully to sit up and he was complaining!

"I don't think he'd realised yet that he was actually tied to the donkey, but as he struggled, he kept shouting at Sam to let him down and complaining that the donkey was making his head bang."

Adie couldn't resist smiling when she added,

"Sam didn't slow for a moment. Instead, he just told Tom to stop moaning and that it was his hangover, not the donkey that was making his head hurt. But Tom didn't stop moaning until Sam told him we'd be home soon and then if he didn't shut up, we could all discuss his morning's work with his wife.

"I didn't need reminding why we were taking him home, but I'm glad I hadn't the time to think about it. Whether it was the donkey's movement or the reminder that we were about to meet Mum, I don't know, but Tom's colour, which was already pallid, turned grey and leaning over, he was very sick. He started protesting again, but I think he must have been feeling really unwell because, this time when Sam told him to shut up like he really meant it, Tom went quiet and just laid with his head on the donkey's neck. From there until we arrived in the village, where I pointed out the gennel and then our house, all we heard from Tom was an occasional moan."

Mum wasn't in when we arrived, but as the door was unbolted, Sam guided Tom into the house where he made straight for the bed and was soon snoring again. There was nothing for me and Sam to do but wait for Mum's return.

I don't know how long Sam would have waited, but it didn't matter because after only a few minutes, Mum bustled through the door. Sat in Tom's chair, Sam was in the shadows and I stood behind the door, so all Mum saw when she first came in was Tom. She was just beginning a rant when Sam shifting in the chair caught her eye. In alarm she said,

'Who's there?'

Standing, Sam said,

'Hello Mrs Rider. My name's Sam Baker and I've brought your husband home from the Boar.'

She tried to look surprised, but I don't think she was.

'He should have been at the pans, so what was he doing drinking at the Boar at this time of the morning? Comes to that, why did Jabez Payne serve him?'

Sam looked at Tom and said,

'He's been drinking alright, but I think there's someone else who should tell you what he was doing there.'

He beckoned to me to come out from behind the door. It was only two steps, but I tell you Jabez, my feet felt like I was wearing shoes made of lead; they didn't want to move and after what happened next, I believe they definitely had the right opinion."

Finally, I thought, now I'm going to hear what happened. But as I looked at her, I saw her eyes were brimming with tears, so I took her hand and spoke quietly to her.

"You know that whatever happened, I'm here to look after you and Sam's already said he'll protect you so, come on, just tell me what happened."

She looked at me and what I said must have struck home because the tears retreated. Straightening her back, she swallowed hard and began again.

"Well, when Mum first saw me, I thought everything was going to be alright because she called my name and then smothered me in one of her huge hugs. She told me how much she missed me and then, looking at Tom, said she was sorry she hadn't been to see me but I must understand how difficult things were for her."

All this time, she kept holding me close, but she must have felt I was tense because, pulling herself away from me and now holding me instead by the shoulders, she looked straight at me; she knew something was wrong. It seemed we'd been standing like that forever, although it was probably only a few seconds and I don't think either of us dared speak 'cos we were afraid of what might be said. If it had been just the two of us, I think one of us would have broken the silence by talking about something safe, but before that could happen Sam said, "Come on now Adie, remember what we said."

Oh Jabez, it was horrible and Mum made it worse because she looked as though she was pleading for me not to say anything. But Sam was right, so I pulled myself right away from her; I knew this was the moment and so I just started talking.

First I told her how I loved her and I'd always be grateful to her and Tom for taking me and Will in when we had nowhere else to go. Then I said how I really wished things could have stayed the same as they'd always been when I was small but that Tom had made that impossible. I'll never forget how she looked at me and said quietly, 'Why Adie? What has he done?' That was all she said.

Jabez, she sounded scared, but now that I'd started I knew I had to carry on.
I told her how he'd changed over the last year and then I began to tell her the things he'd said or done, or at least tried to. As I was speaking, I could see she was getting more and more upset.

Although I had imagined much, apart from the damage Tom had caused, I really knew nothing of what had actually happened before I returned from Foulk Stapleford. But I could see repeating everything that happened was getting harder and harder to tell, and tears were returning to her eyes. So I suggested we had a break, perhaps had a cup of tea, which smiling weakly she agreed was a good idea. Obviously thinking I expected her to make it, she started to get up but I told her to leave it to me, and by the time I returned, she seemed to have composed herself. I handed her the tea and she clasped the mug close which seemed to bring her comfort, and taking a deep breath she continued to tell her tale.

"Anyway, as I was saying, Mum had been looking more and more upset, but now she started to look angry. I thought after all I'd told her about Tom she was angry with him, so I felt more confident about telling her what happened this morning."

She paused for a moment then said,

"I haven't told you about what happened this morning, have I?"

I tried to hide my impatience by saying it had been more important for her to tell Elizabeth than me.

"I suppose so, but it's a lot easier to tell you than her 'cos I kept on having to remember Sam's warning. So although I explained I was awake when I heard a noise downstairs, I didn't tell her I was listening out for you and I didn't tell her that at first I thought the noise must have been you returning early. I still don't know why she didn't ask me where you were, but I suppose she was still so angry she forgot all about you.

"Anyway, when I heard nothing else, I lay there persuading myself it had probably been my imagination. But then I heard the sound of breaking glass and I knew there was someone there, although I still had no idea who. Getting up, I quickly put on some clothes, opened my bedroom door and peered out. Now I could hear unsteady footsteps coming up the stairs and I knew the only way out was down the same stairs. I thought I was trapped, but then I noticed you'd left your room open, so not knowing what else to do I closed my door, slipped into your room and hid behind the door.

"As he came up the corridor, the man was muttering to himself, but I still didn't recognise who it was. It was only as he looked in your room that, through a crack, I recognised Tom. He was swinging your billyclub and I held my breath, petrified that he'd catch me. But I needn't have worried because he took one look round and without stepping in, slurred, 'Jabez' room.'

"Then he turned and started down the corridor towards my room. As he went, there was no doubt I was his target because I heard him say,

"'Alright then Admonition I know you're in there and we've got a score to settle, you and me.'

"With that, he burst into my room. I'd already come out from behind the door in yours, so as soon as he stumbled out of sight, I shot out and made for the stairs. But just as I started down the stairs, I heard his angry cry. Seeing my room was empty, he must have stepped out again, unfortunately just in time to see me turn the corner. He started after me, but I didn't stop and I was at the bottom of the stairs before he reached the top.

"It was while I was telling Mum and got to this part that things with Mum got really bad. All the time I'd been talking about this morning she'd just stood there; she'd looked angrier and angrier though she still said nothing. But then it was as if she sort of burst because she looked at me and screamed,

"'Liar! You're a liar Admonition; why are you making up these horrible tales? Tom's a good man who, like you said, took you in when you were homeless, so why are you saying these awful things about him?'

"Then she said the worst thing. She was much quieter now. I think it would have been better if she'd kept screaming, but she put her face right up to mine and in a whisper, spat,

"'I see it now; I should have believed Tom when he told me about Hannah seeing another man. Like mother like daughter, I reckon you've been chasing Tom and when he rejected you, that's when you started making up all those lies about him.'

"I didn't have words to answer her. I'd thought she believed me but now she was turning everything around and saying it was all my fault."

Tears were returning to Adie's eyes and before I could speak, she dissolved. Through the tears I made out,

"Then she said I was no daughter of hers and I wasn't welcome in her house anymore."

I didn't really know what to say or do, so I just said what I felt.

"Elizabeth must be a troubled woman Adie."

With her head buried in her arms and lying on the table when I spoke, she didn't answer, but something told me she was listening, so I carried on.

"I believe she knows you're not lying, but she hasn't really got a choice, has she?"

Lifting her head, she looked at me angrily and said,

"Why not? She knows I've never lied to her before, so why should I start now?"

"You haven't Adie – and she knows it, but if she admits that what you said about Tom was true, what does that tell her about the man she married? If she accepts what you've told her, I bet there are things that have happened in the past she's dismissed or buried, that otherwise she'd have to face. I know it's hard on you, but I think I'm right, don't you?"

Her eyes were red from crying and when I looked in them, all I saw was too much age for one so young. When she spoke, though she sounded tired, her voice was steady. All she said was,

"I suppose so."

It struck me then that she hadn't told me anything more about what Sam had said, so I asked her,

"Didn't Sam say anything?"

I was glad I'd asked because she brightened and said,

"Well yes, he did. At first, when he saw we were getting on alright, remember Mum hugged me when we first met, he went outside. He said he was going to check the donkey, but I think he felt a little awkward, especially as he still had to tell Mum that Tom wasn't welcome here anymore.

Anyway, when Mum started shouting, he came back in, but he didn't say or do anything until Mum told me to leave."

As she spoke, I heard in her voice Adie's throat tighten and I thought the tears were back, but she coughed, cleared her throat and carried on.

"He told Mum he hadn't heard everything, but he had heard her call me a liar. He told her, now let's get this right."

Concentrating, she tried to remember exactly what Sam had said.

"That, 'given a choice between Admonition and Tom I know who I'd believe every time and it wouldn't be Tom.' Then he said, 'But we all make our choices, don't we Elizabeth?' I didn't know what he meant at the time but now I think he was saying the same as you.

"Then he told me to go and wait with the donkey while he talked a little more with Elizabeth. I don't know exactly what he said but as he came out the door I heard him say, 'Don't forget to tell him what I told you and make sure he believes you. I think you know what will happen if he doesn't.' It was nice to hear him say he believed me over Tom's lies and it's good to know that you do as well."

She smiled weakly at me then added,

"I just hope that one day Mum knows I was telling the truth."

I told her I had a feeling that one day, though I didn't know when, the truth was going to come out. For now, I reminded her, I still hadn't really learnt what had happened in the Boar that morning.

"There isn't really that much more to tell, although I think things might have been different if you and Sam hadn't got here when you did.

"Once I knew he'd seen me I stopped trying to be quiet and ran down the stairs, but I still didn't know what I would do when I got to the bottom. Because I knew when you left for Foulk Stapleford you had gone out the back, I knew the front door must still be locked, so I went through to the bar. I could hear Tom coming down the stairs; it sounded like he was falling down them. When he stumbled into the bar, it was obvious he was very drunk.

"He started chasing me round the bar shouting crude things and trying to hit me with your billyclub. But he was so drunk, I had no trouble keeping out of range; he did break a lot of things though."

She actually looked apologetic, as if it was her fault, so I reminded her it definitely wasn't and told her that there wasn't really much damage anyway. She looked like she didn't believe me, so I added that at least there was nothing that couldn't be replaced. But now I was getting impatient again and I wanted her to finish her tale; after all, I still had something I wanted to say, so to encourage her I asked her how, after Tom chased her around, she'd managed to escape.

Smiling, she said,

"Well, in the end that turned out to be quite easy. After a while, I think because he was getting frustrated that he wasn't able to catch me, he made a desperate lunge for me, missed and ended up on the floor in a tangle of chair and table legs. At that moment, I was close to the way out of the bar, so when I saw he was struggling to get up, I took my chance and dashed for the front door. Even though the bolts were difficult for me, I'd drawn them and opened the door before Tom escaped his self-made prison."

I asked her what she was saying to him when I arrived.

"Oh nothing really, just something about how I didn't know how he was going to explain the state he was in when he got home."

Realising what she'd said, she added gloomily,

"That didn't work out the way I hoped, did it?"

Not wanting her to dwell too much on her morning with Elizabeth, I finally said what I'd been wanting to say.

"I've been thinking, Adie, and there's something I want to ask you."

She looked at me strangely. I knew it was because my face felt hot and I must have reddened; I hadn't blushed since I was a boy back in the workhouse. The certainty I'd felt all morning that I was doing the right thing drained away and I heard my voice tremble as I said,

"I think it might be best if we married?"

There was a pause and then, too loudly, she said,

"Married? You want me to marry you?"

It was obvious that I'd shocked her, but the effort of asking the question in the first place seemed to have temporarily robbed me of all further thought on the subject and I could add nothing that might persuade her. It didn't matter because she wasn't finished.

"I can't marry you, Jabez. I don't think of you that way and besides you're old enough to be my father."

She stopped for a moment and then, as that weary look I'd seen before returned to her eyes, she said,

"You know I thought you were different, but you're not, are you? You're just like Tom and you only want one thing from me."

It was my turn to be shocked. She was getting up and I thought she meant to leave, so I said desperately,

"Adie, please sit down again. I don't think I've explained myself properly."

Cautiously she sat down and in a voice that sounded tired rather than angry, said,

"I don't know what there is to understand. You want to marry me and if I become your wife, that gives you certain rights."

I couldn't be angry with her, given her albeit limited experience of men, her reaction was understandable. So I said quietly,

"That would be true if it was the reason I think we should be married, but it isn't. You see, I wouldn't ask you to share my bedroom, let alone my bed. All I want to do is to protect you from Tom and anyone else who thinks they can try for you. You're right about one thing though, I am old enough to be your father and to be honest, that's closer to who I'd like to be."

She seemed to think about what I said and then made up her mind. Leaning towards me, she appeared far older than her years and when she spoke, it was with an authority I'd not heard from her before.

"Jabez, I want to believe you and I'm sure you mean what you say. That's how you feel today, but tomorrow, the day after, who knows?"

It dawned on me then why she was still saying she wouldn't marry me.

"You think that whatever I say or do now, in the end I'll turn out to be just like Tom."

Eyes downcast, she wouldn't look at me, but said quietly,

"When I was little, Tom was kind to me and I thought he'd always be like that, but look how things turned out."

Frustrated, I told her,

"But that's exactly why I want you to marry me. If you do, then Tom will have to leave you alone. You'll no longer be the orphan he provided with shelter and who, in his twisted mind, he thinks he owns. Instead, you'll be my wife who he would have to consider as my possession."

As soon as I spoke, I knew what I said was wrong because Adie glowered and said,

"I'll never be any man's possession Jabez. You're right about one thing though, Tom does think he owns me and he already believes you've stolen me. So as far as he's concerned, you marrying me will only confirm the theft."

I must have looked dejected because she added,

"Besides, I believe you mean well but you don't really think he'd do anything now he knows Sam Baker is taking an interest, do you?"

An hour later, I had to open the pub and all evening there was awkwardness between Adie and me, so I was glad when the last mug was drained, the final customer left and finally I could lock up.

Adie was clearing the tables when I returned to the bar. Like me, she'd obviously been thinking about my proposal because we both spoke at the same time. Both stopping almost before we started, it was clear we needed to sort things out between us, so I suggested that I made us some tea.

When I returned, Adie had drawn the blinds and was already sitting at a table she'd cleared. Putting the tea down, I pulled out a chair, but even before I could sit down, she began to talk.

"You're a good man Jabez, and I know you mean me no harm, so I'm sorry I said those things about you. I want you to know I'll work for you and I'll live here with you, but I won't marry you; I don't know if I'll ever want to marry anyone."

I had thought she might leave, though Heaven knows where I thought she would go. All the same, I was relieved that she appeared to be staying, so I asked her to forget my proposal of marriage and if she would, just concentrate on helping me run the Boar.

She responded by telling me some of her ideas. She'd obviously thought a lot about how she might help me, not only to run the pub but also carry out my work for Sam. She seemed to have completely forgotten, or chose to ignore, that I didn't want her entangled in that business. Yet despite her renewed enthusiasm, when eventually we went to bed and I heard for the first time the sound of her locking her bedroom door, I realised she wasn't yet certain she could trust me. But as I lay on my bed, tired but unable to sleep, it struck me, she'd locked her door, but all evening since we'd closed, she'd talked about little else than the ways she might help me; she even said she had an idea of how the smuggling might be made a little safer, though she hadn't explained. So I smiled and told myself things might not be quite as bad as they had first appeared to be – I just needed to give her a little time. With that, I turned on my side and allowed sleep to overcome me.

The next morning, leaving Adie cleaning the pub, I went into town, but when I returned around lunchtime, she was nowhere to be seen. All morning I'd told myself there could be no danger in leaving her on her own, that Tom would still be licking his wounds and there was no possibility of him returning to the Boar so soon – especially after Elizabeth passed on Sam's warning. But now, as I moved from room to room and Adie was nowhere to be found, all my confidence began to drain away. Having looked in the kitchen and upstairs, I had just returned from checking the orchard and the stable when the cold thought struck me – I hadn't checked the well. Close to panic, I was just turning to go outside again, when from behind the bar Adie appeared. She'd been in the one other place I hadn't checked; covered in dirt and cobwebs, she'd clearly been in the cellar.

Mostly from relief, I couldn't help laughing at how she looked. But blowing away a cobweb that was creeping towards her mouth, she clearly wasn't amused.

"I don't know why you're laughing 'cos it's a death-trap down there. The floor's bumpy and even with a candle, there's things hiding in the dark just waiting to trip you up."

Brushing down her smock unnecessarily she added,

"And it's really dirty."

I tried not to smile, but the glare she gave me let me know I'd failed, so I said quickly,

"I've been looking for you everywhere and I was beginning to worry. What made you go in the cellar? You've never been down there before, have you?"

"I was looking for something. I've had an idea I think will help you move the salt more safely. If I'm right, you should even be able to move it during the day."

"But you didn't find what you were looking for?"

I was interested in what she might be thinking, although I couldn't see that there was any way I could move salt during the day without being caught.

"Oh yes, I found what I was looking for. It's just too big for me to lift out of the cellar on my own. I need one of your empty barrels; there's loads of them down there."

I tried to hide my disappointment. Barrels had been used to smuggle many things and I knew they would never fool the Excise men. I tried to explain this to Adie but she stopped me.

"What if when they open the tap, all that came out was beer?"

Seeing that I didn't understand, she said,

"If you get me a barrel from the cellar, I'll show you."

She seemed so certain, I did as she asked.

"Right. This is what I think we should do." She rested one hand on the barrel. "First, we need to take the bands off and take the barrel apart and if it's still wet, leave it to dry. Next, and I know this might be difficult, we'll need a thin sheet of wood that's just big enough to divide the barrel in two and it needs to be shaped to fit the sides. Then, when the barrel's rebuilt, it's going to need a larger second bung hole made to be hidden by the grain of the wood. All that will be left to do then is to seal the piece of wood across the middle of the barrel and fill one half with beer and the other with salt. Then, if you're stopped by the Excise men and they want to see what's in the barrel, when they pull out the bung all that'll pour out is beer."

It was an interesting idea, but as I explained to her, there was still a problem.

"I can see how it might work, but it would take a skilled man to re-build the barrel, especially with your, er... modifications. I certainly couldn't do it."

That didn't trouble her; she'd obviously thought I might say something like that.

"Well, isn't there someone you know, someone you trust, who could do it for you? What about Harry and John? They're always looking for work and I bet they'd do it for you no questions asked."

She looked at me expectantly. What she said was true. Harry and John Chester were blacksmiths, not coopers, but I was sure with all their experience, they'd be able to turn their hands to barrel-making. The more I thought about it, the more it made sense, because the smithy burnt a lot of wood and I knew that apart from heating the forge, the wood also produced sealing pitch; I'd once bought some from them to seal a leak in the Boar's roof. But most importantly, I knew I could trust them – Adie was right as well when she said times were hard for them and I knew if I put work their way, any work, they'd be grateful and definitely would keep quiet if they thought they might lose it.

"Alright then," I said. "They should be in tonight and I'll have a word with Harry; see what he thinks. As long as he doesn't know what the barrel's for and I'm sure he won't want to, it should be fine. I'll get him to make one and then we'll show it to Sam."

"Show Sam!" She looked alarmed. "Why do you need to show him?"

I reminded her that Sam had made it very clear he didn't expect any changes in his arrangements unless he agreed to them first.

"So if he doesn't like it, even though you think it's a good idea, even though it *is* a good idea, you still won't use it?"

Although she was annoyed, I pointed out to her that as soon as I delivered salt in a barrel to him, his cousin was bound to tell Sam who, I reminded her, wasn't the type of man to make a threat lightly. She still looked disappointed, so I added that I thought her idea was a good one and I was sure Sam would agree.

As expected, that evening Harry and John walked in. Harry had been a regular at the Boar since Mr Dodds' time, so we knew each other very well. He could tell from my tone that the work I had in mind was not something I wanted to discuss anywhere we might be overheard. So he told me,

"If we're able, we'll do whatever you need. We'll be down at the smithy in the morning. I've got a horse who's thrown a shoe being brought in first thing. I should be clear by nine though, so how about you leave it 'til 'bout half-past, just to be sure."

When I told Adie, she of course wanted to go with me, so she was less than happy when I said I'd go on my own. I reminded her that she wasn't supposed to have anything to do with the salt smuggling and that the fewer people who knew she was involved the better. For the rest of the evening whilst she was her usual bright and cheerful self with my customers, all I had from her was silence and scowls, but by morning she'd decided reluctantly that I was right.

It was barely light when I heard her leave her room and when I joined her downstairs I was greeted with a bright 'good morning' and a bowl of porridge. Whilst I ate, she got on with setting the bar straight, but stopped as soon as I finished eating and came and sat with me.

"I suppose you're right when you say people like Harry shouldn't know I had anything to do with the barrel, but when you show it to Sam you will tell him it was my idea, won't you?"

My first instinct was to tell her it would be better if he thought the idea was mine, but I realised if I was to fully regain her trust, this was one way that might help. So I smiled and told her that of course I'd tell him the design was hers.

She hesitated, then handed me a piece of paper, saying shyly,

"I've done some drawings. I know they're not very good, but I thought they might give Harry an idea of what we're looking for."

She handed me the drawings and, without another word, went back to cleaning the bar. They were very simple sketches without any explanation and I was sure they would add little to the description I would be able to give Harry, but I still promised to pass them to him. Something else dawned on me and I also promised myself that, as soon as we had time, I would teach Adie to read and write.

It was already past nine and as I had promised Harry I'd be at the smithy by half-past, I took the empty barrel we'd left behind the bar to dry out and rolled it to the stable where, with Adie's help, I secured it on the jack.

When I arrived at the smithy, Harry was still shoeing the horse he'd told me about, so I was met by John. He stood with me outside the smithy and we talked about how he and his father's business was going, what trade at the Boar was like and how Adie had taken to her new life; in fact we talked about anything except the reason I was there.

Eventually, the horse and its owner left and as I'd already tethered the donkey and John and I had relieved it of its burden, we rolled the barrel into the smithy. After explaining he'd been so long because he'd persuaded the horse's owner to replace all four shoes, I handed Harry Adie's sketches and told him what I wanted him to do. He stood scratching his head for a while, then turning to John, said,

"I reckon this is more the job for a carpenter than a smithy, don't you son?"

My heart sank. It wouldn't be a problem to find a carpenter, but I didn't know anyone that well, certainly not as well as I knew Harry and John and none that I was sure I could trust.

Fortunately, Harry hadn't finished.

"You're better than me working wood, ain't you John. Reckon you can do what Jabez is asking?"

Before John replied, I thought he should know that this barrel was to be only an example.

"Before you answer your dad, I need to tell you, if this works the way I hope it will, I'm going to need a dozen more barrels like it."

Harry looked questioningly at his son, but all John wanted to know was how soon I needed them.

"It depends really, as I told your dad, what's most important is that the two sections keep wet and dry apart. So if you let me know when the first one's ready, I'll come and pick it up. Then, as long as it works as well as I hope it will, I'll want the rest as soon as you can let me have them.

"Oh, and there's one last thing. I need this kept between the three of us, that won't be a problem, will it?"

Harry frowned.

"We'd already worked that one out Jabez, and no, it won't be a problem."

I wished I hadn't added that 'last thing', but Harry just said,

"To be honest, we're just glad to have the work. We'll let you know when the first one's ready. It shouldn't be more than a week, should it John?"

John had agreed with his father it might take him a week, but after only four days, the pair of them walked into the pub and John told me the first barrel was ready. So early the next morning, after collecting it from the smithy and returning to the Boar, I took the barrel straight to the barn, where Adie was anxiously waiting to see if John's handy work was as she'd imagined. Satisfied with John's modifications, she looked closely at each join and then ran a finger slowly across the length of each seal; after a few minutes, she declared that, as far as she could tell, the barrel was sound. Lastly, she turned the barrel over and both of us admired the hidden plug which, disguised as it was in the wood grain, could only be found by touch.

But to be really sure, and we had to be, the barrel needed to be tested for leaks. Although Adie had looked as closely as she could, we needed to be certain that the two halves were watertight – the smallest leak and the salt would be ruined. Salt was too expensive to waste, so I fetched my fire buckets; I had two, one by the fire and the other by the front door. We filled one side of the barrel with sand from the buckets and the other with water then rolled it across the stable floor so any leaks would show. After draining the water and carefully removing the sand, we were glad to find that the sand was completely dry.

"There you are. I told you it would work."

I had to admit to a proud Adie that the barrel was everything she'd said it would be, but I also reminded her that my opinion wasn't important as we still needed Sam's approval.

"He's not going to stop us using it, is he? He'll see it's a good way to hide the salt, especially for a publican like you, won't he?"

Adie knew I couldn't really answer her, but I assured her that the next time any of Sam's men came in the pub, I'd ask them to let Sam know I wanted to see him. Satisfied, she helped me move the barrel back into the cellar.

As luck would have it, or at least that's what I thought at the time, the very next evening Sam himself walked into the pub accompanied by three of his men. I was barely acknowledged as I served them and they quickly became involved in a quiet but intense conversation. When they called for another round, I couldn't stop Adie stepping forward ahead of me and I knew she was going to say something to Sam about the barrel. But before she had a chance to speak, Sam leant across the bar and whispered at length into her ear. She didn't say anything, just glanced at me and then nodded, but when she finished serving them, she came over to where I was standing at the end of the bar; I could tell she was trying unsuccessfully to suppress a smile.

"We're in luck," she breathed. "Sam says he needs to talk to you. Apparently the Excise Supervisor has caught two of his men red-handed. He doesn't think they'll talk, but he can't be sure. He says he needs to shut his operation down for a while, but I think it's our big chance."

She looked at me and I hoped she wasn't thinking what I knew she almost certainly was. I agreed, it *was* our big chance, our chance to get out of smuggling, at least for a while. But then Adie confirmed my fears.

"Don't you see? If we can prove to him that the barrel works, we could be the only smugglers he keeps using. He wouldn't have to use you just to take salt to his cousin. He could send you to whoever was willing to pay the most and you can insist on bigger payments in return."

As she was standing close speaking quietly into my ear, she couldn't see the alarm she'd caused me, so it was with no less enthusiasm she added,

"Anyway, he wants to talk to you as soon as you close the pub."

With that, she returned to serving some waiting customers, leaving me to acknowledge the enquiring look I got from Sam Baker.

Just as the last time they were in the pub with Sam, when it was time to leave, his men drank up together, rose together and left as one. There may have been less of them this time, but they were no less striking. I don't think it was deliberate, but when they saw Sam had remained alone, the rest of my customers hastily finished their drinks and, with almost identical unity, got up and left.

I bolted the door and when Adie had drawn the blinds, Sam drew up a table. He didn't question Adie's presence when the three of us sat down together, instead began immediately to talk about what had happened.

"Adie's told you?"

I explained she hadn't told me too much because she was worried she might be overheard.

"She told you that two of my men were caught. You know that much?"

I told him that was about all she'd told me.

"But I didn't tell her which two men."

The light was beginning to dawn.

"Not your cousin? You're not saying he was one of them?"

Sam looked grim.

"That's *exactly* what I'm saying."

Usually relaxed and sure of himself, he now seemed tense and uncertain.

"My cousin and the man who works for him on the farm were running that last load to my Liverpool customer. There was a high wind blowing when they left Foulk Stapleford, but at least when they set off, it blew in their backs. But there came a point where they changed direction which meant the wind now blew straight at them. Although their progress was slowed, this wouldn't have been a problem if a sudden downpour hadn't blown straight into their faces. The rain came out of nowhere and completely obscured their vision, so when they ran straight into the Supervisor and two of his men, they had no chance of getting away or disposing of the salt. It came on so suddenly that even though they got an oilcloth over the salt as quickly as they could, rain had already penetrated the sacks and ruined the salt; it was worthless. But the Supervisor didn't take that view and I doubt the Magistrate will either."

He laughed, but there was no humour in his voice.

"Dick won't talk. There's no reason why you shouldn't know my cousin's name. It's bound to come out soon enough. But Rob, even though he doesn't know anything about you, does know some of my other customers. Dick's worked for me for longer than anybody, so over the years he's handled a lot of my deliveries and for at least five years, Rob has helped him."

He smiled grimly.

"Now, because I can't be sure they won't make him talk, I've had to stop all deliveries."

"Jabez' barrel could help."

It was Adie. I'd forgotten she was there. I think Sam had as well. Turning to her and in a voice that left no doubt that he was irritated by her interruption, he said,

"Barrel? What barrel?"

I don't know if she heard the impatience in his voice. If she did, she ignored it.

"Jabez had it made, but it was my idea. He said the next time any of your men came in the pub, he was going to ask to see you; he was going to show you what we had made."

At least Sam's voice was even when he answered her.

"You're talking about using barrels for smuggling, is that right?"

"Yes, but…"

Sam didn't let her finish.

"Using barrels to smuggle anything is the oldest trick in the book and it won't fool that Supervisor. If he's got Rob or even Richard to talk and they've got some very persuasive ways of making a man beg to tell all he knows, then they'll be watching my customers as well as my men. No, sorry Adie. It wouldn't work."

I knew if this was a chance to stop spending the night leading two donkeys to Foulk Stapleford and back, even if it was only for a short while, then it was a chance I didn't want to miss.

"Don't worry Adie. I'm sure Sam will be interested in your barrel just as soon as his deliveries start again."

Ignoring me, she said,

"But I bet they wouldn't watch too closely if they knew it was just a publican delivering ale."

I could see Sam was close to losing his temper, so could Adie. Almost apologetically she added,

"But what if when they do stop him and make him open a barrel or two, all they find is ale. Then they're going to have to let him go, aren't they?"

For the first time, Sam looked curious and my blood ran cold as he said,

"Alright then Jabez. Let's have a look at this barrel. I can see the girl's not going to give up. Where do you keep it?"

"That's another good thing about it." She wasn't going to miss this chance. "It's in the cellar with all the other barrels; you couldn't tell it apart."

He looked at me and said,

"Just fetch it, will you? Quick as you can."

As I got up, Adie said,

"While you're fetching it, I'll get the fire bucket from the fire and maybe Sam could get the one from out the front?"

I began to say that I'd get it as soon as I'd got the barrel, but Sam waved me away, telling me he'd get it and that the sooner we got this over with, the better. After I returned, Adie showed Sam every detail and when she finally invited him to find the hidden plug, she was delighted when he failed.

Carrying the barrel out the back, I again filled one side with water and the other with sand. Space was tight, but we rolled the barrel to and fro and then left the water for a couple of minutes just to be sure. After emptying the water out the backdoor, we finally turned the barrel over, removed the blind plug and poured out the sand. Adie took great delight in pointing out that, just as Sam's salt would be, the sand was completely dry.

I could see Sam was thinking, so I was ready to say nothing and just wait for his opinion, but Adie wasn't as patient and started to speak.

"So what do you…"

Sam raised his hand to stop her, but it was the piercing look he gave her that was the real reason she stopped mid-sentence. Lowering his hand, he turned to me and asked,

140

"Who made it?"

I told him; I didn't know if he'd approve. Whether or not he did wasn't clear, he just said,

"And do they know what it's for?"

I assured him they didn't. He thought some more, then said,

"So how many have you got?"

Finding her voice again, Adie said,

"That's the only one. Jabez said we had to show you before we had any more made."

"That's true," I told him, "but I did explain to Harry and John that if this one was satisfactory," I tapped the barrel, "I'd need another dozen. They said they could do it, but I don't know how long it would take them. This one took four days to make, so I suppose the rest will take about another month to a month and a half."

I wanted him to say that the best part of fifty days was too long and he'd abandon any plans he might be forming. Of course I got my first wish, but he definitely had no intention of giving up his plans. Grasping the barrel, he said,

"Tell Harry that whatever you paid him for this one, you'll pay him double for the rest. But you can also tell him you want the first six in a week, the rest in two.

I don't care how you do it, but you make sure he knows he'd need to get them finished on time, that's if he knows what's good for him."

Whilst Sam was talking, Adie had been on her knees next to me, using cupped hands to shovel sand back into the buckets. But now I felt her bristle and she stopped shovelling. Getting to her feet, she looked straight at Sam and said,

"Why do you do that? Why do you always threaten people?"

He looked back at her. I could see she'd thrown him again and he was searching for a reply. Finally he said,

"I need them to be more frightened of me than of anyone else, pan owners, the Excise Supervisor, Magistrates, even the King if it comes to it. If they're not, then I can't be sure they can't be bribed, threatened or just plain scared into telling all they know."

When she replied, I heard tightness in her voice. She knew the line had been crossed already, but that didn't stop her.

"You can trust me and Jabez. Remember I thought of the barrel and Jabez had it made, we could have kept quiet, then you wouldn't have known anything about it. But we didn't keep quiet. We told you because we thought it might be of use to you – especially now."

I tried to read Sam's face but it was impossible. Unblinking, those piercing eyes were still staring at her, but his thoughts were hidden. Just as on their first meeting, Adie met his stare and carried on.

"Harry and John don't need threatening either. They're desperate for work and know, if they want to carry on getting ours, they're going to have to keep quiet about it. Also, if Jabez tells them he wants the rest of the barrels quickly, they'll make them as fast as they can. It stands to reason, they're going to hope if they do a good job there might be more work coming their way; threatening them won't make them go any faster than the chance to put food on their family's table will."

I was getting used to this slip of a girl speaking her mind, but I wasn't sure Sam ever would. But I'll give him credit – he tried. Turning to me, he said,

"As I said, I want six in a week and six the week after."

Then he spoke to Adie.

"You're young with a lot to learn, so for now all I'll say is that if I want your advice, I'll ask for it."

He started for the door, but before leaving, turned to me and said,

"Jabez, if this works, it could dig me out of a hole, but I need those barrels fast and I need them right first time; get them made and I'll explain."

With that, he was gone and I was left looking at Adie.

"What?" she said defiantly. "Why are you staring at me like that?"

The truth was I admired her, but what I said was,

"I think you must have a death wish. That's the second time you've spoken to him like that and I honestly don't know why he keeps letting you get away with it."

"It made a difference though, didn't it?"

I couldn't see what she meant.

"I don't know why you say that. He still wants half the barrels in a week, the rest in two."

She gave me a knowing smile.

"That's true, but do you remember him issuing a single threat after I spoke out, 'cos I don't."

I had to admit she was right, but that didn't stop me from being outside the smithy at dawn with two empty barrels strapped to the jenny waiting for the blacksmith and his son to appear.

Harry appeared at half past six.

"Mornin' Jabez," he said as he opened the smithy, "I don't need to guess why you're here so early. John's barrel must have been what you wanted and now you want to talk about the rest."

I hadn't yet worked out how I was going to tell him how quickly I needed the rest, but he seemed to be in a good mood, so I just agreed with him and told him John's work couldn't have been better.

Harry smiled and said,

"You're lucky to find me here. I got some gate work in yesterday and I promised it would be finished today, otherwise I wouldn't be here. Hold on a minute while I light the forge. It takes a bit o' time to heat up. Then we can talk about your work."

I was surprised John wasn't with him but Harry must have read my mind.

"John'll be along presently. Today's his turn to clear the muck."

I'd forgotten that Harry and John shared a job in town and that each morning one of them cleared mud and manure from the shop doorways of those whose owners were willing to pay. Even though it didn't pay too well, I was sure they wouldn't want to give the work up, which meant they'd have even less time to complete my barrels.

I decided I needed to tell them the whole truth; what they were making and who for, so I told Harry I needed to talk to both of them as soon as John arrived. I thought I saw a trace of a smile, but he said nothing just shrugged his shoulders and carried on stoking the forge.

About half an hour later, John appeared whistling to himself.

"You're in a fair mood son. People must have paid up."

John stopped whistling and said,

"Not only did everyone pay up, but even that tight bugger who owns the apothecary settled his bill."

Harry laughed. "You can't mean old Jeremiah Hunt? He must owe us for nigh on a year."

"That's exactly who I mean and that's just what he paid us; for a whole year. And that's not everythin', 'cos I found a bob in the street. I nearly missed it. I'd just cleared a doorway and was about to sweep the muck into the gutter when I saw something glitter. It was nearly hidden and it's only because the sun had just come out from behind a cloud that I saw it. Anyway Dad, the ales on me tonight, no argument – at least 'til the shillin's run out. Mentionin' ale, good mornin' to you Jabez. Me chunterin' on, you must be here about your ba…"

"That's right John. Jabez is here to talk about the work he needs doin'."

Harry signalled for us both to keep quiet and then walked quickly and quietly out of the smithy. Moments later, we heard him speak.

"Can I help you?"

Hearing Harry talking to someone, I started to follow John out of the smithy. Neither of us had heard anything and both of us were keen to see who was there. But before I turned the corner into the lane, I recognised a familiar voice.

"No, no, I was just passing and I thought I heard someone I knew, but I must have been mistaken."

I stopped in my tracks. I didn't want another argument with Tom Rider and I certainly didn't want him finding out why I was there. Harry must have been thinking the same way because I heard him say,

"No one here but me and John. It's him you must have heard."

John pointed at their wood store. It was the only place I could go in the smithy where I couldn't be seen. I tried as quietly as I could to conceal myself, whilst John strolled out the front and started talking to Tom.

The store was small, cramped and almost full, but I managed to find a fixed but tolerable position where I could wait for Tom to leave. With nothing to do but wait for Harry and John to re-appear, I began to think about Tom and why he was outside the smithy this early in the morning. It struck me that he must have been following me because the smithy was at the end of a lane, so unless he had business with the blacksmiths, he had no reason to be there. As I thought about it, more incidents fell into place: the morning after that first salt delivery when he was hanging around my stable, how, on several occasions I'd heard noises outside the pub when returning from a delivery, that Sam had told me his men had spotted Tom hanging around the Boar on more than one occasion and finally, I remembered how on the morning I'd overslept and Adie had found and woken me, she'd said that the front door had been wide open when I was sure I'd locked it. It dawned on me that the earliest incidents may have just been plain nosiness, but from the day Adie started working in the pub and certainly after she moved in, he'd been trying to find out what I was doing and I didn't think it was just to satisfy his own curiosity.

Although at first tolerable because I was unable to move, my position was fast becoming unbearable. I was just trying to work out how best I could move without creating too much noise, when Harry opened the door to the store and helped me out.

"Tom's gone. John's just making sure he's not doubled back." He looked serious. "But I think he knew you were here and more than that, I think he's got some idea why."

It didn't worry me that Tom knew I was there, although I wanted to avoid any sort of quarrel with him, but I was very concerned that he might know why. Harry must have seen that I looked worried because he added,

"I'm not saying he definitely knows about the barrels, but we can't be sure how much he overheard and I bet he already had an idea about the salt."

There was no doubt that I'd been rattled by what Harry had said, but at least it was clear that him and John had already worked out what I wanted the barrels for, so at least I wouldn't have to explain that to them.

John returned and after he closed the doors, I explained what I needed and more importantly by when. I'd also decided to tell them exactly who they were getting involved with.

"The modifications you made to the barrel were perfect John, but now I'm going to need some more with exactly the same changes – that's the easy part. Probably what's most important is who's behind this…"

"Sam Baker?"

It was Harry who spoke and I must have looked taken aback.

"It is Baker, isn't it?" he asked.

I admitted it was.

"Only someone involved in salt smuggling, as much as Sam Baker, is going to make this much effort. We don't like getting involved with him, I'm sure you don't either, but we've got used to the idea."

I wasn't sure they'd be so used to it when I told them how quickly the barrels would be needed.

"He wants six barrels in a week's time, another six in two," then remembered,

"Oh, and he says he'll pay you for each barrel double what I paid you for the first one. But I'm sure you know he'll exact a much higher price if you don't deliver on time."

I attempted a smile, but the truth was I was as fearful of Sam Baker as they were, so it slid away almost as quickly as it tried to form.

Harry said,

"I don't suppose it makes any difference, but do you know why he wants them so soon?"

It was too soon for news of the arrests to be known by many and although I knew the Supervisor would make sure it was spread far and wide by the end of the day, I made sure Harry and John were amongst the first to hear.

"The truth is Sam's in a bit of a spot. Two of his smugglers have been arrested and he's had to stop all deliveries. Now he's seen the barrel, he thinks he might be able use them to supply his most important customers right under the Excise men's noses."

Whilst his dad was talking, John had been silent, but now he spoke, the light-heartedness of earlier was gone.

"We'll be pushed and we'll have to change the way we do things, but I think it's possible."

I was pleased that he thought he could do it, but Harry wasn't so sure.

"John, it took you four days to make one barrel. He wants six in a week's time – that's about one a day; and that's without our other work."

"I know Dad, but as I said I think we can do it. I need you to do all the muck clearing in town, 'cos we don't want to lose that work, especially now that it's paying. If you can do any other work that comes in the smithy, then I'll concentrate on the barrels; if I need to work late, then I'll work late. Don't forget, he said he'd pay us double to get 'em all done in a fortnight and we could really do with that money."

When I think back over the fortnight, starting that morning I believe I saw a father begin to hand over the reins of a family concern to his son.

"Now, while I'm working on the barrel in here, we can keep things to ourselves, but I'm not sure how we move them between here and the Boar."

I had already given this some thought and decided the best way to hide them was not to hide them at all, so I said,

"I've been thinking about that. What we're doing isn't breaking any laws, is it?"

John agreed.

"So I think I should bring them down here over the next few mornings then, as you finish them, you or your dad can bring them back. I don't suppose anyone will be that interested, but if someone is meddlesome enough to enquire…"

Laughing, John said,

"Like Tom Rider."

I was beginning to realise that Tom might be more of a danger to me than even the Excise Supervisor. Whilst the Supervisor wanted to catch anyone smuggling salt, especially Sam Baker, it was becoming clear Tom was only interested in ruining me by any means. So I said,

"If anybody should ask questions, we tell 'em I've had some damaged barrels in the cellar for years and the brewery won't pay me anything for them. We'll say it hasn't been worth my while sending them to the cooper's to be fixed 'cos he charges too much, but that you need the work and have offered to mend them for me for a lot less. Everyone knows that most blacksmiths are having a hard time, so it's a story most people are likely to believe – apart from Tom Rider."

Elizabeth
My Hero?

What a few days I've had! On Monday, Tom was out really early on one of them walks he likes to have. When he came back, he didn't say a word, just had his breakfast and set off for the pans. I didn't think much of it at the time because he's been pretty quiet since Will left, even more so since Adie went, but on Tuesday evening, we had a visit from Mr Sweetman, the local Excise man. I didn't know him, but when I answered the door, Tom seemed to be expecting him because he slipped on his jacket and without a word stepped out. They both disappeared into the night and when he returned half an hour later, again he said little and when I enquired just told me I was better off not knowing.

But on Wednesday, all thoughts I might have had about these events and whether they might be connected was forgotten. It was fortunate I was in, because I'd spent the morning in town shopping and after returning, was about to go gathering wood. I was just putting my coat back on when I heard a lot of noise outside the door. Before I could open it to find out what was going on there was loud and urgent knocking.

When I opened the door, there was Tom, looking like death and held up by two men. For a moment, I thought he was drunk, but then I realised his face was etched with pain. The men, who looked like father and son, brought him in and laid him, not too gently I may add, on our bed and it was only then I saw that his right hand was heavily bandaged. I looked to the men for an explanation, although I had a good idea of what must have happened.

"Scalded his hand in the brine, he's lucky he didn't fall right in."

There was a groan from Tom and the men looked at him strangely.

"How did it happen?"

Tom had lapsed into unconsciousness again and it seemed the obvious question to ask them, but they looked at each other strangely before the older one said,

"We don't know. I don't think nobody does. We think he slipped on the hurdle and lost his balance, but we can't be sure. You'll have to ask him yourself when he comes round."

Glancing one last time at Tom, they hurried away.

The first thing I did after they'd gone was to go to Tom and try to undo his bandaged hand. But as soon as I touched it, his eyes opened and gave me a look the like of which I'd never seen before. He hissed,

"Don't touch it."

That's all he said before shutting his eyes again and apparently going back to sleep. He'd startled me so much, I'd stepped back from the side of the bed, but now I didn't know what to do for the best. We couldn't afford a doctor and the one other person who could have helped me, my old friend Betsy, had been gone for over a year.

I decided there was little I could do except let him sleep and try again in the morning. But he tossed and turned so much I spent most of the night trying to sleep in a chair and by morning it was clear he had a fever – I just hoped it wasn't because his hand was infected. I bathed his brow to try and cool him down and then as he started to wake told him he *must* let me look at his hand. At first he refused, told me it hurt too much, so I didn't press him just carried on bathing his brow. I decided to leave it for a while but I knew I needed to see it.

Tom was still slipping in and out of consciousness, so to have any chance of saving his hand, maybe even his life, I had to get the bandage off.

For the rest of the morning, whilst I got on with my usual tasks, Tom lay on the bed unchanged and as he continued to toss and turn, I realised what I must do. Telling Tom I'd be back as soon as I could – I'm not sure he heard me, he was sliding back to sleep or unconsciousness – I hurried out and headed for the Boar's Head. I knew I couldn't expect a warm reception there, but I had little choice. I needed some gin and the town was twice as far.

I hadn't been in the Boar's Head Inn for many years, not since me and Tom were courting. But it might as well have been yesterday for the amount it had changed, even the old sign of a boar's head that hung above the entrance was so weathered and faded that it could have been the head of just about any animal. Walking through the gloomy entrance, I turned right and entered the bar, but stopped almost immediately. Across the room, Adie was kneeling and facing away from me, relaying the fire and so I paused for a moment, but I knew there was nothing else I could do.

"Hello Adie."

That was all I said, but she looked as if she'd been struck. She sprang to her feet and spun round all in one move, but before she spoke it was my turn to be startled when a familiar voice behind me said,

"Hello Elizabeth, can I help you?"

Jabez had entered the bar behind me and I could tell he wasn't pleased to see me. So I said quickly,

"I'm not here to cause any trouble."

To be honest, even though his greeting had sounded less than welcoming, I was glad he was there because I had no wish to talk to Adie.

"I just want to buy a quart of gin; I haven't time to go into town."

He looked curious but said nothing and Adie, when she heard why I was there, slipped into the kitchen. When Jabez gave me the gin and I attempted to pay him, he pushed my hand away and said,

"Keep your money. Just promise me we won't see you again, at least not until you're ready to apologise to Admonition and admit she told you the truth."

I wanted to tell him what had happened to Tom, tell him that he was a good man, but I just thanked him for the gin and left. Adie must have gone out quietly by the kitchen door and she was waiting for me when I came through the front. I didn't want any trouble. I just wanted to get back to Tom – I'd been away too long already. But I needn't have worried because Jabez had followed me out and spoke to her.

"Adie, can you come inside? I need your help readying the bar. We open in about half an hour and there's still so much to do – that fire you were setting needs lighting if we're going to take the chill off before our first customers arrive."

She didn't move, but I had no time to waste. I had to get back to Tom. So looking straight ahead, I walked past her and heard her say quietly,

"You know he's a liar."

I knew I had to ignore her, so still looking straight ahead, I kept on towards home. She called after me,

"Think about what I've told you. You know I've never lied to you."

I thought, *'there's always a first time, my girl,'* but I knew she was trying to provoke me, so I didn't say anything, just kept walking in the direction of the village and home.

Jabez spoke to her again. I didn't hear what he said but I heard nothing more from Adie and as I turned the corner I finally glanced back; they'd both gone inside. I couldn't dwell on what she'd said, I had more important things to worry about, so I pressed on home as fast as I could.

When I got home, Tom was conscious and a little more lucid, but he was fretting because he didn't know where I was. I didn't tell him where the gin came from, but I did tell him my plan. He wasn't sure but I told him I had to have a look at that hand. So handing him his first mug of gin, I promised him that however drunk he got, I'd still be as gentle as I could. I knew I'd have to be patient and let him drink slowly – if I tried to make him go too fast, he'd bring it back up and I wanted him drunk not sick. So as the afternoon changed into evening, he slowly became more and more affected by the alcohol and finally, at about nine, I thought he was drunk enough for me to remove the bandage.

I thought he was out cold when I reached for his hand, but as soon I touched it, his eyes opened and he slurred,

"Don't hurt me Lizzie."

It was a long time since he'd called me Lizzie and it felt nice. I smiled at him and told him I'd be as careful as I could. Then, supporting his arm at the elbow, I very carefully started to unwind the piece of cloth that had served as a bandage. Tom lay motionless as it unwound and I thought that everything was going to be fine, but as I started to remove the final layer, Tom screamed and wrenched his hand away. Luckily, as it turned out, I held on to the bandage as he pulled away, removing the last of it from his hand. Tom screamed again and looked at me. The pain had cleared away the gin and his eyes were full of resentment.

"You meant to do that. You ripped it away."

I didn't answer him, just stared at his hand. I could only see the back which was red raw and his fingers that were drawn up like a claw. Pus ran from holes that were all that remained of the blisters that came away with the bandage when he pulled back his hand. He wasn't likely to let me touch it and even if he did, I didn't know what I could do. However, the gin had taken full effect and Tom now seemed in a deep sleep.

But as I moved away, he stirred and I heard him mutter, 'soap'.

I didn't know what he meant and thought he might be dreaming. But then he suddenly seemed to come to and with a struggle sat up and said,

"You've got some soap, ain't you Lizzie? Some soft soap, I mean, like you use for washing our clothes?"

Bemused, I told him that of course I did. What I didn't understand was why he asked. He still had a fever so I thought he might be delirious.

He realised I still didn't understand.

"I've just remembered. I've seen it done before in the pans. I want you to go into town and visit the apothecary and ask him to give you half a dram of Sal Tartar. When you get back, I want you to boil a quart of water with about six ounces of soap and make up the quart to a gallon with cold water and add the Sal Tartar. Then I'm going to put my hand in it for half an hour. I don't know why I didn't think of it before."

So that's what we did, and while Tom sat gently moving his hand about, he told me what had happened. Apparently, him and Josh, he's the lad whose been helping him since Will left, had drained the brine and were just about to start drawing the salt from their latest make. Josh had picked up his rake and stood on the hurdle. Unfortunately as he reached forward to draw the salt, one of his feet slipped and he would have gone straight in if he hadn't managed to jam the rake in the bottom of the pan. He was still unbalanced though, and would have gone in if Tom hadn't caught him. Unfortunately, as he grabbed the boy, Tom slipped as well and put his hand straight in the hot salt.

"Nobody's fault though, Lizzie. The boy just slipped but I think I might have saved his life. That's got to be worth it for just a burnt hand, hasn't it?"

He smiled weakly at me and I thought,

'You're a liar, Admonition Bostock. My husband is a good man, a hero even and next time I see you, I'll be sure to let you know.'

Jabez
Manchester

Delivery of the barrels went as smoothly as I hoped and I saw no one when I delivered the rest of the first consignment. Harry and John did see a couple they knew from the village when returning the last barrel, but Harry said they'd passed each other with nothing more than a mutual 'good afternoon'.

Sam had made sure at least one of his men was in the pub each evening checking on progress. Late in the evening, following the last of the first week's deliveries, Sam himself walked in. When everyone else had left and while I locked up, Adie closed the blinds. Returning to the bar, I was surprised to find Sam still standing, drink in hand. When I invited him to sit with me, he shook his head and said,

"I can't stay because I'll be bringing tonight's consignment myself. I'll need you to be ready to receive it and then to take it straight to Manchester."

"Manchester!"

I couldn't hide my surprise.

"Yes Jabez, Manchester. I have a customer there who has already paid me for the cost of his order and he won't be happy if I don't deliver."

Sam might have a good reason to send me to Manchester, but I knew it would take me two days to get there and back, so I asked him,

"Even if I'm able to walk all that way, what am I going to do about running this place? I can't leave Adie to run it on her own for two days."

Sam had already thought about this.

"You can ride a horse, can't you?"

Mr Dodds had taught me to ride, but I hadn't ridden since the old horse had died.

"It's been a while, but yes, I can ride," I told him.

"Well then, I'll lend you a horse and you can lead the donkeys. If you travel out overnight, you should reach my customer by mid-morning and without any load, you should be back here about closing time. I'm sure Adie can run this place for one night and a couple of my lads will be in, just to make sure there's no trouble. Now, put these barrels in your stable and tonight, wait for me there. Make sure the beer is already in the barrels and I'll help you transfer the salt."

So that was that. It was clear it would be pointless arguing with him because his mind was made up and moments later, after saying he'd be back in an hour, Sam left. As soon as he'd gone and with Adie's help, I fetched the barrels from the cellar, filled and sealed one side with beer and rolled them all to the stable. We rolled the last two barrels in, then sat on bales of hay in complete silence and waited for Sam to reappear. Not for the first time I heard noises in the dark and also not for the first time, told myself it was just animals moving in the undergrowth.

We'd only been waiting about a quarter of an hour, though sitting silently in the dark it seemed much longer, when the stable door opened and we were joined by Sam, leading a mare and two heavily loaded mules.

"I don't think I was followed, but I can't be sure. We need to transfer the salt to the barrels, load your donkeys and then you need to get on your way. You can use the mare and I'll ride one of my mules home, but it's important we get the salt in the barrels and on its way."

We worked quickly to unload the mules and then carefully filled the barrels. Sam helped to load the donkeys and after introducing myself to the mare, I mounted and, leading the donkeys, got on my way. I wasn't too worried about leaving Adie on her own. I knew Sam would make sure she had no problems, and she'd been more in danger while the salt was in the stable.

Resigned to not reaching my destination until several hours after daybreak, I didn't push the animals and followed the main route into Manchester. The moving of the barrels between the Boar and the smithy in broad daylight had been such a success that it made me more confident. So whilst I travelled in the general direction of Manchester, I also moved towards the west and the London Road. I knew by daybreak the road would be full of carts carrying fresh produce to feed the hungry mouths of Manchester and I hoped to be lost in the crowd.

And that's how things were, because even though I joined the road to London long before dawn, there were already a fair number of carts and mules on the road and by the time it was light, there was no reason why I should be noticed amongst the crowd of vehicles and animals, all moving in the same direction.

I began to smell the town about an hour before I could see it, and by the time we reached Great Ancoats Lane and fields began to be replaced by buildings, the air was full of smoke. All three animals had travelled without complaint, but when we turned into Oldham Street and the smoke became dense and acrid, the jenny began to bray loudly and tried to escape her tether and the jack soon followed her example. I managed to keep control of the mare and dismounted; I couldn't blame the donkeys. No doubt like me, their eyes were sore, their noses caked with soot and their mouths full of the acrid taste of smoke, but I had to get them under control because we were so close to our destination. Though I untethered the donkeys from the mare, I struggled in vain with them and was just wondering if there was any other way I could get the barrels over the final mile, when a door opened and a woman carrying a bucket stepped out.

"You need to wash their faces down and give 'em a drink. They're not use to the smoke, are they?"

She handed me the bucket and with difficulty, they were both still bucking, I washed the donkeys down, and then let each one have a drink. From somewhere the women produced a rag.

"Use this to dry 'em and make sure all the soot's gone from their noses. Have you got far to go?"

I told her I hadn't.

"They should be alright for a couple of miles, so if you're coming back this way, knock on the door and I'll give you another bucket-full."

I let the mare finish the water then, thanking the women, handed her back the rag saying I was grateful to her but that I hoped to find a different way home.

Re-mounting the mare, I set off once again for my destination, congratulating myself that despite the crowd the donkeys had drawn, no one had shown any interest in what I was carrying.

Approaching the end of Oldham Street, I knew that when I turned into Lever Row, the building I was looking for would be only yards away. But before I turned the corner, a familiar face stepped out from a doorway.

"Jabez, wait." The mare was more startled than me. "I've only got a minute, but I need to warn you."

It was our local Excise man Richard Sweetman. We hardly ever saw him, but that was how we all liked it. For years, local people had used my pub to buy and sell a little salt. It wasn't legal because no one paid any taxes, but the Excise didn't trouble us because I was always paid a small amount for allowing the trade to go on and I always paid a share of that money to Sweetman. Sam Baker didn't concern himself with what went on. The amounts involved were too small and I knew he had only accused me of undercutting his prices because he wanted to use me in his own operation. I had no doubt he would have found a way of embroiling me regardless.

When he spoke, Sweetman sounded agitated,

"You've got to turn round and go back. The Supervisor has been following you from the Boar and he knows, don't ask me how, that you're carrying salt. He knows all of Sam Baker's customers. So once he could see you were heading into Manchester, he left me tracking you and went ahead to your customer's where he's hoping to catch you."

Looking towards Piccadilly I could see, turning the corner from Lever Row, the Excise Supervisor with two men I didn't recognise, but knew had to be the two he'd employed to assist him. Knowing the barrels were about to be tested, I said,

"I think he may have had a change of plan."

Sat high on his stallion was a thick set man with a heavy curly beard and a wild head of hair. Though I'd never heard him speak before, I wasn't surprised that when he did, his voice boomed.

"There you are, Mr Sweetman. I see you're holding Mr Payne – that is what you're doing, isn't it? You wouldn't be trying to warn him off, would you?"

Sweetman's answer didn't surprise me. This large man, with his matching voice sat on his great horse, was an intimidating sight and our local man sounded terrified.

"No, I was holding him alright. He spotted me following him and I was just taking him round to where I knew you were going to be."

The Supervisor didn't look like he believed him for a moment, but just then, I was far more concerned that the barrels did the job John had made them for and that the salt remained undiscovered.

Instructing me to dismount and follow him, he led us round the corner into Lever Row and on into Piccadilly. We hadn't gone much further before we were passing the gates of the factory expecting my delivery. There was nobody at the gate and I carried on as if I had no knowledge of the place. I was almost past the gates when that loud booming voice rang out.

"Stop!"

I did as he said.

"Isn't this your destination, Mr Payne?"

I feigned surprise.

"Yes, I think it is. Sorry, this is the first time I've been here. It's the owner's birthday and this year is his sixtieth and he's giving his workers dinner. I've been asked to supply the beer."

I knew he wouldn't believe me. I just hoped he couldn't prove I was lying. When Sam was helping me load the donkeys, we'd discussed what I would say if I was stopped, so at least I had a reason for being so far from the Boar.

"Beers are brewed round every corner in Manchester. Why go to the expense of having beer brought from over thirty miles away?"

I hoped I didn't sound rehearsed.

"It's true there's a lot of beer brewed here, but you see the owner of this factory grew up close to the Boar. He worked in the pans with his parents and, when he was old enough, used to come in the Boar with his dad. 'Course that was a long time ago, well before I came to the pub, but I'm told he remembers the ale with fondness. His son, who's ordered the beer, says his father talks about it every time they drink ale together and always says the ale in the Boar is better than the one they happened to be drinking. His son thought it would be a nice touch to order the ale as a surprise for the celebration dinner. The brew's been the same for at least fifty years. I just hope it tastes as good as he remembers."

I'd been practising this tale so often as I travelled to Manchester that I almost believed it myself. Unfortunately, I couldn't say the same of the Supervisor.

"Take a barrel down and show me."

Sure of what would happen, he didn't try to hide the smirk on his face as I took a barrel down from the jenny. I assured him it only contained beer, but he told me to get on with it.

I hadn't expected him to change his mind. Still, as I watched it flow into the gutter, it did seem a waste of perfectly good ale.

"Alright, let's try another one," he said, "but this time from the jack."

I said nothing, just took a barrel from the back of the jack, stood it next to the one I'd taken from the jenny and opened the tap. I had been worried the ale would stop running before he let me close the tap and the first one must have been quite close. The second was similar. But when he told me to take down the third and I reminded him this order was especially to celebrate the factory owner's birthday, I'd let out barely a mug full when he told me to close the tap. Even more pleasing, I noticed his smirk had faded and was being replaced by a look of doubt, a doubt that grew as I showed him that each barrel contained nothing but ale.

When I closed the final tap, he couldn't contain his frustration. He turned to Sweetman and said,

"I want to see the weasel who's made me trail after this man all night for nothing."

Sweetman looked shocked.

"But you agreed I could keep his name to myself."

"And you promised me that I could trust his information. No, he's wasted my time and so have you. I want to see him tomorrow or you can say goodbye to your job."

Without even another look in my direction, he set off home, followed closely by his assistants. Glancing nervously in my direction, Sweetman looked like he was going to speak. He obviously thought better of it and set off hurriedly after them.

Of course, I was in no doubt Tom Rider was the informant, but just then I was more interested in moving the salt into the factory as quickly as possible. There was no reason for me to worry though, because the Excise men had only just disappeared into the Piccadilly crowds when a group of men from the Factory descended on the barrels. In seconds, they'd moved the barrels through the gates and vanished with them into the depths of the factory.

Hurried into the factory by a man who introduced himself only as the factory foreman, I enjoyed watching his men try to get to the salt in the barrels. The floor was awash with beer before a sharp-eyed young apprentice, who I suppose also had smaller and nimbler fingers than his workmates, spotted and managed to remove the hidden bung from one of the barrels. Immediately, if only temporarily, promoted from the lowliest position to one of great importance, the lad was keen to open the other barrels. But before he could start on the next one, I suggested they were moved on to drier ground before checking that the salt had been delivered dry. The foreman agreed and all six were moved before the apprentice was allowed to open them. Rather than empty each barrel and risk getting the salt damp in the humid factory air, a sample was drawn from each barrel, taken from where the seal ensured the beer and the salt were kept apart. Once the foreman was satisfied that each sample was dry, it was put back and the bung put back in place.

I'd hitched the mare and the donkeys to the factory gate when the Excise Supervisor had insisted on checking the contents of the barrels, so they had been breathing the filthy air a lot longer than I'd anticipated. Not wanting to make them wait until we were back in Great Ancoats Lane, I asked the foreman if he could spare me a bucket of water. Clearly delighted by his salt delivery, he sent the lad who opened the barrels to fetch one. The boy in turn, still basking in his newfound importance, rushed off, returning a minute later soaking wet and with a nearly full bucket. Thanking him, I took the bucket outside and washed the animals, letting each have a drink. As the mare finished the last of the water, the lad came out to collect the bucket. When I thanked him, he beamed and said there was no need because,

"I've had just about the best day of my life, thanks to you and them barrels. They've treated me like I'm one of them and all the time I'm the only one who can take out the bungs, they're going to have to carry on treating me the same way."

I'd already tethered the donkeys to the mare, so after telling him I was pleased I'd been able to help him, I re-mounted the mare and set off home. But as I rode away, I wondered how long it would be before the men devised their own ways to open the barrels. Most of all, I hoped the boy wouldn't go through life always marking today as the best one, but with the suspicion that he probably would.

Shaking off that saddening thought, I reminded myself how successful the barrels had been at not only keeping the salt dry but also completely fooling the Excise Supervisor. I'd already taken the same route as the Excise men, so with the happy thought of how pleased both Adie and Sam would be at my success, I shook up the mare and we set off home at a steady trot.

I made good time returning to the Boar and arrived home in the early evening not long, so she told me, after Adie had opened the doors. There were only three customers in the bar. Two were regulars who showed no curiosity in knowing where I'd been. The other one I recognised as one of Sam's men who, as soon as I confirmed that everything had gone to plan, got on his way – presumably to report the good news to Sam.

Having established that Adie had had no problems in my absence and having assured her that I would tell her all about my trip as soon as we'd closed, I went outside and led three exhausted animals to the stable. Having fed and watered all three, I was just bedding them down for the night, when I heard a noise behind me. I turned sharply and there, standing in the doorway, was Sam Baker. It was barely twenty minutes since Sam's man had left the Boar, which meant he must have been waiting close by. Clearly, he had been anxious to hear that I'd returned and by the look on his face he was keen to hear how I'd got on.

"All went well then, Jabez?"

Shutting the door, Sam moved across to his mare who, having eaten, was dosing. As he stood fondling her ear, I told him about my morning's adventures. Although happy that his salt had been safely delivered, he wanted to know more about the Excise Supervisor's examination of the barrels. He looked more anxious now than before. So perhaps because I was as tired as the animals, I forgot who I was talking to.

"I thought you'd be pleased. The barrels have all been examined and the salt stayed hidden – Adie's idea worked."

I already decided not to mention Tom and my suspicion that he was Sweetman's informant. Sam seemed to relax a little.

155

"You're right; I'll check that there weren't any problems with the salt and then I'll be back to see you and collect my mare. In the meantime, you should get some rest."

Giving the mare one final pat, he went on his way and I headed back into the pub.

Elizabeth
Cold Comfort

When he brought it home, Tom said it was beef. With him being in the mood he was, I didn't like to argue, but I knew it was mutton – and from an old ewe at that. Still, I boiled it for a couple of hours and though it was a bit stringy, it didn't taste too bad. Mind you, it wouldn't matter what I gave Tom. By then he didn't seem to care what he ate or even if he ate at all.

It's been three months now since he was injured and he hasn't worked a day since; looking at his hand, I don't know if he ever will. Though it's healed in a fashion, the skin's so thin and taught that the slightest knock breaks it and lays open the red and raw flesh underneath and the slightest touch is so painful to him; it turns his already pallid face grey.

What I can't understand is why, since two of them brought him home, neither of the workers, or come to that, anyone else from the pan have offered to help us, not even been to see him. I would have thought, especially as he saved that boy, at least his mother would have tried to help us. I've seen her in the gennel a couple of times, but she's deliberately ignored me and slipped away the moment she's seen me. No, the only visitors we've had was when we had another visit from Mr Sweetman, and this time that dreadful man the Excise Supervisor, Mr Herne, was with him. I can't understand why he came 'cos he's only interested in catching salt smugglers and I know Tom's never had anything to do with that business. The horrid man looked really angry when I opened the door and he pushed straight past me. He started shouting at Tom, something to do with the information he'd given Sweetman being worthless. Tom seemed more worried about making sure I didn't know what they were talking about, because he didn't argue with him, just led the way back outside – Herne followed him with Mr Sweetman trailing behind. I followed them, worrying that Tom, who hadn't been outside since his accident, was alright. I needn't have worried, he was already well down the gennel with Herne close behind him. He was still shouting at Tom, but I couldn't make out what he was saying.

When he returned about half an hour later, Tom was alone and as I say, Herne and Mr Sweetman have never returned and nor has anyone else. It makes me so angry. I told Tom I'd go down those salt pans and give them all, especially that Sarah, a piece of my mind, but he's told me I must never do that. He's never told me what Herne wanted, but at least since then he's started going out again.

But this morning I finally broke down. We had no money, nothing left to sell and not a thing left to eat and I really mean it, not a single thing. For a week, we had only oatmeal and we'd had the last of that two days ago; there had been so little left towards the end, all it had done was to turn water grey. When I broke down, I think I shocked Tom because I didn't shout or rant at him, but just sat at the table with my head on my arms and sobbed.

When I eventually spoke, all emotion had been washed away, so I said unsteadily,

"I don't know what else to do Tom. We've got nothing to eat and no way of getting anything. You won't talk to the people who by rights should be helping us and you won't let me talk to them. I can't see that there's anything left for me to do except go to the workhouse."

Tom looked at me. He saw that I meant what I said and talk of the workhouse must have shaken him because reaching for his coat, he just said,

"Right, leave it with me."

With that, he left the house and marched off up the gennel.

He'd been gone for over an hour and I was beginning to worry, when he walked back in and handed me that bit of mutton.

"They told me that's to last us for a week, but I've found a way to earn a bit of money. I hope that'll make you happy."

He spoke so coldly. I didn't answer him. I wanted to tell him I was very far from happy, that I was tired of wondering where our next meal was coming from and that I was sick of having to go begging to the Parish when they ought to be treating him like a hero. But as I said, I kept quiet, forced a smile and set about cooking the mutton.

Jabez
Arrest

After Sam left, Adie didn't really want to talk about the pub. She wanted to hear about my trip and listened in rapt silence while I told her about my escapade. She showed increased pride as I told her about my close shave with Herne, then laughed with delight when I told her how the Supervisor had been so certain that he'd caught me red-handed and looked so disappointed when he failed to find anything but ale. Best of all, we agreed, was knowing that he thought his informant, who we knew to be Tom, had proved to be so unreliable.

The next few weeks went quietly enough and whilst I rested on the first day, still recovering from my travels, on the second afternoon we sat in the bar and I began to teach Adie to read and write. Sat at a table, I thought of my first lessons with Mr Deeming, but not possessing a slate, I found a piece of paper and using a pencil, wrote a b c d e, then asked Adie to copy them – and that's where my problems started.

Adie had said she wanted to learn, but when she could see her first effort, though recognisable, was very different from mine and several more attempts brought little improvement, I could tell she was getting frustrated. So I decided to leave things until the next afternoon, but it made no difference because, even though I tried different letters and capitals, her copies still didn't look anything like mine. After almost a week, Adie wanted to give up and I didn't know how I could help her. Not knowing what else to do, I decided that the next day we should try reading. Sitting side by side at our usual table, this time I'd brought from my bedroom the big old Bible Mr Dodds had left me when he died. I decided the Bible would be the best place to start because I knew Adie would know many of the stories. So I asked her what her favourite Bible story was. She thought for a moment and said,

"The Good Samaritan," she smiled and added, "because he reminds me of you."

I knew that wasn't true. I was very far from being a Samaritan of any sort, but I returned her smile and turned the pages of the huge book to Luke's Gospel and found the story she'd asked for. I thought it best if on that first occasion I read the story slowly, running my finger along the words as I read so she could follow.

As I read, Adie followed closely. So when I finished, I suggested I read it again, but that this time she tried to follow with her own finger. Whether it helped her learn to read I don't know, but it did solve the problem that was stopping her learning to write. As I read, I saw Adie was following quite closely with her finger – though she couldn't read she clearly recognised a lot of the letters and words she was hearing – but I was struck by something strange. So stopping, I said,

"I can see your following quite well, but you're using your left hand. I thought you were right-handed?"

It was as if the paper had suddenly become red hot to her left hand and she quickly changed to her right.

"I'm sorry Jabez, I just forgot."

She looked far more worried than she should, so I asked her,

"Are you really left-handed?"

"No, I'm right-handed. I used my left to do things when I was really young, but my mother told me that was wrong and made sure I always used my right – as I said, I just forgot."

I said nothing but got up and fetched another piece of paper and a pencil. Like before, I wrote the first five letters of the alphabet and asked Adie to copy them, but this time to use her left hand. Looking at me suspiciously, she said,

"But it's wrong. Mother told me, it's evil to be left-handed."

I'd heard this old superstition before, but I knew that's all it was, an old suspicion. So that's what I told her, adding,

"Anyway, there's no one else here except you and me, so why not give it a try?"

Shrugging her shoulders, she picked up the pencil in her left hand and started to copy the letters. As soon as she picked up the pencil, I could see she held it more easily and when she'd finished copying the letters and sat back, we could both see the improvement. Turning the paper over, I showed her some of the previous week's efforts.

"Still think that being left-handed is evil?"

I smiled when I said it, but she scowled and said,

"Just give me the next five, will you?"

Of course she copied these as easily as the first five and would have carried on with the rest had our first customers not started knocking loudly, keen to get their first pint.

Next morning, she raced round getting her jobs done as quickly as she could, chivvying me to get mine done more quickly and helping me as soon as hers were done. When we were finished, she rushed and got the pencil and paper we'd been using the day before, sat at a table and said,

"Right then Jabez. Let's have the next five letters."

I did as she asked, pleased to see the transformation in her enthusiasm. Watching her copy, hesitating only a moment as she took in the shape of the *k*, I was just as pleased to see how quickly her confidence had grown. We worked on the alphabet for the rest of the morning and in the afternoon once again, read and re-read the story of the Good Samaritan.

For several weeks, life went on in very much the same vein. Our days were spent with Adie learning to read and write, our evenings serving my regular customers and, because for several weeks we heard nothing from Sam Baker, our nights sleeping. Over what must have been six or seven weeks, Adie made good progress and had grasped some basic writing skills. For example, she could write her name with great confidence. She also began to read parts of the Good Samaritan, although remembering Ben Camden's failed attempt to deceive Mr Deeming, I did wonder how much she read and how much she'd memorised. But I never had a chance to find out, because one day, out of the blue, there was a knock at the back door and when I answered, there stood Sam Baker.

Pushing past me, he led the way back to the bar, where barely acknowledging Adie's greeting, he turned to me and said,

"I need those other six barrels you had made. I can't get the six back from Manchester. The Supervisor has the place watched night and day. He's still suspicious about your delivery there, you know. I hear he's got an informer who keeps insisting you were delivering salt."

He must have seen the questioning look on my face because he added,

"You have still got them, haven't you?"

That wasn't the problem.

160

"Yes Sam, I've still got them. It's just that Harry and John haven't been paid for any of them yet."

"Nor has Jabez."

Adie was sitting quietly and listening. She had been trying to write 'the Boars Head' when we'd been interrupted, but now she was clearly keen to hear his reply.

Sam looked preoccupied but he said,

"Yes, you're right Jabez." Half turning to Adie, he added, "You both are."

"I'll tell you what we'll do. I'm going to come back tonight after you close and I want you to have put the barrels in the stable. When I come, I'll pay you in full for all twelve. Agreed?"

He didn't wait for an answer but rapidly made for the door and as I heard it shut, I breathed,

"Agreed."

Turning to Adie, I said,

"Right, I think we should get the barrels moved before we open. By the sound of it, we won't have much time after we close."

As the barrels were empty, between us we rolled them quickly into the stable. The evening was quiet, but Harry and John were in and delighted when I told them I would be able to pay them in the morning. As expected, Sam turned up about half an hour before I shut. With him was a man I didn't recognise but I assumed was from his gang.

As soon as all my other customers had left and I'd locked up, Sam paid me for the barrels. As promised, he paid me twice the amount due and though I hadn't asked, he also paid me double for taking the salt to Manchester. Then, after confirming with me they were in the stable, Sam and his companion slipped out the back, took the remaining barrels and were gone.

We hadn't seen or heard from Sam in over two months and we had no reason to expect to see him again for another two. So when, just three days after he collected the barrels, I answered a loud knocking at the front door, I was startled to be confronted by a very angry Sam. The metal bar he held looked threatening and its purpose plain, though I had no idea how I'd angered him. But the anticipated blow never came and in a moment, the real purpose of the bar became clear. When I opened the door, I'd seen only Sam and the bar he was holding, but now, standing a couple of yards to one side of him, was a barrel and I knew it could only be one of mine. Turning to it, he said,

"I thought this barrel was supposed to keep the salt and beer apart."

I realised then the real purpose of the bar because, not waiting for a reply he put its flattened end, something I previously hadn't noticed, under the lid of the barrel and prising it away, grabbed a handful of salt.

"Look at this stuff."

He opened his hand revealing a brown, grainy mess that had the familiar ale smell. I was fast catching up and it wasn't difficult to guess what had happened. But Sam made sure I was in no doubt.

"You told me they wouldn't leak and I delivered this one along with the rest. This morning it was brought back and as you can see, the salt is ruined."

It didn't seem necessary to tell him he'd already proved that point, but he hadn't finished.

"My buyer was so angry. He risked travelling in broad daylight all the way from Chester to bring it back. Now I've got to replace it by tomorrow morning or he'll make trouble for me, he's promised me that, and I don't doubt him. Now, how do you think I'm going to get a replacement while that Excise man is snapping at my heels?"

Because he'd talked from the moment I'd opened the door, I'd had time to think. So after apologising, I asked him to wait and with Adie's help (although she'd stayed in the bar, she'd heard every word) fetched the first barrel John had made, knowing it had an advantage over all the others. Rolling it out the front, I stood it on end and said,

"This is the barrel I had made to show you Adie's idea and if you remember, we tested it in front of you to prove it was leak-proof."

In his rage, he'd clearly forgotten about this other barrel and though still angry, he realised it gave him a solution to his problem. Apparently remembering for the first time that I still had his mare, though he must have seen her when he'd collected the six barrels from the stable, he told me to bring her round and secure the barrel to her. I did as he said and then, without another word, he rode off. As I watched him gallop away, I realised he'd left me with the barrel of ruined salt; something I'd find very hard to explain, should the Excise Supervisor come looking. So with Adie's help, I quickly put it in the furthest and darkest corner of the cellar, promising myself I'd destroy it just as soon as things quietened down.

But things didn't quieten down, because two days rather than two months later, word came that Sam was on the run along with several of his gang. The night after he'd collected the barrel, one of his men had set off to take it, now full of salt, to his Chester buyer. He had gone barely a mile when, turning a corner, he ran straight into Herne and his men; he said he thought they were waiting for him. Because he'd heard about my delivery to Manchester, even though he'd been stopped, he was still quite confident and had expected to go through the same routine. Herne told him to untie the barrel from the mare, but that was where things changed. Instead of telling him to open the tap, Herne stepped forward. He had a bar in his hand that sounded much like Sam's and without hesitating he wrenched the lid off the barrel.

Of course, he found the salt straight away and arrested the man, but what Sam didn't understand was how they knew where to wait for him. It was a bigger mystery that Herne knew how to find the salt. Word was that Sam believed someone in the Manchester factory, or even John or Harry, had told Herne about the barrels. Of course I knew that Tom Rider was almost certainly behind Herne's discovery, but what I didn't understand was why he hadn't raided the Boar; I was sure it could only be a matter of time.

At first nothing happened, giving Adie and me time to talk. We agreed that we must expect a raid at any time and when that happened, planned what we would do and say, especially if one or both of us got arrested. I knew there was something we should do, but previous experience made me hold back. But after a week, rumours started to spread from the Nantwich pans about the Manchester factory, and when on Friday night the Boar was full of talk of the Excise's raid on the factory, I knew I couldn't wait any longer.

As soon as the Boar was empty and I'd locked up, I told Adie to stop clearing the bar and to join me at a table. This time, I wasn't nervous or embarrassed. I knew what I had to say was for the best. So wasting no time, I told her exactly what was on my mind.

"Adie, I've been thinking. I know you refused me when I asked you to marry me, but I think that was because I asked you for the wrong reasons."

I knew I had my own reasons for asking her again, but for the time being, I kept them to myself. I just hoped she'd accept the reasons I gave her.

"But now I think it's really important for both of us that we marry."

She looked at me suspiciously, but I pressed on because I knew we needed to marry before we were arrested and I knew that was likely to happen soon.

"We both know we're likely to be raided at any time. If we're arrested but already married, we can't be made to give evidence against each other. But we need to do it quickly. If you agree, I'll go and see Reverend Grace in the morning and see if he'll marry us tomorrow afternoon."

She looked at me long and hard and then said,

"So I couldn't be made to speak against you?"

"Nor me against you, not if we were married."

"I didn't know that."

Again she stared at me. I wanted to prompt her, give her more reasons to say yes, but something made me wait for her reply; I was so glad I did.

"Why should we wait until tomorrow afternoon? If I go with you in the morning, why can't we get him to marry us straight away?"

I felt only relief. I'd clearly persuaded her that we had good reason to marry and she hadn't suspected my real motives.

In the morning, we both dressed as well as we could and set off for the village. I had on the clothes I'd bought for Mr Dodds' funeral, which may have been alright when I was in my early twenties, but were now decidedly ill-fitting – and in the most unlikely ways. My shoes, which I expected to fit if nothing else did, I managed to squeeze on but was unable to tie, my feet clearly having swollen after so many years of standing behind a bar. I knew my waist had expanded over the years, so I expected my breeches to give me the greatest difficulty. But the waist button fastened quite easily. The problem was that my thighs had thickened, making it difficult to keep the legs of the breeches over my knees. My waistcoat also rode up, but I told myself that was the modern fashion.

For Adie, it was easier. She only owned two smocks and two dresses, one dress she wore in the day and one she wore behind the bar in the evening. Since she believed her evening-wear bore less stains and tears, and there was no good reason why I should disagree, that was the one she chose to wear to our wedding.

We hurried towards the village, hoping we wouldn't be seen but knowing that was unlikely. In fact, although we were hailed by a couple of Boar regulars who, nudging each other, pointed and laughed at the way we were dressed, we were almost at the church before we saw anyone else we knew. But then we saw the very last person we wanted to see, someone who stopped us in our tracks. Emerging from the same gennel that Adie had run from that first time we met, was the man who had been chasing her on that occasion.

Seeing us, Tom stopped and so did Adie. I knew she wanted to say something to him, but I also knew it was more important we completed the task we'd set out to perform and even more so because I was more certain than ever that Tom was the Excise Supervisor's informant. Without a word, I put my arm around her shoulders and steered Adie along the Church path.

Before we left the Boar, I had wondered whether Reverend Grace would be in the church so early and now wonder turned to hope because, if he guessed what we were doing, I didn't want Tom alerting the Excise Supervisor before we were married – Herne was certain to try to stop us.

When we entered the church, hope turned to despair. Though gloomy, the church was so small that I could see all of it. Eight rows of pews, unevenly divided so that six could sit together on one side but only two on the other, sat between plain white walls and were fronted by a baptismal font and a lectern. Behind the lectern, where Reverend Grace would make his fiery sermons and to his and the lecterns side stood the church's only other notable feature, an ancient organ, said to be older than the church itself.

I smiled to myself, remembering how Adie had said I sounded like that organ's wheezing bellows, when she'd run into me on the first occasion we met. But the smile was fleeting as it appeared we were the only ones there. I was about to suggest to Adie that we had no choice but to sit and wait for Reverend Grace to arrive, when movement at the far end of the larger front pew caught my eye. As I turned, Reverend Grace stood up and looked at us – clearly, he'd been on his knees praying and from the back of the church couldn't be seen. In the pulpit, he had a fearsome reputation for breathing fire and brimstone, but when he spoke, although still brusque, he sounded welcoming.

"Good morning, Jabez, Admonition." He gave a small nod towards Adie. "I was wondering when you two would come to see me."

Although he was never seen in the Boar, the church was the villagers' main centre of conversation and gossip, so it was hardly surprising that Reverend Grace had learnt that Adie was living at the Boar. Exactly what he'd heard and what he made of it was about to become clear.

"And you want me to marry the two of you and by the look of things, in a hurry as well. So I suppose there's a baby on the way, is there?"

Adie was quicker to react than me.

"No, it's nothing like that. Well, we do want to get married, but not because I'm having a baby."

As we talked, the vicar reached us.

"But I'm right you're in a hurry, yes?" Adie nodded. "So why is that then?"

Adie hesitated because she knew she couldn't tell him the truth. Quickly, I said,

"Because we're tired of all the gossip. I want to make an honest woman of her."

I could see he didn't believe me. He knew there must be something else, but I could also tell he *wanted* to see us married.

"We hoped you could marry us this morning. We thought that way we could have a quiet service and no one need know until it's over."

With a resigned smile, he said,

"Very well then. I need to change into my vestments and I need to be clear in an hour for our morning service. I suggest I re-join you here in about ten minutes."

So that was that. I'd judged him correctly and ten minutes later, we met Reverend Grace at the lectern and in another ten, he had joined us in matrimony.

As we left, Adie suddenly took my arm and whispered,

"Let's walk like newly-weds."

She pulled in closer and I wondered if the marriage ceremony had affected her. For no reason I could really explain, I looked behind me and then understood her sudden change of mood. Tom hadn't followed us into the church, but must have remained at the end of the gennel waiting for us to reappear. I had failed to notice he was there when we left the church because I was keen to return to the Boar – there was something I needed to do. I told Adie to ignore him and explained why we needed to get back. Adie paled and though she didn't release my arm, she did start walking much faster. Looking back over my shoulder one last time, I was left with the haunting image of Tom grinning at me and as we walked, I thought how in all the years I'd known him, I had never even seen him smile. He must have guessed the reason we were in the church and that should have made him very angry, so the question I kept asking myself was what was making him grin now?

I didn't have to wait long for an answer, because when we returned to the Boar, everything became very clear.

Four of them: Herne, his two men and Dick Sweetman were all gathered around the Inn's front door. As we got nearer, they stepped back two or three paces and I could see that between them, they were holding a large piece of tree trunk and were about to use it as a battering ram. Detaching myself from Adie and breaking into a trot, I shouted,

"What the hell do you think you're doing?"

Of course, I knew exactly what they were doing. They were about to break down my front door, but I hoped hearing me made them hesitate long enough to allow me to reach them. Herne looked annoyed, as turning to me, he said,

"I want to see your cellar. Let us in and we'll find our own way, you and your wife, I suppose that's what I have to call her now, can stay out here with Sweetman."

He didn't appear to realise, or maybe didn't care, but he'd just confirmed that Tom was his informer – his only thought was to get inside the Boar. I unlocked and open the door and he pushed past me, but before he and his men disappeared, he turned to Sweetman and said grimly,

"I'm expecting them to be here when I come out. I'll hold you to blame if they're not, understood?"

He didn't wait for a reply. Instead, he and his men made their way inside. All Adie and I could do was wait for them to reappear. We stood there in silence for what seemed like forever, but probably was not more than twenty minutes, not daring to look at one another in case we somehow gave ourselves away; we both knew what was in the cellar and we didn't want Herne to find it.

Herne and one of his men reappeared first, and from his thunderous look I knew their search had proved fruitless. I expected the second man to be right behind them, but he failed to appear; Herne looked back. He clearly had no idea what was keeping him, but then we all heard the urgent call and Herne and his man rushed back inside. Reappearing shortly after, he was followed closely by both of his men, carrying between them what I knew to be the barrel that had leaked. They put it down and removed the lid so that Herne could lean over and take out a handful of the ruined salt. Holding out his hand, the salt falling from between his fingers, he asked,

"And how do you explain this then, Payne?"

I already knew if the barrel was found, there was little I could say that would help me, so I remained silent.

"Well, nothing to say for yourself, eh? Sweetman, go and fetch the cart. I'm putting them both under arrest."

That wasn't part of my plan.

"You can't arrest Adie. She's had nothing to do with it. She's never even seen that barrel."

He gave me a knowing smile and said,

"I was told you might say something like that. What you say might be true, but I doubt it – we'll just have to let a judge and jury decide. Sweetman, I told you to fetch the cart!"

Richard Sweetman, who had been transfixed since Herne and his two men reappeared, was startled into action. Hurrying round to the orchard, he came back quickly, leading the horse and cart. Herne opened the back of the cart and with a sarcastically polite gesture of his hand, invited us to step up. I made one last, desperate attempt to stop him taking Adie.

"Herne, you're making a mistake. I told you she had nothing to do with it. Let her go and I'll confess. You won't even need to convince a jury."

Herne wavered. I think he was almost persuaded, but then Adie, who had said nothing since we arrived at the inn, ruined everything.

"That's not true. I've known about Jabez' work for as long as I've lived here. I even came up with the idea for the barrel."

Turning to me, she said,

"I'm sorry Jabez. You're a kind man and I know what you're trying to do, but it's not fair. I can't let you take all the blame."

With that, she stepped up onto the cart. Grasping my arm, Herne pressed me to follow. His men lifted the barrel up behind me and driven by a triumphant Herne, we were taken into Nantwich. Adie was taken down from the cart and put into the small gaol they have there, whilst I had to endure a much longer journey. A full two hours later, I was finally placed here in Northgate gaol.

Part Four

Henry
Articles of Faith

In 1748, I began five years as an Articled Clerk. Father paid Mr Dowle one hundred and fifty guineas to take me on. He could have found me a post for much less, but as he said when I baulked at the price,

"Dowle, Anderson and Risk has the best reputation in the County and, in law these days, nothing is more important."

I'd met Jane that first Christmas when we were both at Lord Delamere's Christmas Ball; she'd come with her parents, whilst I was there with Mr Dowle to represent the firm. We began courting about a year after we first met and though we were hesitant at first, both with little experience of the opposite sex, as time went by, we gradually fell in love.

When I asked Jane to marry me, I added that of course, if she said yes, we would have to wait until I was qualified and could afford the responsibilities of marriage. Jane said she would be glad to marry me however poor we were and that she believed the real values of marriage were without price. I've often reflected that if only it were possible, Jane should have made a wonderful lawyer; with just a few words she could go straight to the heart of a matter and stop you in your tracks, or at times like this, also go straight to the heart without even trying.

She'd taken my breath away, but gathering myself, I told her that if we married now, we should not get the approval of my employer, without which I might never complete my Articles. I said I could just hear Frederick Dowle (although I could never bring myself to actually call him by his first name) pronounce on the matter.

"Mark my words, my boy, a lawyer should marry; a good wife provides support and eases the load the job carries, but a Clerk should concentrate on his studies without distractions, particularly those of a wife."

Jane smiled at my poor imitation of Dowle, yet I knew her smile was a brave one. She still agreed to marry me, but we both knew two and a half years was a long time. Still, it helped that we had the approval of Jane's father, because he believed I thought enough of his daughter to wait until I could afford to keep her before contemplating marriage. Neither of us told him that wasn't quite the whole truth, but it seemed close enough, and in no time he was treating me with great familiarity. Jane had been an only child, born to Mrs Waverley when she was forty and Mr Waverley forty-eight, long after they had given up hope of ever having children. So now the thought that there was someone he could treat as a son, coupled with the prospect of grandchildren in his dotage, made Mr Waverley's life complete.

At first, I wasn't at all sure that Mrs Waverley also approved of our proposed union. I asked Mr Waverley for his permission to marry Jane, but unconventionally I asked him when all four of us were together. I was unsure whether Mrs Waverley approved because she said nothing, rather she got up, went straight to their piano and started playing. She was apparently ignored by Jane and her father and I tried to concentrate on Mr Waverley's response, but I must admit I was disquieted.

Jane laughed when, later, I told her of my anxiety.

"You fussock! Mum was hiding a tear." Then, more quietly she added, "I spoke to her as soon as you left and she told me she was very happy and sure you would make a good, if a little too serious, husband."

I wasn't sure I liked being called a fussock, but then she added,

"Didn't you hear what she was playing?"

I must have looked puzzled and so, still smiling, she explained,

"It was Mr Bach's 'Ou du Liebe meiner Liebe'"

My expression must have remained unchanged; my musical knowledge was almost as bad as my German.

Exasperated, she said,

"It means, 'Oh, you love my love'."

Finally I understood. We definitely had the blessings of both her parents and yes, I had to admit, perhaps I was something of a potato pudding.

We married five months after I qualified, and two after I was made junior attorney with Dowle, Anderson and Risk.

Now I don't like to talk about someone's death bringing me good fortune, as with undertakers, it doesn't sit well with the legal profession; but in my case it really is the unavoidable truth. All three partners were venerable. But as Thomas Risk was the youngest and most sprightly, his sudden death, they say his heart gave way, was wholly unexpected.

A period of mourning and respect was appropriate, as was the manner in which the completion of my Articles three months after Risk's death went by almost unnoticed. I had a small celebration with Jane and her parents, but other than that, I just kept working and wondering. My anxiety came to an end three months later at the end of February when Mr Dowle asked me to step into his office.

Mr Dowle was a large, corpulent man with a thunderous voice to match. These characteristics he made into qualities and employed them all to command staff, clients and courts to equally good effect. There was never any courtroom rowdiness when Frederick Dowle QC was on his feet – unless, of course, he orchestrated it.

His office was similarly commanding. A large room, it had oak floors, an inglenook fire and oak panelled walls, all of which framed an enormous mahogany desk. The only other items present were his chair, made comfortable by two cushions stuffed with goose feathers, a further chair for his clients (without cushions), shelves from floor to ceiling containing his books of law and rolls of case papers on one wall, and on his desk a rack of quills, a lamp, his seal and sealing wax. To complete the room, on the wall above his chair and looking suitably severe, a large imposing portrait of Dowle himself kept close scrutiny over all. Light came only from the fire, which burned in all but the hottest months and the desk lamp that struggled valiantly to provided sufficient light for Mr Dowle to read or write. He saw no reason to provide further illumination for his clients, saying that most couldn't read, certainly not legal documents, and the few exceptions could always move closer to the fire. The result was cavernous and intimidating and this was clearly his intention.

As always, he wasted no time.

"Six months since Risk died, a great shock, a very great shock."

Then he seemed to stiffen, become resolute.

"But six months' mourning should be long enough."

He paused and then added,

"Don't you agree?"

Now he looked straight at me. Normally, Mr Dowle's speech contained only demands, instructions or pronouncements; he never sought advice nor counsel and only asked questions to extract information or for clarification. Even now, he remained brusque and to the point.

Although I realised the question was largely rhetorical, I sensed Dowle had been shaken to his foundations by Risk's death – I suppose he couldn't quite avoid his own mortality whilst I couldn't avoid his question. So, taken by surprise and without forethought, I replied,

"Mr Risk is in his grave, sir, and I think our clients will want us to be concentrating on keeping them out of theirs."

Dowle's face darkened. I looked down and stared at a knot in the floor and thought how five years learning my trade should have taught me better. I expected the worst, but what he told me next taught me something that has ruled my life as a lawyer to this day.

When he spoke, Dowle's voice was calm.

"I must agree with you, Carlyle. What's more? I think Risk would have agreed as well. I want you to remember this conversation now you're a lawyer, because in this profession you're going to hear many half-truths, lies and especially from prosecutors, lies dressed up as truth – and it's going to be your job to expose them for what they are. To do that and to do it well, you will always need to act as you just did and say what you believe to be the truth at all times, no matter what you fear the consequences may be."

So that was it. You could have forgiven me for missing it, but I had just become a lawyer. When I left Dowle's office, I was met by Mr Anderson who explained that since Risk's death, a backlog of minor cases had built up. If left long enough, he added, the trivial had a habit of becoming important. He went on to tell me that an affidavit confirming I had completed my Articles would be filed with Chester Court at the beginning of April. It was to be my job to tie up any loose ends, either in Court or on paper.

But more significantly, I now received sufficient remuneration to marry. It wasn't a king's ransom, but it was enough to support a careful wife. So Jane, who saw prudence as one of life's greatest virtues, and I were married and I'm pleased to say that Jane's parents lived long enough to know and enjoy both of their grandchildren.

Jabez
Planning and Preparation

I'd hoped Adie wouldn't be arrested, but now that she had, it was more important than ever I put into place the rest of my plan.

Arriving in Chester, I spent a sleepless night in a cell with about twenty others. Some like me were awaiting trial – the circuit judge wasn't due for a month – and some already sentenced, including two who were completely mad, a few awaiting transfer to a hulk and some of those for onward transfer to a ship bound for New Holland. Carved from rock, the cell was windowless, so unsurprisingly, the air was foul. But it was neither the condition of the cell, nor the nature of my fellow inmates that led me next morning, to give the warder almost all of the money I had in a purse hidden inside my blouse.

Although I was still wearing my wedding attire and I'm sure looked ridiculous, I didn't pay him to supply me with a change of clothes. It was both more urgent and important that I had the privacy of a solitary cell. In addition, I needed paper, quill and ink so that I could write a number of letters.

It took almost all morning to arrange, but by midday I had been moved to a cell on my own and not only been provided with writing implements but also a desk, a chair and a lamp to see by – though there was a small window high in the wall, it provided almost no light. I'd clearly paid the warder more than I needed to and I suppose he thought that by providing me with a little more than I asked, I might be encouraged to spend even more – little was he to know that I had barely enough money left to buy food for a day or two. Still, I hoped that my first letter would help ease that problem.

I'd avoided the legal profession most of my life, like most people, I thought lawyers weren't to be trusted. But now I needed one and there was only one I knew and thought I might be able to trust. Not long before he died, Mr Dodds had a young lawyer called Henry Carlyle draw up his Will, leaving everything to me. I was young, barely twenty-two, when Dodds died and I am sure a clever lawyer could have used my youth to rob me blind. But Carlyle was straight with me. I received everything I was due and his bill for executing the Will was reasonable. So the first letter I wrote was to Carlyle, reminding him of his involvement in Dodds' Will, explaining my current predicament and asking him to represent me. If he agreed, I requested he visited me at his very earliest convenience. While we were planning what we would do if we were both arrested, I had told Adie I would arrange for a lawyer to represent her. I reminded her of this in the second letter and said I would arrange a lawyer to act on her behalf over the next day or two. I gave both letters to the warder who, of course for further reimbursement, said he would arrange delivery. I had two more letters to write and though no less important, they were less urgent.

For the remainder of the afternoon, I rested. In fact as it grew dark, I fell asleep and only woke when the warder brought me the victuals and lamp oil I'd paid him for with the last of my money. I ate a little of my food in the dark before refilling and lighting my lamp. I then started to write the first of the remaining letters. The second had to wait as it was to Carlyle if he agreed to represent me.

I wrote long into the night and the lamp was burning low when I finished, but I was glad it was done because now I only needed to wait for Carlyle's response. Only if he was agreeable would I have reason to write that fourth letter.

Henry
A Foregone Conclusion

Dowle and Anderson both died within five years of Risk's demise. The firm has since undergone little change, because after Risk's death, Dowle's son Charles was made a partner and, upon the death of his father, became the senior partner. He made it clear that the firm's reputation for fairness and incorruptibility built by his father was one he was determined to maintain. Two years ago, after James Smith, one of the five partners in a now expanded firm, left to form his own partnership with his brother, Charles invited me to replace him.

And so it was that as a partner in the firm I began to defend clients who could, and in many cases definitely would, face the death penalty if found guilty. In some cases, the judge, in exchange for a guilty plea, could be persuaded that the value of a theft was less than five shillings and shouldn't carry the ultimate penalty. Instead, they would usually receive a lengthy gaol sentence or spend some years in the colonies. In more and more cases, barristers are trying to persuade judges that the alleged crime involved property worth less than five shillings and should be heard in a Church Court – a Church Court, of course, cannot pass a death sentence. Even in the quarterly Assizes when the death penalty is passed, it is usual for the client's lawyer to petition the King for clemency and except for the most heinous crimes, is usually commuted to a life sentence. I expected no other outcome when I received a letter asking me to defend a local publican.

Jabez Payne and his wife had both been charged with salt smuggling and although the evidence against them was pretty conclusive, I expected both would eventually face seven years, perhaps longer, in New Holland. That, after all, was the typical sentence. But Jabez and his wife weren't a typical couple and neither was their punishment.

Jabez stood impassively as the judge donned his black cap.

Of course, once Jabez was declared guilty as charged, the sentence was inevitable. I had expected the jury to find him guilty, but hoped I had persuaded them it should be for a lesser crime, but with the evidence against him so strong, I could see only two ways of affecting the outcome. Bernshaw, the prosecutor presented only two witnesses; unfortunately they were both key.

The Excise Supervisor told how he'd suspected Jabez' involvement in salt smuggling for some time, but that in the end it was by chance they'd found the barrel of ruined salt in the Boar's Head. He said that when he asked Jabez to tell him why it was in his cellar, he offered no explanation. Prompted by Bernshaw, he added that the barrel was exactly the same as the one found in the possession of a member of the Nantwich gang.

When I questioned him, I didn't trouble too much with the detail of his find. It was pretty clear Jabez had been caught red-handed. Jabez warned me this man was very confident and had the full backing of his employers – my intention was to prove him over-confidant. So after a few preliminaries, I followed a different line.

"Mr Herne, could you tell the court the true value of the salt you allege you found in my client's possession?"

There was a definite smirk on his face as Herne replied,

"It's no allegation, as you call it. We found the salt in his cellar, hidden in a barrel. We weighed it there and then and it came to nigh on five bushels. That's worth a bit over fifty shillings."

This raised a lively reaction from the public gallery as well as some of the jurymen. I had noted the jury was particularly boisterous from the moment Jabez was brought into the dock. It was risky but as old Dowle used to say, a lively jury can be a persuadable jury, so I decided to try and use their mood. According to Dowle, gain their sympathy and then you might persuade a jury that the value of a crime is less than five shillings and your client could claim Benefit of Clergy, thereby allowing the case to be heard in a Church Court. It was mandatory for any other court to impose a death penalty where the proceeds were worth more than just five shillings and a Church Court never tried a case concerning goods valued at more than five shillings. I had an idea I might be able to persuade a jury that a sack of salt was worth less than fifty shillings, but I didn't think even Frederick Dowle, at his imperious best, could have persuaded a jury that a fifty-shilling bag of salt was worth less than five bob.

So I took Herne to what I wanted the Jury to see.

"Remember, Mr Herne, I didn't ask you where you found it. I asked you what the true value of the salt was."

He seemed to relax; he was obviously dealing with a fool. In a disparaging tone, he said,

"And I told you, it was over fifty shillings. I told you where I found it because I just thought the jury would like to be reminded how cunning this man is."

He waived a dismissive hand in Jabez' direction, but I just looked at him fixedly and struck.

"I know what you told me, Mr Herne. Perhaps you should have concentrated on my question because, even though I've asked you twice and, forgive me, I think it's quite a simple question, you still don't seem to understand."

Before he could speak, I went on.

"So let me help you. If the tax on salt was one hundred percent, would it change the real value of the salt? Would it make any difference if it was five hundred percent? It's over three thousand five hundred percent as it is at the moment, Mr Herne, so does that change its real value?"

Murmurs from the gallery, and more importantly from a few of the jury, told me some were beginning to understand how I was proceeding, so I continued,

"You looked bewildered, Mr Herne, so let me explain. Without the tax, which has absolutely nothing to do with the real value of the salt but goes up and down and let's face it mostly up, at the whim of the government, the salt is worth barely one and six.

Do you understand me *now*, Mr Herne? I'll put it to you again. Would you agree with me that the salt you found at my client's property, far from being worth fifty shillings in reality, was worth less than two shillings?"

In reply, I can say only that Herne gibbered. He seemed to have lost the ability to construct a cohesive sentence. Not wanting to miss the chance now offered, I changed tack.

"You told us you found the salt in a barrel hidden at the back of my client's cellar. Is that correct?"

Like my first, he knew this was a simple question; he also knew what had just happened when he answered the first one. So, no longer the confident Excise Supervisor, used to being obeyed, used to everyone hanging on his every word, he hesitated. I knew I had to keep working the wound.

"Come on, Mr Herne. I just want you to confirm that you found the salt in a barrel at the back of the Boar's cellar. How hard can that be to answer?"

Some in the gallery laughed and I could see the jury settling back in their seats; they'd enjoyed the previous exchange and they were looking forward to this one, wherever it might go, or more correctly, wherever I may take it.

Herne rallied a little; some of his bravado returned.

"Of course, I've already said that. I'm just wondering what clever lawyer point you're going to make out of it."

I tried to look as though he'd hurt my feelings.

"I'm sorry you feel like that, Mr Herne. I rather thought my questions were straightforward."

I didn't give him time to answer.

"So we've established that you found one barrel of salt hidden away at the back of my client's cellar. Tell me, when you examined it, what was the condition of the salt?"

I could see he was ready with his answer.

"I've already explained. It was ruined and that's why it hadn't been delivered."

I wasn't going to let him get away with that.

"'It hadn't been delivered.' So where, in your opinion, was its planned destination?"

I knew he couldn't possibly know, but I'd forgotten one thing.

"I couldn't say."

That was the answer I wanted – or thought I did.

"Well, if you couldn't say, don't you think you *shouldn't* say – this is a Court of Law, after all. We're looking for facts, not supposition."

He looked triumphant. I didn't know why; I was about to find out. Herne drew himself up to his full height and said,

"I don't know about that, but if you want facts, it's a *fact* that the six barrels we discovered last week in Manchester were all made to the same design as the one found in Payne's cellar; it's a *fact* that in addition to salt, they all had a little beer left in them and it's a *fact* that three months ago I stopped Payne when he was delivering six barrels, apparently containing only beer but which must have been the same six that I had just discovered.

So there's some facts for you and I think they're facts that prove Payne's as guilty as Baker – and he's as guilty as Satan."

This was new to me, I'd heard about the raid in Manchester but the details of what had been discovered had been unclear. I knew I'd made a mistake because now, in addition to the single barrel in his cellar, Jabez was being tied to a further six found in Manchester. I could have pointed out that there was no proven link, but that would only serve to emphasise for the jury how *likely* it was that there was a link. So I knew there was little I could do other than get this man off the stand as quickly as possible and hope to make enough of the prosecutor's second witness to make the jury forget Herne. So with the sound of the gallery and the jury drawing their own conclusions in the background, I told the judge I had no further questions.

Herne's triumphant look as he left the stand was matched by Bernshaw, and I'm certain as his second witness took the stand, the lawyer believed he'd have the same success with him – from his opening line of questioning, it was clear he expected to keep the Court's sympathy.

Thin and dishevelled, wearing little more than rags, Tom Rider was a pitiful sight – and Bernshaw knew it. He got Rider to tell the jury how he and his wife took in Admonition and her brother William after the rest of their family were killed. Then he encouraged him to explain how he allowed William to work with him in the salt pans until, without any warning, the boy up and left. Finally, he played his trump card.

"Mr Rider, can you tell the court, are you working now?"

Almost with a sense of pride, he replied,

"I haven't been able to work for over a year. Me and Liz bin relying on the Parish to keep us from starving."

"I'm sorry to hear that, Mr Rider."

Bernshaw glanced at the jury to make sure he had their full attention for his big moment. Satisfied, with all the drama he could muster, he said,

"Could you tell the jury why you haven't been able to work?"

"I can do more than that," Rider faced the jury. "I can show 'em."

Up until then Rider had held his right hand behind his back, but now he brought it forward and held it high for the jury and the entire gallery to see. Although it appeared to be healing, the new skin that covered his hand was so thin that it failed to hide the red and angry flesh beneath, and was so taught he was unable to straighten his fingers.

Much to Bernshaw's satisfaction, there were loud gasps, particularly from the gallery, although, because Jabez had told me what had happened to Rider, I knew what to expect. I was much more interested in hearing his explanation of how and why it had happened. Having waited long enough for the full extent of Rider's injury to be absorbed by the whole court, Bernshaw indicated he should lower his hand and then asked him to explain what had happened.

Keeping his hand in clear view and looking piteously towards the jury, he began to tell his tale; although, as it turned out, he wasn't to get very far.

"After Will left, leaving me working on my own, when he could be spared, another young lad came to help me. One day, me and the boy were on the hurdles dragging salt from the pan when the boy over-balanced. He would have fallen in if I hadn't grabbed him, but as I did I slipped on the hurdle and put my hand in the hot salt and this was the result."

Once again he held up his hand for all to see.

"Still at least the boy wasn't hurt; he probably would have been killed if I hadn't been there."

A sympathetic murmur ran round the court, but for one woman sat at the back of the gallery it was too much. Hefty, ruddy-faced and with exceptionally large forearms, she was quite a formidable sight. When she called out, her voice was equally formidable.

"You're a liar, Tom Rider, and everyone should know it."

I looked questioningly at Jabez, but he just shrugged his shoulders; like me, he obviously had no idea who this woman might be. But she hadn't finished.

"The truth is, and you know it, that your hand was held in the salt as punishment for all the evil things you've done." Looking across to the jury she added, "I know because I saw it done and I know why. He's been chasing young girls and ruining marriages, that's why"

As the judge banged his gavel and threatened to have her ejected, as a final shot, she added,

"Saving my Josh indeed, just one more of his lies."

I didn't know who the woman was and she'd left before the trial concluded, so I was unable to talk to her. However, her outburst had achieved one thing, the air of sympathy towards Rider had evaporated and been replaced with hostility. I later discovered and it was clearly known by a significant number in the courtroom, that what had happened to Rider was a not uncommon punishment meted out in the salt pans to anyone they felt was guilty of a serious crime – especially against a fellow worker.

The change the woman's outburst brought about in the court's mood was patent, so now that it was my turn to cross-examine the witness, I tried to build on it.

I was sure Rider was as aware of the sudden hostility towards him as I was, so I plunged straight in with no preliminaries to see if I could catch him off guard.

"So Mr Rider, can you explain to the jury why you are the prosecution's only witness?"

Appearing untroubled, he replied,

"You're forgetting the Excise man."

"No, Mr Rider, I'm not forgetting him just as I'm not forgetting many other things. For example, I'm not forgetting that you have been using the Boar's Head for twenty years, but apparently in all that time saw nothing untoward. And I'm not forgetting that merely three months ago, you not only told the Excise that my client was selling contraband salt, but told them that it was a matter of common knowledge, yet there's no one here, other than Mr Herne, to support your story."

Looking defiant he said,

"I told 'em those things because it's the truth."

Ignoring him, I carried on; I still wanted to unsettle him if I could.

"And I'm not forgetting that it was about six months ago you fell out with my client over his wife. I'm also not forgetting that, overnight, she left your tender care to live with my client.

So, I repeat my question. If it's common knowledge that my client was dealing in smuggled salt, where are all the other witnesses?"

Of course, prosecuting counsel objected; his client 'could not be expected to answer for the number of witnesses called by the prosecution'.

His objection was upheld, but I could see I had the jury's attention and they were beginning to understand what sort of man Tom Rider was. So I first apologised to the judge but then continued.

"You're quite right, milord. It should be for prosecuting counsel to explain why they were only able to find one witness other than the Excise Supervisor. My apologies."

Ignoring the dark looks from Bernshaw, I pressed on.

"So Mr Rider, would you agree that you have been a regular customer of my client for the past twenty years?"

He thought about this and obviously decided this question was safe.

"I s'pose that's about right, yes."

"And over that time, how would you describe your relationship with my client?"

His look hardened.

"Don't know what you mean, relationship. I didn't have a relationship with him. I bought ale. He served it then I drank it. That's about it."

"And his wife, how about her? Did you have a relationship with her?"

Rider was a dowdy character, but the question seemed to raise his colour a little.

"You know I did. I took her and her brother in when the rest of their family was killed."

"Her brother, and do you know what became of him?"

"I've already explained that he left us."

"So where did he go?"

"When he left us, he said he wanted to better himself so he was going to work for Marshall's; work for those who killed the rest of his family, funny way of bettering himself if you ask me."

"He must have been pretty desperate to get away if he went to work for the people he believed killed his family. Might there be any other reason for him leaving you so suddenly?"

"Look, me and Liz did the best we could for those two and he just up and left so he could 'better himself'; ungrateful, that's what I call it."

"And is he still at Marshall's?"

"No, he hasn't been there for years. Sent us a note saying he was going to the West Indies; we haven't heard from him since."

"So you feel he let you down?"

"'Course I do. Look, when he was with us he brought a bit of money in 'cos he worked with me in the pans. But he still expected us to keep his sister when he left and she wasn't earning anything."

I was getting nowhere with this line of questioning, in fact Rider might even be regaining some sympathy. But fortunately he had just introduced for me my next line of questioning; one I hoped would give the jury even more reason not to like him, but more importantly, real cause for them to doubt his word. So I asked him,

"You felt you were owed then, didn't you? Felt Admonition owed you for her keep."

"I don't know what you mean."

His face was really red now so, sensing progress, I pressed on.

"Well then, perhaps you can explain for the jury why she left your home even more suddenly than her brother, to go and live with someone who, at the time, was more or less a complete stranger to her?"

Rider reddened as he answered.

"I couldn't tell you. Maybe he wanted a bit more than a cleaning service in return for the money he paid her."

He was angry but the anger was suppressed; I needed to provoke him a little more.

181

"I don't know what you mean, Mr Rider. Perhaps you could make yourself a little clearer; for the jury's sake, if not for mine."

From their salacious mutterings, I was sure that everyone in the court knew exactly what he meant, but I hoped to show precisely what type of man Tom Rider was and just how jealous he was of my client.

"She was still only fifteen when she moved in with him, and I reckon there must have been only one thing on his mind right from the start."

"She was old enough and there was only one thing on his mind. Is that right? Really I'd say there was only one thing on *your* mind, Mr Rider, the one thing that was on your mind when you caught her in the gennel. A completely innocent and unsuspecting girl who trusted you, but who, when there was no one else around, you told owed you – and exactly how she was going to pay.

Yes, that's right, Mr Rider. My client knows. Mrs Payne told him all about the way you treated her."

I could tell I'd achieved my aim, so in a final salvo I asked him,

"But she escaped your clutches, didn't she? And you knew you'd lost her forever, didn't you? That's why you argued with him, isn't it? And why you told the Excise he'd been smuggling salt for a long time? Why not be honest, Mr Rider, just this once? Because I'm sure it'll make you feel better. You're driven by jealousy of my client and the truth is no one can believe a word you say."

The court was in uproar. The public in the viewing area and even the jury were cheering and clapping and haranguing Rider. In fact it took the judge a full five minutes to get the courtroom back under his control and when he did, Rider was looking like death. It didn't matter that he denied everything I said; nor did it matter that the judge threatened me with contempt. The jury knew exactly what they thought of Rider and I knew that that was precisely what I wanted them to think.

As for Jabez, he just stood quietly, not saying a word. You might think he was unaffected, but I had got to know him quite well in the months he'd been waiting to go to trial, and I'm certain there was a glint of satisfaction in his eye.

Rider stepped down and left the court with the jeers of the gallery ringing in his ears. I didn't have time to dwell on my success; I had a client to defend and it was now time for me to present the case for the defence. It was a surprise to me that Jabez had agreed to take the stand without any argument, but because both sides had seen no advantage in calling Admonition, like the prosecution I had only one other witness. So before we heard from Jabez, I called Sam Jervis.

Finding Sam had been straightforward because Jabez had learnt of him from one of his customers who knew he was a regular in the Black Lion in Macclesfield – but getting him to attend court had proved more difficult. I had spent several evenings in the pub plying him with gin and ale, but even then he continued to refuse to come to court and I had resigned myself to presenting our case without him. But then, only three days before Jabez was due to appear in court, unannounced he appeared in my office. It turned out his reluctance to appear was caused by his association with Sam Baker. Though never a member of the Nantwich Gang, he had occasionally been used in the past by Baker to make deliveries and he had been worried that if he appeared in court, especially for the defence, Herne might gain a sudden interest in him. Fortunately, I don't know how, Sam Baker learnt of my request and sent Jervis a message telling him that Jabez should be supported in any way possible.

In his testimony, Jervis repeated what he'd been told by Tom Rider, and coming as it did straight after Rider stood down, it caused even greater mayhem in the court and any residual sympathy for Rider was lost. As he stepped down, I saw Jervis glance up to the gallery where someone had caught his eye. Following the line of his gaze, I saw, standing with a face like thunder, was Rider's wife, Elizabeth. She, like everyone else, now saw in Rider what we'd all seen when he was on the stand and had now been confirmed by Jervis. Lips pursed, and without a word, she turned, forced her way out of the gallery and left the court.

Finally, I turned to Jabez in the dock. I knew we couldn't win the case, but I still hoped to win the jury's sympathy.

"Mr Payne, can you tell us, how long were you the landlord of the Boar's Head?"

Jabez sucked his teeth.

"Now you're asking."

After a moment he carried on,

"Old Dodds left me the Boar in his Will. Now, when would that have been? I remember it was the same year they bought in that Enclosure Law and threw all those poor farmers off their farms. So, what's that? Twenty-five, thirty years ago; something like that."

"So were you related to Mr Dodds in some way? Is that why he left you the Inn?" I asked.

Jabez smiled.

"Not at all. I didn't have any relatives alive and so far as he knew, neither did Mr Dodds. In fact, I think that's really why he went looking for an apprentice in the first place.

And as far as I was concerned, my mother died when I was six and my father abandoned me outside a workhouse when I was seven. Luckily, the workhouse took me in. If they hadn't, I think I would've been done for."

I hoped the Jury would catch that here was someone whose life had been so wretched that he was grateful he'd been taken into a workhouse.

"So Mr Payne, perhaps you can tell us what this has to do with you becoming the landlord of the Boar's Head?"

"I was just coming to that." Jabez seemed a little irritated that he'd been interrupted.

"I'd been in the workhouse over five years when, without warning, I was instructed to pack and told I was to start work the next day as a pauper apprentice. These were the words we all dreaded to hear because where the workhouse was located, becoming a pauper apprentice for nearly all of us meant only one thing, the Manchester Mills. We'd heard all sorts of tales about those places: brutal overseers, long hours, poor food and little rest. Because they were so tired, we knew many apprentices through a moment's loss of concentration, had lost fingers, whole arms, maimed in many ways; a few had even been killed. The only other place I'd heard of someone being sent were the mines. In fact, my best friend was killed by an explosion in a North Wales copper mine."

All this background was useful for gaining sympathy and to show how Jabez had made something of himself, but I didn't want the Jury getting bored. So to move him on I asked,

"So that's how you started at the Boar?"

"That's right. Packing took little time as I didn't have much, nothing but a spare smock and a book our tutor had given me. So in the morning, after a quick breakfast, I went straight to the gate. The master was standing there with another man who I didn't recognise but who, of course, turned out to be Mr Dodds. The master spoke to me. He said,

'Thanks to the parish, for whose generosity I hope you're grateful, you've received a free education while you've been here and we've taught you to read. Mr Dodds here is looking for an apprentice to help him run his pub and he particularly wants a boy who can read, so that's why you've been chosen.

Now let me be clear. You'd better suit lad because I don't want to see you back here. Nor will Mr Deeming. (He was our tutor.), because you've been chosen his word.'

I didn't know Mr Dodds and didn't know whether I'd 'suit', but at least I wasn't going to a mill or a mine and that suited me very well."

There was a ripple of laughter. I looked around. All of the gallery and most of the Jury were listening to Jabez with rapt attention. There were only two members of the Jury, sitting together and talking to one another, who were clearly less than persuaded by Jabez' tale.

I tried not to let them unsettle me and turned again to Jabez, who was continuing his story.

"… I settled in to what was required of me. As I grew older, Mr Dodds allowed me more and more responsibility, and on the day he told me I'd completed my apprenticeship, he also gave me a copy of his Will leaving everything to me.
He died about a year later and the pub became mine."

I knew there was more he wanted to tell, but I judged the jury had heard enough to form what I hoped was a favourable opinion of Jabez; or at least the majority of them had. So I decided now was probably the right time to address the question of the salt.

"Now Mr Payne, I want you tell the court about the salt that Mr Herne says they found in your cellar."

I fully expected Jabez, as we'd agreed, to tell them he'd known nothing about it until the Excise men raided the pub. He was supposed to claim it must have been put there by someone who wanted him caught. So I was taken aback by his answer.

"It was part of a delivery but the barrel was faulty and beer spoilt the salt. It was in my cellar waiting to be destroyed."

"But you weren't aware it was there?"

I didn't know what he was doing, but he clearly wasn't following our plan – what he said next sealed his fate. Unblinking, he looked straight at me and said,

"Of course I did, it was me who put it there. I was supposed to deliver it to someone – and before you ask, I never learnt his name."

Bemused, I didn't know what to say; my client had just pleaded guilty to a capital crime. But Jabez hadn't finished and now what he was doing became clear.

"I put it down there so that Admonition didn't see it. I never let her in the cellar for any reason. I made sure she didn't see or know anything about what I was doing."

It was obvious Jabez was sacrificing himself in order to save Admonition, but he was still my client and I had a duty to do my best for him. I had thought Bernshaw might have intervened at this point, just to be sure Jabez understood what he was saying and that none of the jury had missed anything. But he just sat with the hint of a smile on his lips, listening; he knew Jabez needed no assistance in hanging himself.

So I had one last try. I knew we were going to lose but I still hoped for some mitigation.

"I think the court understands your claim that your wife took no part in the smuggling, but I don't think any of us understand why, after all those years as the landlord of the pub closest to the salt pans, *you* became involved. There must have been many opportunities over the years, so why now? Tell us, were you coerced in any way?"

In all the time he was giving evidence, this was the only time Jabez faltered. But after just a moment he replied,

"No, of course not."

I'd seen the hesitation, so I pressed him.

"So why get involved?"

"Because the pub was losing money."

He seemed resolute again.

"I did it to save the pub."

"So no one made you do it?"

"No one."

I was at a loss and didn't know what else I could do. I'd given him every chance to make his sentence a little lighter, but he'd refused the opportunity on every occasion. I told the judge I had no further questions and left it to Bernshaw to do his worst.

He knew he didn't need much more from Jabez. He really had only one question to ask him.

"I know you told Mr Carlyle you didn't know the name of the person you took the salt to. However unlikely that statement is, for now let's assume it's the truth, but you must remember where you met."

I could tell Jabez was unimpressed by this line of questioning. He looked straight at Bernshaw and said,

"Believe what you like. It's the truth I never knew the man's name. I was supposed to take the salt to a bend on the Gowy near Foulk Stapleford but I never went there. Remember the salt was spoilt."

I could tell Bernshaw was annoyed. I suspected with himself – it was an obvious answer to a predictable question. But he hadn't quite finished.

"Alright, Mr Payne. You may not know who you were taking the salt to, but you must know who delivered it to you in the first place."

Jabez had clearly anticipated this question as much as he had the first and was just as ready with his reply.

"No, I don't. I only saw the man who made the proposal to me on that one occasion. He told me he or someone he knew would leave a barrel in my stable over night with a note of the delivery location on top of it. I was instructed to never go into the stable after midnight or before I fed the donkeys in the morning."

Exasperated, Bernshaw realised he was never going to get Jabez to admit Sam Baker's involvement. His answers were too well rehearsed, but I'm sure he consoled himself in the knowledge that Jabez had confessed. He told the judge he had no further questions, but Jabez wasn't quite finished and addressing the jury he said, "I just want you all to know Admonition wasn't involved. She didn't know anything about what I was doing."

After Jabez stood down, the judge instructed the jury to consider their verdict. While we waited, I suspected it would not take them long to come to their decision. Jabez told me there were three members of the jury who sometimes drank in the Boar and who he believed were decent men, but as he said, if they spoke up, it could only make things worse for him and probably cause trouble for them. I told him that, because he had confessed, he could only hope they wouldn't lead the charge to send him to the gallows.

But Jabez' only real concern was that Admonition should not suffer the same fate as him. His emphatic instructions to me were to sacrifice him in order to try and save her, and if he should receive the death penalty, there should be no petition for clemency. When he spoke, the fiery look in his eye made it very clear he meant what he said.

"All efforts should be concentrated on Adie."

I had never before heard him call her anything but Admonition. My impression was that there marriage was one of convenience, and that may have been the case, but clearly he loved her very much. From her point of view, I think perhaps he had really been the father she yearned for.

The jury took less than five minutes to pronounce him guilty. Although the three identified by Jabez took no active part in the jury's deliberations, the two who had seemed wholly unimpressed by Jabez' story and believed his actions were treacherous were the most vociferous. The guilty verdict was unanimous and the jury made no appeal to the judge for leniency.

Following my client's instruction, I offered nothing more. With little else to consider, the judge donned his black cap and in five minutes, Jabez was being marched back to jail to be clapped in irons and await the execution of his sentence.

Elizabeth
A Dish Served Cold

He'll pay; just you wait and see. That was my only thought when I left the court; but it wouldn't be right away. That would have been too soon. I decided when he came home I'd be nice to him, tell him I didn't believe a word that woman said. I'd tell him I knew that lawyer was lying as well, just to try and save his client.

Of course, I thought no such thing. It all added up and I suppose I knew it all along. If I'd just been stronger, he'd have changed his ways or I'd have made him leave. That poor girl called me mum, the most wonderful thing she could have said to me and she asked for my permission for Heaven's sake. So I became her mum and I should have protected her. But what did I do? Just pretended it wasn't happening; I even called her a liar.

Tom's never given me a child. Seventeen years we've been married and after the first year he didn't try that hard and for the last five he hasn't tried at all. But then Adie came along. All she needed was affection and when she received it, gave it back wholeheartedly. She wanted me to be her mum and I was glad because I finally had the child I'd always wanted. For seven wonderful years, even after her brother left, we were happy and still would be if it wasn't for Tom.

But she left. I know she didn't want to go but he gave her no choice. I see that now.

He'd just come in and hadn't said a word, so I asked him.

"Well, what was the verdict?"

"Guilty."

"And his sentence?"

"Hanging."

I wasn't surprised, but I couldn't hide from the truth I'd been avoiding any longer; in two days' time, Adie faced the same charges. When I said as much to Tom, he told me I needn't worry because Jabez had taken all the blame on himself, kept insisting she didn't know anything about it.

But I could tell there was something else, something he hadn't said. Moments later, as icy fingers ran down my back, I realised what it might be.

"Tom, tell me you're not going to be a witness at Adie's trial as well."

For the first time since he'd been back, that old angry defiance returned.

"'Course I am. The agreement was that I appear for them in both trials, the Excise won't pay me if I don't."

I couldn't believe what I was hearing.

"You'd take money to see that poor girl sent to prison, or worse. I've heard plenty this morning about you I don't want to believe, but now this. How low can you sink, Tom Rider?"

Still defiant, he said,

"We need the money; you know I haven't earned a farthing since I did this."

He held his hand in front of my face.

"And as I told you, she'll be alright 'cos Jabez has taken it all on himself, claims she knew nothing about it."

He might be right, but he couldn't see it made no difference.

"I couldn't care less about the money. I'd rather end up in the workhouse than have Adie think we had anything to do with her being charged with a crime – especially one that could see her hung.

You'll tell that Bernshaw you've changed your mind or I'm leaving you."

He laughed. He actually laughed at me and then, in a tone that showed how much he despised me, said,

"Do what you want. I'm taking that money."

Of course it was an empty threat and he knew it because there was nowhere I could go. But I promised myself that if he appeared in court and Adie was found guilty, I'd find a way to get even with him, no matter what.

As things turned out, someone else took matters out of my hands.

That same night they came for him. There was a quiet knock at the door. I don't know what time it was, but it woke me from a deep sleep and I was rising to answer almost before I was awake. But as I sat on the edge of the bed pulling my shawl around me, Tom's hand grabbed my shoulder and pulled me back on to the bed. He whispered,

"Leave it Liz. They'll go away."

I'd never before heard such fear in Tom's voice, so I didn't resist. But when there was a second knock, louder than the first, Tom pressed down even harder on my shoulder and it began to hurt. Spurred by the pain, I remembered how angry he'd made me and pulling his hand away, I started to get up again.

"For God's sake, Liz, don't answer it. You don't know who's there."

But what he'd done in that courtroom and what he intended to do to Adie, came flooding back and made me deaf to his pleading; besides, like him I had a good idea of exactly who it was.

So I said coldly,

"That's the point of opening the door, isn't it? Find out who's there?"

I opened it and standing in front of me a man, his face covered with a mask, who in a muffled voice simply said,

"We've come for Tom."

The voice was familiar, but because it was muffled and before I could work out where I'd heard it before, Tom flew past me, desperate to escape. Out of the darkness, four men, all wearing masks, stepped forward smartly and grabbed him. Tom cried out.

"Help me Liz. You've got to help me. Oh God, they're going to kill me."

It came to me then who that voice belonged to and I realised Tom was probably right. I took one last look at him, but his look of desperation meant nothing to me and I shut the door – my work was being done for me. I heard him start to cry out again, but then suddenly, mid-sentence, he stopped – I suppose one of the gang members must have knocked him senseless. As for me, I went straight back to bed and my only thought before falling asleep was: 'I think the prosecution are going to be one witness short for Adie's trial.'

Henry
Looking to the Future

I visited Jabez in prison every day after his conviction. Charles Dowle himself represented Admonition, but the two of them used me rather than Charles as a messenger. Of course, I continued trying to persuade Jabez we should petition the King for leniency, but to no avail.

"I told you, forget the petition," he said. "I want you and Charles to concentrate on Admonition; nothing should be done that might jeopardise her case. Do you hear me? Nothing."

That's what he'd told me the first time I broached the subject, and this was the one and only time I saw Jabez agitated. Of course I knew Admonition had been heavily involved in the smuggling operations, at least by the time they were married. She had hinted as much when she was briefing Charles, but by now I understood what Jabez was doing.

Since his arrest back in June, Jabez had been held in solitary confinement in Northgate gaol. Upon conviction, they were going to put him in the appropriately named 'dead man's room'. Carved from rock, this cell is a stinking hole. Built below ground, it's the holding place for the condemned, so it was no small blessing that Jabez had, through me, access to enough money to persuade the warder to make other arrangements for him. At least he had a barred window which let in some light as well as a little air, though not enough to stop the smell. The better cells, like Jabez', at least have a bucket, but even he didn't get to empty his bucket every day; mind you, the communal cells have nothing but a commonly agreed corner. Jabez seemed to have got used to the smell. I suppose you get used to anything when, day in day out, you experience nothing else. But I found it overwhelming and even though I carried a vinaigrette whenever I was in the gaol, I had to cut many of my visits short when the smell became too much for me.

His money came from the sale of the inn. He hadn't received its true value, but enough to pay Dowle, Anderson and Riske's bill (The name has never been changed) for both himself and Admonition; bribe the sheriff – in all conscience, I couldn't describe it any other way, and still have enough left to buy a little food. He'd also paid and arranged to be buried back in the village church where he'd long since bought the plot next to Mr Dodds.

He appeared to have got used to a lot of things, although resigned is probably more correct. On my visits we usually talked details of Admonition's case but, on occasion, he would allow me to tell him how things were on the outside. Most memorably, only days before his execution date I heard and duly informed Jabez of Admiral Nelson's great victory at Trafalgar. He was delighted and proud, but as it was so close to his execution, I withheld from him the news of the Admiral's death. When after I left him for the last time, I reflected on his reaction to the news of Nelson's victory and concluded that for anyone to dare to accuse this proud and patriotic Englishman of treason should itself be a capital offence.

Admonition's trial was over almost before it began. At least that was the view of Charles Dowle when he returned mid-morning from Chester Court. He said that all the time he was trying to examine witnesses, he could hear the jury discussing the age difference between his client and her husband. At the same time, the prosecution seemed to be content just going through the motions – they didn't even seem concerned that one of their key witnesses had failed to appear. It was clear that they had successfully caught and prosecuted a number of the Nantwich Gang, and whilst their leader was still on the run, he was now wanted for murder as well as salt smuggling, so it was only a matter of time before he would be caught. In addition, Admonition's husband was facing the gallows and it was known he didn't intend to fight the sentence unless Admonition was similarly convicted. From their brief summation, it was clear the prosecution would settle for a lesser sentence.

Charles told me his most significant work had taken place before Admonition reached the court and even then his job was made easier by a note from Jabez pleading with her to confirm she had no knowledge of the smuggling. Charles pointed out to her that Jabez was not going to petition the king for leniency and his death would be pointless if she didn't claim innocence. Although she refused to swear on the Bible and then deny her complicity, she did agree to not being called and the prosecution offered no objection.

The jury took two minutes to find her guilty and Charles was relieved when the judge didn't don his black cap to deliver his verdict.

I had to tell Jabez that Admonition had been found guilty, but I was also able to tell him that the prosecution accepted he had claimed sole responsibility for any wrongdoing. They recognised he had maintained this position, even after being sentenced to death, and had also refused to give his attorney permission to petition for clemency, in case it had a detrimental effect upon his wife's defence.

Although they didn't believe her non-involvement, the prosecution were prepared to acknowledge his sacrifice and reduced their request for an execution sentence for Admonition to one of fourteen years transportation. Jabez was disappointed she'd been found guilty, but took solace in knowing she didn't face the death penalty and I gently pointed out that they could have pressed for and probably got a longer sentence – even life.

The last time I saw him prior to his execution, Jabez was still calm and I was determined to stay with him as long as possible, no matter how bad the smell. That night, after I finally left, he was taken from his cell and across the small bridge that led to the apartment especially built for prisoner's to spend their last hours. In the morning, prior to his execution, he was taken to Little St John's chapel, which was attached to the apartment, and received his last rights. But on that last night, before we parted, he said he had one last request to make of me.

I assured him that if it were possible and legal, I would do anything he asked.

Although there was little chance we would be overheard, lowering his voice, he said, "I think what I'm asking is legal, but if it isn't, I'll understand if you don't want anything to do with it. It's only because I believe you to be an honest man, Carlyle, that I'm asking you in the first place. So if you do think what I'm asking is illegal, all I ask is that you tell no one else of my request."

Although I couldn't be absolutely sure until I heard what he had to say, I nevertheless reassured him that anything he told me would be in confidence.

Reaching inside his smock, he extracted two sealed documents; he told me he'd had to pay the sheriff far too much to seal them for him. Handing me the first, he told me,

"This is for Admonition, but I only want you to give it to her when she returns to England. It will be of no use to her before then."

Assuring him I would keep it safe until her return, I slipped the letter into my jacket pocket. Satisfied, Jabez then handed me the second.

"This is for you and you alone. It explains what I want you to do on her return, but it's important you don't open it until you know that she's back."

I took the letter from him, but I was curious to know why I should wait fourteen years before opening it. Jabez explained that if others discovered the letter's contents, both Admonition and I could be in danger. The lawyer in me wanted to know more, but I could tell Jabez had said everything he intended to, so suppressing my curiosity, I put the letter with the other.

Before I left him for what we both knew was to be the final time, Jabez thanked me for all I had done for him and trusted I would follow his instructions regarding the letters. I tried one last time to persuade him to let me petition the King, but smiling, he shook his head and told me he felt he'd atoned for what he had done to Admonition and that he was now ready to meet his Maker. Knowing there was nothing further I could say or do, yet still with a heavy heart, I left him.

Elizabeth
A Fate Deserved

Adie's gone and I know I'll never see her again. I went to her trial because I wanted to speak up for her, tell them how her life had been. I wanted to tell them that if it hadn't been for Tom, she would have still been with me and wouldn't have even met Jabez Payne, let alone got involved in all that salt smuggling nonsense. But they wouldn't let me. They were much more interested in asking me where Tom was. I told them I had no idea; after those men dragged him off, (I know it was the Nantwich gang, but I saw none of their faces, so I didn't tell them that,) I never saw him again.

Anyway, they know where he is now, don't they? 'Cos they found him drowned in the Boar's Head's well, a couple of days after he was taken. Bound with his hands tied to his feet, they say he'd been weighed down with boulders so that he drowned quickly. But I'm not so sure that's true. I think he was probably stoned after they threw him in the well 'cos the Nantwich Gang's known for killing people that way. But it doesn't matter to me how he went. The main thing is that he's gone and I'm glad. There, I've said it. I know some will say I should never talk like that about the man I married, but I've learnt a lot more about him since he was killed and though I don't want to talk about it, I will just say I now know I was married to a monster.

I tried to see Adie in prison after she'd been convicted, but she refused to see me. She told her lawyer to tell me it was too late, that when she'd come to see me, I'd pushed her away, called her a liar and it would be best if we never saw each other again. Mr Dowle told me he didn't think that was really the truth. He thought because she knew she was leaving England and might never return, she believed for us to see each other would be pointless and upsetting.

I don't think he's right even though what she said was true. I did do and say those things. I still wonder whether they are the real reasons she doesn't want to see me. You see, I remember a conversation we had a long time ago when she told me she thought her name was a curse for anyone she grew close to. Then I told her it wasn't true, but now I'm not so sure. After all Tom was murdered, Jabez' been executed and I'm about to head for the workhouse because I have no money and no way of earning any. So I wouldn't be surprised if she was thinking her name is to blame. I still can't believe a name can be a curse but I think that may be the real reason she won't see me and maybe, just maybe, she's right and that it's best for both of us if we stay apart.

Anyway, I do know I will miss her deeply and I know things would have been so different if only I had believed her about Tom. But I didn't and that's definitely *my* curse.

Henry
Ignorance, Neglect and Contempt

My old chair, a blazing fire and a large brandy. Balm on a ragged day, that's what Jane calls it and over twenty-five years, she's learned to judge my moods like a seasoned helmsman judges the weather. If she could see dark clouds were gathering, she'd turn my sights to somewhere brighter, our plans for the evening (We love to go to the theatre.) or, when they were young, something one of the boys had said or done. If she judged I needed distracting, that the clouds would sail on by if only I would look away from them, then she pointed me straight in the direction of the boys themselves; I might help John with his Latin (He always disliked Latin and that's maybe why he hasn't followed me into Law, becoming an engineer instead.) or perhaps I'd play marbles with Kit, his young brother.

Jane understood that dealing with difficult clients, robust prosecutors, bribed witnesses and wrong decisions by juries, were all part of a defence lawyers day; we both did. What is more, I think Jane would say that the man who came home to her in the evening was usually the same as the one who left her in the morning. But on those few occasions when I came home with a storm still raging about my head, then that's when she applied the balm.

Both boys have left us now. John is in Manchester where he's an engineer working in a cotton mill, whilst Kit will shortly be on his way to New Holland as the surgeon on a ship.

But now, for the first time, Jane's balm just isn't working. I've seen many go to the gallows and if I've defended them, to me it seems only right that I should be present to witness their demise. There were some who were executed that I've thought were harshly sentenced and a few, mercifully a very few, who I genuinely believe were wholly innocent. There have also been a number, whom I still defended to the best of my ability, even though I knew them to be guilty. I must also confess that in some of those cases, I've believed the sentence fitted the crime.

Nevertheless, whatever my view might be, the mob who attended these executions always behaved the same way. Whether the prisoners looked strong, weak, happy or sad, whether they cried, laughed, (It's true. I really did see a few go to their grave laughing.) pleaded for mercy or screamed their innocence, they were always met by a crowd jeering and baying for blood. That is until today.

The Boughton crowd had already seen one poor soul go to meet his Maker that morning and had responded in their usual manner. But for Jabez, things were remarkably different. As the cart bearing him came into view, the crowd fell silent. There were none of the usual ribald comments, none of the jeers or the cries for his death.

As he looked around the crowd, Jabez looked bewildered. I'm sure he had prepared himself for a reception much as I described, but the silence continued as the cart reached and stopped at the foot of the gallows.

Then, as he was helped down from the cart and began to climb the scaffold, a lone voice started to chant.

"Jabez. Jabez.
Jabez. Jabez."

I looked in the direction the voice was coming from and there, at the front of the crowd, fearlessly chanting Jabez' name was Sam Baker, the leader of the Nantwich Gang. I say fearless, because I knew there was a price on his head; not only had he and some of his gang members not yet been captured, but all had been tried in their absence and found guilty of salt smuggling. Since his tied and weighted body was pulled from the well at the Boar's Head, they were also sought on suspicion of murdering Tom Rider.

As he continued chanting, a second voice, then a third and a fourth joined him. I looked around and recognised all of them as members of the Nantwich Gang and I knew that each one was risking his freedom – or worse. As I watched, others in the crowd joined in, until soon the whole crowd was chanting his name.

I looked towards the gallows where, by this time, Jabez had reached the platform where the hangman was waiting. He looked around as the crowd's chanting reached a crescendo. As I've said before, in all the time I spent with Jabez, I truly believe I got to know him better than most and I'm sure, even though he faced imminent death, I saw the trace of a smile on his lips. Then, with the crowd still calling his name, I saw the hangman, who looked equally nonplussed, speak into Jabez' ear; Jabez shook his head. After a moment, the hangman placed the noose over his head, plainly Jabez had refused the hood; I suppose he wanted the sight of the crowd calling his name to be the last thing he saw.

After first removing the leg irons, the hangman took no time in pushing him from the platform; I suppose he saw it as a kindness not to delay. A groan rose from the crowd as Jabez' legs jerked twice. Then he hung lifelessly. I've seen men, women and children struggle for up to five minutes against strangulation; the less they weigh, the longer it can take to kill them. Unfortunately children, unless weighed down, are particularly likely to suffer. Mercifully, Jabez' neck had broken and in moments he was dead.

His body was taken and as he'd arranged, given a decent burial next to Jack Dodds in the graveyard of his local village church. Living five miles outside Chester, I usually take a carriage home, but on this occasion I decided to go by foot to see if walking would clear my head and perhaps let me understand the unique scene I had just witnessed.

But the walk failed to have the desired effect. The questions that filled my head then were still with me when I got home; their persistence was also the reason Jane's balm failed to work. There were two questions that plagued me then, and I think always will. First, if every man woman and child called out for him, if everyone believed his hanging was wrong and if some had even risked their lives to voice their support for him, then why is Jabez Payne dead? Of course, the other question I have to ask, the one that weighs heaviest, is: why wasn't I able to save him?

I must have sat there most of the evening, brandy in hand just staring into the fire. Did I make any progress? Some I think. To start, it's clear to me that had Jabez allowed me to petition the King, his sentence would have been commuted to life in prison or to a lengthy term of transportation; that's certainly true of similar cases I've known. But I think there were two reasons Jabez went to the gallows rather than let me plead for him. First, I know how guilty he felt about allowing Admonition to become embroiled in his smuggling and he truly thought if he claimed all responsibility, Admonition would be set free. Second, (and this is my judgement rather than something he said) he'd seen life in prison and knew that once convicted, conditions for him would be even worse: I believe Jabez saw prison or, Heaven preserve us, the hulks, simply as a drawn out execution and he'd therefore chosen what he saw as the shorter sentence.

So I have at least satisfied myself that there was nothing more I could have done to save him. But what I cannot resolve is why, even if he was guilty of everything they accused him of, they should consider Jabez' crime and that of so many others like it, meriting such a draconian sentence.

I know it's illegal to own it and even Jane doesn't know I have a copy, but I've recently been re-reading Thomas Paine's *The Rights of Man* and one phrase stays with me more than any other, 'Ignorance, neglect, or contempt of human rights are the sole causes of public misfortunes and corruptions of government.' Not only do I agree with Paine, but I also believe that until things are righted, we will continue to see good men like Jabez Payne go to the gallows.

Part Five

Admonition
Survival

Thank God! Today we sailed.

The Sydney Cove is going to be our home for the next five months or so, and after the disease-ridden hell I've been in for the past four, anything has to be better. So before the journey really gets underway, let me go back a little and explain what happened after my conviction.

After sentencing, I spent around a month in solitary confinement. Exactly how long I can't say, because with no sun and little light, it was hard to tell where one day ended and the next one started. But I must just say how grateful I am to Jane Carlyle, because after I was sentenced to fourteen years transportation (At least Jabez lived long enough to know I was not to face execution.), Henry brought me a parcel of clothes from her. He had told her I only had those that I stood in, so she had taken pity on me.

The parcel contained: a gown, two chemise, two shifts, a pair of boots (worn, but still serviceable) and best of all, a warm jacket. They were all old and I think Jane knew or, at least Henry must have told her, that brand new clothes would raise too much interest from prisoners and wardens alike. Henry also must have noticed that she and I were of similar height and frame because everything fitted, although the boots did pinch a little.

I took my old clothes off and put on all the new ones; I thought wearing them meant they couldn't be stolen. The new clothes had been wrapped in an old piece of cloth which I wrapped my old ones in; six months in gaol had taught me that nothing should be wasted. Then, over eight days, shackled and in the back of an open wagon, they moved me to a prison hulk moored in the River Medway off a place called Chatham – I'd never heard of either, but to me they seemed just as far from home as I imagined New Holland to be.

There were eight of us in that wagon, all sentenced to transportation. Although it was still early September, it was unseasonably cold and Ann, the only other woman in the wagon, wore barely enough to cover her dignity and shivered uncontrollably. When I offered her my parcel, she said she had nothing to offer in exchange. I thought one day I might regret it, but I let her have it anyway. She grabbed it like I'd given her roast beef – I suppose she thought I might change my mind. She then put everything on over her old rags and even wrapped the old cloth around her shoulders. Her feet had been unshod so I could see that, even though they were much too big for her, my old shoes were especially precious to her.

Over those eight days, I discovered all of us were sentenced to varying lengths of transportation. Ann, who was thin, sallow and coughed incessantly, was sentenced to seven years, but to me she didn't look like she'd survive a few months living on a hulk, never mind the rigours of transportation. In fact, when we were rowed out to the *Brunswick*, the Commandant refused to allow her on board, insisting instead that she be taken to the hospital ship moored nearby. I was never to see Ann again nor, even though I enquired, was I to hear anything of her. It's true that on recovery, she could have been taken to a different hulk, that sometimes happened, but more often, if someone doesn't return to a ship it's because they've succumbed. Now that I'm away from that place I allow myself to accept Ann probably died, but I still like to hope that she survived.

The *Brunswick* was to hold us until a ship became available to transport us to New Holland and I survived for four months there, avoiding many dangers including theft, rape, hunger and disease. But the worst risk was from asphyxiation. The ship was so overcrowded that when we arrived, we were made to join about twenty others and make the best we could of sleeping on the top deck. Death, transportation and occasional releases led to a fairly steady turnover of convicts which meant that after a couple of weeks, I was moved down to the orlop deck. Whilst living on the top deck, I'd been glad to be wearing all my extra clothes, particularly when early morning mist rolled across the ship and chilled me to the bone. But now at night, when we were locked in the orlop, we were so crowded we stripped down beyond decency. The lucky ones found a hammock by a porthole and hung on to the porthole's bars no matter how hard others tried to displace them. I found it impossible to reach the portholes but survived because another convict, who told me she'd already been on the *Brunswick* for over four months, explained to me the best way to survive.

Lolly, who said she was twenty-three but looked much older and stood at about four foot six inches tall, told me she'd been born into the theatre. Her parents were part of a travelling troop which provided all types of entertainment, from jugglers to tightrope walkers, from acrobats to small plays performed by just two or three actors. Her father was a big man and from as far back as Lolly could remember, he'd performed a short play with her mother, telling the story of Samson and Delilah. It had been of great relief to her father when Lolly was old enough to join them on stage and they could change their act. Up until then, he'd needed to keep his head shaved and wear a wig on stage so that her mother could appear to cut it off whilst he slept. But then when Lolly was still young enough to be able to play a small boy, they played many stories, some from the Bible, others they made up, about Mary and Joseph and the young Christ. Although not as popular as Samson and Delilah, most of these stories had still been well received.

But as she became older and just as luck would have it, buxom, she could no longer get away with playing these roles even to the most drunken and boisterous crowd. They struggled to find or invent successful plays for an elderly couple and a young woman. After being booed off the stage yet again, they were in despair when Charlie Hamlet knocked on their caravan door. He told Lolly's father he'd done a bit of acting down in London; as he said, with a name like his, how could he do anything else. He said he'd seen the trouble they'd had on stage and wondered if they might do better as a foursome. Lolly said that her father had liked his boldness and had agreed to give him a try. Charlie was three years older than Lolly and she couldn't help a rueful laugh when she told me she'd liked him as well, but not for the same reason as her father. At twenty, he was dark, tall and handsome, but most of all he had a way with words, and as Lolly said, 'She didn't stand a chance.'

Charlie had been with them for only six months when Lolly fell pregnant and three months later they were married. She never knew if he was telling the truth about having done some acting in London, but it didn't matter she said, because he was a natural. They were doing well again. So after the baby was born, they decided to try some Shakespeare. They tried several scenes with all four of them, but by far and away the most successful ones were those Lolly and Charlie did on their own. In fact, so successful were their extracts from *Romeo and Juliet,* especially their balcony scene and their final deaths, which had drawn standing ovations from three full houses, the troop agreed to give them a benefit night. Coming just before Christmas, the extra money meant they had a fine old time and Lolly told me Christmas that year was the best she'd 'ever 'ad in all me days'.

But, she said, all that success went to Charlie's head and he decided that Lolly and the baby, who they'd called Charlie like his dad, should go with him to London and see if they couldn't find some theatre work there. So leaving her parents behind to do the best they could without her, Lolly and the baby went with Charlie to London. Charlie soon found work for them both – made sure of by the reviews he'd kept of their *Romeo and Juliet*.

Problems started when Lolly fell pregnant again; no theatre owner wanted an obviously pregnant *Juliet*. Later other members of the cast were willing to look after young Charlie when his mother was on stage, but were much less willing to look after him as well as his new baby sister. When only three months later she became pregnant for the third time, Lolly was told she would no longer be required by the theatre; Charlie could still play *Romeo* but they would have to find a new *Juliet* for him. Lolly didn't mind, Charlie was earning enough to keep all of them and expecting their third child so soon after the other two, she was weary enough without working in the theatre every night. But when one night Charlie didn't come home and was still missing the next morning, she minded. Lately he'd been coming home later and later, telling her how the show was so successful that the curtain calls were making him late. But Lolly had her doubts and so now, carrying the two babies and with young Charlie toddling along beside her, she went straight to the theatre where her husband worked.

When she got there, the place was in disarray. The theatre owner showed her a note; she recognised Charlie's hand, but when she went to take it from him, he snatched it back.

"Romeo and Juliet have run away together and this note from 'im says they're not coming back. I ask you, what can I do?" He looked at his pocket watch. "I've got a show to put on in less than six hours and my main act has run away."

Though she knew it was pointless, Lolly did ask if the note said, or if anyone knew, where they'd gone. Tight-lipped, the owner had told her that if he knew that, he would have found and throttled them himself.

But Lolly wasn't interested in the theatre owner's troubles because she knew that without Charlie she was going to have enough problems of her own. Charlie had gone, taking that eighteen-year-old childless floozy with him. Even though she could see the draw, Lolly couldn't hide the bitterness when she told me the girl had obviously been playing *Juliet* to his *Romeo* off stage as well as on. She wished the girl good luck because, as she said, Charlie would no doubt do the same to this foolish girl as he'd done to her and Lord knows how many before her.

Although she'd been left with three small children and no income, Lolly knew she had a small sum saved and hidden, enough to feed the four of them for a couple of days. So, heading home she promised little Charlie, who, like her, hadn't had any breakfast, they'd have some bread and drippin' as soon as they got back home. Of course, when she got home, the money, like her husband, was long gone and she had nothing to give her son to eat other than a couple of crusts. Unable to feed herself at all, she worried that unless she ate soon, her milk would dry up, leaving her with nothing to give her babies. So, that evening, in desperation and hoping they wouldn't stir, she left the children sleeping and went to the local tavern where the innkeeper allowed her to sing as long as there weren't any complaints from his regulars. He said she could keep any money they threw.

Lolly sung herself hoarse, but at the end of the evening, though there had not been any complaints, she had barely enough for a loaf and maybe a little tea and she still had to find the money for the rent which was already three weeks overdue. So when a man she didn't know made her an offer, she had little choice but to take him back to her place.

Fifteen minutes after she'd got him home, the man had paid her what they'd agreed, finished what he came for and with barely a word, adjusted his dress and left. In quarter of an hour, Lolly had made twice the money she'd worked all evening to earn.

So, though she didn't like it and despised the men who bought her favours, it became her business. Walking them quickly home, their money already safe in a hidden pocket in her dress, by encouraging their eagerness with promises of what was about to be, she found that if she applied herself, they would be leaving again barely ten minutes after she'd got them home. She found the daughter of a neighbour willing to look after the children while she was out, a girl who was ready to disappear the moment she heard Lolly and that night's companion approaching the door.

Now she could afford to feed the four of them and keep a roof over their heads and Lolly's life remained tolerable until the night she took home what she called a 'posh'en'. Tall and thin, he wore a kid-skin waistcoat above brown pantaloons, white stockings and over all, a close fitting blue jacket trimmed with gold braiding. All of this was topped, she said, by a powdered wig which stood like an oversized meringue a foot above his head. Standing close to him, as he obliged her to do, Lolly could see below the white powder that caked his face. His skin had been deeply scarred by a calling card left by a smallpox visit. To complete this handsome vision, when he smiled, most of his teeth were missing, while those that remained were in the last stages of decay.

But he'd given her a crown, one of good quality according to Lolly, so he could spend the whole night with her. Lolly didn't like men to stay the night, not with the children there, but as she said a crown's a crown, so this night she made an exception. She said there was no need for her to warm this one up, because he spent the walk to her door telling her of his plans for her. Lolly had begun to wonder whether she really did want this man's money, but the truth was he was so drunk that by the time she got him home, he just fell unconscious on her bed. He stayed that way until morning when, murdered by a hangover, he had no desire to trouble Lolly any further.

Just like her very first customer, he said almost nothing before leaving. Instead, he headed straight out with, he told her, the single intention of finding a cab. Lolly was left to muse over what she thought was the easiest crown she'd ever earned. But she couldn't have been more wrong, because less than half an hour later, there was a loud knock at the door. She'd just given Charlie his breakfast and was getting herself ready to feed the babies who were already crying out their hunger. So covering herself again and ignoring the babies' protests, she opened the door. Standing there, still looking the worse for wear was her visitor from the night before and next to him was a Bow Street Runner. Looking expectantly at the Runner, her visitor instructed,

"That's her constable. That's the woman who stole my money; I want you to arrest her."

Stunned, Lolly didn't understand. She assumed he wanted his crown back, so she reached inside her skirt and took it from the pocket where it was still hidden and tried to give it back to him. But he refused to take it, telling her that was the only money she'd actually earned and as she knew, it was his purse containing five sovereigns she'd stolen.

Lolly protested her innocence, she *was* innocent, but the Runner had been paid to arrest her and he wasn't about to lose his money. So he gave her just long enough to ask the girl who'd sat with the children, whether she would look after them until she returned, before he marched her away and put her in front of the magistrate. Whilst of course, her guilt couldn't be proven, once he learnt her profession, the magistrate didn't hesitate in pronouncing her guilty.

She didn't know why, but no one took the crown from her and it remained safely hidden in her pocket. Which was just as well, because when the girl who had the children visited her, she was able to give her the coin and ask her not only to send a message to her parents, but also to look after the children until her parents arrived. She missed her children. She had tears in her eyes as she told me this part of her tale, but she knew they'd be safe with the girl until her parents arrived and that they'd look after them until she was released.

She was sent to the *Brunswick* long before her parents would have got her message and even when they did, she didn't know when they'd be able to travel to London – if at all. Still, as she ruefully told me, they had seven years to travel. In the meantime she'd decided to concentrate on survival on the hulk and that was dependant on her learning the rules, both official and unofficial, as quickly as possible. Because she'd learnt them quickly, she was able to tell me how to survive the night down on the orlop deck and a lot more besides.

"The trick is to be still. Take your clothes off and roll 'em up to make a pillow. Get in your bunk and try not to move. The less you move, the less you have to breathe and the less you breathe, the less air you're going to need. If you're lying on your clothes, it's a whole lot harder for the thieves we've got on here to steal 'em."

She looked down at my feet and then added,

"But whatever else you do, only take those boots off if you want to lose them. Boots, especially good ones like those, are worth more than gold here; they'd grab a pair of those even before they took your food. In fact, you better sleep with one eye open or one of them dippers will take them off your feet while you sleep."

So that's what I did. Every night, most of the others (except those who rushed to claim a bunk by a porthole) only went down into the darkness reluctantly. But when they commanded us to go below I went straight down, stripped to my boots and undergarments and then, having rolled my clothes into a tight ball, took the ball as my pillow and got straight into a bunk. I lay there motionless, in a place just either side of that line which separates sleep and wakefulness. This way, although it was unbearably hot and breathless, each night I survived until morning and it was thanks to Lolly's advice that only once did someone try to steal from me.

I'd been sleeping down below for about a week when I was wrenched into full wakefulness by someone trying to remove my boots. Feigning sleep, I remained motionless and waited whilst the thief undid the lace on the left one. It was in the moments between when one lace was untied and before the thief began to untie the second, I struck out. I kicked as hard as I could with my right foot. Although I didn't know what my boot connected with, I heard a satisfying cry of pain and whoever it was, shuffled hurriedly away.

I never discovered for certain the identity of the failed thief, but I did notice that one of the captured French soldiers, who'd increased our number in the past week, had a fresh bruise over his left eye. Of course, I knew I couldn't prove anything, but of far greater importance, the bruise served as a deterrent for others and I never again had any problems with thieves; thanks to Lolly, there were easier targets than me.

Damp and cold in the day, cramped and airless at night.
These conditions, combined with the need to be continually on the look-out for thieves, amongst the crew as well as the other convicts, were beginning to take their toll. But then the chance of blessed relief came.

One morning, when there was a sharp wind blowing from the sea straight down the Medway, I'd managed to find a little shelter on the lee side of the wooden stump that was all that remained of the mainmast. It was because I leant against the mast with my back to the wind that I didn't see the naval clerk until he was upon me. These clerks were as untrustworthy as any of the convicts, ready to take advantage, particularly of someone who had fallen foul of the maze of rules that governed life on the hulks.

But these men were also known for being able to arrange anything – at a price. Not only did they control the black market on the ship, they could also make a convict's life a little easier in other ways. The easement of irons was favourite, whilst supplements or improved rations were almost as popular. Even if a man wanted to be taken off a work party – or put on one (Boredom was one of the hulks' worst punishments.), that was also something the clerk could arrange. So, though he startled me, it came as no surprise when this clerk whispered to me.

"So what do you want for them boots?"

Once it was realised that attempting to steal my boots was likely to end painfully, I had been asked this question many times. The difference now was that this man could get me what I really wanted. What's more, one glance at his feet, the remains of his shoes held on with strips of rag, told me he really needed my boots. I guessed he was due an inspection and I knew that if he wasn't reasonably attired, including his feet, when the inspection took place, he'd lose his job.

I didn't need to think about my reply.

"The next consignment going to join a Transportation ship leaves in four days. Make sure my name's on that Bay draft and you can have my boots."

Now it was his turn to be startled.

"But the list is complete. No more names can be added."

I knew he might have to bribe one or two to achieve it, but it was always possible to add a name to the Bay draft. I had known names to be added as late as the night before a draft left, so I said,

"I'm not interested in anything else. You get me on that list or you can forget about the boots."

He tried to argue, but I could see his heart wasn't in it; he really wanted my boots.

Begrudgingly he said,

"I'll see what I can do."

The next day I asked around and confirmed the clerks were due an inspection. Now having complete confidence that the clerk who wanted my boots would make sure I was on that ship, I traded a chemise and one of my shifts for a passable pair of shoes.

In the morning, the clerk caught me.

"Don't ask me how, but I've got your name added to the list."

206

I didn't need to ask. I knew exactly how he'd got me on the list. The only thing I didn't know was how much he'd had to pay.

"So are you goin' to give them to me, then?"

Four months on the *Brunswick* had taught me a lot, so I said,

"Make sure you're by the gangplank when they take us off. I'll give them to you then."

He wasn't happy.

"But how do I know you won't just leave the ship still wearing them?"

Of course, there was no possibility I would take any risk that might delay my departure, something, if he wasn't so anxious, he probably would have realised. But I had seen him and the other clerks take advantage of so many who had nothing to bargain with, so it gave me great satisfaction to see him suffer.

"You'll just have to trust me and make sure you're close by the gangplank when we leave."

The next day crawled by as I worried someone would notice that my name should not be on the list. I needn't have been concerned because nothing was said and the day passed as monotonously as had most of the others.

That night, for the first time in three months, I took off my boots and replaced them with the shoes. I didn't like to examine my feet too closely. Three months in those boots meant they weren't going to be in the best condition. I tied the boots together, put the laces round my neck and put the boots down the front of my chemise; though I knew I wouldn't sleep that night, I was taking no chances.

The night passed uneventfully and at first light, when letting us out on deck, they called those of us on the draft together and marched us towards the gangplank. Standing alone by the plank was the naval clerk. I waved farewell to Lolly, who looked surprised at first but then smiled and clapped; it was clear she thought that I had done the right thing by not even telling her I was going. I took the boots from round my neck and started swinging them around by the laces. As I passed the clerk, whose eyes had not left the boots since I started swirling them, I let them go. To be honest, I hadn't expected them to travel so far and it was only because he was paying such close attention that the clerk was able to stretch out and catch them by the laces before they disappeared over the side and vanished in the oozing quagmire below.

He swore at me, but I just smiled back. I knew we both had what we wanted.

Still in shackles, twelve of us and a guard were put into the back of another wagon no bigger than the one that brought me from Chester and began the journey down to Falmouth. Even though we were cramped already, we stopped at Woolwich to pick up one more convict. At first we had no idea why we were stopping, but when the door opened and the guard stepped down, we got a glimpse of the pub we'd stopped outside. As he shut the door behind him, even though it was still early in the day, we assumed that was his destination.

But moments later, we heard him talking to someone whose voice we didn't recognise. Soon their voices were raised and we could hear every word. It was clear they were talking about a third person and they were haggling over money – it seemed our guard wanted a pound to take the extra passenger. But then the tone of the other man's voice changed and he said,

"Look, Mary Baldwin is on your draft list and Mr Peters paid your clerk fifty pounds to make sure of that."

We couldn't believe it. Why would somebody have paid a year's wages just to get this Mary on a draft list? Anyway, the door suddenly opened and a disconsolate guard followed by Mary climbed into the wagon. A second man poked his head in the wagon and told Mary he'd be riding with the driver to make sure she arrived in Falmouth safely. Before he shut the door, he fitted her with shackles and, as I was sat next to her, connected them to mine.

When we pulled away, all thirteen of us and even the guard, who obviously hadn't got his pound, were silent. Glancing sideways, I could see our new passenger, in addition to being very valuable was, for a convict, very well dressed. I knew all the others had heard what I'd heard and seen what I'd seen, so I was sure they had just as many questions as me. But no one said a word. Like me, they didn't know who or what we were dealing with. Fortunately, Mary was very different from the person she might have been and as we travelled, she told us all about the time she'd spent on a hulk and especially about Simon Peters.

Her story was surprising.

Mary
Descent into Hell

The 27th June 1806 was a Friday. That's true that is, and I might be the only person who remembers. I suppose for most people the day just slid by like any other, but for me I can definitely say it marked the start of the worst time in my life. I don't mean the sentence, it was the third time I'd been caught thieving (This time, not that it matters, I'd been caught with a role of cotton I'd taken from outside a haberdashers in Poplar.) and fourteen years' transportation was about the best I could expect. To tell the truth, I'm glad to be going. If I stayed in England, there are only two ways I was goin' to go; more thievin' with more jail, finally entertainin' the crowd at Tyburn. Or walking the streets and drinking myself to death just so I could face with a cheery smile, all those ugly men who'd want to pay me for my time. No, New Holland holds no fear for me. But before I joined the *Sydney Cove*, I spent five months on the *Warrior*, a hulk moored off Woolwich and had I known what a hell-hole that was going to be I might have felt different about my sentence.

A heavy mist rolling in off the marshes lay over the Thames when they rowed us out. So even when we were only yards away from the hulk, a silhouette was still all we could see. So it was the stench that hit you first, and long before the *Warrior* loomed out of the fog, the unmistakable sweet smell of death and damp decay overwhelmed all the other noxious smells rising from the river. Clambering on board the hulk, the dead n' dying lying all over the deck, made it very clear where the smell had come from. Picking our way through the bodies, only the occasional groan told us who still waited for the blessed relief that death would bring.

The top deck contained the dead and all but dead, but when they took us below, we entered what I can only describe as a *living* death. There were no candles and what little light there was entered through draughty gaps in the ship's side. Filth and vermin were everywhere and the endless movement of convicts trying to ease their chains completed the feeling of descending into hell. Every convict, and there were more than I could tell, wore leg-irons and I soon discovered that when they broke a rule, big, small, real or invented, a convict's irons would be either tightened, doubled or have a ball added to them. What's more, anyone foolish enough to be caught trying to remove or adjust their chains would be introduced to the cat – a meeting, if they survived, they were unlikely to ever forget. The cat o' nine tails, in case you haven't met him, is a whip like no other. Coming from the handle, nine thongs of knotted rope, all between two and three feet long, mean each lash from the cat delivers nine of them to the unfortunate offender. So a convict sentenced to just ten lashes with the cat really receives ninety and I have to tell you there's not much skin left on his back after that.

The food they gave us was pretty poor as well. Boiled ox-cheek, pease pudding and mouldy bread is what we got on that first night and on most nights after that. Our diet only changed if they ran out of ox-cheek, in which case they gave us oatmeal. They also gave us mouldy biscuits when the bread ran out. Pease pudding never ran out 'cos if supplies ran low, they just thinned and stretched out what was left until they got new supplies.

If the guards, conditions and food they gave us weren't bad enough, then my thieving, cheating, fellow convicts completed the whole sorry picture. If these low creatures thought they could make a ha'penny by stealing from you, they would, and if they believed they could get better food by telling a guard you were plannin' to escape, they wouldn't blink at that either. Worst of all, they'd say they were your friend, and to seal your new pact with them, slide a knife between your shoulders. So, all in all, it didn't take me long to see that if I was to avoid being murdered, and if gaol fever didn't get me, there was only one way I'd survive.

Despite his name, Simon Peters wasn't a religious man – far from it. But he *was* the head guard and the other guards were as afraid of him as the convicts. A mountain of a man and as bald as a coot, his beard only half-covered the scar he'd gained from a knife wound. The slash of a blade had been a convict's desperate final act before Simon crushed the last breath from him. That blade, having removed one of Simon's earlobes, had travelled across his cheek and finished by widening the right side of his mouth. So all in all, he wasn't a pretty sight and his temper was just as ugly. But I wasn't about to cross him; no, I made sure he knew exactly what I had in mind right from the start.

Most of the guards lived in one large cabin, but Simon Peters shared a smaller one with just three of his favoured guards. Keeping an eye on the cabin, I saw that three of the four went out every day to check both convicts and the rest of the guards, the fourth staying to watch over the cabin. So on the day Simon stayed behind, waiting as close to the cabin as I could without raising suspicion, and when I was sure the other guards were otherwise engaged, I slipped through the doorway. I knew the guards were usually gone no longer than twenty minutes, but that was more than long enough for what I had in mind.

Ducking back out of the cabin fifteen minutes later, leaving a bemused but smiling Simon, I re-joined the other convicts. The day's inspection was still unfinished, so returning to my bunk with my freshly eased chains, though I got knowing looks from a couple of women, I went unseen by the other guards.

So that's how things went. Every four days, for the few minutes he was alone, I would enter Simon's cabin and slip him from his breeches. I knew how to tickle a man's fancy and Simon was like a puppy when we were done. I never left without reward or promise of reward that, pleased to say, he was always glad to supply.

The chains I wore had been so tight that I knew if they weren't eased, my legs would be permanently disfigured. But once they were loosened, I next needed protection and that's why I'd chosen Simon Peters. Any guard could ease my chains and most could protect me from the other convicts, but only he could do both *and* protect me from the attention of the other guards. So on my second visit, he loosened my chains and promised me the protection I required, and I was then able to concentrate on improving the quality of my daily life. Over the next few weeks, my food improved. I was given better clothes (including new boots), extra bedding against the cold and even a second pillow. But after three months, he gave me somethin' I will never forget, somethin' he gave only out of kindness.

Although the *Warrior* was already full of death when they put me on board, it was mainly the result of maltreatment, pitiable conditions and a poor diet. But then gaol fever started to spread through the ship, taking convict and guard alike. It spread like wildfire and pretty soon those guards, still unaffected, despite dire threats from Simon, started to abandon us and we would have followed 'cept the authorities placed a guard from the local barracks round the ship. As the weeks passed and more and more fell ill and died, those of us still fit were becoming desperate, knowing it was only a matter of time before we succumbed.

All this time, Simon was becoming ever more wild and angry. Most guards, unless dead or dying, had slipped away, until only Simon and his chosen three remained to make sure we stayed under control and didn't escape. Most of the guards may have gone but Simon, by threatening and cajoling both convict and guard alike, though never asking the guards to do anything he wouldn't do himself, managed to retain some order.

But after only a few days of living this new madness, one where we were made to carry dead and dying bodies up on deck and where four men watched us day and night, making sure that none of us escaped, the morning dawned when Simon failed to appear and I was summoned to his cabin by one of the other guards.

Simon was lying on his bunk and I'd seen enough cases of typhus and how it progressed, to know it wouldn't be long before he joined all the others who had succumbed. Despite a high fever that made him sweat from every pore, he was shivering uncontrollably. His vision was cloudy and he was unable to focus properly. Delirious, he talked nonsense no one could understand. But then he closed his eyes for a long moment and when he opened them again, they had cleared. He asked for water, and having drunk thirstily, whispered to one of the guards who, instructing the other two to join him, left the cabin. Summoning me to his bedside, he took my hand and I could see he was making an immense effort to stay lucid. Gripping hard, he said,

"I know why you come to me and I know it isn't because you care for me. You just want me to make your life easier. But Mary, that's what I like most about you, you're a survivor and you'll do anything you need to do to get by. Strange as it may seem, that's the reason I've come to care for you. But now I'm dying."

I squeezed his hand. There was no point in telling him he would recover because, like me, he'd seen too many die not to know his time was almost up. So I just let him finish what he wanted to tell me.

"I'm not going to be able to protect you any longer and anyway, if you stay in this God forsaken graveyard, it won't be long until you go the same way as me."

Since he started talking to me, his shivers had stopped but he seemed to be burning up even more than before. I tried to bathe him but he stopped my hand.

"Don't fuss Mary. I haven't long and I need to tell you something before I die; it's important if you want to live."

Now he had my full attention.

"You saw me talking to Ben before I made the three of 'em leave; he's a good man and you can trust him. At first light, he's going to take you from here to join a wagon that's coming from Chatham. It will be carrying convicts going to Falmouth to join a New Holland-bound transport ship. You should be heading there anyway, but I think they've decided to leave you and all the rest here to let the typhus do their job for them; it'll save 'em a lot of trouble and more importantly, money. Anyway, when the wagon gets here, there'll be room for one more and I've had your name added to their bay draft list. Ben will make sure they don't forget."

Then he looked straight at me and I realised he was smitten; that big ugly man, who could kill as easily as swatting a fly and with no more thought, who knew our weekly dalliance was never going to be anything more, had fallen for me. But then he just smiled at me, closed his eyes and turned on his side and I knew he'd said goodbye for the last time.

Early next morning, I was woken by Ben. Warning me to be quiet, he indicated I should follow him up on deck. The orlop was still in darkness, but I was already dressed and so followed him as quickly and quietly as I could. Reaching the deck unheard, I breathed out, only then realising I'd been holding my breath since I'd left my cot.

Hurrying, I caught up with Ben as he reached the river side of the ship. Looking over, I could see another of our guards bringing a small wherry alongside. Ben breathed,

"Alright then Mary. You first."

A net had been hung from the side of the *Warrior* and because the hulk lay in mud at an angle away from the river, climbing down the net wasn't too difficult and I was helped into the wherry by its oarsman. Scrambling down the net after me, Ben joined us in the boat and took one of the oars. The wherry sat low in the water, so although it was beginning to get light, the morning mist that sat on the river kept us unseen. The two oarsmen rowed us slowly and quietly some way upstream, before drawing us into the opposite bank where, along with Ben, I stepped out onto a small beach and from there up an iron ladder to the dock. Surprising some early morning dockers, we slipped between two warehouses and stepped out into the High Street. I hadn't looked back after I stepped from the wherry, so when I realised he hadn't followed us, I guessed the other guard, having done what was asked of him, had simply rowed it back to its mooring.

I suppose I could have tried to give Ben the slip, but what would have been the point? As I said, England held no future for me, at least not one I could look forward to, and if I did manage to escape, I'd have no future and I'd be a fugitive in my own country for the rest of my life. So I just walked beside him, keeping to the early morning shadows thrown by the High Street buildings and hoped we'd have no problems meeting the Falmouth wagon.

Ben brought us to a halt outside the pub where I was to be picked up. Helpfully, like the hulk, the pub was also called the Warrior. We had been standing for about ten minutes, with Ben growing more and more edgy, when we saw this carriage appear at the top of the High Street.

'Course I didn't know it was our carriage, but Ben did, and though the cart was moving quickly, he stepped boldly into the road and turned to face the driver, his arm outstretched in front of him. At first it didn't look like the cart was going to slow down. I don't know what Ben would have done if it hadn't, but then I saw the driver stand and pull on the horses' heads. When the carriage came nearer, I could see the driver was pulling with all his strength, but I still couldn't be sure he would stop in time.

If Ben was worried, he didn't show it. He just stood motionless watching the horses coming towards him. I screamed out his name when I was certain he would be ploughed into the road, but I must admit I never really saw how things ended 'cos when I screamed, I must have shut my eyes. When I opened them, I was amazed to see the carriage stationary and Ben rubbing the steaming head of the lead horse. I swear if he'd moved at all, he'd only taken a step forward. I won't say much more 'cos he's sitting there, but the carriage door opened, our guard here stepped down and you must have heard all the arguing between him and the driver, but what you won't know is what settled the argument.

It had me wondering at first I'll tell you, but then I heard someone clear their throat right behind me. I looked round and saw the guard who had been our other oarsman and the remaining guard from the *Warrior,* standing right behind us, batons in hand. They didn't say anything. They didn't need to. The batons seemed to win the argument without further discussion.

Admonition
Hammocks

We've got to learn to sleep in swinging hammocks.

We arrived last night and they moved us onto the ship straight away. It's nothing like the *Brunswick*, but the *Sydney Cove* is still fairly cramped below deck and they keep us in chains all the time we're down there. Worst of all, we've got to learn to sleep in hammocks on a moving ship. We'd slept in hammocks on the Hulk, but unlike the *Brunswick,* the *Cove* wasn't stuck firm in the mud and swayed with the swell. It meant I didn't get any sleep at all, I was so afraid of falling out.

This morning I discovered most of the others felt the same – but Mary was one who definitely hadn't had any problems sleeping. As in the wagon that carried us from Woolwich, her leg shared a chain with mine, so when we retired for the night, the chain was too short for us to sleep any other way than next to each other. I knew she hadn't had a problem sleeping, because it seemed I had barely got into my hammock before I could hear her snoring. So this morning, I asked her what her secret was.

"Me dad was in the Merchant Navy. When he come 'ome one time, he brought his 'ammock with him. He told me mum 'e couldn't sleep in their ordinary bed no more, so 'e slung his 'ammock over their bed." She laughed. "Mind you, I think 'e must have fallen out a few times 'cos I'm only the third-born of fourteen.

Anyway, in the daytime, we kids used to fight with each other to lie in it, and like the rest of 'em, I got really good at climbing in quickly and hanging on when the others started it swinging. Dad explained to us that on a ship, 'ammocks were safer than a bunk 'cos they swung with the ship. A bunk, he said, could throw you out but an 'ammock just rocks you to sleep. Unlike all the other men I've ever known, Dad never told me somethin' that didn't turn out to be true."

She'd laughed like when she was telling us about Simon Peters, and I can't remember when I'd last heard laughter before then, it certainly wasn't while I was on the hulk. But I've also decided that what she said makes sense, so I've decided that tonight, even though we're at sea now and the hammocks are really swinging, I'm definitely going to try to use my hammock like Mary.

It was only this afternoon, when we were allowed on deck to get some fresh air and a little exercise, that I noticed how many women are on board. In fact, apart from the crew, I haven't seen any men. When I asked Mary if she'd noticed, she said she hadn't but then added,

"But if you want my opinion the fewer there are the better.'

I agreed with her, but told her why I thought a shortage of women was probably the reason we were gathered together to be sent to New Holland. I asked her,

"You and me were on a hulk for about the same time, four months, yes?"

She nodded, "Well, I don't know about on the *Warrior*," I said, "but on the *Brunswick* about once a month, some were carted off to join a transportation ship."

She said it was more or less the same in Woolwich.

"Now," I said, "ask y'self. What was the split? How many men and how many women were taken?"

"I dunno," she said. I could see she was trying to think back.

"About the same?" she asked, then before I could reply, answered her own question,

"No, definitely more men. I remember, before I was taken from the *Warrior*, almost all the men had already been taken for transportation. 'Cos of the gaol fever they 'adn't put any new prisoners on, so most of those left were women. When I think about it, I'd say about twice as many men were taken as women."

Looking straight at me, she said,

"So what do you fink that means is waiting for us in New 'olland? Wives, maybe?"

I knew by then she was thinking the same as me, so I just came out with it.

"Maybe, but a hundred or so women are never going to be enough to provide wives for every single man out there. There must be hundreds, thousands even, of men on their own. No, they don't want us to be wives, not mostly anyway. We both know they think of us all as being prostitutes and I think that's exactly what they'll expect us to be when we get out there."

As I say, she knew I was right.

"So what ye finkin' of doin' then, Adie?"

She looked at me expectantly. I didn't really have an answer, but I told there was one thing I was certain of,

"I don't know, but I do know one thing. No one is going to make me do anything like that – not if I don't want to."

She didn't argue with me, but even then I knew Mary would find her own way.

Mary
The Bay of Biscay

We'd been at sea about a week and every day the weather was much like the day before – a light breeze and a cloudless sky. Every morning they released our chains and allowed us up on deck for an hour or so, but for the rest of the day we were kept chained to one another in the hold. Confined to that gloomy, vermin-infested dungeon most of the time, it ain't hard to see why all of us lived for that precious hour when, basking in the sun, we could breathe deep without fear of taking in disease. So at the end of a day when the weather was unchanged, we had no reason not to look forward to being back on deck again the next morning. But overnight there was a major change and we woke early, our hammocks swinging in a full blown storm. The storm raged for five days.

On the first morning, three half-drowned seamen scrambled down the ladder and took off our chains. But before they struggled back up again, one of them told us the chains had been removed on the Master's orders to save us from injury. The Master had also ordered, so no one got washed overboard, that we should be locked in the hold until the storm was over.

So for the next five days, we were at the mercy of the storm, tossed in whatever direction the sea fancied. Some of the women found lengths of discarded rope and lashed themselves to the mainmast, but soon found the rope was rotten and failed to hold them. Others removed clothes which they used to tie themselves to any part of the ship that would take it. Most hoped that by lying down they would save themselves from too much movement, but in no time this became impossible as well because the hold leaked like a sieve. So when a huge wave went right over the ship as if the hatch weren't there, the hold filled over our heads.

We were lucky though because the water subsided quickly, otherwise I think some of us would have drowned, but it still stayed far too high to allow anyone to lie down. So for five exhausting days, wet, cold and sleepless, we were thrown like peas in a drum to all parts. We were only given food or fresh water twice; on the second day and again on the fourth when the hatch opened and a bucket, suspended from a rope, provided us with a small barrel of water and some sea-soaked biscuits. Hunger forced us to eat the biscuits and we were so thirsty we would have fought each other over the barrel if we'd been able to stand fore-square long enough to exchange blows.

On the fifth morning, we noticed waves weren't hitting the ship so often and when they did, it was with much less force. Finally, early in the afternoon, the hatch opened and Mr Carlyle, the ship's surgeon, shouted down that we were free to come up on deck. Some of the women had been injured and though no bones had been broken, all of us were fit to drop. But whatever state we were in, none of us wanted to stay in the hold a second longer than we had to, so we all managed to scramble up the ladder. The sky was still heavy and the sea tormented, but the wind had dropped and there were no longer any large waves.

While the surgeon tended the injured, four of the women who were still able, were chosen to cook us some food. When we finished eating, we were all sent back down and put in chains again. Returning to the hold, one of the first things we noticed was that all the vermin had disappeared. We soon realised that, as the women who'd been sent to clean up told us they'd found only three drowned rats, the rats would soon be back. Still, it was three days before a tell-tale scream from one of the women let us know the rats had returned. Now I'm not saying we would have volunteered for the five-day nightmare we'd endured, just for three days without rats, I don't think any of us ever would. But those three days, was the only time in the whole trip we could put our food down safely or leave our shoes on the floor while we slept. Their return meant that by the time we reached New Holland, hatred for any rat who was stupid enough to let itself be caught guaranteed it a bloody end.

As we went south, the weather got warmer. Otherwise it was unchanged – a steady breeze and clear sunny skies, or storms with high winds and high seas. Luckily, though the wind always seemed to blow as strong and the waves grow as high as in the Bay, the storms never lasted more than a couple a days.

But then the weather changed. We never noticed at first because when we were allowed up on deck, it was just a hot, still day. That was the difference though, and me and Adie didn't notice it for about four days – we hadn't realised just how still it was. When we did, I talked to one of the sailors and he told me we were in what they called the 'horse latitudes'. That scared me, I don't mind saying, because I remember me dad talking about them. Dad used to tell us stories about his times at sea before we went to bed and I never forgot the horse latitudes, because it was the one time I'd heard him say he'd thought he was going to die. He told us his ship had been stuck for a month with barely a breath of air and in the end without no water and they'd thrown overboard anything that wasn't vital, just to lighten the ship.

It was in the fourth week that a few desperate sailors wanted to launch a Jolly, even though they were still two hundred miles from the nearest land. Dad said they would have as well, if the captain hadn't refused to let them take any water with them. Dad said they were too weak to row two hundred miles, even if they'd taken all of the ship's water and that the captain had probably saved their lives.

Anyway, after a month the look-out picked up a faint breath of wind and the ship drifted just about far enough south for that breath to push them into the Westerlies. The captain kept on as much sail as the strong but steady gale that blew them towards South Africa would allow without capsizing the ship, and they made Cape Town just as dusk fell. Dad said they lost a total of four men on that trip and all had been lost in the Horses. Just like on Dad's ship, the Master on the *Sydney Cove* raised every sail we had and for two weeks they just hung like wet washing. Even though we were nearly out of water, I said nothing to anyone about me dad, not even Adie.

The third week had just begun when the crew started throwing any heavy but not essential items overboard and by then I had seen how deep in the barrel the sailor giving us our water reached over, to know it wouldn't last to the end of that week, let alone a month. It was late one afternoon at the back end of that third week that things began to change. We were all in the hold. They hadn't chained us for several days – I thought they were probably as weak as we were – and most of us were sitting round wherever we could. But a few, including Adie, were lying in their hammocks, which I suppose is the reason she was the first to notice.

"My hammocks moving, there must be a bit of a swell."

As soon as she said it, I knew she was right. Relieved, I said,

"If there's a swell, there must be wind."

Others noticed the ship was moving and one, because the crew hadn't raised it, climbed the ladder and started banging on the hatch. A few seconds later, the hatch was opened by one of the crew, who sounded annoyed when we heard him tell the woman to get back down. Climbing down the ladder after her, but only far enough to tell us a storm was building and we would be kept where we was until it was over, he climbed back out, pulling the ladder after him. Cries from some that they were thirsty went unheard, or more likely, were ignored.

As it happens, we was only without water for a couple of hours. Due to the movement of the ship, the ones who'd been in their hammocks all got down and were holding on to lengths of honest rope we'd found and already tied onto the ship wherever we could. The storm was blowing hard when the hatch opened and a water barrel was lowered down. A familiar voice told us to move it out the way and then the ladder was lowered and our surgeon hurriedly descended.

"The storm's already blown us into the path of the Westerlies and as soon as it's over, we'll be using the winds to sail into Cape Town; the Master says we should be there in a day once we're free of the storm.

Now that's the last of our water," he pointed at the barrel, "so, as we don't know how long the storm will last, you need to make it last as long as you can."

With that, he turned and climbed the ladder again then, struggling against the pitch and roll of the ship, raised the ladder behind him.

As soon as the hatch was shut, Adie stepped in front of the barrel and, leaning over, grabbed the ladle. Straightening, she turned and with the ladle in one hand, the other holding the edge of the barrel, she shouted over the noise of the storm,

"I think there's enough here for a ladle-full each, but I don't know if there's any more than that."

"Well I need a drink now." It was the woman who'd climbed the ladder. "We've not had any storm that's lasted more than two days since that first one in the Bay of Biscay. So that means we should be on our way to Cape Town sometime tomorrow."

She looked at Adie like she'd cause trouble if she didn't get her way, but Adie looked straight past her and spoke to the rest of us.

"Now you all know how much we've got, so now we need to agree a time when we all want to drink."

Looking for the first time at the woman who had demanded her water, but still speaking in a voice loud enough to be heard by everyone, she said,

"We need to agree on one time because, even if only one of us ladles out the water, she's never going to be sure that anyone who asks for a drink hasn't already had one. So I suggest we drink either now, this evening, or first thing in the morning."

She asked for a show of hands and it was clear most agreed they'd take their chances with the storm and have their ration right away. As it turned out, that was the right decision, 'cos even though when the last person emptied the ladle the barrel was almost dry, the storm dropped in the night.

Most of us took to our hammocks then and got some rest, but it seemed I'd only just shut my eyes when the sound of the hatch opening, followed by the ladder being lowered, woke me up again. Two of the crew began to climb down the ladder. Above them I could see dawn was breaking and as soon as they reached the bottom, they started fitting the chains back on us. When they finished, they headed straight back to the ladder, but as one started up again the other turned and said,

"We've been travelling towards Cape Town for the last three hours and the Master says we should be there by nightfall. So he's commanded us to fix the chains back on you – you'll be kept down here until we're back on our way to New Holland."

He paused before adding,

"As soon as we get to Cape Town, we'll be replenishing our water supply. When that's done, we'll send down a barrel."

I felt like Lazarus when they finally let us back on deck, I can tell you. We'd been held below for four days while supplies were taken on board and we were back out at sea before they let us breathe fresh air again. Up on deck we found that the wind was blowing hard, but not so hard we couldn't sail under full canvas most of the way to Sydney Cove. I suppose I could tell you more about our daily drudgery, but that's all it was – drudgery. In fact, because the wind was too hard and the sea too rough, we spent most of the time chained up in the hold, which got more and more disgusting every day.

It was during the only time that the wind dropped between when we left Cape Town and our arrival in New Holland, that we experienced the one incident worth remembering on that last leg of our journey. We were in the Southern Ocean when we woke one morning to find ourselves becalmed. About an hour later, the hatch opened and a couple of sailors came down and released our shackles. They told us we could go up on deck, which was just as well 'cos we'd been stuck down there for nearly a week and the foul smell from our buckets was overwhelming.

When we got on deck, me and Adie went different ways; I went to the port side, which turned towards New Holland, while she went to starboard which still faced out to sea. With the drop in the wind, the sky was clearer and the sea flatter, meaning we could see a lot further and in the distance we could just make out land. At first we thought it was just some clouds, but one of the other women had a word with a sailor she'd been getting very close to and it turned out that we were passing Van Diemans Land. We were just taking in the fact that we should reach Sydney Cove in the next three days when the most memorable and terrifying event of the whole journey occurred. With the ocean so still, I had noticed how clear the water was, and it was while I marvelled at how very far down I could see, that a small but growing shape way down in the depths caught my eye. Soon, about thirty feet from the ship and rising steadily towards the surface, the shape was already impossibly large and still growing. I looked around and was surprised to find that not only were all the women who'd been straining to see their first sighting of New Holland were now staring into the ocean, but that all the rest had come across from starboard and were looking down in the same direction.

Moments later, the monster broke the surface and continued to rise higher and higher, until it towered over us. What then happened appeared to happen in slow motion. When all of the creature had left the ocean it hung in the air, torrents of water cascading from its body before its weight, slowly at first then gathering speed, returned it to where it had come from. As most of the water was sucked down after the creature, creating a hole above it, we first experienced nothing more than a drenching from the little water that escaped the hole. But after a long moment, one long enough for us to relax, a deluge rose from the hole and engulfed us all in a wall of water. Because we were held by the ship's rail, no one noticed that with all of us stood on one side, the ship was already listing dangerously. Now the weight of added water that soaked our clothes, left the deck awash and swamped the hold, left our ship on the verge of capsizing. We held onto the rail to keep our balance, but then the voice of the master rang out above the roar of the water and the screams of those who could still breathe.

"Get over the other side. We've got to balance the ship or we'll capsize."

Some of the women who heard him and understood what he was saying started to scramble up the hill that the deck had become, others followed. But that was the tragedy; although enough women scrambled across to allow the ship to right itself, because two set off while the ship was still at its steepest and the deck at its wettest, both slid back and under the rail. No one saw them go and if they cried out, no one heard them. It was only about a quarter of an hour later, when women who knew them were unable to find them, that we realised they were lost.

Then, even though the wind was picking up again, our surgeon insisted the master turn the ship around and we all hung over the rail straining our eyes into the increasingly choppy ocean depths. We looked for over an hour without any sighting of either of them. It was only then, when we knew they must be drowned, that no one protested when the Master insisted that we return to our original course.

It was three more days before we reached Sydney Cove and another before we reached our final destination, the Women's Factory at Parramatta.

Admonition
Sydney Cove

One Hundred and Fifty-Eight Days, that's how long the Master told us it was since we left Falmouth and now we'd arrived in the place the ship that brought us here was named after. One hundred and fifty-eight days means almost six months of my sentence already served. So, for me and Mary, who had been given the same sentence as me, add the six months we were either in jail or on the hulks and there were only thirteen years left.

When we were first on the *Cove,* they chained me and Mary next to each other. Stuck that close to someone for so long, you either get on like me and Mary, or tear each other to pieces like some of the others. As Mary said,

"It's just like bein' married."

Talking of being married, Mary's 'old man' as she called him, was run over by a carriage. He'd hung on for a couple of days, but as he'd lost both his legs, Mary said she was glad when he died.

"No point getting all sentimen'al, is there?" She said, looking like she meant it. "'E couldn't 'ave worked anymore and I would 'ave 'ad to keep 'im. It was gonna be 'ard enough to keep meself."

Mary, who told me she was twenty-three, had married at eighteen and been with Tom for nearly three years. They didn't have any children, which Mary said was a blessing the way things had worked out.

Tom had worked as a Scavenger round the City of London, clearing horse muck from outside rich people's houses and keeping anything he found worth having. She told me,

"Always smelt of the stuff 'e did, but we didn't do too bad. We 'ad a roof over our 'eads and never went 'ungry. There were a lot who couldn't say that."

Some say that's why we get on; both of us having lost husbands, but I don't think that's the reason. I'm glad to call Mary a friend because she's never afraid to speak her mind, whatever the cost and I think I'm a bit like that. The last time I heard her speak her mind, we weren't far from port.

Now, I don't know exactly how many are on *The Sydney Cove*, but I do know that all but four are women. Apart from the two women who were lost a couple of days ago and the two who died of dysentery in the first week of the voyage, the only other one we lost was a poor young girl who died two weeks ago giving birth. Apart from that, we've all survived.

But that girl was only thirteen and you should have heard Mary.

"Thirteen and transpor'ed 'cos she cant the dobbin."

"Cos she can't what?" I asked – I had no idea what she meant.

For a moment she looked irritated. I'd interrupted her just as she was getting into her stride. But then she realised she was using slang. I'd learnt some Cockney phrases on the *Brunswick* and picked up a few more from Mary, but this was a new one. Laughing she said,

"Cant, not can't. She cant the dobbin. She was caught stealing ribbon from a shop. Didn't matter that she hadn't eaten for three days, was living on the street and that it was only the second time she'd been up in front of the beak."

I didn't know if all of that was true, but I didn't want to risk interrupting her a second time.

"Oh no, he was much more innerested in the fact she'd been workin' on the town. 'Depraved' the magistrate called her."

Now she was in full flow.

"Depraved! What about all the men who used 'er and what about 'im who made money out of 'er? Then there's the one who give 'er the pox and the one who made her pregnant. What's 'appened to them? All of them got away scot-free. That's what 'appened. They lied, she died and I know who I say was depraved, and it definitely ain't that poor child."

She was right of course. All the women agreed with her and do you know, I think even the surgeon agreed with her – the poor child certainly didn't die because of a lack of care from him. He made sure she had meat every day, for the rest of us it was only on Sunday, and she had fish whenever any were caught. He also made sure she had half a lime each day. She hated it and complained that it was too sour, but he made her eat it, told her it would stop her and her baby getting scurvy. Then, when her time was close, he moved her to the cabin where the two with dysentery had been confined. She'd been frightened at first, but he told her good sea air had been blowing through the place for nearly six months and there wasn't any trace of the smell of disease in there anymore.

By this time she trusted him, so she went without further argument. I don't think she'd ever received such kindness – especially from a man. And do you know what? I think that was how most of the women on the ship felt; certainly not one of them complained that she was getting special treatment.

As a ship's surgeon, he must have been used to seeing death, but I'm telling you, losing that girl and her baby hit him hard. He made the Master give her a proper funeral and because he was in charge of our religious teaching as well as our health, he said a prayer. Nice it was. As Mary said,

"She may have died, but the decent way 'e treated 'er gave some of 'em here a reason to go on livin'."

223

We'd made port late in the day on 18th June and the Master told us we would be held on board until morning. None of us really minded. We'd been at sea for almost six months and the ship had become our home. Only very few, the one's serving a second sentence, had any real idea of what New Holland held for us – though of course, we'd all heard stories. So when morning came, I think it was nervousness more than missing men that made some of the women call out bawdy comments when local constables, led by an armed officer from the local garrison, arrived to take us off.

They made us line up on the dock in pairs and fitted us with leg-irons, before marching us along the only road leading from the docks. Dolly, the woman in front of me, who was serving her second sentence in New Holland, complained that the last time she'd been here they'd all been ferried down the creek by boat. But she'd been partnered with Mary, who took no time in pointing out to her and anyone else in earshot, that the creek was in full flood and there was no way they'd be able to hold a boat steady for long enough for all of us to get on.

"Anyway," she said, "after six months cooped up on that ship, I reckon a bit of a walk won't do us no 'arm."

Mary never admitted regretting what she said. She and Dolly had had a few spats on the ship coming over, but we'd gone about half a mile before she turned to me and pointed towards the horizon. The sky above us was the bluest, clearest sky I'd ever seen, but ahead the horizon looked as though a thick black pencil had been used to mark its edges. As we watched, we'd all seen it by now, the line thickened until darkness covered half the sky, and even though it was still some miles off, we could see clearly that torrential rain was heading our way. All of us, including the guards, looked around for somewhere to shelter, but as far as the eye could see there was nothing but scrubland. We had no choice but to await the rain's arrival; we didn't have long to wait.

We'd been walking about ten more minutes when the first few drops began to fall. Heavy with rain, black clouds covered the whole sky; their heaviness seeming to weigh on us and although the constables shouted at us to go faster, when the rain started to fall in earnest we all came to a halt. Some of the guards and a few of the women had something to cover their heads, but most of us didn't have anything and we all became affected in the same strange way. One by one, we threw our arms in the air, turned our faces to the sky and gloried in the fat, warm drops that hit us in greater and greater numbers.

As the contagion spread, we all started laughing and then, despite the leg-irons, we began to dance. We must have been a strange sight, something like a hundred women soaked to the skin and all performing this odd, lop-sided dance, each to a separate tune no one else could hear. The constables stood watching in amazement and I'm not sure how long they would have let us carry on if things hadn't started to get out of hand.

All that rain turned the red dust which covered the track into cloy, slippery clay and I suppose it was inevitable that one of us should lose their footing and fall. Dolly, who had complained about having to walk, now danced more wildly than anyone and of course, when she slipped and fell, Mary fell with her. As they scrambled to help each other up, one of them would lose her footing again and they'd both sit back in the mud.

Several times they tried to get up but each time, as they slid about, the ground became even more slippery, making sure each attempt to rise was bound to end in failure. Eventually they gave up and just sat on the ground laughing at each other, their differences forgotten. They were tears of laughter I think, but it was hard to be certain with the rain and mud running down their faces and when Dolly started throwing handfuls of mud at Mary, she of course returned the favour. The other women stood laughing at them, and even then I don't think the constables were that concerned. But when handfuls started to go astray and hit the women standing closest to them, they responded in kind, slipping and falling as they tried to avoid the mud now aimed at them. With one pair after another joining Dolly and Mary on the ground, it became too much for the constables.

The officer in charge, who unlike the constables was armed, lifted his rifle and shot it in the air. The loud retort from the gun arrested us all and those on the ground tried more seriously to get up, but even when those still standing tried to help them, more often than not things went the wrong way and they joined the women on the ground. The shambles was getting worse and the officer knew he was in danger of losing face as well as control. So this time when he raised his gun, instead of firing skyward, he aimed at the ground in front of us. He hit the ground so close that mud spattered, by the bullet, sprayed the legs of the nearest women. Having got our attention again, he told those of us still standing to line up at the edge of the track where the ground was a little less muddy. Stepping carefully to find the cleanest ground, everyone did as they were told. The officer then commanded the constables to help the remaining women to their feet, instructing them to join the rest of us.

When eventually we were all on safer ground, we began to move off again. Thankfully, although its force had lessened the rain still fell steadily, washing away most of the mud that had stuck to us during our games. We trudged onwards, the path rising steadily until our tired legs, weary because they'd spent months walking no further than the length of the *Sidney Cove*, were brought gratefully to a halt outside our destination, the Female Factory.

Part Six

Henry
Parting Gifts

Though weak, I'm content. I've just completed two letters that will settle the last of my affairs and now I face death knowing there is nothing more I need do.

For some time Jane had smiled at my breathlessness, blaming it on my expanding waistline. But I was unable to hide from her the true cause when, as we walked together in the garden, the first violent coughing fit struck me. Snatching my handkerchief from me, she saw the tell-tale spots of blood. She looked straight at me. Though neither of us spoke, we both knew I had become consumptive.

It's been nine months since that fateful walk and I suppose we both hoped the condition would progress more slowly. But it wasn't to be, and about three months ago I began to withdraw from the Practice. Led by Charles Dowle, who took from me my most pressing cases, my partners have, without complaint, taken the rest. I am so very grateful to them because it means I have been able to spend more time with Jane. For me, the most difficult and distressing sight to witness has been the effect my condition has had upon her. She tries to be strong, but every night when she thinks I'm sleeping, I hear her crying. I try to tell her these things must be and that I shall leave her well provided for, but though she says she knows and tries to smile reassuringly, still I hear the night time weeping and it breaks my heart.

Yesterday, to Jane's great dismay, I decided to take a coach into town because I needed to visit a bank. So seeing I was determined to go, she insisted on accompanying me, which was fortunate because by the time we came to returning, I found I was unable to walk to the coach without her support. I didn't want to cause Jane further distress than my illness already had, but it was essential that I withdrew all of the money Jabez had left in an account he'd opened for Admonition. Although he'd been dead for twelve years, I'd never forgotten the last time Jabez and I met and the letters he'd entrusted to me. Nor had I forgotten the strictures he placed upon them, which now presented me with a dilemma. By my calculation, assuming there were no extensions to her sentence, Admonition would be free in about two years and even if she then decides to return to England, it would be unlikely she'd be back in less than three. My dilemma was resolved when I realised not only would I be long dead by then, but that she might also choose never to return at all.

Jabez had told me I should give Admonition his letter on her return and only to open the letter he'd written to me when I knew she was back. But now I realised fourteen years was more than enough time for Admonition to change her mind and decide to stay in New Holland. This, with the knowledge that it was very unlikely I would be here if she did return, meant I was quite sure Jabez would have wanted me to open the letter he addressed to me a little early. So, sitting behind my desk with the letter in front of me, I knew that no matter how I tried to justify my actions to myself, I was going against a client's last request. What's more, it was a request I had expressly promised to honour. So as I broke the seal, I still felt very unsure that I was doing the right thing.

As soon as I unfolded the letter and even before I could read it, a small piece of paper fell on my desk. Straight away, I saw it was issued by the Critchley and Turner Bank in Macclesfield and, on closer examination, that it contained the number of a strongbox. Many of our clients used banks, including Critchley and Turner's, to hold their legal documents and the most common documents they held were their Wills. As we were often named as executor, I was familiar with the note from Critchley's acknowledging a deposit. The bank was some distance from the Boar's Head, so I imagined Jabez wanted his dealings with them to remain private.

I could glean nothing further from the note, so I turned to the letter. Jabez' writing was small, neat and clear and it surprised me how someone who grew up in a workhouse could write so well. He started the letter by thanking me for representing him in court and hoped I understood why he had refused to allow me to petition the King for clemency. But most of the letter explained the contents of the strongbox and how I could gain access to it. He wrote that when he suspected the Excise men were closing in on him, he took all the money remaining from the payments he received from Sam Baker, which was most of it, and deposited it with Critchley and Turner, a bank he'd never before had any dealings with. He added that he knew if the Excise men caught him smuggling, he would, at very least, receive a very long prison sentence and any money held by a bank in his or Admonition's name would be confiscated; so he'd devised what I must admit was an ingenious plan.

Although he'd had very little dealings with the legal profession, he remembered that I had written Jack Dodds' Last Will and Testimony. He also remembered he still had the copy of the Will that Dodds had given him when it had been drawn up. Crucially, it carried my signature as executor, so when he completed the Plate Ledger at Critchley's, he gave my name as signatory and left his copy of Dodds' Will with my signature as proof of mandate.

Jabez firmly believed that if he took complete responsibility for the smuggling, charges against Admonition would be dropped, or at worst result in only a light sentence. Expecting that to be the outcome, he thought he needed to explain only the arrangements to me and then, when people had begun to forget about the case, I would simply give her the money with his letter and help her to start a new life. But when things failed to work out as he hoped and he knew Admonition wouldn't, under any circumstances, be able to access the money for fourteen years, he realised he needed to adjust his plan. Judging that he needed to protect me from the likely illegality of the money until it was time to pass it to Admonition, he also understood that the less I knew about the strongbox and its contents the better. He knew it would be cruel to tell Admonition about the money whilst it remained well beyond her reach and I now understood fully why he'd instructed me not to pass on his letter to her until she was free.

I had no option but to get to the bank because once I was gone, no one else would be able to gain access to the strongbox. I had no problem withdrawing the money because although I'd been young when I drew up Dodds' Will, my signature had changed little over the years and now the money resides safely in a secret compartment in my study desk.

My own Will ensures that all my financial matters are clear and whilst I have made a number of small bequests and two larger ones to John and Kit, everything else I've left to Jane, ensuring she'll be secure for her remaining years. On his return from New Holland, I shall show Kit both the letter I've just completed for Admonition, the letter to her from Jabez, as well as the money locked in my desk. Then I'll ask him, when he goes back to New Holland, to use his best endeavours to try and find Admonition and give her both letters. I haven't opened Jabez' letter to her. It's bound to be much more personal than his letter to me and I feel sure my letter will clear up any contradictions. I'll also ask Kit to arrange for the money to be made available to her when she's set free. Although it has been twelve years since she left these shores, finding her should be possible as she will still be serving her sentence. I know the ship she was on sailed to Sydney Cove and it's most likely that on arrival she was taken from there to a place nearby called the Female Factory, although it is also likely she will have moved on from there. The authorities in Parramatta, the nearest settlement, should hold a record of her whereabouts, so I'm sure Kit will be able to find her.

I know my life is to be cut short by this miserable consumption, but in many other ways I've been and still am a lucky man. While work has mostly brought me satisfaction and with it, the money that has allowed me to live comfortably, my two boys and Jane have really made my life worthwhile. Neither of the boys has found a wife yet, but both have settled into jobs that suit them and I believe they're happy. Jane has been beside me for over thirty years and her kindness, composure and level head have seen me through even the most difficult of times.

But now, like me, the inkwell is almost empty. The dry well and this wretched cough prevent me from writing anymore, so there is nothing more I can do except, for the last time, put down this quill and resolve to make the best I can of the days I have left to spend with Jane.

Admonition
A Taste of Freedom

It was something I hadn't expected. After all, when we got here, we both knew we were bound to end up in different places. It was just that one day we were both stuck in that squalid hold and the next, though she'd only known him for an hour or so, Mary was saying she was marrying some farmer. The following morning she was gone, leaving me not knowing if I'd ever see her again and I was bereft. And that's really what surprised me.

The women who'd been in the *Factory* a while told us conditions had improved since it was re-built after a fire had gutted the place. God only knows what it had been like then, because conditions were still worse than on the *Sydney Cove* and in some ways even worse than on the *Brunswick*. For a start, on the hulk, although they made us wear chains, we were otherwise free to move around on the top deck during the day. But in the *Factory* the women from the *Cove* who hadn't already been assigned elsewhere, took the number of women expected to live in a couple of rooms big enough for about fifty, up to nearly two hundred. To complete the pretty picture, the *Factory* roof leaked and the privvies, there were only two, stank.

When there was work, we spent our days weaving or making rope, but for more than half the time, stocks of wool or flax ran out leaving us idle until more arrived, which could take weeks. When that happened, the days seemed to go on forever and we passed the day sleeping or just lounging and hoping the next day would bring new supplies. But when we had nothing to do, spending every idle hour, both day and night in the same overcrowded place, most of us not yet used to the heat, there was bound to be friction.

Rachel said she'd been there the longest and that was the reason she was the leader among the women in the Factory. Whilst she might have been 'top dog', several women had been there longer than her; it was other reasons that made the women in the Factory do as she bid. She was broader, taller and just plain stronger than anyone else, and there were some who hid behind Rachel's size and made sure there was no dissent. But it was the simple truth that no one ever dared challenge her, no one took the risk and that's what kept her on top; that was until Amy arrived.

Transported from Cork with a group of other ne'er-do-wells, Amy O'Brien arrived only a month after the *Sydney Cove* deposited almost one hundred of us into the already full Factory. Since we'd arrived a number had been assigned elsewhere providing much-needed labour, mostly on the farms that were spread thinly across New South Wales and us with much needed space.

Unfortunately, the newest arrivals had more or less replaced the ones who'd been moved on and that's why Rachel paid them special attention. Of course, if anyone had pointed out to her that no one in the Factory, including these latest additions, had any choice but to go where they were put, I suppose she might have behaved differently, but no one ever did because everyone was too frightened of her. She hadn't really paid much attention to Amy, but as the young Irishwoman was barely four foot tall and by nature very quiet, that wasn't surprising. Small and quiet she might have been, but as Rachel

232

was to discover, Amy bowed to no one and when she was ready she made very sure Rachel paid her the closest attention.

Amy had been with us about three weeks when she decided to sleep in Rachel's 'spot'. I'm in no doubt she knew exactly what she was doing. She'd already seen how resentful most of the women were towards Rachel and so had chosen the thing that caused the deepest and widest resentment against her. Whereas the rest of us spent each night cramped in spaces so small it was impossible to turn over, Rachel slept raised a little above all of us and lying on three bales of raw wool. Able to stretch out to her full length if she wanted, she was also free to turn to either side without disturbing anyone – especially herself.

One night, Rachel was late joining us. She'd spent the day on a detail ferrying supplies to the Factory from a ship docked in Sydney Cove and Amy saw it as the chance she'd been waiting for. When Rachel came in about an hour after we settled down, she disturbed everyone in her path, moaning loud enough about her day to make sure we were all awake – she wasn't to know we were all agog, waiting to see what would happen when she got to her 'bed'.

"What the… Get out of my place before I throw you out. You're lucky I'm too tired to do anything about you now, but you can be sure we'll be having a little chat in the morning."

I couldn't see Amy from where I was lying, but I could make out Rachel as she stood looking down at the bales. She obviously expected Amy to pull herself up and scuttle away into the dark. But that's not what happened. In fact, at first nothing happened because Amy just lay there, apparently the only person in the room still asleep. Amy snored, we all knew she was awake but she really did, she actually snored and someone, I never found out who, couldn't contain their laughter. This infuriated Rachel and she bent over and shook Amy roughly. What happened then went from comic to threatening and finally to the deposing of a tyrant and the start of a whole new atmosphere in the Factory.

Apparently just roused, Amy turned slowly over,

"Waser matter? Why've you woken me up? It's comfortable here. You should try it sometime."

According to those who were nearest, it was only then that she opened her eyes and apparently for the first time realised who she was talking to.

"Ah, Rachel, it's you. Glad to see you're back from the Cove, but if you don't mind, I don't really want to talk just now. I'm sure whatever it is that's on your mind will keep until morning."

With that, she lay down again and turned on her side, away from Rachel. This was too much for Rachel who, with a roar of frustration, grabbed Amy's arm and dragged her from the bales. But as she was swung from her bed, Amy reached out and grabbed a handful of Rachel's hair. Her grip was surprisingly strong and as she left the bales and flew past her she kept a hold, so the scream that followed wasn't from Amy as she flew across the room, but from Rachel who had provided Amy with a brake. When Amy stopped moving, a lump of Rachel's hair fell to the ground. Rachel looked down at it and put her hand to her head and gingerly rubbed where it hurt. She looked past Amy, her gaze ranging round until it settled on one of the women she used when she thought she might need support, and in an oddly steady tone, she commanded,

"Bring me the mirror."

The 'mirror' was a small piece taken from a pier glass that had once been part of an order for the Governor's Residence. Back in 1800, Governor Macquarie decided to extend his residence and the pier was part of a mirror arrangement he intended to install in Mrs Macquarie's new dressing room. All the mirrors, including the pier, had survived the journey from England and it was only as they were being transferred from Sydney Cove to Parramatta that the cart carrying them slipped into a deep rut and the pier had slid off. Unfortunately, a rock that stood proud in an otherwise stone-free surface had smashed the mirror into many pieces and the driver had been flogged for his carelessness. Though he'd been treated unjustly, the driver didn't dwell on his treatment. Instead, he got up early the next morning and went back to where the accident happened and collected all the larger pieces of mirror and sold them in Parramatta. One of those pieces had found its way into the Factory.

Rachel held up the mirror and moved it around slowly, so she could see all of the bare patch; there were pinpricks of blood welling up all over the surface. Bending down, she picked up the clump of hair and it started to break apart in her hand. For some reason, this relit the fire in Rachel and she reached out to grab Amy, but all this time Amy had never taken her eyes off her and so as soon as Rachel's hand came towards her, she was ready. Catching hold of her arm, she used Rachel's momentum to pull her past and as she went, stuck out her leg. Amy still had hold of her arm so when Rachel hit the ground Amy, bending Rachel's arm to an impossible degree, landed with both knees in the small of her back. Rachel let out a silent scream, silent only because Amy had knocked all the breath out of her.

This was all too much for her cronies and led by those who could see the obvious pain on Rachel's face, they all started to pick their way through to rescue their protector. But as they weren't all together yet, others buoyed by Amy's example and recognising the chance she'd given them, stood up and prevented any help from arriving. When she realised no help was coming, Rachel had no choice but to gasp her submission and once Amy was satisfied, she was not going to meet further resistance, she relaxed her grip and Rachel slowly got up. Never taking her eyes off Rachel as she also got carefully to her feet, Amy was always ready if she was attacked. But the fight had left Rachel and whilst she viewed Amy with a new respect, her last act as leader was to signal to those who still might offer her support that they should lie down again. Picking up her blanket, which Amy had left folded neatly at the foot of the bales, Rachel made to move away, but then she heard,

"Rachel."

It was Amy and she'd spoken quietly; there was no threat in her voice. Rachel turned and Amy smiled and with open hand offered her the bed.

"It's your bed. I never wanted to take it from you."

Rachel looked bemused as Amy picked up her own cover and moved back to the place she'd occupied earlier. Rachel may have been unsure as to what had just happened, but to the rest of us it was crystal clear. She no longer had any control over us. Amy had made sure of that, but she also had no desire to replace her.

So over the next few months, I can't say life in the Factory was easy. There were times when the work seemed never-ending, others when we had nothing to do, and we were always overcrowded. But there was no trouble; the first sign of trouble Amy, if necessary backed by Rachel (unsurprising if you think about it), made sure it came to nothing.

Finally, after about eight months, the morning came when I was summoned to the Supervisor's office to be told I'd been assigned to the service of the Governor. Because I could read and write a little, my first assignment turned out to be my easiest. Starting with the women in the Factory, before moving on to all other convicts of both sexes in the Parramatta area, I checked that the information held on them was complete and up to date. Where new information was received, most commonly notification of marriage,

234

reassignment or quite often both, it was my job to update that record. But where records were simply incomplete, I was only required to identify them and the missing information and then pass both to my Supervisor.

Whilst I returned each night to the Factory to sleep on the hot and crowded floor, by now something I'd become used to, each morning I was allowed to walk to work accompanied only by two or three other women similarly assigned. As I'd been unassigned long enough to become a familiar sight among the others, though I'm quite sure many didn't even realise the change in my status, nobody objected to me adding to the crowds each evening. But that walk every day in the bright, but still cool, morning air is something I still remember with fondness and probably always will. You see, it wasn't just the cool air, pleasant as it was after a stifling night in the Factory, but the feeling of freedom that, every day, for twenty minutes came with it. Escape was pointless because there was nowhere in New Holland for me to go and England was further away than I could imagine, but that never took the shine off the feeling of being truly unchained.

So with a little bit of freedom in the morning, an interesting job during the day and a safe place to sleep at night (Amy was never assigned.), whilst I hung on to a secret dream, it was nevertheless a way I could have seen out my days, let alone my sentence, quite happily. But it wasn't to be.

I'd been in the Records Office for about eight years when Lt Edward Granger, newly arrived in Sydney, became our Supervisor. The lieutenant was a qualified engineer. The project he'd been sent all the way from India to command had been delayed indefinitely. Rather than sending him straight back to India, the army decided he should stay in New Holland until the future of the project, to clear dangerous shoals in Newcastle Harbour, became clear.

The problem of what to do with him was solved when our Supervisor fell sick and the Governor and the lieutenant's commanding officer realised they could solve each other's problem by appointing Lieutenant Granger as the Records Office's temporary Supervisor. Edward's father had, by dubious means, built a sizeable Estate on the west coast of the Scottish Highlands, after a drop in the value of kelp had forced a number of landlords to sell at rock-bottom prices. Edward's older brother, Stephen, would inherit the Estate, but before joining the army Edward had been responsible for the Estate's administration, an experience he agreed suited him to the work of the Records Office.

Our Supervisor never recovered his health and died in that Summer's heat. Edward was more than happy to stay as our Supervisor because by then he'd met and fallen in love with Catherine, the daughter of the local shipping agent. He stayed with us for three years, during which time he talked often of his plans for when he left the army. The day after Catherine agreed to marry him, he started to include her in those plans and as their relationship deepened, their plans became more and more detailed.

Of course, it was only after Edward and Catherine had decided: first, the date they would marry, then when the Lieutenant would resign his Commission and even after that, when they'd found some land where they could build a homestead, funding for the clearance project came through. Lieutenant Granger had little choice and he knew it; the decision had been made and he would have to go to Newcastle. Knowing there was nothing else he could do, the lieutenant served notice that he would resign his Commission in exactly one year.

There were three women from the Factory working in the Records Office and when I heard that I was the Governor's choice to accompany the Lieutenant to ensure his paperwork was completed fully, I was delighted. My own plans were still not fully formed, but I knew that whatever they turned out to be, they could only be helped if they were supported by the Lieutenant. Spending the last year of my sentence, and his last before leaving the army together, could only make that more possible.

We were due to leave immediately, but torrential rain made the road impassable until June, so we barely had time to settle in Newcastle before he told me that he and Catherine had set the date of their marriage for October. That didn't surprise me, but what came as quite a shock was when he told me that when he and Catherine were married, they would be moving to Morpeth and I should no longer be required. My shock must have shown because he said,

"You'll be alright, because we're getting married at St John's in Parramatta. I've made arrangements for someone to collect you from the Church and take you back to the Factory.

It can't be long until you're a free woman, can it?" I told him that I had about four months of my sentence left to serve, and he said,

"Clearly, once you're free, if I can help you in any way I will."

I didn't tell him that I had hoped he'd take me with them to Morpeth, but what I wasn't to know, couldn't have known, was that his decision to leave me behind was the best thing he could have done for me.

Mary
Ellis

Ellis Johnson was both a grazer and a loner, content because one suited the other.
He'd served fourteen years for coining, most of it assigned to a free farmer and then, his
sentence served, had put into action the plan he'd spent all those years devising. He told
me about it the first time we met and loads more times over the years I knew him.
Sometimes he'd forget things, sometimes he remembered new things he hadn't told me
before and other times he remembered things I think he only wished had happened;
whatever the whole truth, this is what he told me.

Before he was transported, Ellis had lived all his life in Birmingham where, as a
skilled craftsman, he made an honest living producing shoe buckles for the gentry. He
turned to a life of dishonesty when the shoemaker, who bought all his buckles, was
himself forced into bankruptcy by so many of his well-to-do customers not settling their
accounts. Of course that meant he couldn't pay Ellis' bill, leaving him penniless. He did
find bits of work but nothing regular, so in desperation he turned to the only trade his
skills would allow. He first rented a cellar from another metal-worker and then set up
with all the implements he would need for coining – an iron press, a die for guineas and
others for whole and half-crowns, a cutting tool for making the blanks and an edging tool
for milling the coins.

Though he didn't live where he worked, it was still a risky business and Ellis made
it worse for himself by being good at his work. When I questioned how that could make
things riskier for him, he told me his coins were so good the Royal Mint would have
trouble identifying them as fakes. And though he tried to keep to the shadows, making
sure that any repairs to his tools or amendments to his blocks, which he did himself, he
had to rely on many others for supplies of charcoal, brass, copper and other metals. One
of his suppliers was a man who went by the colourful but appropriate title, Pegleg
Johnson. Pegleg supplied Ellis with charcoal, but he had many other customers, and Ellis
was a long way from being his biggest; that honour went to Tom Fordham.

A jeweller by trade, Fordham worked with three others to produce mostly guineas
and crowns. But their quality was second-rate, and even though they produced a lot more
coins than Ellis, they found he was taking trade from them. So when Pegleg told Tom
where Ellis was based, it didn't take long for Fordham to make sure the authorities knew
the address as well.

In a way, Ellis said, he was lucky because counterfeiting is a Capital offence. He
only avoided the rope because, though they found all his tools, he'd run out of coins and
his bronze and copper suppliers (also customers of Pegleg strangely enough) had been
unable to supply him with any metal for the previous week. It meant that though they
could prove he had the equipment to make them, they could find no coins and no metal
to make them with. As there was no chance of finding a witness willing to testify against
him, Ellis could only be sentenced to transportation.

Arriving in New Holland, Ellis avoided the evils of rum which gripped most convicts
and learnt a new way of life. Helping to keep five thousand sheep, protecting them from

rustlers and even learning how to shear them, meant when his sentence was complete, Ellis was ready to put his plan into action. He'd saved all the money he was allowed to earn working overtime, so that on release and as a free man with no debts, he'd been able to buy two hundred hectares of cheap land, with enough money left over to be able to buy a hundred young ewes.

The land he bought was cheap because the ground was stony, the vegetation sparse and there was no obvious water supply. He also knew if the farm was to survive, apart from finding water, he needed to find a ram or two, something he couldn't afford to buy. Before solving those problems, he went ahead and built a bush hut, he didn't build it to last, but he hoped it would give him shelter until he had time to build something more substantial.

He then walked into the nearest settlement and breaking a lifetime's pledge, bought a quart of rum. Returning to the farm, he walked across to his nearest neighbour and then a further two miles to the home of the owner of the biggest farm in the District, inviting them both to join him that evening over a neighbourly glass of best Bengal rum. It wasn't really best Bengal that he'd bought, but that didn't matter, because to Ellis it was everything he needed it to be. A clear and strong spirit of unknown origin, he knew it was likely these men would share the thirst for strong spirits, experienced by most of their fellow settlers. They wouldn't worry whether it came from Bengal or the Dundas Valley.

He was right and as he expected, first Dan Cobb then Jack Cornwall didn't hesitate in accepting his invitation and that evening, as the light faded, they appeared together at his door. Greeting them, full mug in hand, Ellis poured two more large ones from his jug, placed them on the table and invited both men to sit. There then began a right old time of trading stories, from both faded memories of the Old Country and tall and growing taller tales of their time in New Holland. All evening Ellis made sure his guests' glasses were kept topped up, his own filled from a smaller jug of water he kept hidden behind the rum. With the jug of rum half empty, a strong alcohol-fuelled friendship had grown between the men and Ellis judged that both his guests were drunk enough for him to steer the conversation in the direction he wanted it to go.

At daybreak, Ellis had already gathered his sheep together, and as the sun began to climb, he drove them the short distance to his neighbour's property. Passing Dan's hut, he wasn't surprised there was no sign of life. So pressing on, he crossed the land of his other new friend until, on the far side, he reached his destination. A small stream that ran through the corner of Jack's land, trickling over broad flat stones, before winding its way to join the Duck River, which itself, was already heading for Parramatta Creek. His grateful sheep needed no further invitation and stepping across the stones, all drank deeply from the stream. When they'd taken their fill, Ellis began to lead them back home and that was when a shot rang out. Instinctively, Ellis raised his arms in surrender, all the while looking round, trying to find the source of the shot; he'd already guessed who fired the gun. Then a familiar voice rang out.

"What in the Devil's name do you think you're doing?"

Standing in the shadow of the farm's only barn was Jack Cornwall, his rifle raised and pointed at Ellis. Even at fifty yards, Ellis could see Jack's hands were trembling, probably because of the previous night's excesses, and he knew the farmer, whether he meant to or not, could very easily fire again. So although Ellis kept his arms raised, he smiled and trying to look relaxed, said,

"Morning Jack. Good to see you. Sorry if I startled you, but I wanted to take advantage of our agreement straight away. It was good of you to grant my sheep access to your water. I think if you hadn't, they would've started dying in the next day or so."

"Agreement? What agreement?"

Jack remembered little of the previous evening and Ellis laughed when he told me this part of his tale. He said Jack looked bemused and that meant his plan was working.

Now, because he thought it was safe to do so, he started to lower his arms, but as soon as he did, Jack cocked his rifle. Hurriedly raising them again, Ellis explained he was just reaching for his shirt pocket where he had his copy of their agreement. Then slowly, he began to lower his arms again, but this time he looked questioningly at the farmer and in reply, Jack replaced the safety catch and lowered the rifle. Once he was sure he wouldn't be shot, Ellis showed Jack the note he'd written the night before which they'd both signed. It said that in exchange for allowing him to water his sheep daily at the stream and lending him two rams when his ewes were in season, Ellis would give him the first two lambs born to his flock, three the next year and five each year following. Watching him stare at the note, he said he could see Jack struggling to clear the fog that hid his memories of the previous night's events, but whilst he remained lost, Ellis gently took back the note reminding him he had his own copy.

Gathering his sheep, who'd scattered when Jack fired his rifle, he started to drive them home, leaving Jack searching his pockets trying to find his copy of their agreement. Crossing back over Dan's land, Ellis still saw no signs of life, but he expected no trouble from that quarter anyway, having promised Dan two lambs (to do with as he will) just for right of access. He knew he'd tricked them both, but he also knew the deal was a fair one. Jack and Dan knew it as well so didn't give him any more trouble.

So that first Spring, Ellis was as good as his word and when his ewes lambed, he took the first two across to Jack and two more to Combe Acres – the grand name Dan had given his farm. Then, after slaughtering and salting down just enough meat to feed himself for a year, he sold the remaining male lambs and kept the rest of the females so he could start to grow his herd. For the next few years, he continued in much the same way: expanding his flock; keeping his side of the deals he'd struck with his neighbours and saving as much of the money from the lambs he'd sold as he could. The only change that happened in the third year was that his older ewes were now ready for shearing. This not only gave him a little extra income, but also provided him with the means to make a little extra bedding for the cold winter nights.

Slowly, year by year, Ellis' farm expanded, but after five years he knew it would stop growing unless he had more land. Jack Cornwall's farm had also continued to prosper and grow, his increased wealth advertised by his young bride and newly-built farmhouse. Combe Acres on the other hand did not advertise prosperity, nor did its owner. In fact Dan Cobb and his farm both showed neglect, and whilst the symptoms for each were different, the root cause was the same. In the early days, Dan had worked hard trying to grow flax in the poor, parched soil, but no matter how hard he worked, the soil just couldn't support the crop. Ellis said that when the flax failed for the third time, Dan just gave up trying and instead, dedicated all his time to the rum which he'd been drinking in increasing amounts, to numb his disappointment.

After five years, Combe Acres was fast returning to the wild it had never been very far away from, and the sun-bleached bush hut had so many holes in its sides and roof it didn't keep out even the slightest breeze or the lightest shower. But Dan didn't appear to see or care and most days he'd be found outside the front of the hut, sitting on his only chair, drinking rum. He'd only go inside when he was too drunk to stay steady on the chair and then he'd collapse on his bed, where no rain or wind could rouse him.

That was until the night a high wind blew Dan's hut completely away. Ellis heard the noise as pieces of hut careered across the land, but the wind alone still didn't wake Dan and it was another hour before he came banging at Ellis' door. The torrential rain which had arrived on the coattails of the storm had finally woken him and drenched and bedraggled, Ellis said he'd made a pitiful sight.

Ellis sat him down in front of the fire and handed him a glass of rum from the bottle he'd kept untouched for the past five years. Although Dan was grateful, as he'd been drinking all that day, the rum only served as a top-up, and in a few minutes he was drunk again. Then, in the moments Ellis had his back to him laying more wood on the fire; exactly how drunk Dan was became clear. Turning when he heard a dull thud, he found him lying unconscious at his feet. Too heavy to carry, even if he was willing to give up his bed – which he wasn't, Ellis just pulled him a little closer to the fire. But then he had second thoughts, not to give up his bed mind, but he knew when the fire died down, it would get cold inside the hut, so he found a fleece he wasn't using himself and threw it over the sleeping Dan.

Next morning, leaving him sleeping soundly, Ellis took his sheep across to the stream and when he returned Dan was just coming round. Bleary-eyed, he dragged himself into a sitting position where, propped up against the nearest wall, he gazed around the hut. Finally, looking at Ellis he scratched his head and said,

"How in the name of all things Holy did I end up here?"

Ellis said he looked at him in disbelief and asked him if he really didn't remember anything from the night before.

Dan shook his head.

Ellis glanced out the front and said,

"I think you need to take a look at your hut?"

Fear and probably the first few fragments of a memory struck Dan and he pulled himself to his feet and stumbled outside. Moments later, he was back and uninvited, sat down in the nearest chair. Holding his head in his hands, he said nothing, but seconds later his shoulders started to shake and large tears began to fall to the ground between his feet. Ellis said that he didn't know what to do. True he'd heard men cry out from the lashes that were the commonest form of punishment in New Holland, but though he knew of no man who'd been able to keep silent whilst lines of flesh were torn from his back, he'd never heard one of them cry.

Truth be known, he was embarrassed and because he couldn't think of anything else, Ellis said,

"Come on now, Dan. It was only a bush hut. I bet the two of us can knock up a new one in a couple of days. Meanwhile you can always stay here."

Dan looked up and Ellis said he could see his rheumy eyes held nothing but despair, and when he answered, his reply reeked of it.

"You're a good man, but it'd be a waste of time. My crop's failed three times and I haven't even tried this year. I've no money left to try again and the little I did have, I've spent on rum. No, as soon as I can sell my land, I'm heading for town, see what I can pick up there."

They both knew, with money in his pocket, all he'd pick up was more rum and that when the money ran out, he was bound to be thrown in jail for vagrancy. Living that way, life would be short, but without any money, probably even shorter. Either way Ellis wasn't that bothered. Life had been hard – still was – he'd shown Dan as much goodwill as he'd shown any man and here was an opportunity not to be missed – so he took it.

"If you're sure you want to sell, I'll buy your land, so long as it's at the right price."

Because of its position and lack of water, Ellis knew the land wouldn't be of much value to anyone except him or Jack Cornwall. Jack had already expanded by buying land that followed the stream, so Ellis knew he could offer anything he wanted and if he wanted to sell, Dan would have no choice but to accept. Ellis was a decent man but he couldn't afford to be sentimental, so he made what he knew was a fair offer in the circumstances.

"Your farm's about the same size as mine, ain't it? 'Bout two hundred hectares?"

Dan nodded hopefully. Ellis knew he was anxious to get his hand on the money. He had a thirst and it was getting stronger.

"Right then, I'll tell you what I think it's worth."

Of course he reminded him that locked between Ellis and Jack's land and with no water supply, his land was of little value to anyone else and that Jack was only interested in land close to water. Then he pointed out that, due to his neglect, Dan's land had returned to being little more than scrubland and they both knew how much work it would take to make it suitable for sheep. He told me that by the time he finished, even though he offered him half the money he'd paid for his own land, Dan didn't hesitate.

"I'll take it. Just give me the money and we'll seal it with a glass of your rum," he looked greedily at the bottle, "then I'll be on my way."

Knowing Dan's thirst for rum was running high, Ellis just went along with him.

"Alright, if that's the way you want to do it."

He took a jar down from a dark corner of one of the roof struts an' counted out the money – 'e never told me how much. Dan grabbed it and, without even counting it, stuffed the money into his pocket and said,

"Right. Pour the rum then and we'll drink to our deal."

Ellis said Dan's eyes were alight with anticipation and he knew one glass would lead to another, then a third and before you knew it, Dan would be too drunk to leave. So he said,

"Just the one then, Dan. If you're going to town, you've got a fair journey, especially if you're going to make it before nightfall."

Even before he spoke, Dan had swallowed his drink in one and said,

"You're right, Ellis. But before I go, I just want to have a look around and see if there's anything left worth saving." He smiled sadly. "I don't expect so. I didn't have much in the first place."

He turned to leave, but reaching the door, said,

"There's no chance I could take the rest of that bottle, is there?"

Ellis thought a moment, then said,

"I tell you what. You go and look for your possessions and then, when you're ready to leave, come back here and I'll let you have another drink. But the bottle stays with me."

Dan looked at Ellis knowingly – he knew better than to argue – but he was right about his property 'cos even though he looked all over his and Ellis' land, he found next to nothing apart from his old coat, which had somehow got caught in the fallen branches of a dead eucalyptus. So about an hour later and now wearing his coat, he drank what Ellis said he'd made sure was a generous glass of rum and then set off towards the track that would eventually take him to town. The last Ellis saw of him was just as the path took a dip when he stopped and turning, gave him a final wave.

He now owned all the land next to Jack Cornwall, so Ellis immediately set about removing the fence that separated his old land from his new purchase, allowing his sheep to graze wherever they wanted. He'd used most of his savings paying Dan, so there was little more he could afford to do until the next autumn when he knew he'd make a little from selling the season's new lambs. But in the meantime, a new plan started to take shape in his mind.

Looking at the place where Dan had built his bush hut, Ellis realised it was in a much better spot than his own. Sat in a hollow which protected it from the elements on three sides, only poor building and neglected upkeep, allowed Dan's hut to blow away. So he collected all the scraps that might be useful to him and began to think about the house he would build in its place.

'Cos thinking was all Ellis could do until he had more money, for three months he just tended his sheep and tried to grow his kitchen garden. But Ellis was no gardener and nothing grew more than an inch out of the ground before the sun, which was getting stronger and hotter every day, burnt it away. His sheep were more successful though and now, with the extra land, he knew he could allow his flock to double in size.

Before he decided how many lambs to keep, Ellis needed to shear the sheep, see how much he got for the fleeces and then decide how many more lambs he needed to sell in order to build the house. The sun was getting hotter and the sheep's coats were growing thicker, so they were grateful when Ellis began to relieve them of their wool. The job took over a week, but when he finished, Ellis had just over two hundred fleeces.

Over the years, Ellis had slowly got to know Jack Cornwall and the two of them had developed a cautious friendship. Living so far away from the town, or even the nearest small settlement, they knew it was important that they cooperated and so this was the third year that Jack had bought Ellis' fleeces from him and sold them with his own. This particular year, Ellis rode in with Jack and with the money he made, he bought everything he needed to make a start on the house.

When he returned home, the sun was already going down, so there was little he could do except unload the cart. But next morning, straight after he'd taken his sheep to the stream, he outlined the foundations and that afternoon began to dig them out. He worked on building the house through the summer and autumn and after he'd sold as many lambs as he needed to, he finished the house and moved everything in from the bush hut. He'd already decided to use the old hut in the winter as a place for his sheep to shelter if the weather got very cold. Most years weren't too bad but he'd already lost five lambs one winter a couple of years before.

When the house was finished, Jack's wife sent him across with a pie as a sort of celebration. He thought it very neighbourly, especially as he barely knew her, and it got him thinking about how he might want to take a wife of his own. But finding one wasn't going to be that easy 'cos as far as Ellis knew, Jack's wife was the only woman living within fifty miles and in the whole of New Holland, he'd heard it said there were ten men for every woman. So he decided the idea was fanciful and he should forget about it; that was until shearing time came round again and Jack took his fleeces into town for him. Returning, Jack came and gave Ellis his due but he also told him that a ship had just come in with another hundred convicts. But this one, he said, was different because all but a few of them were women.

He'd been talking to the overseer at the Female Factory in Parramatta, who told him about the women who'd just arrived on the *Sydney Cove*. No one had told the overseer how many were arriving, so it hadn't taken long for the Factory to run out of wool for them to weave, and with nothing to do the women were likely to fall out and start fighting each other. About twenty of the women had already been moved on and he knew most of the rest wouldn't be with him for long, but he still had eighty on top of the sixty-odd already in the Factory. Then Ellis laughed and in what I later found out was a fair copy of Jack, said,

"Don't tarry mind. The overseer said they were all being taken, either by military men to help their wives with the domestics or farmers looking for a wife."

But Ellis didn't need coaxing. That evening, he took his cook pot, filled it with water from the stream and heated it over the fire until the water was as hot as he could stand. He poured the water into a bucket and stripping off, washed himself down with a bit of old rag. He dried himself then washed his clothes in the same water. I don't think he was much less dirty than he'd been before his bath, as he called it, but finding out it was the first time he'd had any sort of bath since he'd been on the farm, that he'd made the effort and was proud to tell me about it, made me like him from the very first time we met.

When he'd arrived at the Factory, explaining who he was and why he was there, the supervisor was happy to oblige. He chose six women, including me, from those whose records showed they were not already married. Then shepherding us into a small side room, he brought Ellis in to meet and have a bit of a chat with us. To tell the truth, I'd already decided I didn't really care what he was like, so long as he got me out of that place. It turned out he seemed decent enough, and as I said, he'd made an effort. Anyway, we all talked to him, a few weren't interested but four, including me, definitely were.

The supervisor stayed with us when we met Ellis, to make sure everything was quite proper with no hanky panky. It didn't matter though 'cos the other three flirted with him something shameful. They reminded him they'd been at sea for six months without any men, not counting the four wizened little mice who were the only male convicts on our ship, and they told him they could tell *he* was *definitely* no mouse.

But to me, it was plain to see they were making Ellis uncomfortable and though I couldn't be sure, I guessed he hadn't had much contact with the opposite sex. So when I talked to him, I just asked him about his farm. That was something he was more than happy to talk about and on what turned out to be the first of many, many occasions, (and I suppose the reason I remember so much detail) told me how he'd built the farm and its stock. I listened while the others, seeing he wasn't interested in them, sat looking bored.

After about a quarter of an hour listening to us talking about nothing but the farm, they'd had enough and asked the supervisor if they could leave. But he decided it was time we should all return to work and it was only a few minutes after we'd returned to the main room when I was summoned back to the side room where I'd first met Ellis. It was just as well 'cos the three who'd already tried so hard to win him were getting more and more angry realising, thanks to me, their chance of escaping the Factory was slipping away. Looking nervous, Ellis was accompanied by the overseer whose words I've never forgotten.

"Well, Baldwin, Mr Johnson has decided he would like to take your hand in marriage. He's an honest, hardworking man who's just looking for someone to help run his farm. So what do you think?"

Though everything had happened so quickly, I knew it was my chance to escape the Factory and I didn't know when I might get a better one, so I didn't hesitate in saying I was happy to marry him. Pleased that he'd succeeded in reducing his numbers, even if it was only by one, the supervisor said our marriage would be arranged for the morning.

As we was driving to the farm, Ellis told me he'd been taken aback by how quickly we'd moved from first meeting to marriage – even if I agreed he hadn't expected our marriage to happen for at least a week or two, but all he said at the time was that he'd find somewhere to stay in town and he'd be back as arranged.

When I told Adie what I'd done her reaction at first was a bit frosty, but she said she understood. Then she said something strange.

"You are just doing it to get out of here, aren't you? It's not 'cos you really want him, is it?"

I knew what she meant and I was pretty sure I knew why she asked – but I wasn't certain, so I told her I expected he would want what all men wanted and if I was going to be his wife, he had rights. But no, she was right I told her, I'd do just about anything to get out of that place. She stared at me for a long time. She knew I was telling the truth but I think she hoped to see more. Suddenly she grabbed me and whispered,

"You won't forget me, will you?"

I told her, that of course I wouldn't forget her and that I hoped we'd meet again when we were free, if not before. She sort of smiled. She'd lost the frostiness but I don't think that smile was all together truthful. Anyway, we didn't talk much after that and I spent the rest of the evening talking to the other women about what I'd done; some said they wanted to do the same thing, others teased me, whilst the three who were turned down by Ellis, took every chance they got to tell me he was a wrongen and that I'd live to regret what I'd done. I didn't know if what they said was true, it might be, but what I did know was that they were definitely jealous and would give anything to swap places with me. There was nothing they could do about it and it wasn't much later when, one by one, we begun to settle down the best we could. I slept like a baby on what was to be, for a few years at least, my last night in the Factory and as a single woman.

In the morning I was escorted the half mile to St John's Church by two guards. It was obvious the Minister was well practised in performing weddings involving women from the Factory, 'cos the service was short and quick. Me and Ellis were on our way to his farm less than ten minutes after we'd entered the church.

We drove several miles before either of us spoke. Lost in my thoughts, I'd been wondering what would become of Adie – after all, chained together for six months we'd grown close. I was thinking that I didn't even know if I'd ever see her again, but I did know one thing, I was really going to miss her. But then it struck me strange. There I was just married, sitting next to my new husband, but my thoughts were full of another woman.

It was Ellis who finally broke the silence. We'd been travelling for several hours when he suddenly laughed to himself. When I looked round at him, he said,

"I was just thinking. I've meant to clear up the house for weeks and never got round to it. Now I'm bringing a wife home and I'm wondering what you're going to think of me when you see the state of the place."

Now it was my turn to laugh 'cos he didn't know much about my life and where I'd spent it over the past year. I said to him,

"Ellis, if you'd spent time in a jail, where it was always dark and you could never tell night from day, then on a hulk for six months doing anything and everything you could just to survive, and finally, another six months, most of the time chained up in a ship's hold, then you ain't going to be too worried about living in a bit of a mess."

Ellis thought about this then said,

"I didn't know you'd been on one of those God-forsaken hulks." Looking serious again, he added, "I suppose there are a lot of things we don't know about each other."

I remembered Simon Peters and, smiling to myself, thought, 'I'm sure you wouldn't want to hear all about him.' All I said was,

"I s'pose so."

Ellis gave me a curious look. Perhaps he'd noticed the smile, but he said nothing. A silence fell over us like a heavy blanket and lasted for what seemed hours, and probably would have gone on a lot longer, had our journey not been suddenly interrupted. I must admit the gentle movement of the cart trundling along slowly behind the rhythmic sound of the horse's hooves, had almost rocked me to sleep, when suddenly, the strangest sight I'd ever seen made me sit bolt upright.

To the right of us, about a hundred feet away from the track, a patch of scrub stood higher and wider than most that we'd past. We were almost level with it when a creature, the likes of which I'd never seen before, burst through the far side of the scrub and set off to cross the track ahead of us. Our horse was startled, but Ellis managed to hold its head as in moments, the creature had crossed the track and was heading over the open land on the other side. It had an enormous pair of legs and bound 'cross the land like a giant frog. It looked like it was moving slowly, but it cleared large bushes with ease and covered the distance from its hiding place in the scrub to the track in only three strides. It actually moved faster than any animal I've ever seen and soon was far off in the distance.

I looked at Ellis and for a second time couldn't believe my eyes. Unbelievably he was just looking forward as if nothing had happened. But he must have sensed I was staring at him 'cos without taking his eyes from the track, he said,

"I suppose that was your first kangaroo; you'll get used to 'em. You'll see a lot of 'em round here. They're harmless enough, so long as you keep out of their way that is."

He was right of course. In all these years, I've got used to seeing these strange creatures lolloping through the scrubland, but I don't think I'll ever stop being amazed at the way they move so fast while still looking like they're going so slow.

That kangaroo put the fear of God up me I can tell you, and I've since heard of carts and kangaroos coming a cropper, usually the animal comes off worse, but it don't mean there's not been plenty of people hurt or killed even. But that kangaroo started us talking, just like we did when Ellis first come to the Factory. We began with the simple and safe stuff, but by the time we arrived at the farm I'd told him all about being married to Tom, about why I'd been arrested, what life was like on the hulk and on the *Sydney Cove* – I even told him about Simon, but I said nothing about Adie – not a word. I thought he'd say something about Simon Peters, but he never and I don't mean just then, I mean he never mentioned him in all the years we were together.

When we arrived at the farm, dusk had turned to dark – and it was *very* dark. Ellis, who after all the years he'd lived there, knew every rut, rock and root that might trip me up made me wait while he jumped down and brought a lamp from the house to light my way – made me feel like a proper lady he did. As soon as we got indoors, he went all round what turned out to be the main room, lighting more lamps. As he lit the way, he pointed out the kitchen and where his bedroom was, all the time he kept apologising for the mess. I dunno about the mess, I just couldn't believe he'd built it all on his own while still tending his sheep and keeping his farm.

Inviting me to sit at the table he'd also made himself, he disappeared into the kitchen, returning a few minutes later with a large leg of lamb and two platters. Drawing a knife from his belt, he cut a few generous slices from the leg and shared them between the platters. Passing one to me, he took the other himself. I hadn't eaten all day and hadn't realised how hungry I was until I took the first mouthful. Suddenly ready to eat that kangaroo we'd seen, I swallowed the rest without a pause and it was only as I polished off the last mouthful that I looked up. Ellis had stopped eating and was staring at me. He picked up his plate and pushed half the meat still on it onto mine. Embarrassed, I protested, but he insisted saying,

"This is the first time you've eaten today, isn't it?"

I had to admit that it was.

"I ate this morning," he confessed, "before I came to the church and I should have made sure we had food for the journey. Now you eat what's there and if you want any more, just let me know and I'll cut you off some more slices."

I thanked him for his kindness but told him he'd given me more than enough. Satisfied, he finished his platter and I ate what he'd given me.

As I said, once we started talking, except when I was wolfing down the lamb of course, we hadn't stopped. But as the evening grew longer and the time grew nearer when we'd have to go to bed for the night, we became more and more quiet. Eventually Ellis showed me the way to the dunnark and leaving me there with the lamp, made his way back inside.

Returning, the lamp seemed to attract every flying insect in New Holland. I tried to concentrate on the uneven ground and any obstacles that littered the way back. But then something the size of a small bird flew into the lamp, finally making me lose my nerve. I ran the last few yards and flew through the door, shutting it behind me as quickly as I could.

A startled Ellis looked at me as, breathing heavily, I lent with my back against the door. He asked me,

"What's happened? Is somebody chasing you?"

As I said, I'd lost my nerve, so almost shouting, I said,

"Not someone, something. I've never seen so many insects, not even on a dung heap. But that last one," I pulled on the door to make doubly sure it was shut, "that thing can't 'ave been an insect. I swear it was as big as a sparrow, except it wasn't like any bird I've ever seen 'cos it had two sets of wings."

Ellis laughed and said, "Sounds like you've met one of our Hawk Moths. They're harmless and I don't think they're really as big as a sparrow."

Seeing me glaring at him, he hurriedly added, "Well, not any I've ever seen. Of course there's nothing to say you mightn't have seen a bigger one. Anyway, the important thing is that they're harmless."

Twice he'd said they were harmless, so I had to ask.

"So you're saying there are other creatures round here that ain't harmless?"

He looked at me seriously.

"I suppose you haven't been here long enough to learn too much about the place. Still, they must have told you about the Red-Backs… They have told you about them, haven't they?"

I shook my head. I'd never heard of these monsters: I was imagining some sort of cross between a bear and a big red cat. I'd seen a bear one time up Bankside, he was being baited by a big ugly dog – horrible it was. I'd never seen a big red cat though, but after that moth and the kangaroo, I thought anything was possible in this God-forsaken land.

"I'm sorry," he said. "I should have checked you knew about them before you went to the dunnark. They're spiders and they like dark places, such as the underside of a privy seat. One bite could kill you."

I couldn't believe what I was hearing.

"You mean you let me use the privy and just happened to forget to tell me I might be about to sit on a spider that'll kill me? So are there any others that you've forgotten. Perhaps some poisonous flying insects you want to tell me about or maybe there are creatures in this wretched country that are going to want me for their supper and just slipped your mind?"

Ellis tried to look serious, though I could tell he was trying not to laugh. But I was in no laughing mood, so I said,

"Look, I don't know what it was like where you come from, but in London the worst bite you're likely to get is from a flea. Might make you scratch a bit but that's all. Here, in one day, I meet a stupid giant rabbit with legs like a frog with an even stupider name, a moth the size of a sparrow and then you tell me that at any time I sit on the privy I might get me arse bitten by a spider so poisonous it'll probably kill me. To top it all, you seem to think that's funny."

Ellis could see I was still angry, so he didn't laugh at me, though he later told me he'd only kept a straight face by not thinking about my description of a kangaroo. So instead, he said,

"I know there must be a lot of things that are new to you, but trust me, most of them aren't dangerous and tomorrow I'll tell you what to look out for."

He looked at me seriously and I knew I didn't need to say anything more about it, so coolly I just said,

"Thank you, I think that would be a very good idea."

"Right," he looked relieved, "we've had a long day and we need to be up early tomorrow, so I think it's time we got some sleep."

And that's what happened. Ellis led the way into the bedroom and silently we both took off our outer clothes and got into bed. I don't know what I expected to happen next, but it certainly wasn't for him to start snoring as soon as his head hit the pillow; but that's exactly what did happen – and what a right royal row he made.

I remembered my first night with Tom. In fact I remembered most nights with Tom and the only way I got to sleep early was by learning some of the tricks I'd later used on

Simon. Anyway, when I knew I wasn't going to be troubled by Ellis, like him, I settled down to sleep.

In the morning when I woke, I was on my own. Dressing, I went through to the main room and it was then I heard a distant whistle. Stepping outside, I could see Ellis walking behind his sheep, bringing them back towards the farm. When he saw me, he waved, but before reaching the house, he turned the sheep across to an area which looked as peppered with rocks and thirsty vegetation as everywhere else on the farm.

He came back about half an hour later, by which time I'd found my way around the kitchen and made us some breakfast. It was his turn to be hungry. I guessed he hadn't eaten before he went out, but unlike me the night before, he did stop eating long enough to talk. The first thing he said of any consequence was to ask me if I slept alright. I told him I had, which wasn't a lie, but then I expected him to say something about why he'd fallen straight to sleep. Instead, he started talking about the farm again and how he hoped I'd find time, where he'd failed, to grow a kitchen garden. I said I'd try but warned him that I'd never grown anything before. In fact, I told him, living in London all my life, I'd never seen a vegetable growing and I only had the greengrocer's word that they came out the ground. He laughed and carried on talking about how his flock was growing and what things I might try to grow. I left other things alone, deciding I'd wait and see what the night brought.

But that night was exactly the same, so was the next; in fact, for a whole week, things remained unchanged – we'd go to bed and almost before I was lying down, I'd hear the sound of Ellis snoring. After a week, I was beginning to think it was how things were going to be and the following day there weren't any clues that that night would be any different. So I was almost asleep when I first felt Ellis move, and he was on top of me before I was fully awake. When I opened my eyes, he was looking down at me, and there was no more passion there than he might show if he was examining one of his sheep, and I wouldn't have been sure of his intentions if they hadn't been pressing hard against me. By the time he lowered himself onto me I was wide awake, but barely half a minute later, his body tightened and as I tensed against him, he collapsed, a choked groan forced from his throat.

He rolled off me and we lay there, neither of us speaking, the silence only broken by Ellis' fast but slowing, breathing. When it returned to normal, he spoke out of the dark. It was the first time either of us had said anything since we got to bed.

"That's what you were expecting, wasn't it?"

As we lay there in the dark silence, I knew he was waiting for a reply, but I was thinking about how it had been with Tom. I thought about his hot breath and his slobbering all over my face. I thought about all his sweaty humping and bumping on top of me and the smell from his day's work which 'cos it was warmed by his night-time, what should I call it?… his night-time labours, was overwhelming. And he'd do that every night if I didn't catch hold of him first. I tried to tell myself I enjoyed it; whether or not I did was something I don't think mattered to Tom. But the truth was I didn't enjoy it, and what's more, I didn't see how any girl could. So when I thought about what had just happened with Ellis, I only had two thoughts – he'd been quicker than Tom and at least he hadn't stunk of dung. So when I finally answered him, I told him,

"I don't think I was expecting nothing. If that's what you want to do, I'm your wife now and I ain't never going to try to stop you, but if you don't want to, that's alright with me as well."

Ellis raised himself on one elbow. Through the darkness I could see he was looking straight at me when he said,

"Do you really mean that? You don't mind if we do or if we don't?"

249

"Yes, that's exactly what I mean."

I didn't know what else to say. Ellis was looking into my eyes. I think he was trying to see if I was really telling the truth. He stared at me for what seemed an age, but then he must have seen what he was looking for 'cos he lay back in the darkness and said,

"I've never thought much about it before, never needed to, but I think if it's alright with you, I'd rather spend my days working on the farm and my nights sleeping."

I was glad that Ellis had said what he said and from that night on, we grew into a partnership where we worked together on the farm. I even had some success with the kitchen garden, and while we cared for each other, probably more than most married couples, we just didn't do those things in bed married couples were supposed to do.

We had an understanding on more than just the bedroom. Ellis spent most of every day either tending his sheep or clearing scrub from what had been Combe Acres. I kept house and tried to grow some vegetables – I had a bit of success for a couple of years with a few carrots, but mostly I did no better than Ellis had. In the first year, we found we worked well together and both of us worked on turning his old mud hut into a barn. But most of all, we always talked a lot, not only about the farm and Ellis' hopes and plans for the future, but also about our lives back in the old country; some happy times, but many more bad ones and we both were certain we never wanted to go back. Days, turned into years and little changed except that, for me, each day passing meant there was one less remaining on my sentence. But everything changed a couple of years before my sentence was up.

Summers were always hot and dry, but even though the stream on Jack's place was reduced to a trickle, there was always enough water for both his and Ellis' sheep. That had been until last year, when for a couple of weeks before the rain came, we survived on the brown water, thick with sludge, drawn from a borehole Jack had dug and shared with us. The sheep managed to survive by licking the moisture from the underside of rocks they disturbed in the stream bed; it had been a close thing but all the sheep survived.

But this year was worse – much worse. Things went much the same as they did the year before – it hadn't rained for at least six months when in mid-December, the water in the stream, which had been barely a trickle for weeks, finally stopped altogether. As he did last year, Jack dug another borehole and the sheep found enough moisture in the stream bed to survive. But a few days later, we all thought Jack had wasted his time. The day started with a clear blue sky just as it seemed to have done forever, but the first sign that things might turn out differently happened in the middle of the day. We spotted a few timid grey clouds appearing on the horizon, and by early evening the sky was so dark it might have been the middle of the night. We were all happy 'cos we knew what was coming, and right enough, as we sat eating our evening meal, the heavens opened and we thought the drought was over. But that wasn't how it turned out. In fact by morning not only had the rain stopped, but the ground was bone-dry and the sky was blue and cloudless again. It's true that for a day or two there was water in the stream, but by the third morning it was dry again. The sheep were back to kicking over stones in the stream bed and we were all back to drinking whatever Jack and Ellis could pump from the borehole. Every day we hoped the rain would come back and each day when it didn't, we told each other it was bound to be with us by the end of the month. We had no real reason for thinking that way. It was just that when we were all down after the rain came and went again, Jack had shown us his wife's diary from last year. In it she'd written in large letters, "RAIN ARRIVES AT LAST". It was her only entry for 16th February, but as the date a year later came and went and we still had no rain, I remembered that on the opposite page the entry for the next day read simply: 'Rain still falling. I think we're going to be alright now. Close shave though, I don't think the sheep would have lasted much longer.' The next day, as if to prove that her prediction might well have been right, Ellis told me we'd lost three overnight.

After another ten days, things were desperate. There was little water for us and none for the sheep: only a few of them were still alive. Ellis, who had always told me his thoughts about everything, grew quieter and quieter with every day that went by without rain. When less than fifty sheep were still alive, Ellis took the remainder and put them in his barn, though they still had no water, at least they were out of the sun.

But without water there was little chance of them surviving and after three more days, only fifteen were still alive. The following evening, when Ellis returned from the barn, he told me five more were dead. I'd been getting used to him saying almost nothing, but telling me about those sheep was the only thing he'd said to me all day – and that wasn't the only way he behaved differently. Without saying nothing, he'd disappeared into the kitchen, coming back with the remains of the rum he plied Jack and Dan with all those years ago. I'd never seen a drop of strong liquor pass his lips and that bottle was still half full when Ellis brought it from the kitchen. But about two hours later, the bottle was empty and a very drunk Ellis was slumped, I thought unconscious, across the table.

As I said, I'd never seen him like that before, but I'd seen enough drunks in my life to know – at least I thought I knew – that the best I could do was to leave him where he was to sleep it off. So that's what I did and it was ten minutes later I had my back to him when he grabbed me. He took me completely by surprise, otherwise I'm sure, especially the state he was in, I would have been able to resist him. But as it was, he dragged me into the bedroom and forced me onto the bed, face down. Pushing my right arm painfully up my back, he told me he'd break it if I tried to resist. I know it might sound stupid, but it was only then I realised what he was doing. As he started to pull up my dress, instinctively I tried to twist around, but as I did, an excruciating pain shot up my arm as Ellis increased the pressure.

"I told you I'd break it."

His voice, now thick and slow from the drink, also sounded desperate. I sensed he was unbuttoning his trousers and knowing I couldn't resist, I waited for the inevitable – but it never came. It seemed like forever but was probably less than a minute before I realised what his problem was. I shouldn't have laughed I know, but I couldn't help it. I think it was relief mainly, but when he heard me laughing at him, Ellis let out a roar of frustration, spun me over and with all his might delivered a slap right across my face. Though he hadn't knocked me out, I was stunned and just lay there while he swore at me. Getting no reaction from me, he stumbled out of the room trying to sort out his trousers as he went and I heard him pick up his shotgun – I was sure I was done for. But instead of coming back into the bedroom, I heard him opening the front door.

As I regained my senses, it dawned on me what he was going to do. I also knew it was a kindness 'cos even if they had water now, it was unlikely any of those remaining ten sheep would survive – they were all too far gone. So I lay there and waited for what I knew must come.

I didn't have to wait long, because barely a minute after Ellis left, the first shot rang out, followed moments later by the second. Normally, as the slaughter began the other sheep would have bleated in panic, but there was an eerie silence as Ellis, rifle re-loaded, shot the third and the fourth; the remainder were either too weak to protest or were just ready to die. I lay there and listened as three more pairs of shots put the last six out of their misery. It dawned on me then that now he'd killed the last of his sheep and at the same time put an end to all his hopes and dreams for the future, he would return to the house and that it was unlikely his mood would have improved. But this time I decided I'd make sure he wouldn't catch me by surprise.

I left the bed and hurried through to the main room. Even, thanks to Ellis' attentions, with my right eye closed, I could still see well enough with my left to find the metal rod we used as a poker. Taking it from where it was propped against the wall next to the fire, I went and stood behind the door and waited for his return. But it was then I heard the eleventh shot ring out, and somehow I knew I'd just been made a widow for a second time.

Admonition
From Beyond the Grave

On the morning of the 27 October, we drove to St John's, but before Lieutenant Granger went inside to await the arrival of his bride, he handed me over to the Factory Supervisor.

Arriving back at the Factory I felt lost. My hopes and plans for after my release had been dashed when Lieutenant Granger told me he wouldn't be needing me in Morpeth. Now, already unhappy, I faced a hard final three months in the Factory. I was toying with the food they'd given us, realising that was something else I'd have to learn to put up with again, when I heard a loud and familiar voice outside. I pushed my way through to the door, but before I got there, it opened and in she stepped. For a moment she just stood there looking at me, but then she let out a shriek and before I knew it, I was wrapped in her arms.

It was wonderful to see Mary again. She looked older and the New Holland sun hadn't done her any favours, but she still looked fit and healthy. We talked and talked. It was like we'd never been apart and it was plain to see she was still the single-minded Cockney I was parted from all those years ago. She teased me as I told her about the lieutenant and then she told me all about those twelve years on a sheep farm with her husband, Ellis, and what had become of him. But what she told me when later that night we found a space to sit quietly together ended by giving us the main reason we're sitting here celebrating now.

It was difficult not to be overheard, but Mary looked all around and when she was sure no one was listening to us, she pulled me closer and spoke barely above a whisper.

"Do you remember the ship that brought us to New 'olland, the *Sydney Cove*?"

It may have been nearly thirteen years since we landed but, as I told her, we'd spent six months on that ship. Most of the time the two of us shackled together in the hold, and I was hardly likely to forget it. She laughed at that, drawing the attention of a few. But they soon looked away again and she continued.

"In that case, you'll remember the ship's surgeon?"

I nodded.

"Well, two months ago, I'd only just arrived back at the Factory, he ran into me. He'd been here the week before looking for you, and the Supervisor told him that you'd been sent to the Sydney Garrison and he would have heard if you'd been moved on. But when Kit, that's the surgeon's name, visited the Garrison, they told him you'd gone with your lieutenant (she was still teasing me,) when he was seconded to a dredging project in Newcastle. Kit said he didn't have time to find you then and still get back to Sydney Cove before his ship left. So he came back here, intending to leave this letter for you with the Supervisor."

She handed me the letter; I didn't recognise the handwriting, although the seal looked familiar.

"But before he went to his office, he checked the register and remembered me from the *Sydney Cove*." Lowering her voice even further, she breathed, "He knew you and me was friends, so when I told him I was going to be free soon, he asked if I could try and find you and give you the letter; which of course, I told him I would."

I smiled and said,

"That's turned out to be easier than you thought."

She smiled but otherwise ignored me. It was obvious what she had to say next she thought was too important.

"He introduced himself, said his name was Kit Carlyle."

She waited for my reaction, but when she could see the name meant nothing to me she whispered, now so quietly I had to lean forward to hear her and to read her lips in the dark,

"The name Carlyle doesn't mean anything to you?"

I thought for a moment then slowly shook my head.

"Your husband's solicitor?"

I'd actually forgot that me and Jabez had married. Mary just stared questioningly at me, waiting for a reply. Then it dawned on me.

"Of course, Henry Carlyle. You don't mean to say him and the surgeon are related?"

"Were related; father and son, but I'm afraid old Henry's dead."

I could tell she was excited by what she still had to tell, but she managed to keep her voice low as she said,

"And that's who the letter's from. But here's the thing. Kit said he's put all of the money in the New South Wales Bank and when you're released, it'll all be yours. He wouldn't tell me how much mind, but he did say it was left you by your late husband."

I now realised why Jabez had been so anxious for us to be married. He wanted to be sure there would be no challenge to me inheriting his estate. I didn't know how much there might be, but Mary had twice said Kit had talked of 'all the money'. What I was certain of was that any money Jabez had left me would have come from the salt smuggling. So however much there was, I had to keep quiet about it because, married or not, if the authorities ever found out where it came from, it would all be confiscated. So even though I was desperate to know how much he had left me, we'd have to wait until they let us outside in the morning when it would be easier to find a quiet spot where we wouldn't be watched. Mary didn't argue. She later told me I'd made her happy enough by talking about both of us reading the letter.

It was getting very late, so we decided to try to get some sleep, although by then most comfortable places had been taken. Lying down was impossible, so we propped ourselves up either side of a pillar. Sleep was equally impossible and I spent the long night just waiting for daybreak and the chance to read Henry's letter.

Mary
Back at the Factory

After Ellis' suicide, the authorities took me back to the Factory and to tell you the truth, I didn't mind. The land was barren and silent apart from the occasional birdsong or call of a wild animal and with no prospect of replacing the sheep; just surviving would have been hard for me. What's more, I knew with only about four months of me sentence left to run when I returned to the Factory, I'd just serve out my time and then see if I could find a farm that needed a housekeeper. Anything else a farmer might want, I'd be a free woman so we'd 'ave to see. What I did know was that anything was better than returning to England. As it was, things turned out differently from how I imagined; in fact, they turned out *very* different.

After I heard that extra bullet fired, I froze to the spot. I knew Ellis might have failed to kill one of the sheep with his first shot and needed a second to finish the job, but it was another thought that held me, and I was trying not to think of it. When a few minutes later he still hadn't appeared, I told myself he was probably getting rid of the carcasses.

It must have been a full hour before stiffness in my legs forced me to move away from the door and sit in a chair, though I still held on to the pipe. I sat there for a few more minutes before I even allowed myself to accept Ellis might have injured himself and not be able to get back to the house. Sparked into life by that thought, I forced myself to open the door a crack and listen for any sounds that might give me a clue as to what Ellis was doing, and more importantly, where he was. But everywhere was quiet apart from the distant parched bleat of Jack's few remaining sheep. Hearing and seeing nothing else, I left the house and started to walk slowly and quietly towards the barn, all the time listening for any sound.

But I heard nothing and when I reached out and cautiously opened the barn door, I faced a bloodbath. It wasn't so much the sheep. Each one of them had been shot once through the head, a little blood oozing from the bullet hole the only clue that they weren't just sleeping peaceful. The same could not be said of Ellis. His body lay slumped in the chair, his rifle on the floor by his side, blood covering the sides of his face and more blood and I don't know what else congealing on the wall behind him.

As I moved closer, I could see the top of his head was missing. I turned away and started back towards the door, but before I got there, I heard loud drumming on the roof of the barn. I realised it had been going on for some time – I just hadn't noticed, but I still made my way to the door; staying shut in the barn with Ellis' body wasn't something I fancied. When I got outside again, I stood, eyes shut, my face raised to the sky, rain competing with my tears which had begun to fall. Then, even though I was crying, I started to laugh. I know it sounds wrong. After all the man I'd been married to for a dozen years had just topped himself. But for months I hadn't seen in him the man I married. Since the drought had started to grip the land, he hadn't really spoken to me and then he'd tried to rape me. When he failed even to do that, he'd put me in fear for my life. So out loud I said,

"Well, Ellis, it serves you right. I don't know if the rain coming would have made a difference to you, but you didn't give yourself a chance to find out, did you?"

"What do you mean, didn't give himself a chance?"

I nearly jumped out of my skin, I can tell you. Jack Cornwall was standing behind me, rifle in hand, and I hadn't heard a thing. I just pointed at the hut and said,

"He's in there."

Jack opened the barn's door, hesitated for a second and then went in, closing the door behind him. He wasn't in there long mind, 'cos reappearing, white-faced, a couple of minutes later his voice trembling, he said,

"It's too late to do anything now, but tomorrow I'll bury the sheep for you. Then I'll have to report Ellis' death to the authorities in Parramatta, let them decide what's to be done."

So that's what happened. The next morning Jack buried the sheep, then rode into Parramatta, not getting back until the small hours. (I couldn't sleep thinking of Ellis' dead body only yards away, so I was up when I saw a light shine from Jack's house letting me know he'd just returned.) The following day, an officer from the Sydney Garrison and half a dozen men appeared at my door. The officer never said much but went straight to the barn (Jack must have described where Ellis could be found.), returning almost immediately, his handkerchief covering his nose and mouth. I guessed Ellis was getting a little high after two days' baking. He ordered four men to take the sheet off me bed and wrap Ellis' body in it. Telling them to put the body on the cart they'd brought for the purpose, he said they should then start off back to the Garrison.

When the chosen four had made their reluctant way to the barn, he gave me ten minutes to put together a bag of my possessions.

"Only things that belong to you. Everything else needs to be sold to pay for his burial."

So that was that. I packed some clothes and an old pair of clogs into a bag and was ready to leave in five minutes. The only thing I had worth anything was my wedding ring and I wasn't leaving that behind; our marriage might have been a strange one and ended badly, but for most of the twelve years we were together, we got on just fine; no, the ring belonged to me. Anyway, the officer saw it when he checked me and my bag and looking straight at it, he said to me, "Alright, that's all in order. Now hop up on the cart and let's get you back to Parramatta."

It was late when we got to the Factory, so I never saw what it looked like 'til the next day. When they signed me in, they put me in a small side room, saying they'd decide what to do with me in the morning. I didn't care. It had been a long journey and I'd hardly slept for three days. So as soon as they left me, I flung myself on the small bed which, apart from a pot, was the only thing in the room.

I must have fallen asleep almost immediately and I only 'woke when the sun, streaming through the room's only window, tracked 'cross my face. I'd barely sat up when the door opened and the Matron walked in. She was a short, thick-set woman, but the thing I remember the most was her colour. Well, to say it right, it was her lack of colour – she was the whitest woman I'd ever seen. I couldn't understand it. I thought she must live in a cave or something, but it turned out she was an albino. I was staring at her. I expect that's probably why she spoke to me like she did.

"Up you get then. I suppose I should call you Johnson. Anyway, there's someone here to see you. The gentleman saw your name from where you were signed in last night. Don't get your hopes up. He was here last week looking for Admonition Payne. He says he recognises your name and remembers you and Payne were together when his ship brought you out here.

Anyway, look lively, Mr Carlyle's ship leaves on the evening tide and he's still got to get back to Sydney Cove."

Sleep-confused, I got up and tried to straighten my clothes, but the Matron was in a hurry.

"Come along. There isn't time for all that. You mustn't keep Mr Carlyle waiting."

With that, she bustled out and I hurried after her. The name Carlyle rang a distant bell, but the only thing I really knew was that the Supervisor must have forgotten I'd changed my name when I married Ellis and had registered me as Mary Baldwin, otherwise Mr Carlyle would never have recognised me name.

I was thinking how surprising it was that he recognised me name after so many years. I was after all just another transported convict and he must have known thousands, when Matron stopped us outside an unmarked door.

"This is normally Mr Brown the Supervisor's office," she said, "but Mr Carlyle asked to speak to you alone. He's already inside waiting for you."

She tapped on the door and without waiting for an invitation opened it and guided me in. I recognised the ship's surgeon from the *Sydney Cove* straight away. I remembered how he'd been so kind to that poor pregnant young girl who'd died in childbirth on the journey 'ere. Unnecessarily, the Matron introduced us, so after we said hello and agreed we knew each other, Kit asked her to leave us. Ever so polite he was. She didn't take umbrage at all, just smiled and curtsied as she left.

There was a desk in the room and after she left Kit drew back a chair and invited me to sit on one side of it; made me feel like a proper lady he did. Sitting down on the other side, he started to tell me why he was so keen to find Adie. He said it was his father's dying wish that he should try and find her and give her his letter. Factory records showed she'd been sent to Sydney Garrison, but when he got to the Garrison he found she'd gone to Newcastle with a Lieutenant Granger and they didn't know when she'd be back. Trouble was it didn't matter when she got back 'cos his ship was leaving on the evening tide. He knew he wouldn't be back in New Holland for a year or more, and by then Adie would be free and there was no telling where she'd be – for all he knew, she could be back in England by then. That's when he asked me if I could try to find her after my release and give her the letter. He told me the money mentioned in the letter was now in the Bank of New South Wales where they also held a copy of her signature. She needed only to sign for it and the money was hers – mind you, he didn't tell me how much was there.

Of course, he was happy when I told him I'd try to find her, and he looked mightily relieved when I took the envelope. I'd always hoped me and Adie would meet again someday and now he'd given me an excuse to try to make it happen.

Anyway, I knew there was nothing I could do for a couple of months, but I planned to go to Newcastle as soon as they released me, but when Adie turned up at the Factory, everything was suddenly straightforward. I give her the letter as soon as I was sure there were no prying eyes and the next day we shared a quiet spot where she could read the letter and find out how much money Kit had deposited in the bank.

As soon as she had the answer, Adie started telling me her plans. These were plans she thought she'd have to give up, but now there was no reason she couldn't follow. They were plans she hoped would include me, and we spent every minute we could over the few weeks talking over the details. After about two months, I got my ticket of release and then spent another troublesome month in Parramatta waiting for her to join me.

As I told Adie, it might have been only a month, but it seemed as long as the whole of the rest of my sentence. In other words, it could have gone better!

Admonition
Freedom

Today I'm celebrating; no, *we're* celebrating. It's been two years since my release and so much has happened. I barely know where to begin. But I suppose I must start with that letter from Henry Carlyle and the first thing to say about that is that as soon as I broke the seal and began to open it, a second letter fell out. Like Henry's, the second letter was addressed to me and even after so many years, I recognised Jabez' small and neat handwriting straight away; it was strange to think that both of the men who'd written those letters were dead. Of course, I'd barely known Mr Carlyle, but me and Jabez had been close; at the end we'd even married.

Although I knew Jabez much better than Henry Carlyle, knowing him only as the person who passed notes and messages between me and Jabez, it turned out his letter was the more important of the two. Jabez' letter was short and sentimental, concerned mostly with expressing his regret for having ever involved me in salt smuggling and it was clear he expected me to return to England where Henry could explain everything to me in person. Mr Carlyle's letter was much longer and of far more use to me, it's too long for me to memorise, so I'm letting you see the whole thing.

Dear Mrs Admonition Payne,

My name is Henry Carlyle and as you may recall, I was the barrister who represented your husband at his trial. I write to you in order to fulfil a promise I made Mr Payne and which I believe may be of advantage to you upon your release. Although your present circumstances are not known to me, I calculate that you must be approaching the end of your sentence. Clearly, if you are reading this, my son has found you and I can only hope that, despite the rigours and privations that life in New Holland must have presented, you remain in sound health.

Before I explain the matters regarding your husband, it is with great regret I must first inform you of the death of your brother, William. I recently advised a client regarding his purchase of a plantation in the West Indies. Whilst discussing the purchase, my client had been informed of the recent tragic loss in a hurricane of a vessel hired to carry a salt shipment from the plantation to the United States of America. The ship had gone down with all hands. Amongst them was the plantation's agent, one William Bostock, previously of Northwich, Cheshire. My client was able to provide me with sufficient detail to confirm that this William Bostock was indeed your brother. I know this news will come as a great shock to you and that it will provide you with little comfort to know that the success of the plantation's unique salt production venture, had been in no small part due to your brother. Regardless of all else, I hope you will accept my sincere condolences.

Now, if I may turn to your husband. In addition to defending him, I should explain that in the few months I knew him, I had many conversations with Mr Payne. He told me how he met you and in his way came to love you, why he married you as well as the unusual nature of your marriage. In his last days, he turned our conversations to

259

explaining the truth about the work you both did for Sam Baker, why he'd become involved in the first place and how he had always regretted your involvement.

Mr Payne believed that on your release you intended to come back to England and he felt that only when you returned should I reveal the information contained in this letter. Although he insisted that nothing further should be written down at any time, my own failing health prevents me from fulfilling that particular instruction. It is unlikely I will still be here, should it be your intention to return to England at the end of your sentence. I have also enclosed a letter to you from Mr Payne which he asked me to give you and which he swore contains nothing that would incriminate either you or me.

Mr Payne asked me to explain the following:

He said that although you never enquired, he knew you were aware he received payments from Sam Baker and the first thing he asked me to explain was what happened to that money.

He realised that if he spent the money in significant amounts questions were bound to be asked, so he hid most of it beneath the floorboards in his bedroom. The remaining small amount he added to the weekly takings which, as usual, he paid into the bank. He took only the amount needed to compensate him sufficiently for the trade he'd lost since the mines had opened.

What he intended to do with the money in the end he didn't say, and I'm not sure if he knew himself, but he did tell me that when he realised the Excise Supervisor was closing in, he knew he had to act quickly. So, on the following Monday, just as he always did, he went into town and amongst other places, visited the bank and paid in the week's takings. But in other ways, his day was very far from usual. Rather than walking to town, he had ridden one of his donkeys so that after finishing his usual errands, instead of heading home, he was able to ride on to Macclesfield. There, once he was certain he'd not been followed, he visited the Critchley and Turner Bank, somewhere he'd never been before, and requested a strongbox. He took all the money he had hidden and placed it in the strongbox, naming me as the signatory.

It is because I believe the time left to me is short, yesterday, I withdrew all the money from the bank, a sum of £412 and a small bag of coins. In addition to delivering this letter to you, I have also asked Kit to deposit the money in the Bank of New South Wales (I am advised it is the most secure in New Holland.) and that he should sign it over to you for when you are free – I have taken the liberty of giving him one of the notes you sent Mr Payne so they can verify your signature.

Mr Payne also made it clear to me that your whole life in England had been difficult and I can barely imagine how hard it must be for you in New Holland, but I hope that on your release this money will provide you with the means to lead a comfortable life, whether you choose to stay where you are or return to England.

Kindest regards,
Henry Carlyle

For me, the month after Mary left seemed endless. She was free and there was nothing for me to do except worry that the money might have been stolen. But the month passed eventually, and the morning finally came when I walked out onto the streets of Parramatta. We'd arranged that Mary would be there to meet me, but when I stepped through the Factory's doors, she was nowhere to be seen. Then, from the shadows of a building across the road, I heard a short, sharp whistle. Moving towards the shadows I could see a figure, but I couldn't make out who it was, so I wavered. Seeing me stop, the figure moved into the light and now I could see it was Mary, what wasn't clear was why she was hiding. I also couldn't understand why, in just a month, she had become so dishevelled: her clothes were torn, her hair tangled and knotted and dust covered her from head to toe, but before I could say anything, as loud as she dared she called,

"We must get away from Parramatta. I can't be found anywhere inside the town boundaries."

I didn't understand. She had served her sentence. Surely, she was free to go wherever she wanted?

Knowing what I might be thinking, she said,

"I found a place jus' on the edge of town. Let's go there an' I'll explain what's been happenin'."

With that, she stepped back into the shadows and cautiously started to make her way towards the outskirts of town. Leaving me little choice other than to follow her, she first led us the short distance to the Parramatta River and then, after making sure the way was clear, took us the half mile to St John's graveyard. When we left the graveyard and started to cross open scrubland, she seemed to relax; I assumed we must have left town, though I didn't know how she could be so sure.

Moving beyond the graveyard, Mary quickly picked up a rough but distinct track and we had barely gone a couple of hundred yards when she stopped by a small but dense Wattle tree. From the far side of the tree, unseen from the track, she retrieved a small sack. Moving a little further from the track, she put the sack down and cleared away the ashes of an old fire. Before she began to build a new one, she pulled an old kettle from her sack and said,

"Can you take this and fill it down at the creek?"

I followed her gaze across the scrub and could just see the tell-tale glint of water a few hundred yards away.

"It'll be dry soon," she said, "but right now it's flowin' enough to make pools that are drinkable and still deep enough to take the kettle. I was given some tea, I'll use the last of it to make us a brew."

Who gave her the tea was another question I wanted to ask her. I'd only seen tea in New Holland when the Governor had visitors from England, but as I walked to the creek, I knew I had more important matters I needed her to explain.

Mary was right about the creek. There was still a small but flowing stream in the middle of the creek bed and I soon found a deeper pool where I could fill the kettle. When I returned, Mary took the kettle from me and hung it over the fire on a frame she'd made herself. Inviting me to sit on a rock, she said,

261

"Right, I'll make the tea and then I'll tell you what's happened to me since they let me go from the Factory."

That was more than I could take. I'd waited patiently, but now I needed to know what had happened to her and more importantly, whether our plans were affected. So I told her,

"No, Mary, the tea can wait. I want to know why you're living rough and why you're afraid to be seen in town."

Leaving the kettle over the fire and sitting down, she sighed before beginning her latest tale.

"It's simple really. When they let me out of the Factory, I had no money and nothin' to sell apart from me wedding ring; they'd made me leave everythin' else when they took me from the farm. But I thought if I was careful, the money I'd get for the ring would keep me 'til you got out. What a mistake that was! When I first tried to sell the ring to a publican, 'e told me that there was no gold in it. At first I thought 'e must be lying, so I then tried to sell it to a shopkeeper instead, but 'e told me the same, a fancy gold colour but no actual gold. Without any money, I couldn't buy any food and I couldn't afford a room for even one night, let alone a monf.

Not knowin' what else to do, I spent the night in a wagon at the back of Government House. I would have been alright 'en all if the wagon's driver 'adn't spotted me there when 'e brought the 'orse first thing in the mornin'. Before I woke, 'e'd found the 'ouse guard an' 'e arrested me for vagrancy. Two hours later, I was up in front of the magistrate who gave me two weeks in the local gaol and told me on release I was not allowed anywhere wivin the Parramatta limits. In the gaolhouse, they had a map on the wall markin' the town boundaries. When they let me out, I found this place 'ere, the nearest place to the Factory I could remember from the map, that was still outside the boundary.

So that's it really. I've bin 'ere for the last couple o' weeks livin' on anything I could catch. Ellis taught me how to set traps an' I jus' waited for your release."

"You remembered I'd be released today?"

"I remembered you were being released exactly thirty days after me."

Smiling weakly, she added, "I couldn't think of a better plan."

I couldn't help it but I must admit I was relieved. Mary might have had a rough time since she got out of the Factory, but I'd been worried she was going to tell me that for some unforeseen reason, my plans had been dashed for a second time. Relief helped me make up my mind and I said, "Right. That settles it."

I knew it was time to stop talking and start putting our plan into action.

"We'll steer clear of Parramatta and head for the Parramatta Road. When we get to Sydney, I'll draw the money from the bank and we'll find somewhere to buy some new clothes. After that, we'll find the best boarding lodge we can. We'll wash in hot water and we'll use fancy soap, then we'll dress in our new clothes and order the best food the lodge can provide."

I grasped her hands, looked straight into her eyes and with a certainty I hadn't known I felt, said,

"Mary, I promise you, neither of us will ever again be accused of a crime and no one will ever dare to suggest that you're a vagrant. In fact in a year's time, I'll bet they'll be calling us the finest ladies in Morpeth."

Mary laughed and said,

"I don't know 'bout that, but I like the idea of soap and 'ot wa'er, livin' out here the dirt and sand gets in every nook and cranny, if you know what I mean."

Shifting her chemise to make sure I understood, she went back to making the tea. We didn't talk much more then, except I had to ask her how she got the tea.

"That's the one bit 'o luck I 'ad – that's if you want to call it luck. I tried one more bar with the ring and the bartender told me the same fing as the other two 'ad. I was jus' leavin', ready to give up, when a man sittin' alone in a corner of the bar called me over an' invited me to sit down.

Summin' about 'im made me fink 'e weren't askin' me to sit down for the usual reasons a man might ask a girl on 'er own in a bar to sit down, so I did as 'e asked. Then 'e surprised me, 'e'd obviously bin listenin' to me talkin' to the barman cos 'e asked to see the ring. 'E took a quick glance and said,

'Bartender's right. It's not worth much, but I think I could use it. Tell you what, let me keep the ring and in exchange, I'll give you a quarter of tea.'

It wasn't much, but at the time I fought I could prob'ly sell it on – but o' course I didn't 'ave time before I was arrested. Mind you, it made gaol a bit easier when I could offer the gaoler a cup o' tea – it was 'im who give me that old kettle."

She took the kettle off the frame and emptied it. As she put it back in her sack, she sighed and said ruefully,

"Not much to show for twelve years o' marriage, is it? A beaten old kettle?"

But then she straightened, hitched the bag on her shoulder and said,

"Come on, what's past is past. Let's go and get your money."

Reaching Sydney just as the bank was shutting, Mary, who said she wasn't going to spend another night risking arrest, ran ahead of me to speak to the man guarding the entrance. I don't know what she said to him, but he looked at me curiously and said something in reply; whatever she'd said to him must have worked because she called for me to hurry. We'd been walking all day and the last thing I wanted to do was run, but by then, as I was little more than a hundred yards from the bank, I managed to break into a weary trot.

Following us in, the guard closed and locked the door. There was only one other person in the bank, sat behind a desk, a notice declaring him to be the cashier. With Kit's note in hand and summoning as much confidence as I could, I addressed him,

"My name's Admonition Payne and I'm here for my safe deposit box."

To my surprise, he seemed to have been expecting me. Although when I thought about it, he can't have had many instructions like those he'd received from Kit Carlyle. With barely a word, he opened a safe set in the wall behind him, I noticed the guard had raised his rifle to provide, what I suppose passed for security, and took out a small box plus a letter. I recognised my handwriting and I was ready to provide my signature when he handed me the quill – a glance enough to confirm I was the letter's author, he handed me the box and a key to open it. Thanking him, I picked up the box and took it to a nearby table. It was only as I put it down on the table that I realised Mary wasn't with me. When I turned she was standing in the doorway next to the guard and when she saw me looking at her questioningly, she said,

"It's your money, Adie, not mine."

I couldn't believe it. For two months, it seemed all we'd talked about was our plans for when we were released, and they all depended on this money. Now, when we were finally both free and able to make them happen, she was saying the money was nothing to do with her. I suppose I must have looked quite angry because, before I could speak, she came across and stood next to me. She didn't look at me but mumbled,

"Sorry, Adie. I was just saying."

I didn't reply, just picked up the key, opened the box and there it was – £412 tied with a linen strip and a small bag of coins. Of course, I couldn't be sure it was all there, but there was certainly more money than I'd ever seen. Taking it out of the box, I undid the strip and passed about half the money to Mary.

"You count that lot and I'll count the rest," I said. "We need to know if it's all there, though Lord knows what we do if it isn't."

We smiled at each other and Mary said,

"Let's just count it, shall we? Before we start to worry about any of it being missing."

Of course there was nothing missing, so I re-tied the money and after we'd hidden it at the bottom of Mary's bag, we made to leave. But as we reached the door, the guard spoke to Mary.

"You haven't forgotten what you promised?"

Pulling me back from the door, Mary said,

"Sorry Adie, I promised 'im half a crown if 'e waited for you and let us in. I know it's a lot of money but I wannid to make sure we didn't 'ave to spend the night on the streets of Sydney."

I agreed with her and said so, but I thought the guard could do a little more for his money than just hold the door for us. Retrieving a coin from the bag, I indicated to the guard we should step outside. There I said to him,

"Half a crown is a lot of money for holding a door open."

He didn't say anything, just stood there with an expectant look on his face. But he hadn't disagreed with me, so I carried on.

"Am I right thinking you're soon going to be finished here for the day?"

He looked at me suspiciously, but had to admit that once he'd helped secure the bank, he'd be away for the night; he expected to be done in about ten minutes.

"Right," I said, trying to sound certain, "we'll wait for you here and when you're finished, I want you to find us a shop where we can buy some decent clothes. After that, we need somewhere to get victuals and a bed for the night – I mean somewhere where two women can sleep safely in their beds."

The guard looked thoughtful for a moment then said,

"Well, I was promised the money for keeping the door open, but I'll tell you what I'll do. I think I can find a shop for you and there is a place you can stay; I know the landlord well and I can have a word."

It wasn't a fair deal, but we didn't have much choice, so I agreed reluctantly. Mind you, he was as good as his word and after taking us to what turned out to be the only shop selling women's clothes in the area, he took us across town to an inn he knew well.

We waited while he spoke to the landlord, after which a young girl who turned out to be the landlord's daughter, showed us to our room. The room wasn't the luxury I'd promised, but Mary said it was still the best place she'd slept in since she was arrested in England. Before she left us, I asked the girl if she would bring us a jug of hot water and a piece of soap so we could wash. Hurrying away, the girl returned minutes later with a steaming jug of hot water, a small piece of soap as well as a towel she thought we might want.

As soon as she was gone again, we washed and changed and then, dressed in our new clothes, went downstairs and back into the bar where the landlord was waiting for us. He told us that the bank guard had already left, but before leaving he must have told the landlord something of our good fortune because shepherding us through to his private parlour, he invited us to sit at a table already laid for two. Plainly anxious to please, he said,

"I thought you two ladies would prefer a bit of privacy and I've got some Bengal rum if you want it; the real Bengal I mean, costs a bit more than regular rum, but to be honest, that stuff is about as rough as it comes."

I thanked him and told him the Bengal would be fine and Mary asked him if we might have some food, because we were starving. The landlord beamed and rubbing his hands together, said,

"I can let you have a couple of beefsteaks I was keeping for me and the wife. They cost a bit more mind, but they're yours if you want them."

I was beginning to get irritated; so was Mary, because after I told him we'd have the steaks, she couldn't resist looking straight at him and saying,

"Like Adie said, we'll 'ave the steaks but it'd be nice if that was the last time we was told summin' was goin' to 'cost a bit more'."

By the look he gave her, it was clear she'd offended him and he'd just started to remind Mary that he and his wife were giving up their dinner for us, when I heard a very familiar voice start to sing. Interrupting the landlord, I told him I was certain Mary didn't mean to cause offence, and ignoring her scowls, asked him to delay the steaks for ten minutes. Taking no notice of their questioning faces, I left the parlour and went along the passage to the entrance of the public bar. Standing behind the door, I could hear the voice even more clearly and was certain I knew whose it was. So pulling the door open just a little, I could see the owner of the voice coaxing the men to throw her pennies. At first I thought I'd been mistaken. After all, the woman's face was bloated and red from drink, and wherever there was flesh showing, there were clear signs of syphilis. But she was about the right height, the voice was unmistakable and as I looked closer I realised, I really was looking at the pox-ridden remnants of Lolly Hamlet.

Having decided there was nothing to be gained by speaking to her, I told myself she wouldn't remember me if I did, I didn't realise that to get a better view, I'd opened the door more than I meant and before I closed it again, she called out,

"Adie… Adie Payne, is that really you?"

She'd stopped singing in mid-verse and some of the men, especially those claiming they'd thrown money, were grumbling that she'd not finished their song. But Lolly was deaf to their complaints and tottered towards me.

When she reached me, I tried to hide my shock at her condition by feigning surprise at finding her in New Holland. She hugged me, the smell of alcohol overwhelming, and told me how good it was to see me. I said it was good to see her as well, but also noticed the grumbling had got louder, so I said,

"Lolly, why don't you go back and finish your singing? Then you can join us in the parlour for some dinner."

She looked back into the bar. It was as if she'd forgotten the men were there. With a real effort, she managed to focus on them and said,

"You're right. They love me here, say my singing reminds them of home. I'll give 'em a couple more and then I'll come and find you."

She paused for a moment, then with a sly look, added,

"You couldn't get us another rum, could you, Adie? I need something to wet me whistle – singing is thirsty work, you know."

I promised I'd have one sent through to her, so satisfied she tottered back into the bar. I returned to the parlour and Mary, with the sound of 'Meet me by the moonlight' echoing down the corridor.

In the parlour, the landlord's daughter was waiting to know whether we were ready for our steaks yet and Mary was looking at me expectantly. I asked the girl if she could take a tot of rum to Lolly and then see if the steak might be cut three ways as she'd be joining us for dinner. After she left to give Lolly her rum and her father my request, I explained to Mary that I'd met Lolly on the *Brunswick* and how she'd just about saved my life.

"I think I owe her for that," I said, "even if I'm only buying her dinner," and then I added,

"Anyway, I want to know what happened to her after I was taken from the hulk."

Mary was interested to hear more, so I spent the next quarter of an hour or so telling her all about Lolly and especially how she had helped me. But then the singing stopped and as it did the girl re-appeared with three steaks; her father must have known Lolly's final number because moments later she swayed through the door, rum in hand and dumped herself in the only free chair. I explained how I'd met Mary and we'd become friends while chained together for most of the journey to New Holland. But I was much more anxious to learn what had happened to Lolly since I was taken from the *Brunswick* and how she came to be in Sydney – and I knew I needed to ask her before the rum rendered her unconscious.

I shouldn't have worried because she was more than ready to tell her story. She explained that she'd served three more months on the hulk before being released. When she went back to the place she'd been living before she was arrested, someone else had rented her room, which didn't surprise her, but when she found her old landlord and he told her he didn't have anything else for her, that did surprise her; in all the time she rented from him, she'd never known him not to have a spare room available. She knew her children were safe with her parents, but she had no idea where they were, but her immediate problem was to find somewhere for the night and the means to pay for it. She had no choice. She went back to her old trades – the old pub, the old songs and the same old clients.

Things should have been fine, she said, because she made enough to keep a room for the night and to feed herself and as long as she steered clear of any toffs, she could put up with the men.

"But then this started to show." She ran her hand over one side of her face. "I knew I had it before they put me on the *Brunswick*. I reckon it was that toff who give it me."

Of course, we both knew it could have been any of her clients, but I think it made her feel better to blame him.

"As the pox got worse, so did my trade. In the end, I wasn't earning enough to pay the rent and the landlord was threatening to throw me out."

We'd all finished our steaks and our drinks were low, so I asked the girl when she came to clear our plates, to bring us another round. Thanks to the food I suppose, just then, Lolly looked a little more sober, so I asked how that led to her being transported.

"Well, that's just it. I started thievin'; I had no choice Adie."

She looked defiantly at Mary, as if she thought she was going to disapprove. But Mary just smiled and said,

"We all do what we have to, to get by, don't we?"

Glad of the approval, Lolly spoke to Mary instead of me.

"I did alright for a while, stealing lace and silk and so on and I sold it to one of my old clients who worked in that line of business.

But then I got careless. I stole a roll of curtain material from outside a haberdashery. I got away alright, but instead of shifting it straight away, I got greedy and thought I'd get a better price for it up the West End. So the next day, roll of curtain under my arm, I was on my way across town when I ran slap into the haberdasher. I didn't stand a chance 'cos though I dropped the roll and tried to run away, he kicked up such a row that people were grabbing me from all sides and as soon as you like, I'd been caught and marched in front of a magistrate.

That's where I finally had a slice of luck – and it was about time. See, I knew if I was caught thievin' again I could expect to have my neck stretched or, if I was lucky, a life sentence here in New Holland. But when the magistrate saw me, his ruddy face went pale. You see, we recognised one another. The last time I'd seen him was in my room and just like he was in the courtroom, he'd been wearing his wig – the difference was when there was just the two of us, he wore nothin' else. He liked to pretend I'd been tried in his court and found guilty and he'd invent all sorts of punishments for me you'd never find in any law book. Oh yes, there were many tales I could tell about 'Your Honour' (as he liked to be called when playing his games) and I was ready to tell the court all about 'em – and he knew it. So when it came to passing sentence, he wanted me as far away from him as possible and for as long as possible. But he also knew that the harsher the sentence then the less I had to lose, and the more likely I was to tell of the little games he liked to play – harmless enough, but not what people expect from a magistrate. So that's why he only sentenced me to seven years' transportation."

Me and Mary joined in her laughter, but even though she was very drunk, Lolly suddenly became serious.

"I finished my sentence two years ago but I knew I couldn't go home – there was nothing there for me. At least here I can make enough money to survive; they like to hear me sing 'cos I know all the old songs and they remind 'em of the place they still call home."

Looking a little sad, she raised her almost empty glass and said, "And some of 'em still buy this stuff for me."

With a tremendous effort, she stood up and holding on to the edge of the table announced, "And now I've got to go because I've got a client waiting for me in the bar."

Meandering to the door, she added, "That's if he's still conscious."

With that, she was gone.

Mary looked at me and said, "I know you, Adie, and I know what you're thinking. You want to help her. But you can't – she's just too far gone. I've seen women like her before. A couple more months and the pox will have driven her mad, and in six months she'll be dead."

I knew she was right of course, but I thought to myself that there had to be something I could do for Lolly.

Jabez had once given me gin. Though I hadn't liked it, other than that, the rum we'd drunk that evening was the first strong liquor to have ever passed my lips. It's certainly true I took to the rum more than I had the gin – unlike the gin, I hadn't spat it into anyone's face! In fact, I took to the first mug so well that I'd been more than happy to accept a couple of refills. Mary told me that after Lolly had left, I'd rambled on about the future and what it might hold for her and I hadn't stopped going on about finding some way to help her 'til long after we'd returned to our room for the night. I think that was also one of the reasons why, when we were back in our bedroom, I'd failed to take in that Mary had stopped unlacing her boots and instead, was staring, unashamedly, straight at me as I undressed.

When I'd stripped to my undergarments, I was more than glad to clamber into bed. But as I lay down the room began to spin, the feeling of spinning getting worse when I shut my eyes. The only way I managed to hold the room still was by turning on my side and holding on tightly to the edge of the bed. With the room held steady, the effects of the rum and tiredness at the end of a long day (but especially the effects of rum!), meant I was ready for sleep when Mary slid into the bed beside me and I'd nearly drifted off when she spoke softly into the nape of my neck. Intimately close, she breathed,

"I liked your hair more when it was long. Perhaps you'll grow it again."

As she gently laid her hand on my hip I wondered why, in all the months we'd been chained together, she hadn't ever said anything about my hair.

I didn't ask her why. Instead, I lay still and hoped she'd believe I was already asleep, but she gently increased the pressure on my hip and I realised she sensed I was still awake. I had seen women together in the Factory and been unsure of how it made me feel and though I was still unsure, I knew I really didn't want to resist Mary. So, although I also knew it would start the room spinning again, I let go of the side of the bed and turned over onto my back. When I opened my eyes, Mary, who was already on her belly, raised herself on her elbows, leant over me and kissed my forehead. But because, as soon as I'd open my eyes the room had spun faster, by the time her feather light kisses had travelled down from my brow, over my nose and mouth to my chin and returned to my mouth, becoming firmer as she pressed my lips to part, I was forced to tear myself away from her.

I wasn't rejecting her kisses, but an even stronger force was overwhelming me. Struggling to my feet, I stumbled through the dark to the windowsill where I remembered I'd left the empty washbasin. I reached it just in time and, leaning over, was very, very sick. Though I earnestly promised God I'd never again drink gin or rum, a promise I may add I've kept ever since, I continued to be sick until my stomach was completely empty. Even then I retched several more times before my stomach settled and, drained to the core, I was able to feel my way back to bed.

We've laughed about that night many times and Mary, who always swears I was asleep before I got back into bed, says she knew there was no point in trying to wake me again. I have to admit I have no memory of anything from when I reached the edge of the bed until the next morning, when I awoke with my head feeling like someone had driven a six-inch nail from the centre of my forehead to the back of my skull. To add to my discomfort, I also had a dry throat and a desperate thirst. Silently re-making my vow of the previous night, I bravely opened my eyes and, flinching in the early morning light, was startled by Mary who, fully dressed, was sat on the bed holding a mug.

"I've been down and got a jug of water so I could wash out that basin. I had a feeling you wouldn't want to face that job this morning." Smiling, she added, "I saved you this in case you were thirsty."

She held out the mug and I gratefully drained it. Handing it back, although I could gladly have laid back down again and slept until noon, I forced myself to get up and start getting dressed – as I told Mary, if we were to get to Morpeth in one day, we needed to set off soon and we still had to find two horses to get us there. Of course, I had another reason for wanting to get out of that room in a hurry. I might have had only misty memories of the night before, but I knew I definitely didn't feel in a fit state to discuss them.

Going downstairs, my head thumping with each step, I went through to the bar and spoke to the landlord, leaving Mary talking to his daughter.

A pound, that's what the landlord demanded – he'd accept nothing less. But for that, as well as accepting it as payment for our night's stay, he agreed that when she could no longer work he would look after Lolly, feed her and provide her with a roof over her head. However, he told me, she'd still have to go to the asylum if the madness really took a hold of her. I knew that's how it had to be. So satisfied I'd done the best I could for Lolly, I asked him where I might buy two good horses. It came as no surprise when he told me he had a couple he could sell me if I cared to come out the back to the stable to have a look at them. Of course he wanted top price for them, but to be honest, they were fine mares and I knew they should get us to Morpeth in one day, as long as we got on our way soon.

I paid him what he asked and then went and found Mary. After I told her about the mares, without a word she picked up her bag and we went out the front of the inn to where the landlord was holding the already saddled horses. We mounted a little hesitantly, as neither of us had much riding experience, but soon enough we had waved goodbye to the landlord and were heading, at a steady pace, in the direction of Morpeth. As we didn't have a map, we took the landlord's advice and stuck as closely as we could to the coast until we reached Newcastle. From there, he told us, we should pick up the Hunter River and follow it inland.

The journey passed with only one incident before we reached our destination, and that was of our own making. Our horses were sound and even though we rested and watered them every couple of hours, we still managed a steady trot for most of the day. Creeks and rivers sometimes forced us inland, but many were dry or almost dry, so we were often able to cut straight across them. For long distances, the coast was edged with sandy beach and sometimes the simplest way forward was to drop down from the cliffs and let the horses cool their hooves in the sea where it lapped the shore.

The first time we'd reached the water's edge, Mary's mare had hesitated. It was clearly a new experience for her, but because mine barely broke stride as the water reached her knees, Mary's needed little further encouragement to follow. They were soon striding along side by side and in fact, without being pressed, both horses were moving markedly faster and it took little to spur them into a full gallop.

We must have travelled the best part of five miles in the water, by which time Mary was riding a few yards ahead of me, when it hit me and a cold shiver ran down my spine. Hauling my horse to a slow trot and cursing myself for my own stupidity, I headed for the dry sand. By the time Mary had noticed she was riding alone and managed to turn her horse around to follow me, I had dismounted and was already walking towards a boulder big enough to hide me from prying eyes.

"What you doin'?" Mary panted. "Why d'you stop so suddenly an' wivout sayin' nothin'?"

I didn't reply. I just kept walking to the boulder and still muttering to herself, Mary dismounted and followed me. Reaching the rock, I was pleased to find I'd guessed right, because I was able to walk the mare into the narrow gap between the boulder and the cliffs without any difficulty. Although, apart from us the beach was deserted, I wanted to be doubly sure we weren't seen by any prying eyes. As it turned out, the spot was perfect, we were too close to the cliff to be seen from above, we were hidden completely from the sea and we would see anyone on the beach long before they saw us. It was only then that I untied Mary's bag from the saddle. I took out all of her possessions, noticing that whilst the few items of clothes I took out first were very wet, all the rest were, by degrees, dryer and dryer. Finally, I gingerly picked up the money which we had hidden at the bottom of the bag. Mary had realised my concern when I took down the bag and now was equally anxious to see how much damage the seawater had done to the money. To our relief, although most of the money was damp, only the notes nearest the bottom were actually wet and these I carefully peeled away from the rest and laid on stones to dry. We decided to stop where we were and rest the horses. We also shared the last of our fresh water with them and though we had no food for them or us, at least the space between the rock and the bolder provided all four of us with some shade.

After about half an hour, the money was dry and Mary's clothes, which we'd also laid out, were no worse than damp. So we wrapped the money in the clothes, repacked the now almost dry bag and set off again towards Newcastle.

Reaching Newcastle late in the afternoon and knowing we were pressed for time, we were glad we found the Hunter River quickly and could head inland.

We arrived in Morpeth just as the sun was disappearing behind the hills that had lined the horizon for most of our journey. Complete darkness fell shortly afterwards and realising we would be unlikely to find Lieutenant Granger until the morning, we decided to try and find somewhere to spend the night.

The town seemed to be little more than a single road, sparsely lined with a range of small, roughly built buildings, almost all lying in darkness. However there was one building, sat about halfway along the road, that seemed different from the rest. Even from the end of the road, we could see light escaping from around the front door, and as we got closer, we could also see there was a second floor. When we were just a few yards away, we could hear the murmur of men's voices and on reaching the front door, we saw, almost hidden by the shadows, a handwritten sign declaring 'rum' and beneath it 'beds'. I looked at Mary and she shrugged – we both knew we weren't likely to find anywhere better.

We dismounted and Mary tethered the horses while I took the money from her bag, and after taking a guinea from it and hiding the rest beneath my chemise, I took a deep breath and led the way inside. There were six tables with two or three men sat at each one and as we entered all conversation stopped, every man turning to stare at us. There was a small hatch which served as a bar and where a bored landlord lounged. So ignoring the stares, Mary walked straight up to the him and said,

"We need some beds for the night and some food. We also need somewhere safe to keep our 'orses – they're gonna need food and water as well."

The landlord still looked bored, but at least he was standing up now.

"I'll need to see the money first."

That was all he said and so, annoyed because although we were offering business he couldn't have expected he still appeared disinterested, I moved up next to Mary and said,

"And we'll need to know how much you're asking."

He might have been bored, but he didn't intend to miss a chance to make a bob or two.

"It'll be a shilling for each of you two and two n' tuppence for the horses."

It sounded a bit steep, but I wanted to get out of that bar as quickly as I could and I was sure Mary felt the same, so I handed him the guinea I was holding and while he got my change, I told him we'd take supper in our room. I wished I'd had something smaller than a guinea to give him, because he made a great show of counting out my change.

"I'll get the lad to bring your food up once he's seen to the mares. Don't expect too much, I'm usually only asked for rum and a bed."

The 'lad' appeared from somewhere out the back and took us to our room which, apart from two cots, was dark and empty. He lit us a candle he was carrying and said he would be straight back with our supper. Holding up the lit candle, I could look round the room properly. Built like a lean-to, through gaps in the paperbark walls, I could see it was supported on three sides by other rooms made much the same way. The fourth side was the only one that faced the weather and the elements had shrunk and twisted each timber, so now the wall provided little protection and I could quite easily see the street through the gaps. I looked at Mary, expecting her to say something about the wall, but she was looking the other way, studying the door. I couldn't see why, but whatever the reason the wall had to be a more pressing problem, especially if the distant sound of thunder we'd heard as we left the parlour was an early warning that rain was coming. So I asked her,

"What are you looking at, Mary? Didn't you hear that thunder? If it means rains coming, this wall will never keep us dry."

She must have heard the irritation in my voice, but her reply was just as terse.

"It's not any rain we need to worry about. What I want to know is what we're gonna do when they break in, 'cos that landlord made sure they all saw 'im give you change for that guinea an' I bet they're gonna come lookin' for it, and anything else we might 'ave. An' I bet they ain't gonna be polite about it, niever."

Before I could answer, the lad returned holding two plates. On each plate, there was a little bread but this was dwarfed by a pile of cold lamb. Mary took the plates and, after handing them to me, went to work on the boy.

"So, 'ave you got a name then, lad? It wouldn't feel right. You 'avin' been so nice to us 'en all, not to at least know that much about you."

As she spoke, she lightly touched his arm and then, looking into his eyes, gave him what she told me after, was her most winning smile."

The boy's face reddened to the roots as he stuttered,

"D-D-D…Daniel."

"Well, Daniel, both me an' Adie 'ere, are grateful for 'ow you've treated us and Adie's got a bob for you, ain't you Adie?"

She turned and looked at me and though I thought giving him a penny was more than enough, I put the change the landlord had given me on one of the cots and quickly found a shilling and passed it to her. Taking hold of his hand which, if it was possible turned him an even deeper shade of red, she placed the coin in his palm and closed his fingers over it. After lightly patting his hand, she slowly released it. He was now looking as if he might burst and at once I understood why Simon Peters had become so besotted with her. Like Simon Peters and probably Tom before him and as I was yet to realise, me, she now had Daniel eating out of her hand.

"But I need you to do one more thing for me and if you do it, then there's another sixpence in it for you."

Unfolding his fingers, he stared at the shilling, the look of surprise on his face enough to make me wonder if he'd ever held one of his own before – I was certain he'd never before earned one so easily – but I had to object when I heard how easily he could earn another sixpence. Daniel nodded his head and staring at the floor, mumbled,

"'Course I will, but you've paid me enough already. I don't want no more."

Mary knew she had won his heart and there was no need to flirt anymore, so she said,

"All I want you to do when you go back downstairs is to just keep your eyes and ears open."

It was then I tried to object but Mary raised her hand. She didn't even look at me,

"Wait, Adie. I'll explain in a minute." She returned her attention to Daniel. "And if you hear anyone say anythin' that might mean they plan to rob us, first chance you get I want you to come up 'ere an' tell us. Would you be able to do that?"

"Course I will. It should be easy 'cos I'm working in the bar tonight and I'll hear if anyone says anything like that." Then with a look of panic, he said, "I must go now. They'll be wondering why I'm taking so long – he doesn't like me talking to his customers any more than I have to."

With that, he turned and started to return to the bar, but Mary called him back and in barely more than a whisper, said,

"Just one more question. If we needed it, can you get 'old of a ladder?"

Though he was anxious to get away, he smiled, clearly happy that once again he could please Mary.

"I've got one in the stable. I use it to get in the hayloft."

Still whispering, Mary told him that was excellent news and then in a louder than normal voice, added,

"Thank you for fixin' Adie's shoe, Daniel, but you better get on your way now. I don't want to keep you from your duties."

For a moment, Daniel looked confused, but then he grinned and with a 'you're welcome miss', hurried away.

With him gone, Mary shut the door and said,

"Right, I don't think we should waste any time. You put that money away, 'cept for a sixpence o' 'course. Then we'll eat and be ready for when 'e comes back."

My face must have betrayed what I was thinking, because she then answered the question I hadn't even asked yet.

"Oh, and yes, I'm sure he'll be back and we'll need to be ready as soon as he lets us know what's happening. I'll get him to leave his ladder up against our window and then saddle up our horses and get them ready for us to go."

I knew she was probably right, so even though I wasn't hungry any more, as there was no telling when we'd have food again, I forced myself to eat. Mary ate as quickly as I did, but we'd barely finished when I caught a slight noise outside our window. Coming so soon after Daniel had left us, my only thought was that it had to be robbers come early to try and catch us off guard. So after first signalling to Mary what was happening, I picked up our pot and crept up to the window, intending to empty the contents over as many heads as I could. But before I reached it, Daniel's anxious face appeared in the window.

"I didn't have time to warn you. There are four of them getting ready to come up. You've got to go right now."

Loud banging on the door proved his point for him and with an unnecessary "come on!" he started to move back down the ladder. It was unnecessary because followed by Mary, who had the rest of our belongings, I was already climbing onto the ladder. Reaching the bottom, Daniel had run across to the stable and was bringing the mares across, both already saddled and ready to go.

"I guessed you might be needing these earlier than you thought, so I got 'em ready when I was supposed to be bedding them down for the night."

Suddenly, as I mounted my mare, there was the sound of fracturing wood followed by loud voices as they discovered we'd gone. I realised our mistake, but before I could open my mouth to call to Mary, Daniel, who had seen it even sooner, had covered the short distance back to the ladder and swung it away from the wall. He wasn't a moment too soon, because as the ladder crashed to the ground the landlord's face appeared at the window.

Mary called Daniel out of the darkness, but as he turned towards her, the landlord must have recognised her voice and spoke to the others in the room with him.

"Quick, they're still here. Get out there and stop them."

I knew if I'd heard what he said, then Mary must have done as well, but instead of hurrying to mount her horse, she started talking urgently to Daniel. After what seemed minutes, but was probably only seconds, she took hold of his hand and I saw the glint of silver as she gave him the sixpence she'd promised. Closing his fingers over the coin, she gave his hand one final squeeze, then letting go, finally started to mount her horse. She turned to give Daniel one final wave but he'd already disappeared into the night, so she kicked her horse into a gallop and with an infuriating,

"Come on, Adie, let's go," set off down the road. I had no time to protest that I had been ready and waiting while she caste her spell over Daniel, because at that moment the door from the pub burst open and two men, followed closely by the landlord's wife, ran out. I kicked the horse and for a moment outrage gathered in her, before translating straight into a gallop. Her first pull was so strong that I almost lost my grip and after a couple of hundred yards, we caught and passed a surprised Mary, travelling at least a further mile before I managed to re-gain control and bring us to a halt.

By the time we stopped, Mary was a good distance behind us and I couldn't repeat what she said when she caught up. The only repeatable, but also the most important thing she said, was that Daniel had given her directions to the Lieutenant's homestead.

With Daniel's directions, finding Lieutenant Granger was straightforward. Normally, we would have asked the landlord if he knew where the lieutenant could be found, but our night-time flit meant that wasn't possible. Anyway, I'd tried to give the impression I knew him very well and so was bound to know where he lived. Daniel, who had definitely taken a shine to Mary, had been able to tell her that on leaving the army, the Lieutenant had received a land grant just outside Morpeth, where he and Catherine had built their homestead. He also gave her directions, which, even in the dark, were simple enough to follow.

We were greeted at the homestead by a plainly pregnant Catherine, clearly delighted to see me.

"Edward told me to keep an eye out for you ever since we moved," she said, grinning happily. "He told me he knew you'd be along one day."

It turned out that the Lieutenant had been made a magistrate since they moved to Morpeth and this often kept him from home.

"But I know he would hate to miss you," she said anxiously. "You will stay and eat with us, won't you? Edward will be home before it gets dark."

Our only reason for being in Morpeth was to see the Lieutenant, so of course we stayed. We sat and talked, and me and Mary told Catherine all about our lives, even back to our lives in England and why we'd been arrested and transported. Catherine was interested in all we had to tell her, but really she was consumed by her pregnancy. The baby, she said, was due in July. It was natural, she said, that Edward hoped for a son, but though we had to promise not to tell him, she secretly hoped for a girl.

"There are so few women around here," she complained. "A little girl would be a companion for me."

She gave me a rueful smile and I thought how lonely she must be, waiting each day until her husband came home for some company.

Edward came home around six. Delighted to see me and glad to meet Mary, he confirmed (several times) that he'd told Catherine to expect me. Keen to hear our plans now we were free, he said he would help us in any way he could. So I told him about the money Jabez had left me, although I didn't tell him how it had been earned, and said we were hoping he could help us find a suitable place in Morpeth to open a guest house. He thought this over for a minute or two, asked us a couple of questions about the nature of the establishment we intended to run – whether we were intending to offer beds for the night and then what about stabling. Finally he declared,

"Not Morpeth, I don't think here would be the right place for you. It's got an inn already and I don't think its landlord would appreciate the competition. No, I think I've got a much better idea."

Excited by his own thoughts, as he ploughed on he didn't see the knowing smile that passed between me and Mary.

"About five miles down the river, there's a new settlement going up on an island called Carrington. It's not much yet, there's only about fifty people living there at the moment, but it's bound to grow."

He went on to explain that Carrington already had a natural port and though it wasn't widely known, Edward had learnt that a wool production firm would be opening soon.

"The thing is, they haven't got a guesthouse," he smiled and then added, "and they're going to need one."

If we were interested, he said he would accompany us to Carrington in the morning. Of course we were interested. It seemed an opportunity not to be missed. So, taking Edward's suggestion, we wasted no time and went to Carrington early the next day. It was barely daybreak when we set off. Carrington was still waking up when we arrived, and when Edward led us through the centre of the settlement straight down to the river front, he was able to show us the plot he had in mind. It was at least twice the size of any of the places we'd seen in Morpeth and that meant we would be able to build well back from the river, avoiding any chance of flooding and Edward pointed out just how close to the dock we would be. Lowering his voice, he added that he believed the wool production company would be built just beyond the dock.

I looked at Mary and asked her,

"Well, what do you think?"

She grinned and said,

"It's a perfect spot, but I think you already know that."

She was right of course, so turning back to Edward, I said,

"So what do we do now?"

"Well, that's easy," he said. "We go back to the homestead and you can explain to me exactly what you want. I'll try and sketch what you describe, then, if you're happy with what I've sketched, I'll prepare the drawings. Now, I know some reliable men who can build it for you and if you're happy for me to do it, I'll oversee the work as well, so in fact all you'll have to do is pay the bills."

So that's what we did. We described how the building was to be on two floors with a bar, lounge and kitchen downstairs, with upstairs only bedrooms. Because the plot was big enough, we asked for a stable not only for our mares, but one also large enough to take any of our guest's horses. Edward asked many questions then drew and re-drew several sketches and it was almost midnight before we got to our beds – at least me, Mary and Catherine did. Edward said he would follow shortly but that he first needed to make secure the homestead. But when I got up early the next morning he was still sitting at the table where we'd left him, the floor around him covered with detailed drawings of every part of our guesthouse. Looking dishevelled and still wearing the clothes he'd worn the day before, he'd clearly been up all night.

As I entered the room, he put his quill down and looking at the drawing, said,

"Good."

He said it to himself with a note of satisfaction, but then looking up noticed me for the first time.

"Good morning, Adie. I hope you slept well."

I told him I had, and he said,

"I hope Mary will be up soon, I've finished the drawings, so as soon as the plot is yours, we can arrange for it to be built."

We stayed on with Catherine and the Lieutenant right through the autumn and in the July, to the delight of them both, Marianne was born. Edward was bewitched by his daughter from the moment they met and completely forgot he'd wanted a boy. Had there been any fleeting moments of regret, they were soon washed away when he saw the look of love and satisfaction, on Catherine's face.

We were glad for Catherine but I think Mary, like me, regretted she had no children of her own. We had little time to dwell on any regrets we might harbour because in early September the Boar's Head was finished – we owed Jabez' memory that much; after all, it was his money that had paid for it.

And work hadn't finished a day too soon, because after we'd bought enough stock to get by, we opened with barely two pounds left. We opened our doors and waited expectantly for our first customer… and waited. We knew custom might be slow at first, at least until the wool production company started to be built, but we had hoped a few of the fifty or so current residents of Carrington would be curious enough to pay us a visit. Even though we'd told everyone when we were opening, we told each other they might have forgotten tonight was our first night. Consoled by that thought, we decided to close early, and I went to bolt the door. I'd just reached for the first of the three locks that would make the door secure overnight, when a form crashed through and landed at my feet. As it got to its feet, the bundle of rags became recognisable.

'Daniel' was all I said. I'd recognised him, but I should have been forgiven if I hadn't, because apart from the state of his clothes, he'd clearly been severely beaten. We later discovered he was covered from head to toe in cuts and bruises and had a couple of cracked ribs.

But right then, all I could see was his face covered with blood, his bottom lip split and bleeding and his left eye completely closed. It had taken me only a moment to take all of this in, but before I could speak again, Daniel shut the door and while wrestling with the locks, pleaded,

"Adie, please help me. They're after me and if I'm caught, I think they'll kill me this time."

There was real fear in Daniel's voice, so while he pulled the top bolt, I tackled the bottom one. As soon as we were done, he collapsed in the nearest chair.

Transfixed, Mary had only watched up until then, but now, she asked him, "Who are they?"

When he didn't answer her question, she asked again,

"Come on Daniel. Who is it?"

I don't know whether he was ready to speak, but we'll never know because a moment later there was a loud knocking at the door and an angry voice called out,

"Open the door. We know you've got him in there. Let us have him and I promise you'll not have any trouble."

Mary looked at me, like me she'd recognised the voice of the innkeeper from Morpeth.

"He stole from me and he's got to pay for what he took."

"He's lying. I never stole anything from him." Despite all the damage, Daniel's face had drained. "I'll tell you everything that's happened, but please don't let him in. He'll kill me."

A surge of anger coursed through Mary and she told Daniel to go and hide behind the bar.

The lad didn't need telling twice. Without a word and after just a glance of gratitude, he scuttled away.

The innkeeper was getting impatient.

"I'll count to three and if you haven't unlocked this damn door, we'll break it down."

Looking round, Mary spotted and retrieved the short-handled axe we used to split logs too large for the fire. She clearly had no intention of giving up Daniel without a fight, so as the innkeeper's count reached three, I rushed to our kitchen, returning with the largest knife I could find. Just as I returned, the locks resisted a third blow and it was clear the door surround was well made and the bolts of good quality. But they were already starting to move and after the fourth blow, I could see with the next one or, at most the one after, the bolts would fail. Mary had clearly come to the same conclusion because she readied herself for the inevitable; I did the same.

By some miracle, only the bottom bolt had failed. The top and middle bolts had held, but I knew the innkeeper was right when I heard him cry,

"Alright lads, one more push should do it."

I looked at Mary. She just said,

"You ready?"

I nodded, although I didn't see how the two of us, armed only with a knife and an axe, were going to resist a gang of determined men. Out of the corner of my eye, I spotted some movement and looking round, saw that Daniel had come out of his hiding place and picked up the shovel from by the fire. I turned to him, I knew we had little time,

"Daniel, I know you want to help but I don't think you can. Anyway, they can't be sure you're still here, can they?"

He smiled ruefully and said,

"Oh, they know I'm here alright. They wouldn't be trying so hard to get in, if you weren't trying just as hard to keep them out. No, they've told you why they're here. If you had nothing to hide, simplest thing would be just to let 'em in. I bought this trouble down on you, the least I can do is help you defend the place."

Raising the spade, he stood defiantly. I knew I couldn't change his mind, so I turned towards the door. But before anything could happen, we heard the crack of a rifle followed by a shout. Both sounded some way off and it was impossible to work out what had been said, but whatever it was, the next blow to the door never came. Instead, we heard the sound of hooves approaching rapidly and when they reached the door, a familiar voice spoke. At that moment it was the voice I wanted to hear more than any other.

"Adie, it's Edward. Everything's alright now. You can open the door."

Mary answered him,

"Edward. Thank God. Am I glad it's you. The door's almost off, I think the easiest way to open it would be if you give it one last blow."

I could hear Edward talking to whoever was with him and then, after he told Mary to stand back, there was a crack and the door was off. With Edward, I recognised four convicts who worked on his homestead. His gun trained on the innkeeper and looking nowhere but at him and the two men with him, he spoke to us,

"None of you are hurt, are you?"

Mary glanced at me and I shook my head.

280

"No, we're fine," she said and breaking into a grin, she added, "and even better for seeing you."

I suppose because I hadn't spoken, he took his eye from the innkeeper and looking at me, said,

"So what's the problem here then, Adie?"

Just as I started to tell him how I didn't know much more than him, the innkeeper interrupted me. Again he started telling how Daniel had stolen from him and if we just handed him over, the three of them would be on their way.

Daniel, who still stood with the spade raised, took a step forward. I thought he was going to hit the landlord, evidently so did the landlord, who instinctively readied to defend himself. Edward didn't move. He simply cocked his rifle. Ignoring both of them, Daniel said,

"You're a liar, Matthew Francis. I'll tell you all what happened."

He explained that after he'd helped me and Mary to get away, he'd been forced into one of the bedrooms and kept there until he managed to escape. He said he'd been regularly beaten by the landlord and up to five other men.

"Including those two most of the time." He glared at all three of them. "Four nights ago they beat me up so badly I knew they wouldn't stop until they killed me."

He went on to tell how the next night he'd worked loose one of the wall panels in the bedroom and despite his injuries, drop down to the road and slipped away into the night. Even though he'd twisted his ankle when he jumped, he walked all night, only finding a place to hide at first light, so terrified was he that they might catch him.

"And it was just as well I did," reliving the moment was reminding Daniel of how scared he'd been, "I was dozing in a ditch by the side of the road, waiting for night to fall again, when these three rode past." He pointed the spade at the landlord, "I had no time to get away. I just had to hope they wouldn't look in the ditch – if they did they were certain to spot me."

He went on to say he'd been lucky because they were engaged in a heated argument about whose fault it was that he'd escaped. Anyway, he had decided there was nothing else he could do but try and find me and Mary. He'd hoped to find us at Edward's homestead but if we were no longer there, at least find out where we had gone. So, while he'd kept well away from the road, he always kept it in view because he knew that was the way to find the homestead.

Edward interrupted at this point.

"That's why I'm here. I wasn't home when the boy called, but Catherine told me all about him yesterday evening. She told me he was in a terrible state and that apart from the fact that he'd obviously taken a severe beating, he also looked like he hadn't eaten for days. That had upset her the most because, try as she might, she couldn't persuade him to stay for some food, he was only interested in finding this place. So I thought I'd come over this evening see if he found you and see how your first night had gone at the same time. Then, when I was approaching, I saw these three trying to knock your door down."

It was a week before Daniel told us all that had happened on that day when he burst through our door and it was an even longer time before he told us everything that had happened after we parted. In the meantime, Edward dealt with the innkeeper. All the time he'd been talking to us his rifle was always trained on him and now he turned and spoke straight to him.

"Now, I'm going to make myself very clear and you better be listening just as carefully. You know I'm a magistrate, don't you? I haven't asked Daniel to tell us everything you and your band of ne'er-do-wells have done to him, but I am going to ask him to tell me the names of all those who've been involved in your cruelty towards him. If any of them or you, or anyone else come here looking to cause trouble, he'll be telling everything in front of a judge and jury. If you want to avoid that, all you have to do is keep away from this place and make sure this lot stay away as well." He swung his rifle in an arc across the front of them. "Now, have I made myself clear?"

The innkeeper nodded again. He didn't look happy but he wasn't about to cross the local magistrate.

While his men made sure the door was secure for the night, Edward got Daniel to tell him the names of all the people who had helped the innkeeper imprison and beat him. Once that was done, he told Daniel he'd be writing to each of them, just to make sure they understood what will happen if they cause any trouble for him or us.

Finally, before he left, Edward told us he'd send two men in the morning to fix the door properly, adding that he and Catherine would be over the next evening to see how we were getting on.

When we were on our own again, I told Daniel that I'd talked to Mary and we'd agreed he could stay with us as long as he liked – it wasn't true, I hadn't spoken to Mary, but I was certain she'd agree if I asked her. The problem of where he might sleep was solved when he begged to be allowed to sleep in the stable. He said his experience in Morpeth meant he never wanted to sleep in a bedroom ever again.

We had been too tired to talk about Daniel that night, but in the morning whilst he mucked out and fed our mares, we had enough time to decide what we could offer him. Before he finished with the horses, the two men Edward had promised to send, arrived to fix the door and I thought we needed to be alone when I talked to Daniel about money. When I was able to speak to him, I repeated my promise that he could stay as long as he liked if, in return, he would look after our horses and those of our guests and also help us in the bar in the evening. I explained that we wouldn't be able to pay him anything until trade picked up, so we would understand if he decided to leave. I added that whatever his final decision, I hoped he would at least stay until he was fully recovered.

As we couldn't pay him, I'd thought he might need to think about what he should do, but he answered so quickly; he must have known what he was going to say long before I'd finished speaking and, of course, I was delighted, as was Mary.

"Adie, you and Mary have shown me nothing but kindness from the first time we met, and my only regret is that I didn't leave the inn with you. I'd love to stay with you both and I don't mind if you don't ever pay me, so long as I can carry on sleeping in the stable."

I hadn't expected to be able to pay him until work began on the wool factory, but a surprise that evening changed everything. Before it was dark, Edward arrived with Catherine and the baby as he had promised, and with them were the four convicts who had accompanied him the night before. Catherine was delighted to see us and glad to hear what we had agreed with Daniel, but she said they couldn't stay for long. I was disappointed they would be leaving so soon, but there wasn't time for regret before we heard a carriage pull up outside. Daniel went out to hold the horses and then lead them round the back to the stables. The four passengers came into the inn, greeted Edward and Catherine, then ordered what turned out to be the first of several rounds. The four of them had barely sat down before two more men rode in, tethered their horses, nodded at Edward and ordered a bottle of rum. There were soon ten more people, all of whom greeted Edward and a few who said hello to Catherine as well. The Grangers left soon after, but people continued to arrive for the next hour.

It turned out that Edward had found ways to contact everyone he knew in the County and invited them to the Boar's Head for the evening. Looking round the bar, I had to agree with Mary that for whatever reason, most of them must have turned up. The money we took that night was to be the most we took on any night until the factory opened nine months later. Much more importantly, many who were there that night came back – some not often, but a number became regulars and most of those I'm pleased to say are still with us today. We were also able to give Daniel a little money from the start, although I'm certain he meant what he said and would have stayed with us anyway.

Daniel is still with us today and I don't believe he has ever had any thoughts of leaving. He's still in love with Mary but seems to understand why, even though she is always kind to him, she'll never want anything more from him. Since the factory was finished, Carrington has grown and grown and because of our plum position, even though the waterfront has filled with hopeful bars, inns and guest houses, our business has remained a success. Given that we are just two women and a boy running the most successful inn in Carrington, for some time me and Mary have expected efforts, either fair or foul, to be made to persuade us to give up the Boar. But there has been nothing, not even polite enquiries.

Edward and Catherine visited us often, bringing little Marianne with them. She walks now, and is beginning to talk a little; Adie and Mary she manages to say quite easily, but Daniel she still has trouble with, mind you that doesn't stop 'Yan-Yan' from being her favourite. Seeing her face light up as soon as she spots him and how much affection he shows her, makes me hope that one day he will get over Mary and find someone else to marry and have children with.

For me, as I sit here thinking over the past two years, I realise I can't remember when I last thought about England and the people I left behind. Mary and me never talk about it, instead spending our time discussing the Boar and how neither of us have ever been so well placed and so when I say I'm never ever going back, I know she'd say the same.

And finally, what of my name? The answer's simple, to most who know me, my name is Adie, while Mary and me, by not mentioning Admonition, keep the curse at bay – not that either of us believe it exists of course, but you know, why take the chance?

Epilogue

Bill said she was untrue
Her baby a cuckoo
So she answered his suspicion
Called their next one Admonition

I've not heard that rhyme for more than sixty years. But recently, times past have filled my dreams and this morning, as I crossed from sleep to wakefulness, they travelled with me. Many years may have past, but I remember fighting a girl called Sally who chanted that rhyme again and again, right in my face. She was older than me and bigger too, but as her lisped es's sprayed my face, something welled up inside and I struck out. Clutching her bleeding nose, she stumbled backwards, but I didn't stop. She'd released the pent up fury of an angry six-year-old. Luckily for Sally, Reverend Grace who was just passing on his way back from conducting Sunday morning service, dragged me off her and marched me home. My legs still stung from the slap across them my mother had given me when my father taking me by the arm, led me back to Church and made me apologise to Sally. After I made my resentful apology and now less angry, as we slowly returned home, he told me that people would always be interested in my name, but I should never let it upset me because any message it carried was meant for him not me – if only I'd listened.

For many years I'd given little thought to those I'd left behind in England, but about ten years after I was released, I received a letter from Kit Carlyle. Apparently, the Boar and the two female ex-convicts, who owned it, were becoming quite well known throughout England, so when news reached Cheshire, he took it upon himself to write and congratulate us. He also thought I might like to know the fate of some of those I'd left behind and I must admit he'd made me curious.

According to Kit, life had bought Sam Baker very little peace after my trial. It was already difficult for him and the members of his gang who were still free to avoid capture, but after the display of support Sam led at Jabez' execution, all efforts at capture were concentrated on him alone. He knew that if he stayed in Cheshire, his arrest was inevitable, so he fled the County and headed as far south as he could go.

Reaching Kent, Sam still didn't feel safe, even there he saw an old 'Wanted' poster offering a reward for his capture and he'd already decided to try and get to France. But while travelling round the coast, heading for Dover, he discovered the smuggling of gold that was centred on Deal and more importantly, the extraordinary profit made by the smugglers – but it was also in Deal that his luck finally ran out.

Sam was no sailor, but he found it straightforward finding work once the gold was landed. What he didn't know, what no one knew, was that the publican of the inn whose cellar the smugglers used for storage bore a grudge against one of the smugglers' oarsmen. Wrongly believing the oarsman was having an affair with his wife, instead of challenging either of them, the publican let the grudge fester. And it festered until the day came when desire for revenge, combined with gin and opportunity, led him to talk to an ambitious local magistrate. He told the magistrate not only that his inn was used to store gold, but also when he next expected a delivery. All those involved, including Sam, were caught red-handed and held in Dover Barracks until the next quarterly Assizes were to sit in the Spring. For all of them things were looking bad – they knew they could all expect long gaol sentences – but for Sam matters became a lot worse.

When he was arrested, Sam gave a false name and it was under that name, one John Brown, his likeness appeared in the Kent Gazette. It was a copy of that newspaper a Cheshire councillor was reading on his journey home from Gravesend. Of course, the paper said Sam's name was John Brown and that he'd been arrested for gold smuggling. Back in Cheshire, for months, Councillor Weaver had seen the same image in every newspaper, noticeboard or pinned to prominent trees, and he knew with certainty that the image he was confronted with was Baker's. He knew he was wanted for murder and was under sentence to be hung. So two months later, Sam Baker's identity was confirmed and within days he had been returned to Cheshire and like Jabez, hung on the Boughton gallows.

According to Kit, after her husband's murder, Elizabeth had fallen on hard times and found herself forced to go to the workhouse. In her own words, she'd been rescued by Richard Sweetman, who not only paid all her debts, but when he heard she was homeless offered her a roof over her head in his own home. They had married a few months later and as far as Kit knew ten years on, both content, they were grateful to have found each other.

Any resentments I held against Elizabeth had long since disappeared; I had Mary, I had the Boar and I knew my life could never have been as good had I remained in England. But I must admit I was glad to learn what had happened to Elizabeth. She and Richard are sure to be dead now, but I truly hope that like me and Mary, their contentment continued till death parted them.

Two years ago, Mary died and so I sold the inn and retired to live out my days here in Parrametta. I made part of the sale conditions, that for as long as it stood, the inn should always be called The Boar's Head, in memory of the only man who, as Henry Carlyle said, as a parent may a child, truly loved me and went to the gallows to prove it. But for me *it* will always stand as a memorial to Mary, the only person *I* ever truly loved and I know, because she showed me in so many different ways, that she felt the same about me. We became lovers the first night we slept in the Boar, where we had had no choice but to sleep in the one bedroom ready for use and to share its only bed. Just as in Sydney, Mary reached for me, but this time I was neither drunk nor surprised and from the moment her lips sought mine, I responded readily. Of our customers, few knew our arrangements and of those who did, hardly any raised questions. To the handful who did, the explanation that we were just making sure we had as many rooms available as possible for paying guests, seemed to satisfy them.

Though it might have been home to the Women's Factory, Parramatta was also the place where, walking to and from work at the town hall, I'd had my first taste of freedom and so it is also the place I have chosen to end my days. Daniel had never left us, or I should say never left Mary. So there was also never any doubt that he would stay working at the Boar for its new owner.

So now, when a weak heart is drawing my days to an end, it makes me smile when I remember what a furious little girl she was, always fighting and never quite shedding the belief that she was cursed. Now, I wish there was a way I could tell her what's taken me a lifetime, not to mention a journey to the other side of the world, to learn; we can be unlucky, unfortunate, even oppressed by our circumstances or by those around us, but we are never affected by curses and certainly not by our name – unless of course we choose to believe it.

Admonition